Under A Pacific Sun

A StarWand Publishing book

Second Edition

All rights reserved

Copyright© 2013 by DC Musgrove

Cover art by Ryan D. Musgrove, Copyright© 2013, StarWand Publishing

The StarWand Publishing World Wide Web site address is:

http://www.starwandpublishing.com

ISBN: 978-0-9892240-1-7 Paperback
ISBN: 978-0-9892240-0-0 Kindle

Introduction

It is the late 1940's in the war torn islands of the Philippines. Richard *"Gunner"* McQuaid, a former U.S. Marine fighter pilot, is haunted by the recent horrors of battle during WWII in the Pacific.

Hoping to escape to a more peaceful way of life, he opens an air cargo business on the sleepy tropical island of Lubang. Also hoping for a more tranquil lifestyle, he is joined by two other expatriates; Mattie Adams, a pretty British war widow who runs the General Store in Lubang Village, and James *"Doc"* McCawley, a widowed British Navy surgeon at the Lubang Village hospital.

All is quiet after the cessation of hostilities in the Pacific and for a brief period, life indeed seems idyllic. Until they suddenly run afoul of a vicious band of criminals trafficking drugs and enslaved young island girls, heirs to a century old legacy of the most feared and powerful pirate queen in the history of the South China Sea. Their struggle becomes personal when the pirates target McQuaid and Kiko, an adopted nine-year-old island girl, on orders from the notorious Madam Chin who controls the Flower Boat prostitution business along Hong Kong's Aberdeen Harbor with an iron fist.

And, if life hadn't become treacherous enough, McQuaid and friends discover they have stumbled into the path of a secret Chinese conspiracy to gain control over the war-shattered island nations of the Far East. Suddenly, they find themselves in a fight for their lives and only Gunner McQuaid can save them. That is, if he is willing to make the ultimate sacrifice.

Under a Pacific Sun is a work of historical fiction and the first book in the *Gunner McQuaid* series, which takes place in the Far East countries of the Philippines, China, and the former British Colonies around Hong Kong. The story is surrounded by a rich and colorful backdrop of adventure and intrigue from real people, places, and events of the period.

The story and main characters in *Under a Pacific Sun* are mostly fiction. But they could have existed and are painted against an accurate map of those uncertain and turbulent times in the South China Sea following WWII.

The books in the continuing series follow characters Richard *"Gunner"* McQuaid, Mattie Adams, and Kiko, accompanied by a growing cast of old and new players, struggling to find their way in the war-ravaged Eastern hemisphere. The decisions and actions they take along the way affect not only themselves, but the lives of millions of people around them in the years to follow.

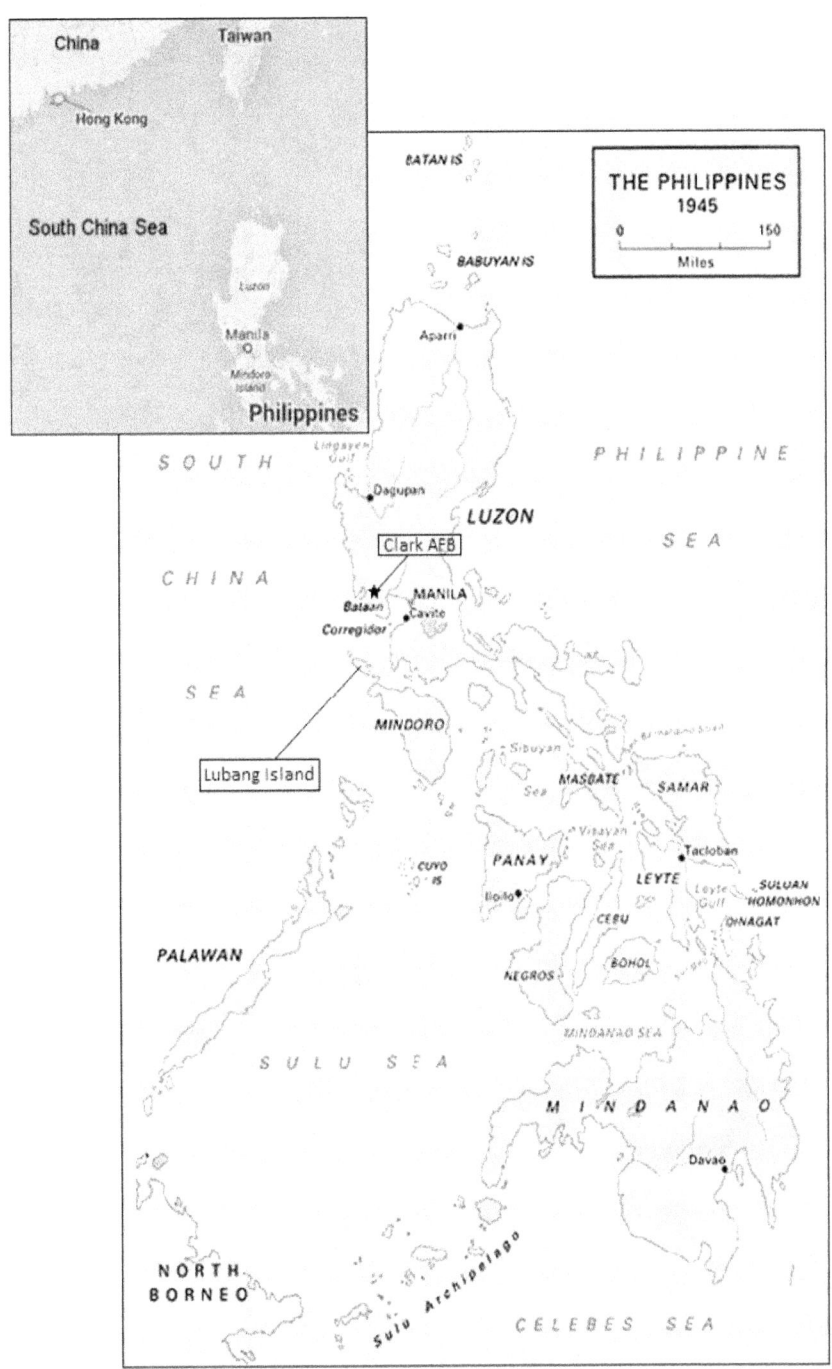

China

Taiwan

Hong Kong

South China Sea

Luzon

Manila

Mindoro Island

Philippines

THE PHILIPPINES
1945

0   150
Miles

BATAN IS

BABUYAN IS

Aparri

PHILIPPINE

SEA

S O U T H

Lingayen Gulf

Dagupan

LUZON

Clark AFB

C H I N A

Bataan   MANILA
          Cavite
Corregidor

Lubang Island

S E A

MINDORO

Sibuyan Sea

MASBATE

SAMAR

Tacloban

CUYO IS

PANAY

Visayan Sea

LEYTE

Leyte Gulf

SULUAN
HOMONHON

Iloilo

CEBU

DINAGAT

PALAWAN

NEGROS

BOHOL

MINDANAO SEA

S U L U   S E A

M I N D A N A O

Davao

N O R T H
B O R N E O

Sulu Archipelago

C E L E B E S   S E A

Chapter One
1948, Lubang Island, the Philippines

McQuaid was pushing the Willys harder than usual along the rutted coast road. Willys were built for war and endurance, not comfort. So, the jeep didn't just bounce over ruts and potholes, it ricocheted off them with bone bruising violence. He managed to keep his seat, but it was like busting an ornery bronc. Likewise, the roaring engine and grinding gears were a raucous and jarring assault on the tranquility of the otherwise lazy island afternoon. Bright colored birds and small animals exploded from his path, fluttering and shrieking, as he careened around blind bends in the road, rousting them from their naps in the sultry heat.

Sun bleached and island browned, he was big for an ex-fighter pilot – over six feet – which made him a snug fit in the jeep's front seat. Although in a hurry, as usual, his driving remained sure and disciplined. Like everything else about McQuaid, there was a purpose to his passing.

Events of the day so far weren't encouraging, nor making his afternoon's schedule any easier. Earlier, he'd landed the large Army C-47 cargo aircraft at a small dirt airstrip on the southeast side of the island. They had unloaded cargo there for the villagers over in Looc. When he tried to take-off again, he discovered his right engine fuel pump was out. The plan had been to drop off medical supplies and fly right back to the island's main airport in time for another load. He wanted to try and get in one last cargo drop at the neighboring Mindoro Island before nightfall. That mission had to be scrubbed the moment he realized the fuel pump failure reduced him from two engines, to just one. Strapped down in the rear bed of the jeep now, he needed to haul the bad pump to the airfield in time to make the flight to Manila for parts using his second company airplane.

He glanced over at his passenger sharing the mad dash back to his cargo base. In general, Kiko appeared unimpressed with his adroit driving skills. Perched on the edge of her seat, she remained calm, but prudent; holding on tight with both hands. They had folded the jeep's windshield flat on the hood to favor a cooler breeze over the stifling humidity. Just able to see above the dashboard, she'd borrowed his old leather flying helmet and pulled the goggles over her eyes. They proved effective in fending off various foreign objects bouncing off the two of them from both the dirt road and a relentless cloud of bugs near the coastline. So far, they'd been able to duck under anything life threatening.

McQuaid chuckled to himself, realizing she reminded him of a dog with the unbuckled helmet chin-straps flapping behind her like the ears of a retriever. He reached over and punched her arm with affection, moving the over-chewed cigar in his mouth to one side so he could yell to her.

"How're you doing, kid? You hanging in there?" he hollered above the wind and roar of the engine. She refused to break her concentration on the road ahead and returned a quick nod in response. Her little jaw was set in a determined line and he noticed a few wisps of jet-black hair, windblown, attempting to escape from beneath the flying helmet. The goggles covered dark and somber eyes that were possessed of a wisdom he knew to be hard won and well advanced of her years. When he returned his attention to the road, he discovered a large mottled green iguana standing frozen in mid step, right in front of them. McQuaid snapped the wheel to one side and was just able to swerve around him, as the lizard glared back at them in defiance. Relieved, he looked back at Kiko again, curious about how she might react to this near homicide for one of her beloved local wildlife.

"Whoa! Close one, huh?" he yelled, hoping to get a rise out of her. Kiko appeared unfazed, but he glimpsed a slight frown cross her face. She continued holding herself ramrod straight and leaning into the wind. Her dirty gray tennis shoes didn't quite reach the floorboards, but he could see her bare legs braced against the frequent sudden jolts and turns. She was an obvious veteran of McQuaid's customary all-terrain driving sorties. His gaze softened in a father's appreciation. Impressed by her undaunted determination and poise, he smiled to himself. Other parents might consider such driving style reckless endangerment. The smile turned bitter, however, when he remembered how Kiko had lost her parents.

McQuaid had taken her under his wing right after the war's end. Japanese soldiers had raided her village and killed most of the villagers. They unleashed their vengeance on the island population in retribution for aiding Americans against them. A young U.S. Army chaplain had related the worst day of her young life to him.

McQuaid had been visiting a fellow pilot in the hospital at Clark Air Base on Luzon, the main island and noticed one of the wards was full of children. The chaplain was sitting on one of the beds next to a small girl who stared unblinking at the far wall. For some reason he felt drawn to her. He walked over and stooped down to bring his face level with hers. She was a pretty child and though her dark eyes were vacant and staring, she sat upright with her head held high. The big Marine's heart went out to her, but he didn't know what he could do to help.

"Why are all these kids here?" he asked, looking up at the chaplain for some explanation. The man wasn't much older than McQuaid. Standing, he drew him off to one side to talk so they wouldn't be overheard.

"They're all orphans from villages around these islands. When we took back the Philippines, we found burned out villages everywhere. The Army was overwhelmed with refugees; many of them children. Most needed medical care. A lot of them suffered from severe trauma and also required psychiatric treatment." The man paused, watching McQuaid survey the rest of the room and then return his attention to the child sitting on the bed.

"What's her story?" he asked. The Chaplain sighed and his gaze returned to her as well.

"A woman from one of the villages brought her here. They'd been attacked by the Japanese near the end of the war. She told me this one hid with some other children, cowering under one of the huts. The woman said she watched a Nippon officer behead her father and then impale her mother with his sword when she fell weeping over his body. Without giving them a second glance, he worked his way down the line of villagers, pushed to their knees, awaiting their turn. He'd just wipe his bloody blade on the dying and move on to the next victim." McQuaid looked up at him, studying his face.

"How old is she?"

"We're not sure, but I think somewhere between six and seven." McQuaid's eyes were haunted.

"She had to watch him murder her family?" Nodding his head, the young army officer's voice fell to a whisper.

"Yeah. The woman was there and saw the whole thing. She described how this Jap swung his sword high over his head and it made a whistling sound when it whipped through the air. The sound of that blade chopping through bone and tissue must have been awful. But she said the little girl never looked away." The chaplain rubbed his mouth with

9

a quick swipe and continued. "She never cries and hasn't spoken many words since. That all happened a few months ago, west of here on Lubang Island." He was watching this Marine for the signs. His eyes fell on the polished silver wings over a starched uniform breast.

"What's her name?"

"Kiko," the chaplain replied, his brown eyes appraising him; patient and hopeful. That had been several years ago. McQuaid smiled to himself again. It had been a fateful decision and one he'd never regretted.

The jeep lurched over a slight hill and a magnificent stretch of pristine white sandy beach emerged from the palms and dark jungle underbrush. They could hear the boom of the breakers and smell the salt-laden sea air. Kiko lifted herself up for a better view. She pointed out a wave-skimming squadron of pelicans gliding along next to them, close enough that the lead bird began to eye them with suspicion.

McQuaid pulled the jeep over onto the shoulder and stopped near the edge; with a sharp drop off to the beach ten or so feet below them. It was a favorite spot of his and overlooked a narrow palm-ringed inlet. Even rushed, he could seldom pass it by without stopping. He turned the motor off and set the handbrake, then hopped out and walked to the bluff's edge with his hands shoved deep in the pockets of his flight coverall. The waves below were breaking in steady sets, hissing back across the wet sand to regroup for another determined onslaught on the beach. A cool breeze off the curling surf stroked his face and offered seductive relief to the relentless heat of the day. They watched seabirds crying and wheeling overhead. Entranced, he stared at the shimmering fire of an orange tropical sun, like a glowing glob of lava, beginning its long fall to the azure horizon. It was breathtaking, but with reluctance his view moved back to the water's edge, searching, waiting for something. It was always the same.

Kiko sidled up next to him unnoticed, until she yanked his trouser leg to get his attention. His gaze never wavered, fascinated by the waves clawing for a foothold upon the shore. The sea seemed desperate to reclaim the land; to return it to her, like a woman clinging in vain to a lover who had turned his back on her.

"Why you sad, Gunna'?" Almost everyone on the island referred to him as Gunner, or just McQuaid. Kiko faced him now, studying his eyes with forlorn. They reflected the sun-speckled blue water and bright white sand, yet somehow remained gloomy and gray like a coming storm. He broke from his reverie, looked down at her and smiled. Kneeling down to her eye level, he pulled the flight helmet off her head with a gentle hand and ruffled her short bobbed hair.

"Nothing's wrong, little pigeon," he said, putting his arm around her thin shoulders and peering back to the sea over the top of her head.

"What you come here for? What you look for all time?" she asked, insistent, pushing him away so she could see his face. She didn't buy his veiled attempt to brush her concerns aside. He knew she kept a vigil over him and seldom strayed from his wing. He looked back down at her face, with the dark pooled almond eyes he knew someday a man would fall into and drown. Her small mouth was full lipped and set in worry about this mystery she needed to understand.

"I wanted to see if anything from the war washed up on the beach," he replied, hoping that might quench her curiosity without need for deeper inquiry. But it wasn't to be – it never was.

"You look for someone, Gunna'. Who you look for?" Her brow scrunched down, hooding her eyes over a pert, freckled little nose, daring him not to reveal the full truth of his pain.

An object in the surf caught his eye among some other bits of the usual flotsam and he stood up, blocking the glare of the sun with the edge of his hand. She turned to follow his gaze.

"C'mon," he replied, his voice faint and distracted. He strode toward the rocky path to the left leading down to the sand below. She scrambled along behind him without another word; three steps for every one of his. He trudged into the surf as soon as he reached the beach, waded knee deep into the foamy water, and grabbed the oblong object, before it could be pulled back by the waves.

Retreating to the dry sand with his prize, he flopped down with it between his legs. It was a sodden wooden box with a simple black military stencil on it: Lt. Harris. The letters were almost worn away by repeated beaching across the coarse sand. He pulled out a pocketknife and was able to pry the lid off to peer inside. It contained what had once been an officer's manicure set and some other personal items.

There was a rotted leather case containing spindly pieces of metal, brown knobbed with rust and welded together by the corrosion. He could make out a metal comb, straight razor, what had once been scissors, and a pair of tweezers. There was also a rusted pocket watch on a chain and a curled brown-edged photograph of a young woman. She waved back at him from the front porch of a plank wood house. With her left hand held toward the camera, she smiled and displayed a small-stoned wedding ring.

Kiko also began to rummage through the box and pulled out the corroded razor to hold up to her face, her eyes crossed in concentration. She tried to unfold the handle with her tiny fingers, but it had rusted tight. Tossing it back in the box, she pulled out another item and noticed him looking at the photo.

"What you find, Gunna'?" she asked, grabbing his arm to bring the picture around so she could see. She gawked at it, wide-eyed, but without comment. He noticed some writing on the back and brought it around to read: "Love always, Judy. August 10, 1944." It felt as if he were spying on someone; looking through the window of another man's world. With a slight pang, he wondered about her husband; whether he had ever made it back to her after the war. With one last view of the face in the photo, he slid it into one of the zipper pockets of his flight coverall and stood up.

"Let's go, Kiko. We've wasted enough time here already." He closed the wooden box, tossed it back into the surf, and glanced at his watch. It was near two-thirty in the afternoon. They had over a half hour's drive yet to make it to the Lubang airfield and almost an hour flight to the Air Force base near Manila to drop off the fuel pump for repairs. Or, better yet, the base might have a rebuilt in stock. They made it back to the jeep in time to hear the short wave radio crackle and Mattie calling them from the office.

"Mattie calling McQuaid, over. Where are you two? We've got work to do here, people!" She sounded like she may have already called several times. He grabbed the receiver from the walkie-talkie strapped onto the jump seat in back and keyed the mike.

"McQuaid here. What've you got, Mattie, over?" He let up on the mike switch and winked at Kiko. "We're going to catch it now, little pigeon," he quipped out of the side of his mouth. Kiko stared up at him unconcerned. She had long since figured out Mattie's bark was way worse than her bite. Besides, she hadn't been driving. Therefore, she was in the clear on anything McQuaid might have made them late for.

"Listen, you two loafers. I've been slaving away over here trying to keep your raggedy excuse for a cargo business open, while all hell's breaking loose. Captain Nguyen's been over here twice looking for you, saying they got an S.O.S. call from a private yacht offshore of Cabra Island. They've lost their engines and are taking on water. He wants you to fly him out there so he can help in time before they all end up having to dog paddle back to the island, over."

"I guess we were out of radio range for a while there and we've had a few problems of our own, over." He swung his legs into the jeep and turned the motor over, grinding the gears while getting it turned back onto the road headed toward home. Mattie hesitated for a moment.

"What do you mean out of radio range? You're on the walkie-talkie? Why aren't you in the air? I expected you back here an hour ago, over."

He keyed the mike again.

"Yeah, well, we lost a fuel pump and I had to borrow the auxiliary jeep at the airstrip over near Chief Mahutra's village. I pulled the pump so we could hot-foot it back and try to get over to Clark by Goose in time to get another one, over." He was referring to the amphibious Grumman Goose they had parked at their base at Lubang Airfield. Both planes were war surplus and he'd gotten them for a steal through his connections in military aviation.

Instead of shipping home like so many other soldiers and airmen, he'd pounced on an opportunity to supply air cargo service to the limping post war economy in the Philippines; now a ward of the U.S. government as well. Carving out an air shipping service in the new American-supported economy would be a coup. The trick was to get the business up and running fast enough to take advantage of a temporary gap in services. Planes and parts had been easy to obtain since military equipment needs had fallen off after the war.

Now, over three years since the Japanese surrender, the shipping business was moving along at a brisk pace, but so were his expenses. Market demand for air cargo services came in lower than expected too. Plenty of Filipinos with small boats were happy to bring cargo back and forth between the islands and for a fraction of his costs. Perishables, medical supplies, and mail were the real money-makers.

He swerved to avoid a clump of brown palm fronds in the road and keyed the mike again.

"I figure we should be there in about twenty to thirty minutes – if you can keep your drawers dry that long, over." Kiko looked over at him aghast and then giggled, realizing he was kidding about Mattie's pants.

"Well, it's only life and death for those people on the yacht, so take your time, sport. Wait, Captain Nguyen wants me to ask you something, over." She was off the air for fifteen seconds or so. "McQuaid, he wants to know, after you pick him up here, how long it would take you to get out there and land in the water next to the boat. I think he's wondering if they could get their rusty bucket out there before you make it back, over."

"I'll be there in twenty and it'll take another fifteen minutes and some change by air. He'd be two hours getting out there and maybe we'd end up having to rescue him too, when that piece of crap he calls a police launch sucks a rod and blows the motor. But if he's feelin' frisky, tell him go on with my blessing, over."

Again, a slight pause and Mattie came back.

"He says if it's that much faster for you he'll take you up on your offer. You were offering weren't you, over?" Nguyen was a pain in the ass and she knew it. They also both knew unpaid favors were a small fee for keeping the local constabulary happy and off their backs. The better relations they had with Nguyen, the less nosy he was about their business. Which suited McQuaid just fine and it was well worth the fairly regular unpaid police work they ended up trading in return.

"Sure. I'd be thrilled to run him out there. Make sure we bring extra yack-sacks. I don't want to see his lunch splattered all over the inside of the Goose, over."

"Yeah, thanks for that picture. I'll make sure we're all set on this end. The Goose is gassed and ready, so bust it on over here, out." He didn't bother to answer back. He was thinking about the yacht and keyed the mike again.

"Mattie, ask Nguyen if he knows whose yacht that is, or where it came from, will you, over?"

She came back after a long pause.

"He says he believes they're a good sized motor launch out of Hong Kong and it's a woman making the radio calls. She told him they are about thirty, to forty kilometers northeast of the Cabra Lighthouse – with three souls aboard. The other two are her husband and a young girl. I presume she's the daughter. He thinks the husband and daughter might be busy bailing if they're taking on water, over."

McQuaid was used to dealing with Mattie's British metric system and so did the math in his head, ending up with their position being twenty to twenty-five miles northeast of Cabra Island's lighthouse, which was a few miles northwest of Lubang Island.

"Okay, Mattie. We'll get there as soon as we can. McQuaid out."

Hong Kong? That was almost seven hundred miles away. He wondered if they'd stopped in Manila first and then floundered some time later after leaving port. In any case, it wasn't a good place to be without engines on what sounded like it might be a luxury motor launch. The South China Sea was renowned hunting grounds for pirates. Maybe that's why the captain of local police was nervous about tearing out there on his only patrol boat.

Pirates were known to outgun the ill equipped and scattered police forces in the large Mindoro Island group of the Philippines. Nguyen had better weapons than most. There were still persistent rumors Lubang Island might have a few Japanese soldiers hidden in the mountains, after being stranded by the retreating Nippon army. Villagers in the south complained of missing chickens and goats on occasion, but they never saw anyone. If they stayed away from everyone and didn't cause too much trouble, they were safe enough. That's if they were out there at all.

The American military had determined they weren't going to spend any resources chasing stories of lost enemy soldiers. Even if true, they'd be low on ammunition, half-starved and too cowed to start any fights. And they knew better than to give themselves up. Too many of the local villagers would sooner see their hides tacked on their huts, than respect their white flag. There'd be little chance of mercy after the years of atrocities the Japanese army had perpetrated on the island populace.

Still, McQuaid kept a loaded Thompson submachine gun in the backseat and he had one of his .45 cal. military issue automatics in a holster on his hip. The heavy pistol was uncomfortable bouncing around in his seat though. With his free hand, he reached down on the floorboard to make sure he had it lying at his feet, within easy reach. You never knew what you might run into around the next bend, just a few years after WWII. It was the Wild West all over again.

He kept several handguns and automatic rifles in both planes for the same reason. He had a small stash of hand grenades in boxes behind the crew seats of both aircraft as well as in the jeep. There was nothing like a hand grenade to even the odds, if confronted in the open and outgunned by any number of renegades who watched the roads, or pirates patrolling inlets around the islands. They held people up for anything of value. It was easy work to scare money out of the locals, or better yet, a few rich foreigners who were stupid enough to travel unarmed.

The first few huts on the outskirts of town came into view and within another couple minutes, they were tearing down the dusty main street, scattering chickens and dogs. A small pack of laughing, chattering children joined them, running alongside, as an escort to Mattie's General Store. McQuaid slid to a stop in the gravel out front, next to a white police jeep. Captain Nguyen ambled out the front screen door, his Aussie hat on his head; side brim up. The police chief wore dark, military aviator sunglasses and his right hand rested on his low-slung sidearm; like a gunslinger.

He tipped two fingers of his left hand to his hat in salute and grinned around nicotine stained teeth and a thin, drooping black mustache. Nguyen reminded McQuaid of a comic book caricature of an oriental cowboy. A gold front tooth completed the picture and flashed in the sun, almost as bright as the glare from the cheap gold badge pinned over his shirt pocket.

Cho, his fat deputy, lounged in their jeep and raised a hand in a limp, perfunctory greeting when McQuaid glanced his way. The Lubang police was a mighty force of three. One of the deputies hung around the station to monitor the radio between naps. They also had a shortwave set in the police jeep, with a long whip antenna that seemed to be in constant motion, bobbing back and forth, no matter how long it had been parked. McQuaid killed the engine on the Willys and hopped out in time to reach the captain's outstretched hand.

"Captain Nguyen, nice to see you've got the time to fly out with me and check on a stalled pleasure boat a few miles offshore. No cattle rustlers or old woman beaters to round up in town today I presume?" He and McQuaid tolerated each other and even needed the other's services on frequent occasions. But neither was under the illusion they had to feign more friendship than necessary. Nevertheless, McQuaid took his hand as help out of the jeep and smiled at his magnanimous air of benevolence over all residents of the town.

"You funny, Gunna'. I like you for now, but sometimes you forget, it is hot and I have hot tempa' too. No?" He grinned again, almost jovial and slapped McQuaid on the back, as they walked up the steps together.

Mattie sat sideways behind the bar, wearing her radio headset. Her glossy brown ponytail stuck out from under the headphones and bobbed up and down, as she carried on an animated conversation with someone on the short-wave. She arched her eyebrows in acknowledgement, when she saw him come in with Nguyen. Lubang's bar/general store wasn't much cooler than outside, despite several ceiling fans blowing the muggy air around. The shade of indoors only made the interior seem cooler, compared to the steamy tropical swelter on the street outside.

Besides the long wooden bar, stretching across most of the room in front of the store, there were some bar stools, tables, and chairs. They were intended to accommodate the crowd that never materialized. To the left and right, were tall store shelves stocked with canned goods and other sundry items. A couple glass counters on the far right, contained butchered cuts of pork and poultry on ice. A long steel drink cooler kept cold beers and sodas handy, right inside the door.

Captain Nguyen was already sauntering over that way to fish out a soda, or beer, depending on the hour. Allowed any two of his choice per day, he had to pay for anything else. It was a little game they all played, to see if anyone could catch him palming a third bottle. Once in a while, he made an unmistakable show of taking a paid bottle and laying his money on the bar in front of everyone. This to allay any concern he might take advantage of Mattie's generous support of local law enforcement. Amused, McQuaid watched Mattie turn in mid-sentence, on the radio, so she could keep an eye on

Nguyen. McQuaid chuckled, dug a nickel out of his pocket, and slapped it down on the bar.

"Captain, let me buy you a soda and pull out one of those beers for me if you don't mind." Nguyen obliged him, thanking him for his soda and then, on second thought, eyed McQuaid askance, as he popped his beer and took a long pull. Kiko had already made her way over to the ice chest and hauled out a Coca-Cola for herself. She was intent on working off the bottle cap.

"Beer okay before you fly plane, Gunna'?" Nguyen asked, sounding a mite too casual.

Mattie, who had finished her conversation, pulled off her headset and was looking over at Nguyen, no doubt wondering what he imagined the response to his question might be.

McQuaid finished a long last draught and banged the empty on the bar. Then wiped his mouth with the back of his hand and stifled a righteous belch to accommodate the sensitivities of the ladies in the room.

"Would you rather I was hung over, or just a little inebriated, flying you this afternoon, Officer Nguyen? I'm not worth a damn as a pilot when I'm hung over, you know."

The police chief looked over to Mattie for some support for his concern. She remained expressionless, but stated for the record:

"He's right. I've seen him damn near swerve off the end of the bloody runway and almost forget to takeoff when he's hung over," she deadpanned. Stifling further debate, she addressed McQuaid on more pressing matters. "That was the woman from the yacht again. She sounded sort of panicked and said the boat is starting to list to port. Maybe you might want to stop fooling around, saddle up the Goose, and haul yourselves out there to offer some assistance?"

"Yep, I'm all set. Got any idea on a course heading off the end of the runway?"

She was way ahead of him and whipped a chart from under the bar, smoothed it out and stabbed a finger at a dark pencil mark. McQuaid noticed their position indicated they were about thirty degrees northeast of the Cabra Island Lighthouse.

"You'll want to fly a course line from the runway toward Manila airport and you should see them around forty kilometers or so, on your right side. The seas are calm, with a light five to ten knot breeze out of zero-three-five degrees. It should be like a stroll through the park for you. I wrote down their broadcast radio frequency here, so you can have her talk you in when you get close enough for them to hear the Goose overhead. I also had Baacay throw the life raft in the Goose. There are an additional eight life vests on board for you; in case you need them." Baacay was their general maintenance and refueling helper over at the airfield. Mattie slapped the bar to finalize her briefing. "Time's a wasting, cowboys!"

McQuaid gave the chart one last cursory glance.

"Has she seen any other boats in the area?"

"No, she even said they shot off some flares to try and attract some attention, but nothing's in sight anywhere."

McQuaid raised a thumb and forefinger to his eyes and rubbed them in frustration.

"Great. Nothing like announcing to the entire pirate population you're a boat in distress in the middle of nowhere."

She refrained from reminding him the pirates also monitored most of the common transmit frequencies.

He yanked his well-worn Brooklyn Dodgers ball cap from his back pocket and pulled the bill low over his eyes. Then he grabbed a couple of cigars out of the jar by the cash register. Casting a knowing look at Mattie, he cocked his head toward Kiko, before heading for the door with Nguyen in tow.

Mattie ducked under the bar opening and nabbed Kiko before she could follow them out.

"You're not going, young lady. I need you to stay here with me today!" Kiko tried to pull away and looked to McQuaid for support.

"Gunna', I go with, okay?"

He turned to see Mattie give him a pleading look and then looked down to Kiko's angry face.

"She's right, kid. You need to stay and help Mattie around here. We'll be back real quick and you can fly over to Manila with me later this afternoon, okay?"

She didn't buy it and tried to yank away, but Mattie had a good grip.

"Stay here," he commanded. "I'll be back soon." With that, he banged through the screen door and leaped into the jeep. Nguyen jumped into the seat next to him and off they went in a cloud of dust and a spray of gravel. He felt bad about leaving Kiko. Most of time, she flew with him everywhere he went. But this wasn't a cargo mission.

McQuaid had made her an honorary employee in his air cargo business soon after bringing her home from the Army hospital. She blossomed under his gentle supervision, helping him load boxes and bags for transport, checking off items on his shipping manifests, running endless errands in town for various supplies, food, cigars and of course whiskey; the other fuel running his makeshift company. Kiko would always spread the handwritten tabs out on his desk after each supply sortie, to make sure he knew Mattie also kept careful accounting of his staples.

It was understood he and Mattie Adams, a British war widow, were partners in the business. Mattie not only fed and revived him after frequent binges between cargo contracts; she also ran the short-wave radio station for the island. This served as the mainstay for air-to-ground communications, also the "telephone" for job requests for McQuaid Air Cargo from clients around the primary Philippine islands. McQuaid had promised to keep his drinking under control and they compromised on their squabbling over differences in styles for raising Kiko. According to Mattie, she "had to learn responsibility," not just the devil-may-care soldiering through life, like a former Marine fighter pilot – her hero.

McQuaid reflected on a most recent argument with Mattie, about Kiko's tendency to sling every article of clothing from her body, in windmill fashion, to whichever corner happened to be handiest. It was a consistent practice before her bath, or on any rare occasion when she needed to change. And since hers was just a small corner near the back of Mattie's store, they wound up in heaps all around her cot. Whereas, she kept McQuaid's cargo office at the airfield so neat, it appeared everything was there for show and never used. This stark contrast in housekeeping infuriated Mattie of course. Kiko, however, remained unrepentant. So, the battle continued on a near daily basis.

With a sigh, he reminded himself she was only nine years old after all. The two adults would need to work out their own issues with each other before they tried to enforce a confused set of rules on Kiko. Any further pondering on the subject was cut short by the sight of the Lubang airfield coming into view.

Chapter Two
Verde Island Passage, the Philippines

Baacay was loitering in the shade under a wing of their second company aircraft, splayed out in his grimy lawn chair. He wore his standard uniform of frayed jungle shorts, a holey, once white t-shirt, and his oversized, floppy straw hat. The Goose, fueled and ready, was waiting on the apron out in front of the Quonset hut they used for a company hangar at the airfield. Along with the hangar space, there was a maintenance office, spartan sleeping quarters, and a parts storage room.

Baacay lived in a small hut behind the hangar, when he wasn't doing odd jobs, changing oil, or refueling aircraft. Without any maintenance work to do, which was rare, he could be found at Mattie's store or a mile or so away, fishing off the pier on the harbor. But more often as not, he was busy handing tools and rags to McQuaid, hanging out of various access panels on one of the two company aircraft, often lagging behind in needed repairs.

He wasn't a qualified mechanic, but McQuaid kept him busy earning his room and board, doing all other minor upkeep and servicing. The Goose had low flight hours and still sported standard military camouflage colors – dark and pastel blues – designed to make it hard to see on the water from the air. They had painted over the star on the nose and other U.S. Navy markings and replaced them with McQuaid Air Cargo in big yellow letters. Otherwise, the Grumman flying boat was Navy standard issue.

McQuaid pulled the jeep into the hangar and walked out on the apron to the Goose for a quick look-around pre-flight with Baacay. She was sturdy, only leaked oil from the port engine, and had good tires, considering the rough landing strips he'd put her down on over the last year. Water landings were the norm, but he liked to hangar her at the airport whenever possible, to preserve the paint and keep barnacles off the hull.

Nguyen followed him around but remained quiet, with his hands clasped behind him. He knew better than to touch anything, but watched with close attention as McQuaid stood on a small stepladder to check the fuel levels in the wing tanks and the engine oil under the access doors in the engine cowling. He said something to Baacay in Tagalog, the prevailing Filipino dialect of the islands. They both laughed and McQuaid understood enough of it to pick up on the joke. Nguyen wanted to know if he was sure he'd bolted the engines on tight, or was still holding a grudge against him from the last time he threw him in jail for chasing chickens around when he was stinking drunk. Their owner complained they were distressed and wouldn't lay for two days.

"Hand me that rag, Baacay. She's slinging some oil under the cowling and I can't tell where it's coming from," he hollered down. Baacay jumped up on the ladder next to him and craned his head in to look where McQuaid's flashlight was pointing. The ever present rag was yanked out of his back shorts pocket and he began wiping around the gasket seal for one of the nine radial engine cylinders. While he was mopping grease and oil from around inside the cowling, McQuaid looked down at a now apprehensive Nguyen and winked.

"Don't worry. I think we'll make it back before that cylinder comes loose," he deadpanned. "She'll fly on one engine anyway, so nothing to be concerned with, Captain." Baacay started to snicker and McQuaid elbowed him. Nguyen didn't seem sure whether he was kidding or not, but offered a lopsided grin in return.

"You funny, Gunna', but I know you are not crazy. Baacay will not fly with you if you crazy, so I am not worried." The gold tooth flashed in the sun.

McQuaid studied him for a moment, his face serious, and Nguyen's smile vanished. As if on cue, Baacay poked his head out and waved the oil soaked rag at him.

"I not fly with you today. No way, Gunna'! I put raft inside. Goose crash – you not need swim. Raft fo' two only. I not go with. No way!" Still shaking his head, he retreated back under the cowling. McQuaid turned his head away to keep from busting a gut.

"Nice," he muttered at Baacay under his breath. He heard a slight giggle in return and coughed loudly to cover.

Nguyen pushed his Aussie hat back on his head and regarded the two of them with narrowed eyes. "I use radio in office. See if dis boat still okay."

McQuaid just waved down to him to go ahead. Baacay topped off the oil and helped him finish his pre-flight inspection. Then he stood by with a fire bottle, while McQuaid cranked the engines. Nguyen returned, slammed the door tight after him, and belted into the right cockpit seat. Soon they were bumping down the Lubang field runway, skirting the larger potholes, which seemed to sprout anew after each thunderstorm. McQuaid had a fresh cigar clenched in his teeth – "to help him concentrate."

The Goose let him know with a familiar feel to the controls, when she was ready to fly and after a quick confirmation check of his airspeed gauge, he eased back on the control yoke to let her go. They passed by the old lighthouse on the point and over the shallow harbor as he cranked up the landing gear. She shook off her earthbound clumsiness and reached for the sky with surprising grace. They were in the air for about fifteen minutes when Mattie called in on the radio.

"Mattie to McQuaid. Come in, over." McQuaid clicked the transmit button.

"Go ahead, Mattie, over."

"Richard, there's a young girl from the yacht on the radio now and she sounds pretty scared!" McQuaid looked over at Nguyen, who was listening carefully. "She says a boat came alongside of them and just started shooting. Both her parents were wounded and the men from the boat are ransacking their yacht. She managed to slip away from them to get on the radio. She doesn't have much time, but says her parents might be dead and they're looking for her now. You need to hurry!" He could tell Mattie was shaken up too. When she was worried, or things were bad, she called him by his first name.

"Tell her to drop one of the bow lines in the water and slip overboard where they can't see her. She can hold onto the line and keep her head underwater if they look for her. They may not know she's aboard if they shot the parents and are just searching the boat for loot. Let her know we're coming and to get off the radio right now. We're almost there." Nguyen had been looking out the cockpit window on the right and pointed.

"Der is boat!" McQuaid banked hard to the right and spotted the boats ahead and several miles off the right wing tip.

"Mattie, we see the boats and we're closing in on them now, over."

The fighter pilot in him began to kick into overdrive. Ramming the twin throttles to their stops, he firewalled the engines. Then he pulled the Goose hard over in a high-G, diving right turn, making the wings groan and Nguyen grunt in protest. The altimeter started winding down and he monitored the airspeed indicator as it clawed upward through the yellow, then into the red never-to-exceed-airspeed range on the gauge. He knew what the Goose could take though, so he shifted his gaze out through the windshield, to watch the ocean looming up to meet them.

Nguyen began a low wailing howl, which grew louder as the horizon vanished and the sea filled their view. Details of the two boats emerged when he banked to the left to line them up with their nose. A smaller, fast motor skiff was tied off to the side of a teakwood motor yacht. He estimated the hull to be fifty to sixty feet and it listed hard to port. Warrior eyes took in everything. Time slowed. Hands and feet became extensions of his plane. A part of his brain began to freeze imagery, assessing skirmish lines between enemies and friendlies. There was a body floating in the water and another lying on the port side deck, up against the gunwales, amidst a spreading red stain. Several faces gawked up at them, open mouthed, as they tried to discern whether the aircraft diving on them was a Kamikaze, or just a bloody fool.

The twin Pratt and Whitney's were roaring now, wind howling like a banshee and the yoke began to shudder under his hands as their airspeed built to destructive forces. Nguyen was busy trying to brace his feet and hands, for what must have looked to him like impending doom. It was just one of many mental pictures coursing through McQuaid's mind. He absorbed it all, calm and detached, plotting his perilous line of descent against the engineering constraints of the Goose. A small corner of his awareness even found Nguyen's actions amusing and yet he also felt compassion for the man, who was bracing for impact. There was no time to explain himself, however. The two boats and their now alert occupants were growing larger by the split second.

Automatic rifle muzzles begin to rise in slow motion, while a couple of the men threw themselves to the deck. It was time to pull the Goose out of her dive before her controls started to freeze and the death grip of gravity dug her claws so deep into his plane they wouldn't be able to escape.

"Easy now, girl," he whispered, while she howled in protest. With care not to overstress the airframe, he began pulling back on the yoke. She bucked in resistance, but he could feel the slight give in tension on the controls. It was as if she was still willing to trust him and respond to his will. They flashed over the boats with a deafening roar, at over two hundred mph – somewhere well past the max speed limit – the needle pegged on the gauge. They were just clearing the tops of the waves before he felt her begin to pull out; regaining precious altitude. Throttling back now, he pulled the yoke to his chest and watched the altimeter wind back up; bleeding airspeed off to within the yellow, then into the green range once more.

A quick glance over his shoulder revealed several of the men running to their boat. Their aim of disrupting the pirates' looting of the yacht appeared successful. But in spite of the G-forces pushing him and Nguyen deep in their seats and his vision dimming from the blood draining from his head, he noticed something else. One of the pirates threw off a tarp covering a deck-mounted machine gun, which he was racking around in an attempt to fire on the retreating flying boat; still a large and lumbering target at this point.

He banked hard to the right and then jinked back to the left again, to throw off the man's aim. A thin line of yellow tracers squirted past their high right wing. Grabbing for the throttles, he firewalled the engines and released the yoke, to bring their nose down to the waves again.

"Dey are shooting, Gunna'. What we do now?" Nguyen yelled over the intercom.

"Get out of your seat and grab my two Thompsons and a few ammo clips out of that footlocker behind you!" The policeman released his seat belts and McQuaid watched him break the submachine guns out of their storage locker, then rack both their slides to arm them and stuff several clips in his pocket for good measure. "Give me one of those, open your side window, and get in position to fire on those assholes when I bring her around again!"

"You are crazy, Gunna'! Dey got big machine gun." Nguyen looked back at him, his eyes pleading for him to reconsider.

"Don't worry, Captain. We'll stay low and keep the stern of their boat between us. They'd have to shoot through their wheelhouse to hit us, even if they could!"

Nguyen seemed to think about that strategy for a second and responded with a quick nod. Then he jumped back into his seat and handed the other weapon to McQuaid. Meanwhile, he was busy keeping the Goose from kissing the waves, as he cranked her around, watching their left wing slicing the air just above the water, while calculating the angle he needed to take to come in behind the pirate boat.

Nguyen was a little slow, but not stupid. And he was, after all, a former Philippine Army officer who knew how to shoot. He slid his side window open and hung the Thompson out with both hands, looked back at McQuaid and gave him a nod he was ready to go. He leveled the Goose off and was coming in just over the waves, about a mile and a half astern of the pirate boat now. Holding the Thompson between his knees, he used his left hand to crank open the pilot side window. Then got the weapon positioned in his left hand, ready to stick out the window. Between the two of them, they would have some decent firepower with the two .45 caliber submachine guns pointed forward. And they had an added advantage of being able to pivot the guns, to track their targets, without having to maneuver the aircraft as much as he would if he was flying with fixed guns on a fighter plane.

Reversing the situation on the pirates, along with surprise and uncertainty of their intentions, he reasoned, should be enough to throw them off for at least one high-speed pass. He hoped that strategy would work out. But they had little time to ponder other options. Not quite in range with the Thompsons, the .30 caliber deck gun opened up again; even though the tracers were well high of them at this point. *So far so good*, he thought.

"You all set, Captain?" he asked over the intercom, not daring to break his concentration by looking over to check up on him. "Okay, count to three and let 'em have it. Try to aim for the stern where their fuel tanks should be. They definitely don't want to be swimming home!" He had to assume the police chief heard him and understood the plan. He was mentally at "two" when he heard the chatter of Nguyen's gun starting to fire. He joined in with his own, trying hard to keep the bucking Thompson steady with one hand, while holding on to the Goose with his other.

They weren't shooting with intermittent tracers in their clips, so he had to try to walk his line of fire up from the waterline, marked by little geysers of water jumping up behind the pirate boat. Each gun only had a thirty round stick magazine, so there wasn't much room for error. McQuaid was able to get off two quick bursts, yanked the Goose up and over the top of the motor launches, and then dropped down on the other side to prevent the pirate's deck gun from getting a clean line of fire.

He only had a split second to assess the results of their work, as the two boats flashed under them. Nevertheless, he was encouraged to observe they had ripped the hell out of the rear of the pirate boat, broken all the windows in their pilothouse and as they passed over the yacht, he saw a small figure holding onto a trailing line in the water off the starboard bow.

Good girl, he mouthed to himself. She had followed his instructions and it appeared she was still safe.

The sickening sound of rounds hitting the rear of the Goose shocked him into sudden action. He shoved the yoke forward, but had to pull up again right away, or run the risk of hitting the waves in front of them. The water was too close to jink to either side. Their best hope was to stay low enough to spoil the gunner's aim. It must have worked, because another line of wide-spaced tracers sailed well past them overhead.

He tested the controls, which still felt taut and responsive, so nothing critical on any of the wing control surfaces had been shot up and the engines were still running smooth. A quick scan of his instruments told him nothing appeared to be overheating and his fluid levels were all good.

"Mattie to McQuaid. What the hell is going on out there, over?" He had kept her in suspense too long and it seemed she couldn't stand it anymore. There was time before he turned to make another pass. He keyed his mike.

"So far we're in good shape, Mattie. We used the Thompsons I had on board to make one low firing pass and scared the hell out of the pirates. I spotted two bodies, which are probable friendlies down; one floating in the water and one lying on the deck. The girl's in the water on the yacht's starboard side, holding on to a trailing line like we instructed. We're turning around for another firing pass to see if we can get the pirates to haul ass out of there, over." Nguyen's head whipped around.

"Dis bad idea, Gunna'! We don't go back. Dey shoot us down dis time!"

"Mattie back to McQuaid. What's he babbling about? What does he mean 'this time', over?"

McQuaid gave Nguyen an angry cut-throat sign with his right hand.

"He's just a little spooked because they blasted away with some rounds that could have been a little scary, but we were low and fast, so they weren't able to get a real bead on us. We tore the back of their boat a new one though, over."

Nguyen raised his hands and rolled his eyes. Then he dropped the almost empty magazine out of his Thompson and snapped in a full one. "Gotta get back to work here, Mattie. I'll let you know as soon as we've picked up the girl and figured out the situation down there, over." He reached up and shoved the throttles forward again, while pulling the control yoke back and over into a climbing left turn. The boats were several miles behind them by now and he'd have time to set up another low firing pass; from a different angle this time.

"Mattie to McQuaid, I'll radio the hospital and let them know we'll have some business for them. You're saying at least one, maybe two dead from what you can tell, over?"

"That's what it looks like from where we sit, over."

"Okay then, please promise me the only additional casualties will be pirates and not McQuaid company employees, over!"

He was busy holding the Goose in a steep bank, keeping the distant boats in sight down to the left of their position, and was starting another rapid descent. Then he handed his Thompson over to Nguyen, who gave him back a loaded weapon and started reloading McQuaid's.

"Don't worry, Mattie. It's almost cocktail hour and I'm tired and thirsty. We'll get back to you in a couple shakes with an update. McQuaid out." He gave Nguyen a grin and a quick wink. The Captain just shook his head and looked out his side window, the reloaded Thompson in his lap and ready.

They dropped down to wave-top level again with the Pratts roaring and he flashed Nguyen a jaunty thumbs-up. "All set to finish these boys off so we can head back to the barn for a cold one, Captain?"

Nguyen just waved his hand in submission and started working himself around in his seat to hang the gun out the window again.

This time they would come in low, with the pleasure yacht between them and that .30 cal. They'd have to wait until he was able to put enough distance between them, for a last hard bank to the left, in order to line up for another firing run at the pirates. He was hoping they wouldn't be able to react in time to hit them head on, or swing that gun around before he could get the Goose low to the waves again after passing over them on the other side.

They were close enough now to see the girl hanging on to the bowline, her head bobbing next to the yacht, still afloat, despite a now dangerous list to her port side. One of the pirates was on the deck throwing some boxes over to one of the other men in their party. His eyes grew wide when he spotted the Goose coming right at him and dove head first into the pirate boat. The .30 cal. started up again, with tracers passing well over their right wing. McQuaid hung his arm out his window again, preparing to fire.

Nguyen started shooting first and horrified McQuaid when he saw a line of waterspouts heading low and right for the girl's head. She ducked and disappeared, as a row of bullets ran right through the place her head had been and up the side of the yacht; the heavy slugs tearing big chunks out of its wooden side. McQuaid kicked the right rudder pedal hard and the Goose yawed to the right, pushing Nguyen's faulty aim away and over onto the heads of the pirates. Then he pulled their nose up and opened up with his own Thompson.

This time, their combined firing zeroed in on the front deck of the pirate boat. Just before they passed over the two vessels again, he saw the pirate behind the .30 cal. wheel around and sprawl to the deck, with a couple holes in his chest and a wound on his head gushing blood. They zoomed over the top and down to wave level on the other side, with the stern of the pirate boat now between them and two other men trying to work their way around the wheelhouse to fire on them with rifles.

"What the hell were you shootin' at back there, Tex?" McQuaid hollered over the intercom at Nguyen, his eyes blazing. "You might have killed the girl and sunk their boat on top of her! Let me have that thing before you blow one of your feet off – or mine." He reached for Nguyen's gun, who handed it over with a rare sheepish expression.

"My mistake, Gunna'. I did not see girl until I shoot. My mistake," he repeated. "You got pirate with machine gun plenty good, Gunna'. He no shoot us again. Hah!" Nguyen was grinning and slapping McQuaid on the back.

But he shrugged him off, worried about whether the girl had been wounded and also a little puzzled by the police chief's baffling poor marksmanship. He had seen the girl without any problem and it worried him Nguyen would have almost had to aim at her, to hit so close. He was banking the Goose around again, when Nguyen pointed back over his

29

shoulder. "Look! Dey go," he exclaimed, with decided relief. McQuaid craned his neck around to look and confirmed he was right.

The pirate boat was pulling away from the yacht and making for land at high speed. Two men were firing back at them from the stern of the boat, but were out of range. He pulled the throttles to idle and hauled back on the control yoke, killing off their airspeed. The pirates continued to put distance between them and the pleasure yacht at a fast clip.

"I guess they've had enough of us," he remarked to Nguyen, who appeared elated they wouldn't have to dive back in guns blazing again. After checking to make sure his airspeed was low enough, he pulled his flap handle down two notches. He set the wing float switches to extend and continued to hold back pressure on the yoke, as the Goose slowed and descended toward the water. A quick check of the yacht's flags told him they were headed almost straight into the ocean breeze and so he set up for a landing as close to the boat as he could. They touched down a little fast, but settled into the water without bouncing. He used the throttles to maneuver closer to the boat. When they were about twenty feet away, he pulled both fuel mixture levers down to full lean and the engines went silent, the props freewheeling for a few rotations before coming to rest. With the engines quiet, the Goose coasted toward the yacht and he motioned for Nguyen to break out the life raft.

"See if you can get over there and throw me one of their lines will you?"

"Okay Gunna'." The swaggering Captain Nguyen seemed to be acting more like a repentant teenager and anxious to offer any assistance to McQuaid, who was in no mood for any more foul-ups. While Nguyen was breaking out the raft, pushing it through the side door of the Goose, McQuaid got on the radio again to Mattie for a status update. She'd be worried about them and he had his hands free for the moment.

"McQuaid to Mattie. We're down safe next to the yacht. We must have scared the pirates enough to run them off. They lit out of here like their tail feathers were on fire, over." He let up the mike button and wiped sweat out of his eyes with the back of his arm. Nguyen was dropping the raft in the water next to the Goose, one hand holding the lanyard and bracing himself in the doorway against the rolling waves with the other. The body they had seen from the air floated into view through the open hatch, bobbing up and down on the waves a few yards away. It looked like a middle-aged man, with thinning gray hair, face down in the water, his arms outstretched out in front of him. A couple large, angry looking red holes in his back oozed blood, turning the water a rust color around him.

"Mattie to McQuaid. Thank God, you're down safe! Did you find anyone alive, over?" He lowered his voice before answering; his mouth twisted in displeasure.

"Well, we'll know soon if Nguyen shot up the girl on that last pass. I can't see her yet. She's on the far side of the boat from us, but I hope she's still holding onto that line off the bow, over."

"What do you mean Nguyen shot her, over?" Mattie asked, also in a quieter voice. She sounded shocked, but picked up that McQuaid didn't want the police captain to overhear them.

"I'll let you know as soon as we get over to pull her out of the water. Seems Nguyen managed to hit everything but the pirates shooting at us on that last pass. He's paddling the raft over now, so he can get a line to tie the Goose off against their boat. I'll check and see if their radio still works when I get aboard. If it does, I'll be able to give you another status report, over."

"Gunna', catch line okay?" Captain Nguyen was standing on the deck with a bowline coiled in his right hand to toss over to him.

"Call you back, Mattie, out." He tore off the headset and lurched over to grab the doorframe between waves tossing the Goose up and down. The line whizzed by the door and he grabbed it to tie off on a cargo cleat inside the cabin. He gave him a thumbs-up and started pulling the plane over to the boat and secured it with a little slack, to keep the wing from crashing onto the listing, rolling deck. Nguyen kicked the raft over to him and he used it to reach the yacht and pulled himself aboard.

The body of an older woman lay facing them, her head lolling; dead eyes staring, rocking back and forth in a puddle of blood pooled against the gunwale. She'd been shot at least twice in the stomach and had a neat hole near the middle of her forehead. Most of the back of her head was splattered against a bullet-riddled cabin wall near her feet. They both looked down at her in a moment of quiet reflection. Then McQuaid pulled Nguyen away toward the starboard side to find the girl.

The line off the bow was visible, trailing down along side of the hull, but there was no sign of the girl. They crouched down and crawled along the gunwale, peering into the depths to see if she had been dragged under the boat. The line disappeared down somewhere beneath the hull. But there was no sign of her. McQuaid threw off his shoes and was just about to dive in, when she burst out of the water coughing and sputtering.

"Quick, hold my legs," he commanded, as he flopped down lengthwise on the deck. Reaching down into the water with both arms, he grabbed her under the shoulders and dragged her up onto the deck like a ragdoll, in one sweeping movement. She lay on her face, palms flat and fingers splayed against the teak wood deck. Gasping for breath, she was retching and coughing up water. McQuaid rolled her over and straightened her up to a sitting position facing him. Dark wet shoulder-length hair, tangled around her face. With great apprehension, she opened her eyes and looked up at him, lips quivering.

"You're going to be just fine," he said and smiled. The girl's face melted and she burst into tears. He pulled her to his chest and held her. "It's okay, baby. You made it. We're here to protect you now," he whispered, rocking her back and forth, doing what he could to calm her. She held onto him, clutching his flight overalls between her little fists, wailing now; her voice was low and guttural, more like an animal than human. He just held her and rocked her. "Let it all go, baby. You're safe now. We've got you."

Nguyen stood by, watching them. McQuaid flicked his head toward the rear of the boat. "See if there's anyone else on board, Captain. I'll take care of her for now." Nguyen nodded and headed off toward the stern, his revolver out.

After a moment or two, her crying subsided and she pulled away from him, sniffling, and looked at his face again. He smiled back at her, hoping to appear reassuring. "What's your name?" he asked gently. Soft hazel colored eyes appraised his, but she remained silent. He could tell by her expression she had understood him. She sucked her bottom lip under and trembled a few more times.

"I am Lijuan." Her words came out as if they were being held captive between a last few heaving sobs.

"You are indeed beautiful," he replied, remembering her name was the Mandarin term for one who is graceful and beautiful. He figured she might be in her early twenties, Chinese thin, small boned, and probably very pretty when she didn't look like a drowned little mouse. As he pulled thick, sodden strands of hair away from her mouth and eyes, she grew self-conscious and blushed. He tried to sit her back away from him, so she could gather her wits before he helped her to her feet. But she shrank back, craning her neck to see past him. "It's okay," he reassured her. "We chased the pirates away. They won't bother you anymore."

Relief flooded her expression and she stood to see for herself. But relief turned to horror when she spotted the body lying on the deck. Her fists flew to her mouth and she screamed. Running over, Lijuan dropped to her knees over the woman. Agonized cries seemed wrenched from deep within her body. Clutching herself with both arms, she rocked back and forth while tears rolled off her cheeks and splashed in the puddle of blood next to the woman's sightless eyes. McQuaid pulled her away and wrapped a big arm around her shoulder to steer her toward the cockpit of the boat.

"You can't help her anymore," he whispered.

Looking past his arm, Lijuan saw the man's corpse floating near the boat; rolling with the gentle waves. Recoiling in revulsion, she turned away and buried her face against his chest. McQuaid walked her aft, steering her toward the steps up into the cockpit and sat her down on a padded bench near the helm. He saw the radio to one side and noticed the lights on the face showed it still had power.

"Sit here for a moment while I call for some help from shore," he told her, while she sat with her back bowed forward, hugging her knees, staring at the deck. McQuaid turned his attention to the radio and confirmed it was still dialed to the emergency frequency Mattie was monitoring. He grabbed the mike off the hook and clicked the transmit button. "McQuaid to Mattie, over." Letting up on the button, he watched the girl while waiting for Mattie to come back. Lijuan sat unmoving, wet straggled hair hanging over and hiding most of her face. She was breathing in short gasps and shivered, her eyes frozen forward and vacant.

"Mattie here, what's going on, Richard, over?"

"It's all finished, Mattie. We ran the pirates off and found the girl alive. She's not injured, but her parents weren't so lucky, over."

"They're dead?"

He glanced over at Lijuan.

"Yep, 'fraid so."

Chapter Three
Clark Air Force Base, Luzon Island, the Philippines

McQuaid left Nguyen on the boat to tend to the dead. Mattie called the police station to send their launch out to pick him and the bodies up. He bundled Lijuan up in the Goose for the short hop back to Lubang Hospital. She was silent and unresponsive on the flight back. Her face remained pressed against the glass of the co-pilot's window and otherwise she never moved from where he'd belted her in with an Army blanket wrapped around her sodden clothing. She had stopped shivering, but he knew she was in shock and he wanted her to keep warm until Doc McCawley could get a look at her.

Former Lieutenant James McCawley, who everyone on the island referred to as "Doc", was another war refugee, also British, who had lost his wife in one of the many London bombing raids. He had set his sights on Mattie for a while, but was empathetic to the death of her husband and the still raw pain of his own loss. They had just settled for being good friends. In a way, they were the three Musketeers on Lubang: the Doc, Mattie, and McQuaid. All war veterans who yearned for the slower, simpler life of the Philippines, with people they had served with; a much closer bond than friends, or distant family awaiting them in their native countries. Only there weren't any families to return to. They were islands unto themselves and so the island of Lubang seemed to provide a welcome refuge from painful memories they would have to endure in returning to the real world. So this became their new home.

Doc McCawley stayed on in Lubang after the war, when he discovered the woeful state of their hospital and lack of seasoned medical staff. He had been a British Navy corpsman, but apprenticed under one of their surgeons, so he picked up most of the medical skills needed around town. Anything he couldn't handle was packed off to Manila, on either the Goose or the C-47, whichever was most handy or flight-worthy. Doc and a couple of his Filipino nurses were waiting at the pier for them when the Goose dropped into the water a couple hundred yards away and then taxied up close enough for Baacay to throw them a line from the dock. Baacay gently took the girl by the shoulders and handed her off to the hospital staff. Lijuan just stared at her feet and stumbled along stiff legged, with her mouth hanging half open and arms still wrapped inside the blanket; a frail and pathetic little bundle. McQuaid exchanged a few words with Doc McCawley, as he began looking her over.

"How long was she in the water?" he asked as he pushed her hair back off her face and looked into her eyes, noting her quivering bluish lips.

"Maybe half an hour and the water temp is near eighty degrees." McQuaid looked past Doc's bowed head and noticed Mattie jogging toward the dock from town, with Kiko tight on her wing. Anywhere important was a short walk away in the small ramshackle town of Lubang. "Not sure the water's the problem, Doc," he continued. His expression turned sour and he moved to shut the side hatch on the Goose.

"Oh?" Doc raised an expectant eyebrow above his owlish steel-rimmed glasses and glanced back at McQuaid. His thinning gray hair was in absurd disarray, standing out at all angles atop his head, from the wind on the short ride over from the hospital in their truck. But his green eyes were alert and concerned, in the hope of obtaining any additional scrap of information that might help him with his medical assessment of the young girl.

"Both her parents were killed by the pirates. I'm sure she witnessed the whole thing." McQuaid ran his hand through the short stiff hairs on his head and rubbed the back of his neck. "A tough day all around for her I'd say, wouldn't you?" Doc offered an absent-minded nod in reply and told the nurses to get her in the old Army truck they used for their ambulance.

"We'll give her the full treatment and knock her out for a spell too. Some rest will do her good." He took a slight step back, as Mattie reached them and came to a graceful stop next to McQuaid. Kiko, on the other hand, came in hot, sliding in the gravel and trailing a plume of dust behind her. She latched onto his leg, like a tail hook snagging the 3-wire on a carrier landing, before she jerked to a full stop. Her eyes were clamped shut, standing silent and clutching his leg. He reached down to hold her head against him in one of his big paws.

"She okay?" Mattie asked in a higher pitched voice than usual. "Was she wounded at all?" He glanced up from Kiko.

"Nope. Just a bit waterlogged and probably plenty wiped out over the whole pirate attack. I'm pretty sure she saw the pirates kill both her parents," he said in a low voice so Lijuan, being led to the truck by McCawley's two nurses, couldn't overhear them. "She had a close call too, with Wild Bill spraying bullets practically on top of her." His voice was hardened by disdain. Mattie pursed her lips and looked after the girl without saying anything. McCawley hung back and spoke to McQuaid in his best physician's voice.

"Nguyen will most certainly want to question her. Tell him she'll be out for at least twenty-four hours and he can see me afterward for permission for a supervised interview at her bedside." He jerked his thumb back over his shoulder at her. "She's going to be in no shape anytime soon for one of his ham-handed attempts at police interrogation." He turned to walk away, pulling his ever-present stethoscope from one of his doctor's white coat pockets. Then he stopped and looked back to address them both. "Better yet, tell him I'll call him to let him know when she's ready," he said, arching an authoritative eyebrow. Without question, he was not to be trifled with as the island's lone physician and even Nguyen gave him a wide berth on anything medical. He turned around and walked briskly toward the ambulance.

"Do you think she even knows anything?" Mattie asked McQuaid with some emphasis. McQuaid just shook his head.

"I'm not sure, but the pirates seemed to be unloading a number of packages from the yacht, which all appeared to be about the same size and shape; like some sort of cargo. I wonder what they were carrying. I'd also like to know what happened to their engines and why they foundered." He stooped down to peer closer at Kiko. She had almost shut the blood flow off to his left leg, with her Koala bear-like grip. Her face was buried in the fabric of his flight overall and she hadn't yet made any move to pull away. Mattie glanced down at Kiko as well.

"She was glued to me at the radio the whole time you were out there, hanging on every word." He gave her a questioning look. "She worries about you, McQuaid," she said with a slight smile.

Turning back to Kiko, he brushed the hair back from her face. But her eyes remained squeezed shut. He reached down and gathered her up in his arms, kissing the top of her head.

"I'm okay, little pigeon. You don't have to worry about me. I'll always come back for you," he said, his lips touching her hair. Mattie laid her hand on his shoulder, but turned away to wipe at a tear. McQuaid stood up and they walked back to the General Store arm-in-arm. Mattie held the screen door for him as he carried her in and laid her down on her cot. At last, Kiko let go of him and squinted up at him when he sat down next to her.

"Can I have Coca?" she asked, brightening. They both grinned back at her.

"Sure, kid. Why not?" he replied ruffling her head, and then stood up and walked over to the soda cooler to grab a Coca-Cola out for her. He snapped off the cap on the opener on the side with a practiced hand. Mattie stepped in close to whisper to him.

"Are you still planning on taking her with you on the flight out to Manila this afternoon?" She glanced back at Kiko's silhouette on the cot to make sure she hadn't been overheard. He followed her eyes.

"What d'you think?" he asked. Mattie sighed and wiped her hands on the back of her jeans.

"I don't think we have much choice, do you?" she replied. He took a slow, pensive sip of the Coke considering this and then wiped his mouth with the back of his hand.

"Not really," he admitted. They both laughed and McQuaid rubbed her shoulders with his free hand.

"She'll be all right. I'm betting she falls asleep on the flight over. We'll need to saddle up soon too, if we're going to get there in time to scrounge a fuel pump at the air base," he said glancing at his watch and noting it was near four o'clock. He handed the Coke to Mattie, who also took a token sip, letting her hand rest on his for a moment.

"I was worried about you too," she said, looking up at him, her eyes moist. He looked back at her feigning shock, as if he couldn't imagine such a remark.

"You think I was going to let some puny pirate pipsqueaks shoot me down with their little popguns? I'm a Marine fighter ace, woman!" He rolled his eyes at her, pretending dismay to cover his slight embarrassment over what was a rare intimate moment between them. She looked back at him without answering, her lips pressed together.

Kiko sat up and yelled.

"Hey, where my Coca?" They both burst out laughing and the mood was broken.

"Right here, you ungrateful little scamp! Keep your drawers on will you?" he boomed back at her but couldn't keep a straight face long enough to carry it off.

A half hour later, McQuaid was in the pilot's seat of the Goose again, with Kiko belted into the co-pilot's seat, her trusty flight helmet in place and goggles over her eyes. He had already cranked both engines and motioned out the window to Baacay to cast off the line and secure the aft hatch.

Baacay was to fly along with them – having loaded sundry cargo items aboard for sale and assigned to buying supplies to replenish stock in the store for Mattie. She had given him a long list, which he was careful to stuff deep into one of the buttoned pockets of his jungle shorts. He'd also gotten an invoice from Doc McCawley for hospital supplies he ordered from the hospital on Clark and they were transporting some bundles of mail to drop off at the post office in Manila.

Baacay had also been charged with inspecting the neat little holes in the Goose's tail feathers, but McQuaid determined the damage from the pirate bullets was minimal. They'd apply sheet metal patches later, when they had some down time. After a quick top-off of the wing tanks from a few jerry cans he'd trucked over from the airfield, the Goose was deemed airworthy enough to await their return for repairs.

Baacay leaned out of the rear door, threw the tie-down line onto the pier for Mattie, and gave the dock post a good shove with his foot. Then he exchanged waves with her, ducked back into the plane, and dogged the hatch behind him.

"All done, Gunna'," he yelled up to the cockpit and heard the port engine rev up in response. McQuaid held the right rudder pedal to the floor and advanced the opposing engine throttle to depart the dock in a slow right turn. He gave Mattie a thumbs-up out the window and then a sappy salute. She laughed back at him, her hand shielding her eyes against the glare of the sun on the water, now in the final quarter of its long fall to the sea.

Mattie watched them taxi out past the piled rock jetty that protected the anchorage, where nearby dinghies and small fishing boats bobbed around in the swells. She always felt a twinge of sadness when McQuaid left the safe confines of their small island. Out in the harbor to her right, she noticed some of the fishermen standing on the decks of their boats, also watching the Goose taxi out. Still primitive islanders in many ways, they gazed at the large amphibious plane in wonder as it passed by them. A few were bent over nets, but stopped their work to stand and wave. McQuaid's arm was out the window waving back to them.

Mattie smiled around squinted eyes, looking almost directly into the sun. *Life is good here*, she mused. Things were more primitive and slower paced than England, but this was as much her home now as her family farm in Dorchester had been, so many years ago. At least it seemed like it had been many years anyway. Memories of her childhood rushed in, along with a sharp pang of grief. Reflecting on the past, she remembered having to give up their farm when her parents failed to return from what was supposed to be a brief anniversary trip back to London. They had first met in a little coffee shop there, some twenty years prior. But, as so many others caught in the surprise bombing raids, they had simply vanished without a trace.

She missed the soft English rain, morning smells of breakfast, fried ham, eggs, and porridge with cinnamon in her mother's kitchen, and her dad's pipe smoke. He'd come stomping in through the mud room from the barn, where he'd been milking cows, or one of his other endless farm chores, rainwater streaming off his slicker. But somehow, he kept that old pipe lit through wind, rain, snow, or sleet. And he always had a smile for his daughter and wife, no matter how tired he was. With a twinge, Mattie realized it was one of a number of things that struck her about McQuaid. She felt protected and warm whenever he was around.

Her eyes were still fixed on the Goose while she stood rooted to the dock. They began a wallowing turn into the wind, waves splashing high up her sides, the engines loud and throbbing as they started to pick up speed. Mattie was no aviator and flying in airplanes had always made her quite nervous. She held her breath, waiting for the lumbering flying boat to transform itself into a thing of the air. Flying was a magical adventure to her. It made no sense, no matter how patient and thorough McQuaid's explanation on the "simple" principles of aerodynamics. To Mattie, piloting airplanes was like taming a flying dragon; something only a rare breed of man could master. It seemed as if they were able to merge their minds and souls with their metal beasts, to ply them somehow to do their bidding, when lesser men were crushed in their claws, or sloughed off, falling to their deaths.

The Goose pitched in the waves a few more times, then she seemed to gather herself and rose out of the sea, soaring into the copper sky with a sense of majesty. She saw them banking eastward, the low reflected sun flashing off the metal and glass. Waggling their wings in a final salute to the earth-bounders, watching in humble reverence from the shore, the flying boat merged with the fading light. Mattie was reluctant to turn away, feeling a superstitious need to keep them in sight as long as she could. With a sigh, she waved one last time, shaking off her silly obsession, and started walking toward town. There was plenty to do at the store without wasting any more time down at the dock and she didn't want to keep any possible customers waiting. The droning of the plane's engines merged with the lapping sound of the waves against the pilings and then only the harbor sounds remained.

Back in the Goose, winging toward Luzon Island, McQuaid was holding the throttles to full power over his head, watching his airspeed gauge slowly wind up to a respectable number. He reached over and snapped the electrical switches to retract the wing floats, holding the airplane in a slow bank to the right and eyeing the radio compass until his course settled on zero-one-zero degrees. Leveling off at twenty-five hundred feet, he aimed well right of the setting sun, now reflecting off the gauges on the dash in front of him. He removed his dark green aviator sunglasses and stowed them in the overhead visor.

Glancing over at Kiko, he noticed she had assumed her customary pose, sitting bolt upright in the co-pilot's seat. Her head was tilted back, stretching her neck up and sighting down her nose to see over the instrument panel. She held her lower lip sucked under her top teeth and he could see she was transfixed by fierce concentration. McQuaid chuckled and was about to say something to her, when she sensed his attention and turned to face him with a shy smile.

Caught in a rare instant of elation, her face reflected a child's awe for the mastery of flight above the clouds and freedom from the mundanity of human affairs that shackled others to Earth. Like McQuaid, she seemed to have a deep appreciation for this and never grew tired of it, no matter how many times they flew together. Theirs was a brief and poignant human moment of shared bliss, without regard for age or gender. He just beamed back and winked.

Baacay appeared in the cockpit behind them, flinging his arms over their seat backs, also looking out through the windshield at the glare of the sun on the water and the receding blue ocean beneath them.

"Good day to fly, heh Gunna'?" he shouted at him cheerfully, then reached over and squeezed Kiko's shoulder.

"Every day's a good day to fly, Baacay!" he yelled back, recounting the ageless pilot's retort, to those who were more accustomed to viewing the sky from the confines of the ground. Baacay just nodded, already mesmerized by the reassuring throb of the engines, the warm wind rushing through the open side windows, and the drumming vibration through the deck beneath their feet. If an airplane could be happy, the Goose would be humming a cheerful tune at this tranquil moment in time.

After about thirty minutes, they could begin to see details of the Luzon coastline ahead, with its low-lying rain clouds cresting the hills above Subic Bay, where even three years after the hostilities had ceased with Japan, a large fleet of American warships still jammed the piers and lay at anchor around the harbor. McQuaid had dialed in the radio beacon for Clark Air Base some time back and was following the needle on his Radio Direction Finder (RDF) to home in on the field.

When they crossed over the beach, he eased back on the control yoke to begin his climb over the lower ridgeline of Mount Samat Peak, banking to the right to steer between the mountains and Manila Bay to the south. Green knobbed and jagged peaks stood aside to let them pass. Over the last ridge, they could begin to see the welcome checkerboard of sunlit farm fields, chased by a procession of cloud shadows darting through the valley beyond.

McQuaid's mind's eye drifted back to a time, a scant few years ago, when this same area had been far from pastoral. Corregidor, a fortified island guarding Manila Bay, passed below them to the right, where American and Filipino soldiers made their final stand in defense of the Philippines. Later, thousands of them, wounded and dying, were herded over eighty miles to Japanese detention camps in what became known as the infamous Bataan Death March. The ghosts of those bayonetted and left to die by the roadsides were said to haunt this valley, searching in vain for the men who'd deserted them.

"Look!" Kiko was pointing at a tight formation of aircraft approaching well above and passing to the left of them, several miles away from the north. His practiced fighter pilot eyes had picked them out a few minutes earlier and classified them as friendlies. Of course, there hadn't been any enemy bogies to fear for some time now. But the indelible lesson learned from Pearl Harbor was: *never* let your guard down.

He glanced up at them again and counted several B-29 bombers, with a small fighter escort – F4U Corsairs, the powerful blue gull-winged fighter he had flown into combat a few years back. Corsairs were a Navy/Marine fighter, so McQuaid figured they were probably flying in to Clark on other business. They must have buddied up to escort the slower bombers to their home station at Clark.

Clark Air Force Base was a massive military complex of over fourteen square miles, with long paved runways. They were a recent convert to this new branch of all-air military renamed the U.S. Air Force; whereas they had been a combined Army and Army Air Corps through the end of the war. The bombers were attached to the incoming 13th Air Force, replacing four of the previous bomber groups. They had also upgraded to B-29s from the older Army Air B-17s and B-24s. Their 18th Fighter Wing heralded the newer, faster and more nimble P-51 Mustangs, and some heavier, stubby P-47 Thunderbolts. The 18th was a support air protection group against any potential threats to the base and the bombers; though none was expected during peacetime.

Clark Air Force Base was the single largest airfield in the Pacific theater. They had wrested it back from the Japanese who overran Luzon Island and captured the base in 1942. It wasn't until 1945 that it was once more safely in U.S. hands, after much blood loss on both sides. McQuaid had flown in and out of Clark many times as a Marine fighter pilot – even strafing and bombing enemy aircraft on the ground while it was still held by the Japanese. Memories, good and bad, crowded his mind while he dialed in the tower frequency to work into their approach and landing pattern. Unlike Lubang's sleepy little airfield, Clark was a bustling hive of activity, all day and much of the night.

"Clark tower, this is McQuaid Air Cargo, flying a Grumman Goose, at four thousand feet, twenty miles northeast of Samat Peak, inbound to Clark – request landing instructions, over." He grabbed the volume knob, poised to adjust it up or down, depending on their signal strength. They came back clear and crisp.

"Clark field tower reading McQuaid Air Cargo, runway 1 is active; wind two-three-zero degrees at ten mph. Make left traffic for a southbound landing on runway 1 and report midfield. Adjust altimeter to field pressure at 29.82, over." McQuaid grabbed a pencil out of the visor and wrote down the landing instructions, field conditions, and barometric pressure on the ever-present notebook he kept in a side pocket, more out of habit than concern for memorizing the numbers. He radioed back the instructions for approach and landing approval, then reached forward and adjusted his altimeter gauge to the field pressure of 29.82 – to match the field altitude.

He grabbed the overhead throttles and pulled them to half, holding back on the control yoke, as the Goose began to slow and settle. He could see the field now, dead ahead and almost ten miles away. He'd have plenty of time for a slow descent to landing pattern altitude of fifteen hundred feet. Banking slightly, he lined up parallel with the north/south facing runway 1 for landing south, which would be a series of left turns for the opposite approach to the runway ahead and now slightly to the left of them.

The bomber and fighter formation had called in ahead of him; being much faster. Military took priority over civilian flights, so the tower would clear them in first. That meant a long, slow extended final approach and a few circling turns, until he got the clearance he needed to turn to the runway heading and begin his final approach.

"McQuaid Air Cargo, this is flight leader for Marine flight 209, you wouldn't be THE, ex-Captain Gunner McQuaid by any chance would you, over?" This came through in customary fighter pilot radio vernacular, as a monotone, staccato burst of words. But, he still picked out a familiar slow Southern drawl. Even through the radio distortion, the voice was unmistakable as that of his old wingman Captain Jake Wilmouth, perhaps even a Marine Corps Major by now.

He and Jake hadn't seen each other since they had both served aboard the USS Essex, after the battle for Luzon, and were in more than a few tight spots together as fighter pilots. They were *brothers from different mothers*, as wingmen were often called. Trained to mirror each other in flight and protect each other to the death in battle, there was no closer brotherhood than brothers-in-arms. He thought Jake had left for the states almost three years ago. Their nicknames were legendary in the close circles of fellow Marine fighter pilots. His call sign had been "Gunner" and Jake Wilmouth was "Snake."

"That you, Snake?" he asked, keeping his voice even and professional, though he felt like shouting.

"Yep, though I'm sad to see only one of us has the common decency to fly something that doesn't look like my grandma's rocker with wings!" There was never any quarter given nor asked for among Marines.

"Corsairs don't pay my bills, Snake. If you had a real job, you'd already know that."

"Clark tower to Marine flight 209, advise you maintain radio protocol and take your chatter to the 'O' Club later, boys."

"Roger, Clark Tower – Marine 209 flight leader – sorry 'bout that. The beer better be cold if you're recommending it, over." Jake had replied in the appropriate pilot code. Modest, but unshakable.

"Clark Tower to Marine 209, only the Air Force gets the cold beer. We send the Navy into town. Knock off the chatter. You're cleared number four to land, after the B-29 flight, over."

"Copy, Clark Tower, Marine flight 209 cleared number four to land."

"Clark Tower to McQuaid Air Cargo, hold short five miles northeast of runway 1, circle until further advised, over."

"Copy, Clark Tower, McQuaid Air Cargo. Will hold five miles northeast of runway 1 and circle until further advised. On landing, request immediate taxi to the 'O' Club." He only received two quick mike clicks in response, which was more than he expected. But they were all fellow soldiers first and it was peacetime, so strict radio procedure was more relaxed, as long as their antics didn't get out of hand.

It wasn't long after, while making their slow circles north of the airfield, when the tower radioed and cleared them to land. He sent Baacay back to double check the cargo for anything that might bump loose on landing and then to belt into one of the jump seats. He lined up on runway 1, lowered the gear, dropped one notch of flaps, and began his final descent. They touched down and taxied over to where the other flight had parked and shut down nearest one of the Corsairs. "Snake" Wilmouth met him with a bear hug when he hopped out of the rear hatch.

"Gunner, you look old and fat, but you're a sight for sore eyes!" They stepped back from each other and clasped arms in the way old warriors do. Baacay held Kiko back in the cargo bay of the Goose, to give the two friends a moment to themselves.

"How the hell are ya, Snake?" McQuaid's face was split with a huge grin. He was both relieved and very glad to see his old wingman. Fighter piloting continued to be a dangerous business, even in peacetime. Wilmouth was shorter than McQuaid, but broader shouldered and sported a severe military flat-top haircut; the brown just flecking gray at the temples. If ever there was a picture to exemplify "dashing," it would be the portrait of Jake Wilmouth. He was brutally handsome, complete with glacier blue eyes and even a hero's cleft chin. No doubt he made the ladies drool – assuming of course they could get past his annoying West Texas cowboy swagger. But in spite of himself, he was infectious and grew friends with ease. And there was no better friend, if ever you were in need.

They had lost track of each other after the war and time had passed too fast to stay in touch. McQuaid was curious about him remaining in the South Pacific.

"I thought you'd be flying a desk in San Diego by now. What are you, some kind of hero, sticking around out here in the middle of nowhere? In case you hadn't noticed, the Japs all went home."

Jake grinned and shook his head.

"Nah, they promoted me and I'm heading up a training squadron at Guam. I fly over to Clark every once in a while, just to see what a big island looks like." McQuaid couldn't imagine him relegated to training "nuggets" and they were all based stateside anyway. But Wilmouth deflected the obvious question before he could ask. "Tell you what, speaking of the middle of nowhere, why are we sweating out here on the tarmac, when we could be cooling down over at the 'O' Club? The beer really is cold there you know." Just then, he noticed Baacay and Kiko in the back of the Goose. "What you got there, prisoners?" he drawled and stepped closer to see for himself.

"Major Wilmouth, this is my maintenance hand Baacay and my number one co-pilot, Kiko." He winked, when Jake gave him a quick look. Baacay jumped down and offered his hand.

"Nice meet you, Missar Snake," he said straight faced. "Dis Kiko here," he gestured back at her and helped Kiko step down from the Goose. Jake shook Baacay's hand, then pulled his flight cap off and offered a low knight's bow to Kiko.

"I'm awful honored to meet you, young lady," he said in his hammy version of chivalry. Kiko threw both hands to her mouth and giggled, then hid her eyes. "Ah, I see yore a shy lass, aren't you?" He cast a scornful frown toward McQuaid. "Just let me know if you ever need someone to protect you against this oversized gorilla. I hear he gets real mean if you don't feed him enough bananas!" Kiko burst out laughing and pointed her finger at McQuaid.

"You no like bananas, Gunna'!" She giggled again, as McQuaid pulled her to his side with a big arm around her and shaking his head at Jake.

"I think this one could use a big chocolate milk shake over at the 'O' Club and I, for one, could use that cold beer instead of standing around out here listening to abuse." He motioned to Baacay. "Tie her down and let's get over to maintenance before they close up, so I can see about a new fuel pump. Grab the old one out of there and then follow me. The sooner we take care of business, the sooner we can be cooling our heels in the shade." He squinted toward the maintenance buildings. "I hope I still have some friends around here that can help an old fighter pilot in need."

McQuaid noticed a flight line truck had peeled out from the line shacks near the hangars and was headed their way. The vehicle seemed to shimmer and dance in the heat reflected off the ramp. Jake followed his eyes and spotted the truck as well.

"Allow me to handle this," he said, as he brushed McQuaid aside. When the truck reached them, he stepped forward to flag it down. The driver was an Air Force enlisted man and stuck his head out the window to offer a casual salute to the Major. Jake leaned in the window and addressed him in his best career officer voice. "I need you to take this gentleman over to maintenance and help him locate a replacement fuel pump for..." He looked over to McQuaid for help.

"An engine fuel pump for a C-47. Should be easy to find around here," he replied, gesturing toward a row of the cargo planes lined up near one of the hangars. "I have a used pump to offer in trade," he declared. Baacay held up exhibit A, so the driver could see the offending pump in question. Jake picked up the dialog right on cue.

"Right – a replacement fuel pump for a C-47. Think you can handle that for me, son?" he asked, looking at the man's name sewed over his left pocket. "Airman 2nd Class Jeppers is it?" he asked, reading off his name.

"Yes, sir," Airman Jeppers replied, climbing out of the truck and gesturing to them. "Hop in and I'll run y'all over to maintenance." He seemed eager to please, but in a seasoned military sort of way. Efficient, courteous, and with an expression suggesting he was unimpressed with rank, he mustered just enough energy to manage them, without over extending himself. McQuaid chuckled to himself. The kid appeared much wiser than his rank. Jake turned to him, arched his eyebrows, and smirked.

"Leave it to the Air Force to run a tight ship," he said, with a slight nod back toward Airman Jeppers. McQuaid just smiled back without comment. He had no rank here anymore and was under no illusion they were obligated to help ex-military, cum-expatriated-American-civilians, any more than necessary.

"Thank you for your help, son," he said to Jeppers, his voice and manner genuine. "I owe a favor to you and the Air Force for this one." He moved Kiko around in front of him. "Do you mind if she sits up front with you, Airman?" Jeppers glanced down at Kiko, who gawked back up at him with her mouth hanging open.

"Would you like to ride in the front with me, little lady?" he asked, appearing tolerant, but without enthusiasm. Kiko shook her head and they all turned to watch as one while she marched over to the rear of the pickup and climbed into the bed. Jeppers looked back at McQuaid for further orders.

"Guess she rides in the back," he responded, pushing his ball cap back on his head. "Major, you and Airman Jeppers can ride up front and we'll take the tail gun position." McQuaid turned back to look at Kiko with a wry smile and wondered at her skill in charming grown men into submission. It was clear she assumed she outranked them all. He shuddered to imagine what she might be capable of in a few years' time.

With the help of Jeppers and a maintenance supply chief, who just happened to know Major "Snake" Wilmouth, they were on their way to the 'O' Club with little time lost and a rebuilt fuel pump in hand. The Officer's Club was on the south side of Clark Air Base, about half a mile inside the front gate. There were several bars, diners, and other hangouts on the base, but the 'O' Club was the place to be if you were a pilot. It was cool, dark, and comforting to McQuaid to be on such familiar turf again. Since Clark Air Base was the largest air base in the Pacific hemisphere, the Officer's Club ascended to being lavish, even by military standards, with a separate bar/lounge and a large, well-appointed dining room.

Being in officer country, there were no "enlisteds," except for those working as waiters, bartenders and cooks. Most were Non-Commissioned Officers (NCOs), three-stripers and above, who were either part of the supply corps or worked there as a side job. There were also a number of very attractive and scantily dressed cocktail waitresses. The men descended on a booth in a dimly lit corner and spread out to relax, order drinks and dinner, while listening to the muted brass of Glenn Miller playing on the radio in the background.

Baacay claimed to be a vegetarian, but he ordered poached cod and a large green salad. Both pilots ordered steaks and a hamburger with fries and a chocolate milkshake for Kiko, who immediately ignored her food and attacked the milkshake.

One of the cocktail waitresses, a gorgeous young Mandarin Chinese, greased to an undulating stop in front of their table. She bent under the single hanging lamp swaying low above their table, dropping drink napkins in front of them. Her scooped blouse hugged pent-up breasts straining against a flimsy top button, which as a mechanism for chaste restraint, appeared near the brink of catastrophic failure. Dark feline eyes assessed them from under heavy lashes. Glossy, blue-black hair framed her face and fell to a tiny, wasp-like waist. It occurred to McQuaid, she may have poured herself into the short white silk skirt, which covered little of the long, latte colored legs. Somehow she remained graceful atop a dangerous looking pair of high, white stiletto heels.

"What can I bring you boys from the bar?" she purred. It took several seconds for any of the three men to respond with something coherent. Kiko looked back and forth between

49

them with concern. Major Wilmouth cleared his throat and took the plunge.

"Hello there, gorgeous. Don't you look smashing tonight?" The corners of her mouth turned up, showing very white teeth against lips painted bright red. "I think we're going to have some icy, very icy cold beers this evening, my dear."

McQuaid hadn't ever known Jake to be intimidated by a gorgeous woman and he wasn't about to be caught off his game this time either. Leaning toward her across the table, Jake crooked a conspiratorial finger and motioned her closer. Dark, seductive eyes appraised him as she leaned in to put her face next to his. Lowering his view to her moistened red lips, a bare inch away from his own, he launched his preemptive strike.

"I don't want to give you the wrong idea about us – and by that I mean me," he crooned, placing his hand over his heart, while holding her eyes with a wolfish grin. Then he waggled his forefinger back and forth between the other men seated at the table. "We're having the cold beers. The little lady here is having a milkshake. After dinner, they will be leaving together, abandoning me – I'm sad to admit – all by my lonesome." He winked back at her and clucked twice through his teeth from the corner of his mouth. Practiced eyes studied his mouth for a moment longer and then her lips curved upward in a knowing shape. Turning her head just enough to place her mouth next to his ear, she cocked a warm hip against his thigh before offering a slow, breathy reply.

"Whatever you say, flyboy. I can see you're a real pushover for sweet, innocent young girls." She stepped back to cast a pointed look in Kiko's direction, then pooched her lips to blow him a kiss. With a long, exaggerated wink, she made her exit to get their drinks, rolling her hips in an excellent vaudevillian sashay, only lacking a drum roll and a rim shot for a proper finale. Jake laughed out loud and grabbed McQuaid in an affectionate headlock. McQuaid laughed too.

"You've still got it, Snake," he allowed, shaking his head.

The steaks were perfect; charbroiled, juicy, thick and rare and the Marines tore into them without mercy. Baacay wolfed his fish down with gusto, his mouth breaking into a broad grin around every other bite. Even Kiko eventually made it to her hamburger. She horrified them all, however, by gushing ketchup all over her fries. But she seemed to relish them swimming in tomato sauce, so they tried not to make her self-conscious. McQuaid checked on her with an occasional furtive glance, to make sure she wasn't getting queasy.

The two fighter pilots fell into swapping war stories about life aboard their old floating home at sea, the USS Essex. They bantered about who made the smoothest carrier landings, who got the most women, and who could drink the most beer without falling down. They talked about strafing missions, providing close air support to the Army and Marine "mudders"; battling the Japanese on the ground. Using their hands as fighter planes, they demonstrated how one or the other pulled off numerous feats of heroics at the expense of their inferior enemy counterparts. They ate fast, talked fast and played to their small civilian audience like a practiced stage act; more than once getting them laughing so hard, McQuaid feared Kiko might wet her pants. Their plates emptied and the beer bottles stacked up until they were almost spent. McQuaid was content to just sit and relish the feeling of intense kinship with a fellow fighter pilot with whom he had gone to battle and cheated death many times over. The evening couldn't have been more perfect.

A different cocktail waitress winged over to see if they wanted another round. She was a beautiful local girl from Manila who spoke perfect English and also seemed practiced at extracting premium tips out of female-starved, over-gassed soldiers and airmen. Leaning against each of the men while taking their drink orders, she giggled, batted her eyes and invited visual strafing on her low cut blouse and tight, bun-hugging shorts. Kiko frowned at the unambiguous floorshow for the men, then elbowed McQuaid when the girl started cooing in his ear and asking whether he had someone special waiting back home for him.

He glared down at her, but got the message, realizing he was falling into that typical sappy, over-sudsed, male blabber she was soliciting. There was little doubt she made every man in the club feel like she was there just for him, especially the ones who were feeling no pain anyway and with money to burn. The two pilots had no problem with this, of course. Kiko however, was getting more restless and annoyed with the other Filipino girl, whose fawning over the men appeared so transparent and divisive to her.

The waitress sensed the tension there and tried playing up to Kiko, making an airy attempt to engage in their native

Tagalog. McQuaid hoped things would stay friendly, but was soon disabused of any such notion. Jewel, their cocktail waitress, asked Kiko something, to which Kiko offered a prompt reply, appearing innocent to both the Americans, while Baacay raised a nervous hand to cover his eyes. He elbowed Kiko and began to rub the back of his neck, as if to relieve a sudden muscle spasm, then picked up a menu and became fascinated with the breakfast page. Meanwhile, Jewel's expectant and toothy smile turned glacial.

She raised a reproachful eyebrow, her jaw tight, and looked over at McQuaid and Major Wilmouth for their response. Both men offered congenial smiles in return, all too aware they hadn't the foggiest clue what Kiko had said to her. With an abrupt move, Jewel spun on her heel and flounced off to the darker confines of the club without looking back. Of equal concern, she was perhaps contemplating sabotaging their next round of beers. Unflustered in the least, Kiko emoted cheerful innocence and returned to sucking on the remains of her milkshake. McQuaid locked onto Baacay.

"Did Kiko say anything to Jewel that might have been...unpleasant?" he asked, his voice low and cautious. Baacay flipped his menu over to the lunch page without looking up. He replied as if he were reciting the daily specials.

"Kiko ask her if she 'puta'. Ask how much cost? Kiko say you and Missar Snake want her. Say she want buy her for you." He laid the menu down on the table, smoothing it flat several times before favoring the rest of the room with a vapid stare. "I need mo' beer, Gunna'. I very dry. When beer come?" he asked, his voice rising a decibel or two. Then, appearing to change his mind, he stood and wormed his way out of the booth. "I go pee. Be back soon," he offered as an afterthought and made for the restrooms at flank speed.

McQuaid frowned down at Kiko, who was just working her milkshake to the bottom of the glass and very busy sucking the dregs. After a few moments of patience, he reached over and pinched the straw closed between his fingers. The happy slurping noises ceased forthwith.

"Heeey, what you do?" She looked up at him, with unbridled indignation.

"Puta?" he asked. Kiko sat back and crossed her arms, pouting. Jake expelled a loud sigh, in an effort to break the ominous silence at the table.

"Why do I have the feeling we're not getting more cold beers anytime soon?" he asked, his chin propped on his open palm, gazing at the two of them under half-lidded eyes. "My Filipino is a bit rusty, but I do seem to recall 'puta' means prostitute. Is that pretty close?"

McQuaid kept his eyes fixed on Kiko.

"That's one version, yes. There is a more guttural definition I won't repeat in the presence of a young lady, though I'm beginning to doubt the lady part." From the corner of his eye, he spotted one of the NCO waiters, who proceeded to motor over and dropped their bill on the table.

"I think you boys were just about done here, right?" He was tall, broad shouldered, unimpressed with rank, and glowered at them, suggesting it really wasn't a question. Major Wilmouth sighed again and moved to pay, but McQuaid waved him off.

"I've got this one, Snake. My kid's my problem – not yours." He glanced at the bill and counted out some cash to cover it, along with a generous tip. The waiter reached down for the cash, but Kiko leaped forward and snatched two dollars back, noting he had been overpaid. Mattie had drilled her for hours on adding and subtracting columns of numbers, both for wholesale and retail prices. It was evident she was a quick study, but McQuaid wasn't in the mood for explaining the vagaries of tipping policies, or in this case more like paying to assuage personal injury.

He looked over at her, a storm cloud gathering under his craggy eyebrows, his eyes dark and foreboding. Kiko took one look at him and put the bills back, then slumped back in her seat again, hugging her knees and facing away from him. McQuaid looked up at the waiter with a pleasant smile.

"Please let Jewel know we appreciated her service and I'm sorry for any misunderstanding."

The waiter glanced over at Kiko then back and nodded his acceptance, grabbed the payment, and made a brisk exit without another word. Jake was smiling back at the two of them.

"Shall we?" he asked, his voice breezy, and then stood to leave. "The night is young and there are other less frigid watering holes. Let's blow this dive. I didn't much care for their service anyway."

McQuaid shook his head.

"Sorry Snake. We've got to fly out early to Manila tomorrow and I still need to swing over to base ops and check weather before we head over to the transit billets to rack out. "Now that I know you're around though, we should get together another time when I don't have such a large formation to look out for."

Jake's eyes clicked to the back of Kiko's head and returned with a knowing look.

"Roger that, Gunner. I saw a few boys from the squadron over at the bar anyway, so I'll bid you all a good night. Fly safe tomorrow and I'll take a rain check. Next time I buy!" He clapped McQuaid on the shoulder and looked over at Kiko. "Nice meeting you, young lady." She turned her head to look back at him, her chin on her shoulder.

"Bye, bye, Missar Snake," she replied, in a little voice heavy with forlorn. They both noticed her dark eyes were glistening. Jake looked back at McQuaid and put his hand over his heart, patting it a couple times.

"She's a man killer, son. Have mercy on the rest of us, will you?"

McQuaid shook his head, chuckling, and watched his friend turn away to move off into the shadows of the club, looking for other fellow pilots to hang with. Heaving a sigh to himself, he watched him go before returning his attention back to the table.

"C'mon Kiko, let's go see if we can find a place to sleep tonight. We need to get up early and fly to Manila so we can buy some fun stuff for you and Mattie to sell in the store." Kiko bounced up and grabbed his hand, dragging him toward the door. All else was forgotten. Baacay was loitering near the front and with him in tow, they stepped out into the warm night and hailed a passing GI in a jeep, to take them back to the airfield.

McQuaid arranged a simple room with a bed and two extra cots for them with the billets officer on duty and left Baacay and Kiko in their room to wash up and get ready for bed. Jeppers had dropped off their away-bag from the plane, so they would have clean sleepwear for the night. He wanted to get as early a start as possible, before things heated up, bringing thunderstorms and other tropical weather, which created unfavorable flying conditions. The hop from Clark to Manila shouldn't take more than a half hour or so, but weather was always a crapshoot. According to the weather forecast, the next day was supposed to be a typical hot and humid morning in the tropics. That meant sporadic rain, intermittent thunderstorms, and for them, either finding a way over, or around the line of storms near the mountains; or diverting way south a hundred miles or more.

Depending on where and how high the storm clouds might form up, he might also have an option to scud-run, darting around low-lying storm clouds, and finding holes to fly through, without running into a blind cloud-canyon with an angry thunderstorm hiding at the end. He'd need to play it safe with passengers though and outflank the storms, or get low through the valley running south of the Mount Samat ridgeline, flying under the storm system. He didn't worry too much about the Goose. What she gave up in streamlining and aerodynamics, she regained in durability. She was built for foul weather, which was one of the reasons he'd chosen the sturdy amphibious Grumman Goose as one of his workhorse cargo planes.

He arrived back at their room to find the lights off, Baacay already snoring, and Kiko curled up in the bed he thought he had reserved for himself. Rather than move her, he opted for the other cot. Undressing as quietly as possible in the dark, he splashed water on his face from the sink and was glad to see someone had laid his toiletry bag out. After brushing his teeth, he flopped down on the cot to sleep; exhausted. Kiko, lying just a few feet away, stirred in her sleep. He wondered why she abused the cocktail waitress. It was a clever sneak attack too, suggesting subterfuge well beyond her age. Just when he thought he was beginning to understand her mind, she bowled him over with something unexpected like that.

He had talked about this with Mattie on a number of occasions. Her take was insightful. Kiko was deeply traumatized by the death of her parents and her survival now revolved around two people she still didn't know very well – and foreigners to boot. He and Mattie still struggled with the cultural differences between Western ways and those of the island nation of the Philippines. McQuaid could only imagine the mind of a child, trying to trust in a future with people who seemed to love her, but had nothing in common with anyone she had ever known. It was hard for Kiko to relax without imagining dangers at every turn. They hoped with time she would grow out of her fears of abandonment and accept that both Mattie and McQuaid were committed to being there for her. It was their bond together; albeit a complicated one, he had to admit, but one that ran much deeper than their partnership in the air cargo business.

Life could have turned out much different for him too, if it weren't for the kindness of strangers. McQuaid wasn't his birth name. He too was an orphan, adopted and raised by a loving foster family on their farm in Iowa. As a boy, he learned to appreciate how the long hard work in the fields shaped him and helped him find his place in the world. His adopted father taught him how to shoot and hunt and impressed on him how talking plain and being truthful was the only insurance of sanity in a crazy world. His adopted mother imbued him with a kind spirit and respect for women.

A crop duster who worked for his father had taught him to fly as a young man and helped him get his pilot's license. Later, the man recommended him at a local crop dusting company and soon he got his first real flying job. McQuaid took to it as a natural and reveled in being trusted with their simpler jobs. But he outgrew them with ease and got promoted to their most skilled contracts in record time. It wasn't long before he gained a reputation as one of the best duster pilots in Iowa. It was dangerous but exhilarating work and led him to join the Marine Corps and become a fighter pilot when the war broke out.

Sleep came over him while remembering his early days as a new Marine pilot. They called the rookies "nuggets."

Chapter Four
1944, the USS Essex, off Luzon Island Coast, the Philippines

There was no light anywhere around him; not just darkness – pitch black – like he was at the bottom of a deep and narrow hole. His arms were squeezed against his sides. It occurred to him he might have fallen into the hole and become wedged tight against the sides. But he didn't seem to be surrounded by dirt. More like he'd been wrapped in something soft and fuzzy, binding his arms inside a long dark cocoon.

McQuaid realized he couldn't feel himself in his body, but there was a perception of spinning and then bashing about from side to side. At first there didn't seem to be any pain. A part of his mind reasoned there should be pain. *Why should I be in pain? I'm asleep.* There wouldn't be any reason to feel pain. Curious. Maybe it was happening to someone else and he was just watching all this in some abstract sort of way.

Wait. There were sounds that could be a voice somewhere in the distance – calling to someone, he wondered? It seemed muffled and he couldn't quite make out anything intelligible, or whether it was even human. They were metallic, scratchy, and distorted noises, more akin to an animal, with sharp claws, scrabbling around on a tin roof. Maybe it wasn't a voice after all. Slowly though, after what seemed like an eternity in the blackness, the discordant noises did resolve into a voice that sounded like it was coming out of a radio. With great concentration, he strained to sort out some of the words. They were getting more loud and urgent; repeating his name.

"Gunner, Gunner!" The voice was insistent. He tried harder to make sense of the rest of words. "Gunner, wake up! You've got to get out!"

Why did he need to wake up – out of where? He was tired – so very tired. It was hard to think about all this. What he needed was to sleep. Why didn't the voice understand how tired he was?

Other sounds crowded into his consciousness now – a roaring or rushing; like a gale force wind past his ears. Groaning and whining noises erupted from somewhere within. They sounded like a caged beast flailing around somewhere in the dark. With a shock, he realized the anguished utterances were his own. A burning hot lump of bile arose in his throat and he started to gag. The spinning and disorientation and his head flopping and banging against a hard surface was making him sick. He swallowed hard, trying not to vomit.

"Gunner, you've got to wake up! Wake up, you stupid son of a bitch, or you're going to die!" He recognized the voice now. That was Jerry – his friend Jerry – something; his friend in pilot training. But that was so long ago. He hadn't seen Jerry for many years. Or was it months?

"Gunner, wake up. If you can hear me, do what I tell you and wake up. Open your eyes and snap out of it!" His legs started to ache and then a white-hot pain shot up his spine. The darkness was swirling, changing from black to dirty gray. The irritating voice kept shouting at him. Somehow he managed to pry open his eyelids. They were so heavy. Gauges on an instrument panel swam before his view and he realized he was in the cockpit of his fighter plane. The horizon whirled around outside his canopy and he could feel his body slamming back and forth in his seat harness. Panic clenched his bowels. His plane was out of control; spinning and tumbling toward the ink blue sea. There was no time to waste.

Straining against the centrifugal forces of the spin, he grabbed the stick in front of him and slammed it to the right, against the aircraft's violent rolling to the left. Then he stood on the right rudder pedal to try and reduce the yawing spin. His vision cleared enough to see his altimeter winding down through eight thousand feet and the airspeed crossing into the red. There was no time for fear – only seconds to live. Unless he could slow his dying airplane, the wings would rip off, making him a helpless passenger, riding to his death into the unforgiving waves below. That wasn't going to happen to him – not to Gunner McQuaid.

The split seconds slowed, blurring his past with the present. Shards of near-death memories from his crop dusting days danced before his eyes. There were many close calls during those hot summers over the Iowa cornfields. Other painful images clawed their way into his mind. He tried to shake them out of his head, but they persisted in haunting him, dragging him back to one horrible moment he could never allow himself forget.

"Don't let go of me, Richard." Her eyes pleaded with him as she dangled over the edge beneath him. Tears streaked the dirt on her cheeks. "Hold onto me!" But he could feel her hand slipping through his sweaty grasp.

"I'm trying," he cried into her face, his heart twisted by her expression. With a dawning horror, he realized he couldn't save her. Her mouth was open, but she seemed unable to utter a sound. He lay prone and stretched over the edge of the outcropping of rock. Barely able to keep his grip on a tree root behind him, his eyes betrayed his fear. She saw it too and knew in that instant, they were seeing each other for the last time in their young lives. A transformation passed over her face and her expression smoothed to one of calm acceptance of her fate.

"No!" Making one last desperate attempt to get his other arm down to reach hers in time, he looked into her eyes, crying and shaking his head in denial. Then she just slipped away, falling, watching him wide-eyed while he stared after her in disbelief. She offered him a sympathetic smile in return and disappeared below without another sound. He imagined her frail body breaking against the rocks. The pain of that memory jarred him back.

He grabbed for the throttle with his left hand and pulled it back to the rear stop, his mind still tortured by the vivid memory of losing his childhood friend. The roaring of the engine quieted, along with the rushing wind. Fully alert now, his reflexes took over, relying on his training to recover the aircraft and try to nurse it back to level flight.

The engine was missing and popping and he could see his canopy glass was starred and holed by bullets. Bright dots skittered across his legs, born from sunrays shining through more bullet holes in the metal sides of the cockpit. And there was blood. He couldn't feel his left leg and noticed his flight coverall was soaked dark red and wet with blood.

"Gunner, you crazy son of a bitch! I thought you were a goner." That was his wingman, Jerry Alder. He could see him now, his blue Corsair sliding cautiously up on his left wing. He looked over at him and raised a limp hand in a reassuring wave. But he didn't feel so good. The gray wool was beginning to close over his eyes again. Intense heat washed his face, snatching him back from the dark abyss.

Flames licked out at his feet from under the instrument panel and filled the cockpit with choking, oily black smoke. He tried to push the canopy back to clear the air, but it wouldn't budge. Using both hands, he tried to force it without any luck, causing his aircraft to roll and fall off to the left again, as soon as he took his hands off the stick. Jerry's plane made a sharp bank away to keep from colliding with him. The fire was searing his legs and he smelled burning leather, fabric, and flesh. The cool darkness beckoned to him. He knew he had to escape before he blacked out again. His hand found the emergency canopy release and the wind rushed into the cockpit, chasing away the blackness. Pulling his legs as far back from the fire as he could, he struggled to release his seat harness, when the plane began to roll inverted again. Getting…so tired. It would be so good to sleep.

"Get out, Gunner. Get out now, before it's too late. Gunner, you've got to get out. Gunner! Gunner, can you hear me?"

"Get up, Gunna', get up. Gunna', you get up now!"

McQuaid jerked his head off his pillow and sat bolt upright in bed, his eyes wild. It was early morning and he was lying on sweat soaked sheets. His heart hammered in his chest. Kiko was leaning over him, shaking his shoulder, her expression concerned and apprehensive. He reached out with both hands and held her face, his voice reassuring and gentle, belying the kaleidoscope of images and base emotions coursing through his mind. The room came into focus around him and his dream receded back to the shadows.

"It's okay, Kiko. I'm awake now. I was dreaming. I must have been talking in my sleep. Thanks for waking me up." She looked relieved and handed him a cup of water she'd poured from the sink. Grateful, he took the cup from her and drained it. Still somewhat woozy, he was puzzled by a horrible growling somewhere in the room. Baacay was lying on his cot facing away from them, snoring his head off. Kiko followed his glance and made a face, covering her ears. McQuaid grinned at her and she laughed, putting her hand over her mouth and pointing at Baacay.

"He loud," she said, giggling. He no hear you sleep talk."

McQuaid nodded, but was still half in and out of sleep and disturbed by his dreams, which were vivid and seemed all too real. Rubbing sleep out of his eyes, he wondered about their significance. As nightmares often do, they distorted incidents of the past, but were also an insight to challenges in the present. A good example of that was the little girl he'd tried to save in his dream. She was real, but he recalled she didn't die falling off a cliff. Her family moved away from their farm in Des Moines and years later, he learned she'd married a man who beat her to death.

One magic summer, as teenagers, they became inseparable and promised each other they would always stay together; they swore never to love anyone else. Millie was her name and she wrote to him for years. Later she even teased him for not eloping with her to live in secret somewhere in South America, like they had conspired to do.

When he found out she'd been killed, he blamed himself. Remembering her sweet young face looking up at him and making him promise never to let her go, was a scene replayed in his mind many times over the years. But he did let her go. She waved to him from the rear seat of her parent's car, tears streaming down her face as they drove away from the farm, out the road through the cornfields and out of each other's lives.

The part of his dream about being shot down as a Marine fighter pilot was far more accurate. He had been shot down by a Japanese fighter, based at this very airfield, when the enemy still occupied Clark since capturing it from the Americans in 1942. His wingman at that time was Jerry Alder and that part of the nightmare brought back many dark memories he thought he had buried, along with his friend, on a rainy morning in the winter of '44.

They had gone through flight training together as "nuggets" back in the states. McQuaid never had a brother and never knew his blood family. He and Jerry became the proverbial brothers-by-different-mothers and later, when they shipped out to the Pacific, they were overjoyed to both be deployed aboard the Essex. They did everything together – fellow farm boys from Iowa. They drank together, fought, and even shared the same girl at one point; a Navy nurse, 1st Lieutenant, Gwen Tarbot. She fell in love with Jerry though and McQuaid, more than a little heartbroken, chose to step aside and give his friend a clear playing field. Jerry was smitten with Gwen and while it was sometimes hard to watch them with each other, he was glad if she wasn't meant for him, then at least she was for his best friend and fellow Marine.

Jerry was from Des Moines and endowed with dark featured, rugged good looks. This, along with country values and an "aw shucks" personality, endeared him to everyone. The two of them had gotten drunk together many times and dreamed of finishing flight school near the top of their class so that they could qualify as Marine aviators. They had traded off girlfriends before. The women came and went, but their close friendship endured the arduous pilot training regimen and later the months turned into years in combat. They were inseparable and on that day in '44, Jerry saved his life by killing the Jap that had snuck by him and shot McQuaid's fighter full of holes, wounding him and leaving him unconscious, while his Corsair fell in a death spiral toward the sea.

Jerry stuck with him, shouting at him all the way down, refusing to believe McQuaid was dead, and willing him back to consciousness before he crashed into the ocean. But McQuaid once again cheated death, unbuckling from his seat and throwing himself free at the last second, when his fighter rolled inverted. He must have pulled his ripcord just before he blacked out again. Jerry circled overhead, calling in his position, as he lay unconscious in his life vest drifting with the waves. McQuaid barely remembered being fished out by one of the launches from the destroyer in their convoy.

Jerry and Gwen took turns, long hours on watch by his bedside in the infirmary, while his battered body healed. But Jerry had to go back to war and then it was just Gwen.

Something happened between them in their long hours together. They talked about everything – home, their families, and the friends they'd lost during the war. Many nights she stayed by him, soothing and coaxing him back from dark and violent nightmares. She climbed into bed with him and warmed his body with hers, when fever and chills made his jaws and teeth ache from chattering. At some point, she wasn't Jerry's girl anymore and fell deeply in love with him. Their happiness was only tormented by the guilt they hid from Jerry when he'd come to check on McQuaid. They struggled to hide their feelings, but in the end, their conscience and mutual love for their friend made it impossible to go on without confessing. The betrayal reflected in Jerry's face wounded them both to their souls.

McQuaid was in a wheel chair by then and scheduled to be shipped out to Guam to fully convalesce. Gwen had to stay behind, but any chance for continued friendship between her and Jerry lay in ruins. McQuaid was in the hospital on Guam for almost three months without a single letter from him. Gwen wrote almost every day. When he finally arrived back on the Essex, and was put on the flight schedule again,

Jerry avoided any unnecessary contact. But that first night aboard, McQuaid and Gwen met in his stateroom.

He paid his cabin mate twenty dollars to make himself scarce, so that they could have the tiny room and a bunk to themselves. As soon as she walked through the door, they rushed together, tearing their clothes off each other. They made love most of the night, until they lay spent, arm in arm, imagining how the dawn might look through the porthole; if the cabin only had one. And then that fateful day happened near the end of the war, in the South China Sea, off the northwest coast of Luzon. McQuaid was assigned to a new wingman by then – a brash young Captain named Jake Wilmouth.

They were in a six-ship formation, all Corsairs, flying out from the Essex, a hundred and twenty miles offshore of their target. It was still drizzling; the air was warm and thick with a furtive sun that burned occasional holes through the brooding clouds with blinding shafts of light. Their battle group was in the final throes of pushing the stubborn Japanese off the island and taking back Clark Field. This would prove crucial to staging successful air campaigns around the islands through the waning years of the Pacific war.

On a previous sortie, they'd launched a pre-dawn bombing/strafing mission against the airfield, crippling their anti-aircraft defenses. Clark had become a major base for the feared Kamikaze suicide fighters plaguing the fleet. The Japs had recently been decimated in the Battle of Leyte Gulf and were using aircraft as missiles in the desperate hope of sinking the American carriers, whose planes rained death down on them regularly once air superiority was achieved by the allies. The Corsairs turned toward Clark, with the airfield in sight now around the still smoking remains of aircraft and gun positions destroyed earlier that morning.

"Tally-ho, boys! Bogies at nine o'clock high. Looks like at least eight to ten 'Zeros', or maybe 'Georges'." That was the slang name for the N1J-Shidens – an upgraded model from the A6M Zero. Alder was the first one to spot them. Either model fighter was a serious threat to the Corsairs, while carrying heavy bomb loads for use against ground targets. These Japanese defenders surprised them, attacking them from out of the sun. They hadn't expected them to muster any fighters and were caught with their pants down.

Flight commander Captain James Binton jumped on the radio. "Jettison bomb loads and prepare to engage." The pilots were quick to drop their bomb loads, which would have made them slow and clumsy in an aerial dogfight, especially against the lighter and more nimble Japanese fighters. It was probable they weren't facing their better combat veterans though. Most of them were already dead through heavy attrition, forced on them by significant allied air victories in the latter half of the Pacific war. Binton was on the radio again.

"On my command, one and two break left, three and four down – up and over, five and six break right. Ready? Break now!"

Alder and his wingman were aircraft three and four in their flight. McQuaid and Wilmouth were five and six. They broke right on command and watched to see if any of the Japs followed them. How the enemy formation responded to their dispersing maneuver, would reveal much about their level of combat experience.

Three of them took the bait, breaking off to follow Gunner and Snake, who were intended to be easiest for the Japs get on their tails. Gunner and Snake were the designated "bait" for their trap. But most of the enemy fighters didn't play their game. Two dove after Alder and his wingman, Ed Blake. But the rest veered left to jump Captain Binton and his wingman, Les Camden, who were closing on their group in a climbing left turn. Maybe they hoped to overwhelm them with a fusillade of fire from five enemy fighters to their two, as they flashed by each other.

While that contest was being decided, the two going after Alder and Blake were taught a quick and deadly lesson in air combat energy management. By the time they got in position behind the two Americans, Alder and Blake were rolled inverted to increase their dive angle and to build airspeed. Then they reversed and rolled upright again into a practiced aerobatic maneuver. On cue, they both pulled a high-G climb into an inverted loop over the top and rolled in behind the two hapless Japanese before they realized what had happened.

Both Jap fighters passed beneath them, as they dropped right in on top of them, less than two hundred yards from their tails. Alder opened up first, walking the tracers of his six .50 caliber machine guns into the fuselage, through the cockpit, and then ripping into the engine of the one fighter. The stricken Japanese plane immediately burst into flames, pieces of the engine flying through the cowling and his propeller spinning away to the right. Without a second glance, Alder pulled up in a steep climb looking for his wingman and saw him shoot the left wing off the other Japanese fighter. It flipped into a violent tumble and broke apart into several flaming pieces.

Meanwhile, Binton and Camden had their hands full. Each had gotten superior positioning on one of the enemy for a head-to-head gunfight. But they were closing on them at such high speed, they could only afford a quick snap shot at their targets before being forced to take evasive action against the remaining Jap fighters, who were gaining advantage on them from above and to the rear.

Camden took a couple hits to his right wing, but didn't appear the worse for wear. He was able to invert and pull in under his assailant. Binton rolled over and broke to the opposite side, hoping to split the group of the remaining three Japs in pursuit. One of their initial targets started trailing smoke and was out of the fight. The other fighter continued his dive to gain airspeed for a climb and hard corner turn around, intending to get in a firing run on Binton again. Instead he shot past Alder, who was so intent on climbing back up from his earlier kill to engage one of Binton's other aggressors, the American missed seeing the enemy fighter streak past him.

The Jap saw him, however, and maneuvered to get the angle on him, just as Alder lined up another one of the Shidens in his sights. He got off a fast burst into him, his tracers leading the rest of his shells into the body of the fighter, and watched with satisfaction as his rounds began tearing chunks of metal out of his enemy. He was surprised to hear Binton yell at him over the radio.

"Jerry, you've got a Jap on your tail, break right and I'll be right there to peel him off you!"

Alder snapped the stick to the right, but before his plane could even react, he felt the sickening thuds of rounds hitting his airframe and wing. One lucky round tore through a hinge for the left wing aileron, jamming it in the down position. Already in a turn to the right, his plane inverted and then proceeded to barrel roll around again, faster and faster. He tried pulling up and applying hard right rudder to counteract the roll, but it only made things worse, bleeding off his airspeed, and he started to stall.

Less than a mile away, McQuaid and Wilmouth had battered both their assailants without mercy, causing them to run toward the airfield to try and escape. McQuaid heard Binton's call to Alder and cranked his fighter around in a sharp turn to see if he could pick him out in the fur-ball of individual dogfights going on around them. He spotted Alder's plane in a slow tumble, out of control and heading toward the water from almost ten thousand feet. He mashed his mike button and yelled at him.

"Jerry, get out of there while you still can." Fire-walling his throttle, he tore after him to try and offer some semblance of assistance; if nothing more than to let Jerry hear his voice reassuring him. "Jerry, just get your canopy open, unbuckle and drop out the next time she rolls over." He heard Jerry's radio mike click and the sounds of him straining inside the tumbling fighter. The canopy rolled back and McQuaid started feeling some hope for his friend.

"I can't...get...my damn leg out. It's caught!"

McQuaid watched Alder's fighter roll over again and again, nose down, hoping to see the pilot drop out of the bottom. But it just continued spinning, getting closer to the ocean. He didn't notice the last enemy fighter, which had escaped undamaged, sneak in for a side angle shot from a blind spot below and to his right. Jap bullets began to hammer the right side of his aircraft, puncturing a fuel tank, which spewed gas all over his fuselage. Another volley ripped away his starboard wing flap.

McQuaid took immediate evasive action, rolling inverted and pulled the stick back hard and then over into a diving left turn. He hoped his control surfaces would hold together, or he'd never be able to pull out of his dive. But the Corsair seemed in good shape considering the beating it had taken and strong buffeting from the now missing wing flap. The blood drained from his head and black spots distorted his vision, as he whipped his stricken fighter into a reverse hard-G left climbing turn, trying to come over the top and behind his attacker.

At the same time, he also struggled to keep Alder's falling fighter in sight, but lost him when it passed beneath him. A flash of blue went right past his head, as Binton's Corsair tore by him, guns blazing, and so close the ejected brass shells from his six .50's clattered against his wing and fuselage. He slapped the stick to the right to give way and heard a muffled explosion behind him.

By the time he could get his face turned around, he saw Binton's plane pulling out to avoid black oil smoke and a flying debris cloud from the exploding fighter he had just hosed with his guns. The battle was over in less than a minute and a half. Eight of the ten enemy planes were destroyed and only one of the American fighters was unaccounted for. No one had seen what happened to Alder's plane in the last few seconds of its tumbling path to the sea.

"Jerry, McQuaid, over." There was no answer. "Did anyone see where Jerry's plane went in?" he asked, his voice rising in desperation. They had all been too busy fighting their own personal battles to keep track of one lone American, who had vanished in all the commotion. McQuaid peeled off and flew low over the water on several search passes near the spot Jerry was last seen. He hoped to catch sight of him climbing out of his ditched plane before it sank beneath the waves. There was no parachute in sight. McQuaid's heart clenched in fear for his friend. *What the hell had happened to him?* There was no debris, oil slick, or best case, a bobbling head, held up by the pilot's Mae West flotation vest – nothing. It was as if the ocean had opened up and swallowed him whole.

They were all low on gas by this point, in particular McQuaid, with the shot up fuel tank. Binton made the call.

"Boys, we've got to head back to the carrier before we all end up in the drink. We're about ten miles off the northwest end of Luzon Island. I'll radio ahead to send a couple fast frigates out here to look for Lieutenant Alder. That's the best we can do for him. Let's head for home."

Those last words were a punch in the gut for McQuaid. How could he leave Jerry out here all alone? He had to stay and find him.

"C'mon Gunner – you can't do anything else here. He's gone. We've got to head back to the boat." Binton's voice was compassionate, but it was an order nonetheless. With a sinking feeling, he knew he didn't have any choice. With one last look down, hoping for a miracle that might reveal something to him, he banked his plane right and fell in behind the rest of their flight heading back to the Essex.

That evening, as the day faded into the gloom of night, he and Gwen huddled in silence near the prow of the ship beneath the flight deck, which was heaving up and down in heavy seas. The vibrant sounds of a bustling carrier under way were a constant background din and surrounded them with reassurance that life went on, despite their loss. They were hanging over one of the gangway ladder rails together, watching a blood red sun disappear into the sea and darkness rushing in, dropping a pall over any hope they held out for their friend Jerry. She was sobbing and he was holding on to her, as much as she was supporting him.

How could he let this happen? McQuaid always imagined himself the champion of anything he set out to conquer. He held himself up as the protector of small animals, children, and the women he had known in his life. They turned to him and when all else was forced to give way, he was the rock that stood fast against any storm. Jerry was as close to a brother as he would ever know. There was no one else he had completely trusted, who would come for him if he were in danger and lay down his life for him if required. They were young and stalwart Marine aviators and the corps had imbued them with a sense of immortality. McQuaid felt broken and at a deeper level, he held himself to blame. There wasn't any more he could have done to save Jerry, but being with Gwen felt wrong. After making off with his best friend's girl, he let him perish and he was gone forever, with no way to square things with him.

He saw the last of Gwen, near the end of December that year, in 1944. She got transferred back to the hospital at Guam, but McQuaid fought on, until the Japanese death grip on Manila was pried loose in January the following year. They had grown apart – each trapped in their private world of loss, regret, and guilt. They never found the right words to talk about it. As much as they had loved each other, they just drifted away, until there was nothing left to hold them together.

McQuaid reemerged from this morbid cogitation, and realized Kiko was staring at him again, doubtless wondering where in the world his mind had wandered off to, with his eyes downcast and heart heavy. He looked back at her and smiled. It was a great relief to return to the present, where life was warm and bright again.

"C'mon, little pigeon. We've got work to do and a plane to fly to Manila this morning. Time's a wasting." He aimed a pillow at Baacay and with great satisfaction, watched it bounce off the side of his head – a direct hit. Baacay snorted and rolled over with a loud yawn, stretching his arms over his shoulders. Kiko covered her ears again and giggled at McQuaid. "Let's hit the showers boys and girls. We're burning daylight and the birds are all in the chow line, way ahead of our sorry tails."

He grabbed a towel off the rack and padded through the door toward the shower room down the hall. "Baacay, make sure she washes everywhere and brushes her teeth good, before you let her out of your sight." He heard him mumble something back in the affirmative, before the door slammed shut behind him.

Chapter Five
Manila, Luzon Island, Capital of the Philippines

It was nearly 7:30 a.m. before they got to the chow hall and McQuaid buried a hasty breakfast of eggs, bacon, toast, and coffee. Kiko and Baacay languished over oatmeal and juice. Rushing them didn't improve their efficiency much, so he just ordered more coffee and waited them out. He'd intended to get his wheels-up by dawn to beat the morning heat, but after pounding beers with Jake the night before, he had forgotten to set his alarm. Several cups of coffee with aspirin were just starting to ease the thudding pain in his head. What bothered him more was breaking a promise to Mattie about overdrinking. Left to himself, he could keep things under control, but losing bottle count swapping war stories with his old wingman had been way too easy.

Glancing at his watch, he realized they were falling farther behind schedule and he still had to run over to the base hospital to pick up Doc McCawley's order from their pharmacy. By 8:30 a.m., they were taxiing to the end of the runway and turning into a stiff breeze that smelled of rain, wet pavement, and mossy earth. Light drizzle spattered the windshield and a furtive sun just peeked through low heavy clouds over the airfield. The windsock pointed west, so they would take off almost directly into the wind out of the sunrise. After a right turn, he hoped to make a direct line to the southwest to Manila airport; weather permitting.

The well-maintained concrete runway provided a smooth takeoff roll, unlike their typical experience with washboard dirt strips and Lubang airport's patchwork of asphalt. Their tires only swished through occasional puddles while the Goose gathered speed, before she eased into the red rouged sky and began a shallow climb to the right. Even though the rain picked up nearer the clouds, he left the cockpit side windows open to feel the warm, jungle-scented wind on his face. The fresh air and pinpricks of blowing rain against his skin cleared the shadows from his brain.

Kiko staked out the co-pilot's seat as usual, but as soon as they were airborne, Baacay came forward and motioned for her to get up to sit in her place and then grabbed her back, propping her up on his lap to see over the instrument panel. Their smiling faces were close together and lit by the morning sun, reminding him of heroes painted on war bond recruiting posters.

A brilliant sunrise broke through the rain and blinding gold edged clouds crowning the majestic Mount Arayat, which lorded over the peasant farm fields bordering its steep slopes. Hopscotched sun splotches illuminated the jungle floor outside the airfield fences. Overhead, great pillars of white clouds towered above them, ten thousand feet or more, as if they were holding up the canopy of gray clouds around them. Even with the black and foreboding cumulonimbus rain clouds crowding into view from the south, it was a glorious day to fly.

For the most part, the short flight to Manila proved uneventful, except for a few lightning flashes and frequent, sharp cannonade blasts of thunder that made both Kiko and Baacay squeal and hide their eyes. McQuaid put the Goose's nose in line with the seven-thousand-foot Mount Banahaw, which jutted up through the overcast ahead of them, southeast of the city. He reached over and dialed his radio direction finder to the beacon frequency at the end of Manila Airport to the south. They were descending into heavy cloud cover, which obscured the farm fields and lakes of the valley with a thick gray wool blanket.

He knew if he stayed on a course line with Banahaw Mountain and his RDF gauge pointed at the Manila airport beacon, he would stay clear of obstructions between the high Samat mountain ridgeline to the west and several mountainous outcroppings to the northeast. As they dropped into the soup of the rain clouds, he shifted his eyes from outside the cockpit, to fly by instruments.

Rain hammered their windscreen and the air around them turned cool and damp. They dug deeper into the storm front and submerged into darkness, with only an occasional smudge of gray for contrast. McQuaid continued to mark their descent on instruments, until they popped out under the black belly of the clouds at about eighteen hundred feet. Manila Airport's rotating tower beacon light came into view in the distance and pointed their way across Manila Bay. He made the call to the tower and was cleared to land. But it was less than a mile from landing, when he could finally make out details of the runway in the pouring rain.

After touching down, they were directed to taxi to a parking spot on the tarmac nearest the passenger buildings. Drenched by the time they tied down the Goose, they all scampered inside to get out of the downpour. It was hot and muggy standing in their sodden clothes, inside the building, watching the hard rain creating geysers in the pools of standing water all around the aircraft. McQuaid figured it would be miserable driving the rutted road into the city.

Baacay used the airport telephone to call for a covered truck to meet them at the Goose. Kiko was laughing, watching his arm-waving antics, punctuated by a rapid-fire shouting match in his native tongue. Baacay was from Manila and knew the city and its people well. At least he used to, before most of it was destroyed in the battle of Manila, only a few short years ago in '45. He never spoke about it much, but McQuaid was well aware Baacay and his family had not fared well, between the allied bombing raids, the Japanese burning of the city, and senseless atrocities committed on the population in the final days leading up to liberation.

Out of a family of six brothers and sisters, only he and a brother made it through the conflagration that all but consumed what was the former crown jeweled capital city of the Philippines. McQuaid had first met him and his brother Rajan, right after the war, running supplies back and forth across the bay between Calatagan and Lubang in their tiny skiff. To McQuaid, their boat always appeared more like an oversized and ill-balanced mound of colorful cloth and other odds and ends they motored over for sale to the islanders.

Before he knew the brothers, they had become friends with Mattie, who would come down to meet them at the dock early in the morning to get first pick of their bolts of cloth, sundries, and canned goods for the General Store. Lubang farmers raised livestock and grew plenty of produce, so she bought everything fresh from the locals wherever possible. But anything considered a luxury item, or manufactured, came via Manila, overland to Calatagan and across the Verde Island Passage waterway to Lubang. McQuaid was impressed with Baacay's infectious good humor and his mechanical skills for keeping their little skiff afloat and the motor running.

He hired Baacay for his air cargo business, employee number three, and made a deal with Rajan to handle the Manila end of their merchandising and shipping business. The brothers were overjoyed to work for the big American pilot, whom they saw as one of the hero liberators of the people of the Philippines and a rich businessman to boot. McQuaid always chuckled when Baacay told him he was rich. He supposed that would seem true; compared to most Filipinos he could be considered wealthy – with a cargo business, two airplanes, and rented hangar space at the airport. But with all his costs, he figured on some days a dockworker in Manila might draw better wages.

Baacay was laughing on the phone now and McQuaid overheard more than a few words he recognized as artful swearing in Tagalog. It was obvious he was talking to his brother Rajan, arranging the truck and lining up buyers for their cargo. He would also have a waiting list of sellers for the list of goods they would need to buy and transport back to Mattie as well. He hung up the phone with a broad smile at McQuaid.

"Rajan say no problem. He have plenty people buy cargo." He cast a sly glance over at Kiko. "Rajan say he have supplies fo' Kiko too." Kiko clapped her hands. McQuaid considered him with hands on hips, somewhat skeptical.

"What do you mean supplies?" he asked. Baacay looked back at him, a little chagrined.

"You know supplies? Kiko not know what supplies he buy fo' her." He held his hands over his eyes to make his point. McQuaid laughed.

"You mean he has a surprise for her."

Baacay appeared confused. "Yah, supplies. He got supplies fo' Kiko. She like. You see, Gunna'." He grinned again. McQuaid just smiled and clapped him on the back with unmistakable affection.

It was almost noon before an old jalopy truck pulled up, splashing through a big puddle right outside the door, throwing a sheet of dirty brown water against the already filthy windows. McQuaid had been eyeing the weather for a while now. The rain had let up but the sky remained dark and sullen under low leaden clouds, suggesting more rain was a probable forecast.

As they watched, Rajan bounded out of the cab of the truck and sloshed through puddles to the door. He was a little taller than Baacay, with typical dark Filipino features and thin physique, wearing shorts, a t-shirt, and sandals. Rajan had always struck McQuaid as being more serious than Baacay, but today he was grinning from ear to ear. He pushed through the door, waving and nodding his head to Baacay and McQuaid and then squatted down at eye level with Kiko, holding his hand behind his back.

"Ho, Kiko," he greeted her laughing. "What you say?" Kiko had met Rajan on a few other occasions, but like most people she didn't know well, she stepped back and regarded him with reserve. Rajan wasn't put off in the least. He whipped his arm from behind his back and held a stuffed monkey in front of her face. "Dis' unggoy fo' you, Kiko." He waggled the brown and black stuffed toy in front of her, with its black button eyes even with hers. Kiko appeared perplexed, sucking her lower lip under her front teeth and staring. She had never seen a stuffed toy before and thought at first, he had bought her a real monkey.

She took another quick step back, keeping a close eye on it, but realized it wasn't real. Her eyes crossed trying to make out its little pink tongue, stitched to its mouth, and shiny button eyes staring back at her. Rajan was laughing now and continued to push the monkey toward her.

"You take, Kiko. Dis' unggoy fo' you. He yo' unggoy now."

Kiko looked up at Rajan, then back at the stuffed animal. She reached out her finger and gave it a gentle poke. It made a squeaky noise and she jumped back startled; then she started to giggle. She poked it again and when it squeaked again, she burst out laughing. Rajan held it out for her to take. "You hold unggoy now, Kiko."

At last, she reached out and grasped it by both its arms in front of her. Then she poked it again and squealed when it made the squeaking noise.

McQuaid stood watching her in fascination. He realized he had never seen her with a toy, as long as he'd known her. Matte had always made sure she had sensible things, clothes, toothbrush, combs, even her own books. But they had never gotten her anything frivolous, like a stuffed animal. Kiko was almost ten now and didn't seem to have time for toys, with all her other activities. Still, he felt sheepish realizing she was still a little girl and this young Filipino man, not even related to her, had bargained away something valuable to provide her with a toy he and Mattie should have known she needed. He thanked Rajan, who just nodded back with a knowing smile.

Just then, another older man scurried through the door from the truck outside. Rajan turned to introduce him.

"Dis' be Ruperto. He friend. He help us unload plane." The man offered them a toothy smile in return. It was evident he wasn't a bit self-conscious about missing four of his front teeth. Ruperto bobbed his head up and down showing great enthusiasm, as if he understood what Rajan was saying about him. McQuaid suspected he didn't speak much English. But once they started unloading the Goose, he was gratified to find the man was indeed a diligent worker.

With everyone helping, the truck was loaded by early afternoon and they were soon off to town. Kiko squeezed between Rajan and McQuaid in the cab up front, leaving Baacay and Ruperto to fend for themselves in the rear. Baacay leaned in behind them, hanging through the missing window from the cargo compartment, assessing the punishment they were about to endure on the narrow and deep rutted dirt and gravel road into Manila.

Rajan was practiced at swerving around overloaded pack animals plodding along in front of them, while avoiding the near bottomless pools of water in low spots of the road. They came upon lines of people walking, assorted colored bundles balanced on their heads, dragging dirty children stumbling along beside them. Some glanced up, as their truck jolted by them with bare inches to spare. On numerous occasions, they would happen upon another truck, or oncoming car. Most were missing windows and rusted and dented on all sides, looking as if they could fly apart if they hit so much as a single pothole.

McQuaid was trying not to watch Rajan's driving and focused instead on the passing landscape of flooded rice fields and other staple crops, beginning to give way to shacks and mud brick buildings; evidence they were arriving on the outskirts of the city.

Before long, Kiko was standing on the seat next to McQuaid, both of them fascinated with the solemn procession of jagged gray shapes of burned out buildings and heaps of rubble passing by them. People scurried around these husks of former dwellings, intent on daily chores, oblivious to this shocking contrast to old Manila. What had been quaint, shade-tree lined avenues of colonial homes and awning-covered business fronts, were now stark and ominous shadows of those finer days.

Bone thin dogs, their hides mangy and mottled with open sores, watched them hungrily from litter strewn alleyways, or were hunched down, panting, trying to stay cool, lying in the tepid slime of open street gutters. They passed through a spongy wall of humid air, almost palpable with the smell from fetid piles of rotting garbage, overlaid with the acrid and sulfurous stench of raw sewage. Rajan drove on, his dark eyes solemn and with a stoic view fixed on the road ahead.

All were thankful it wasn't much longer before they arrived at the wharf, where business was struggling to return to normal. Most warehouses had been patched up, giving stored goods some protection from the elements. But the real commerce was being conducted along the inlet waterways from outriggers and other open panga boats, crowded in close to offer their wares of produce, rice, fish, and poultry. Mobs of people wandered about, both buying and selling. Many were trading food and wares back and forth, favoring barter over the unstable currency.

Rajan pulled the truck in near a war-torn shipbuilder's warehouse and hopped out to talk with a couple thin, hard looking men who'd flagged him down. Baacay also jumped out of the back to wander over. McQuaid stayed put but observed their meeting with great interest. He was well aware that he had valuable goods for trade in the back, which made them a target for thieves and cons plying the harbor front.

He moved his holstered .45 around for ease of access, but noticed several Philippine Army guards wandering by with shouldered rifles and eyes moving side to side, searching for any signs of trouble. Keeping his weapon out of sight, he relaxed a little, relieved to see martial law was still in force. Security was essential in these tenuous times of rebuilding an already fragile economy. On the way through town, they noticed several large-scale restoration projects underway, tearing down or refurbishing many of the bomb damaged buildings, streets, and infrastructure.

The men appeared to be getting along all right. Rajan had passed out some packs of American Lucky Strikes to lubricate the negotiations. Everyone appeared to be smiling, bending over for him to use his Zippo lighter to fire up their smokes. One of the guards started to wander over toward the truck. Both Rajan and Baacay's eyes flicked in his direction and they repositioned themselves, trying not to be conspicuous about keeping him under observation.

The guard stopped at the truck door window next to McQuaid, looked in, and offered a casual nod to both him and Kiko. Kiko held up her monkey and waved one of its arms at him. He regarded her with a humorless smile, indulging her by offering a limp wave in return, then began moving around toward the rear of the truck. Baacay had already peeled away from Rajan's discussion with the men and was standing by the tailgate, He engaged the guard with a few offhand pleasantries.

Ruperto sat in the rear of the truck, looking out at nothing in particular from under the canvass cover with feigned boredom; a practiced Filipino pose whenever police or the military were about. McQuaid decided to step outside to investigate, but unbuckled his pistol belt and dropped it to the floor before opening the door. He motioned to Kiko to stay in the truck and be quiet. She gave him a quick nod. He knew she'd be a trooper and he wouldn't have to worry about her.

Baacay was busy showing the guard they only had the usual trade goods loaded and was waving his hand back and forth from their cargo to the men standing in front and boats along the inlet, explaining their intentions. The guard just nodded his head, looked everything over one more time, then turned and strolled away, looking for trouble elsewhere. Meanwhile, Rajan sidled up and addressed McQuaid in a voice pitched so that only the four of them could hear him.

"Deez men say dey no buy fom me," he groused and spat on the ground. McQuaid was puzzled. They had never had problems finding buyers before and usually for the whole lot of goods they brought over from Lubang. Rajan knew what was selling and instructed Mattie, through Baacay, on the kinds of trade goods they needed to pack over with them. McQuaid stared at Rajan in silence for a moment, trying to decipher the nature of his dilemma.

"They always buy from us. Why not now?" he asked in a low voice. Rajan surveyed their surroundings with caution before he replied. He jerked a thumb back toward the two men he'd been conversing with.

"Dey say pirates tell them no buy from Americano piloto from Lubang. Dey no want trouble. Say pirates watch." Rajan frowned, looked around again, still suspicious of spying eyes, and spat again to punctuate his frustration.

"Pirates?" A dark cloud replaced the quizzical expression on McQuaid's face. He swung around and strode from the truck toward the men, still standing around smoking where Rajan left them. Wary of his sudden approach, they tensed up and took a step or two back when he continued to bear down on them. One threw his cigarette down and said something to the other man, then stepped forward to meet the big Marine. McQuaid noticed he had shoved his hand deep inside his trouser pocket and seemed more confident than he should be, considering the striking difference in their sizes. He assumed he didn't appear much like someone coming over to exchange pleasantries with them. The man might be laying his hand on a knife, or worse, a small pistol. McQuaid didn't break his gait, but pulled up short to give some space to the man, who started looking twitchy.

"Which of you two speaks English?" he asked without preamble. The man with his hand in his pocket seemed to understand, but remained silent. McQuaid tried again, standing his ground. "I need to know why you are afraid to buy from us." Folding his arms across his chest, he fixed the man with an expectant glare, his question hanging heavy in the air between them. The man's expression remained blank at first. Then he appeared to come to a decision and leaned toward him, his jaw outthrust, still keeping his hand concealed in his pocket.

"Pirate man say tell Rajan no buy fom you." He looked around to check the position of the nearest Philippine soldier before he spoke again. "He say you kill brodder of pirate chief with plane. Pirate man say he find you. He kill yor friends. He say he kill you too. We want no trouble. You go home. Stay home."

Baacay and Rajan had walked up and were standing behind McQuaid listening. The man paused for effect, looked past McQuaid, and leered at the two of them. Holding his finger up, he waggled it in front of their faces, making an ominous sign they should beware of not heeding his message. Then he turned and walked away, his companion falling in behind him. McQuaid just stood there, watching them disappear into the throng of people roaming the docks. You never knew with these people whether they were genuine in their fear of intimidation by the pirates, or they had just been paid off.

They worked the dock over the next couple hours and were able to unload their cargo for decent prices and fair trade for goods on Mattie's list, to the boat merchants and people running small commercial stalls in front of the gutted warehouses. They made out okay. But it was frustrating and time consuming.

By four in the afternoon, they were bumping their way back to the airfield to reload the Goose and head back to Lubang. The rain had started up again and become a steady downpour by the time they said goodbye to Rajan and yanked the hatch on the Goose shut. McQuaid pulled a fresh flight coverall and a cigar out of his away bag for the flight back. Kiko and Baacay slipped into dry clothes as well.

Soon they were winging their way toward the coast, maintaining a slow steady climb through the dark curtain of storm clouds and rain beating against the Goose. He needed to make sure they cleared the Mount Samat ridgeline between them and the coastline, in spite of near zero visibility. When his altimeter gauge passed through sixty-five hundred feet, they popped out above the overcast into the glaring red eye of the setting sun. He leveled off and trimmed up the aircraft, while admiring the soft, fluffy texture of the cloud tops below them. The sun had tinted them the color of flamingoes, with the texture of a huge layer of cotton candy. He glanced over at Kiko to see her reaction and was surprised to see her curled up asleep in the co-pilot's seat. Baacay hadn't come forward as usual either. He chuckled around his cigar. They both must be plenty tuckered out, he mused to himself. He yanked his sunglasses out of the visor and pulled his ball cap lower over his eyes to help block some of the sun, and pondered the warning from the two men in Manila.

It was no revelation to McQuaid the pirates had moles at the waterfront. After all, they had to move their stolen goods through trusted agents for cash or in trade for drugs. In some cases, drugs were even preferred over cash. Opium and heroin were the contraband of choice, bringing extraordinary returns per ounce. And unlike a fixed rate currency, their value appreciated with increased local market demand.

He thought back to seeing the pirates offloading packages from the yacht the day before. By their consistent size and number, they could have been packaged drugs; a delivery the pirates might have intercepted. That would be a mother lode catch of the day for them. Or maybe they already knew about the drugs and it was a rendezvous gone bad. He wondered how much the girl knew about her parents' business in Hong Kong, or maybe Manila. Something was nagging him at the back of his mind. He needed to talk to Lijuan again and before Nguyen started grilling her.

He also wondered how the pirates managed to miss spotting her. The boat wasn't that big and they were all over the deck around the wheelhouse where she had holed up to use the radio. Maybe she had been able to stay down in there unseen. He'd like to look over that yacht some more too and talk to Nguyen about what he may have discovered that could have caused their engines to fail and the yacht to start taking on water without warning. A lot of things just didn't seem to add up for him. His contemplations were cut short by the radio in his headphones.

"Mattie calling McQuaid, over." He grabbed the mike and replied.

"McQuaid here. How're things back there, over?"

"Just ducky. Nguyen's on the warpath because the girl clammed up and wouldn't answer any of his questions, so he of course started hollering at her. That always works better, huh? So the Doc threw him out of the hospital and then Lijuan went nuts and tried to kill herself. Now she says she won't talk to anyone except you and last, but hardly least, Chief Mahutra sent some runners over looking for you, saying their village had been attacked by Japanese soldiers. What's your ETA by the way? We could use the reinforcements, over."

McQuaid's jaw clunked shut in dismay. He stared out at the sun, now almost touching the rouge red blanket of clouds below them. It would probably be dark in another hour. But they were a few minutes out from making their descent toward Lubang field, so he figured maybe fifteen to twenty minutes before he'd be landing. He mashed the mike button.

"We'll be down in twenty or so. Tell the Doc I'll get over to the hospital as soon as I can and Nguyen will just have to wait until I can see if Lijuan will open up to me. Then maybe we can figure out why she's so unhinged. I have no idea what the chief is talking about. Was he sure they were Japanese soldiers, or just some renegades living in the hills? How many did he tell you they saw anyway, over?"

"The one runner speaks good English. He says he saw two and they were wearing military uniforms. Not any sort of overwhelming force, but they had guns. They took some food and one of the girls from the village as a hostage, over."

McQuaid reflected on the stories of Japanese holdouts from the war, which were said to be hiding out in the jungle near Mount Ambonong. Chief Mahutra's village, Looc, was located about ten miles southeast of there and near the bay. He punched the mike button again.

"Was anyone hurt and did they make any demands for the girl, over?"

Mattie was expecting the question.

"They want some men from the village to pack food and medical supplies up to them in the mountains. They said they'd let the girl go if they got what they wanted. And no one in the village was hurt, over."

McQuaid figured the chief could spring for the food and he had medical supplies on the C-47, still parked out near their village on a dirt strip. He could kick in some supplies if need be. Once he replaced the engine fuel pump, he could fly back to Manila to buy more and make up for any shortfalls in his scheduled deliveries. That would hurt company expenses, but it was doable. So, as bad as that whole village attack scenario sounded, he figured there was nothing he could do about it in the short term. He needed to focus on the situation at hand – with Nguyen and Lijuan.

"Okay, let Doc know I'll be there before too long and if I can get Lijuan to talk to me, we might be able to smooth Nguyen's feathers some. Tell Doc not to sedate her though. I want to try and talk to her right away. I have a few serious questions of my own, over." He glanced at his watch and reached up to start pulling the throttles back to begin his descent. He was glad to see the clouds were thinning out near the island. To the north, he could see the Caba Island Lighthouse beam now. Good. If the weather would cooperate, things would be a little easier too.

"Okay, I'll tell Doc and take care of the rest of this circus as best I can. See you all soon then. Mattie out."

McQuaid double-clicked his mike button to acknowledge. Kiko had heard the change in the engines and was sitting up and looking out at the clouds skimming by just under the wings. She loved to watch the world disappear when the Goose dropped into the clouds and was always in awe whenever they flew up through rainy gray overcast and then burst out into the blue sky and bright sunlight above.

The weather had in fact cleared over the airfield, so McQuaid lined the Goose up on the appropriate runway, after checking the windsock on top of their hangar. He pulled down the gear handle and heard the reassuring electric whine and then a gratifying bump, as the gear locked down into place. He dropped the flaps about a mile out and then greased the Goose in, for what would have otherwise been a real crowd-pleaser landing. There wasn't anyone waiting to applaud him, however, he noticed with some relief. Maybe they could get some work done in peace before he had to rush over to the hospital. After braking to taxi speed, he pulled off the runway onto the apron near the hangar and shut down.

Just as they were opening the rear door hatch, he noticed a cloud of dust on the access road. It had to be Nguyen, tearing over to meet them in his jeep. He just couldn't stand letting them get into town in a calm, civilized manner. McQuaid was already fuming when he hopped out of the plane and started walking over to intercept him – Kiko in tow. Baacay made himself scarce by chocking the Goose and then started on unloading their cargo. McQuaid worked his cigar around to the side of his mouth, clamping it between his teeth, trying to remain calm.

The police chief screeched to a stop right next to him, his arm draped in casual fashion over the steering wheel, the whip antenna in furious motion, waving around behind him. With a slow, dramatic gesture, he pushed his Aussie hat back on his head with two fingers and leered up at him. McQuaid clamped his cigar a little tighter, while he struggled with supreme patience for Nguyen to get to it. He couldn't wait to hear what he'd complain about first.

"Dis girl not talk to me, Gunna'. She say only talk to you. Why she not talk, heh?" He swung his legs over the side of the jeep and stood up to face him, right hand thumb hooked in his gun belt. Nguyen stood a full foot shorter than McQuaid. "What you know 'bout dis girl, Gunna'? She not daughter of parents. You know dis too?"

McQuaid did not know that, in fact. He didn't get a close look at the man floating face down in the water, but the woman lying in a bloody pool on the deck of the yacht did appear to be Asian.

"I only assumed she was their daughter," he shot back at Nguyen. "Did you get a look at their papers?"

"Yah, da parents have papers. Dey both married. Dis girl, she have no papers. Why she have no papers, Gunna'? Why she not talk to me – only you?" Nguyen's face was red now and he appeared to be working himself up over something he knew about, at which McQuaid could only guess. McQuaid whipped his cigar out of his mouth and threw it at the feet of the police chief.

"How the hell should I know what her problem is, Captain? We were there together – remember?" McQuaid could feel his temperature rising. "Maybe you'd like to fill me in on what you found on the boat, so we'll both know something!" Out of the corner of his eye he noticed Kiko sidle up next to him. He didn't need her in the middle of this and cocked his head toward her, so Nguyen might catch a clue he wanted to take this matter up with him elsewhere. Nguyen, of course, either didn't get it or chose to ignore him.

"Boat sink. We got bodies; no boat." Nguyen seemed uptight about that as well.

"Well that's great. How are we supposed to know what happened to the engines and the cargo the pirates seemed so interested in?" McQuaid shook his head, making it plain he was disappointed in the police chief's salvage work. Nguyen just scowled back at him.

"No boat. We got girl. She tell us what happened to boat. But now she not talk. Mebbe, I take her to jail and we talk, heh?" They both knew Doc McCawley wasn't going to allow that, but McQuaid decided to concede the point. The police chief had the right to arrest her and haul her off to jail, where he could interrogate her without interference and without restraint as well. McQuaid, decided to try a different tact.

"Why not let me talk with her first? It couldn't hurt. If she doesn't tell me everything, I'll speak to McCawley about turning her over to you – if she's not in danger because of her health, that is." He shoved his ball cap back on his head and looked at Nguyen, eyebrows up with expectation. Nguyen appeared to be giving his options careful consideration.

"Okay, she talk to you first," he replied back at last. "But I be in room when she talk, heh?"

"Not a good idea. If she has some problem talking to you, she won't want to talk with me if you're around. She might be afraid of police in general. You do want to find out what happened out there, don't you?"

Nguyen glanced down and seemed to notice Kiko for the first time. She was watching them both, hugging her stuffed monkey, and looked back up at the police chief, with her dark eyes wide and mouth hanging open. Nguyen took a deep breath and blew it back out through pursed lips. He looked back at McQuaid, rolling his eyes and making a show of frustration. Then he grabbed the top of the windshield of the jeep with both hands and levered himself into the front seat.

"You need ride, no?" He didn't look up at McQuaid for an answer and started the engine, then sat there with both hands gripping the steering wheel, staring straight ahead. He glanced at Kiko again. "You ride too, Kiko."

They bumped along in silence for a while on the way to the hospital, McQuaid in the front and Kiko on the jump seat in back. McQuaid hollered over to Nguyen above the engine noise.

"Did you hear about the Japanese soldiers who raided Chief Mahutra's village?" This was a safer subject for the moment and he needed to know what was going on over there anyway. He worried they might discover the C-47 and decide to take it hostage, along with the girl from the village. Nguyen gave him a quick look and returned his eyes to the road.

"Dez soldiers Japanese from war. Dey hide in mountains. We need soldiers fight dem, not police. Dey have guns and mebbe more." McQuaid thought he sounded a little defensive. "We give dem food, dey don't fight. Get soldiers fight dem. Not police." McQuaid understood his reluctance to tangle with them. It was hard to know how many holdouts were up there and his rag-tag police force of three was ill equipped to deal with even a small force of armed and desperate Japanese. But they'd have to do something about them at some point. No matter what, he needed to get out there and bring back his other plane before they found it. They might even think it was still military and try to destroy it, along with his expensive cargo. He hoped he could persuade Nguyen into at least driving him back out there to help him pick it up. An extra gun would come in handy.

McQuaid decided he'd wait on that conversation until after they'd dealt with the girl. She was a problem they both needed to solve for different reasons. He wondered what she knew about the pirates and he was becoming more frustrated with his lack of information about them, especially now that he'd discovered he had a price on his head too. He looked back over at Nguyen.

"Did you know the pirates want to kill me now?" Nguyen's head whipped around; his eyes narrowed.

"What you say? How you know dis' Gunna'?" he asked with genuine concern.

"Rajan had us meet some buyers for our cargo at the wharf in Manila. They told us the pirates warned them not to buy from me. I talked to one of them myself and he told me the pirate leader was out to get me for killing his brother when we shot up their boat." Nguyen tore his eyes away from McQuaid's to look back at the road.

"Too many pirates, Gunna'," he offered back, his face solemn. McQuaid ignored his warning.

"Do the pirates have some sort of base, or hideout around these islands?" Nguyen looked back at him – puzzled.

"What you mean?"

"You know – some place they keep their boats and sleep at night."

"Oh, yah. Dey have many places." The police chief waved his arm around his head. "Dey on many islands. Stay in no place for long time. We try find dem many times. No find dem, Gunna'. You no find dem; dey find you. Dey know you heah all time." He looked over at McQuaid as if he wanted to ensure he had made his point.

"So what am I supposed to do, just wait 'til they show up? I don't wait well, Captain. You know that." Nguyen shook his head.

"No, you need pay dem for dead brodder. Dey take money and go way. Much bedda you pay money, Gunna'." The police chief was animated now and stated all of this with some amount of passion. But it didn't seem like he had any real expectation McQuaid would do anything of the sort.

"That's bullshit and you know it! I'm not paying those bastards. They'll keep coming back for more, even if I did. I need to find their boss. There's only one way to handle this for good."

Nguyen's jaw was set hard and his expression turned angry. With a sudden move, he slammed on the brakes, throwing Kiko into the back of McQuaid's seat with a cry of protest. He set the hand brake and swiveled around to face McQuaid.

"Gunna', you no look for trouble. Dis for army and police." He pointed over the windshield out at the bay. "You kill more pirates, more pirates come heah. Dey find you, find your friends. Dey kill dem. Mebbe kill Lubang people too. You pay. Much bedder you pay. No more shoot pirate boats. No more kill pirates!"

86

He was plenty riled up, but McQuaid detected some fear beneath the surface of the bravado. It made sense to him why he wanted to keep the pirates away from Lubang. Nguyen didn't have the manpower or equipment to wage war against them. And without superior strength, they would be overrun. They needed help and a plan was beginning to form in the back of his mind now. But for the moment, he decided to pacify Nguyen and talk to Lijuan to see what, if anything, she knew about them. He had a hunch she knew plenty.

"Okay, Captain. You're right. I need to set up a meeting with them though. Maybe they'll take something in trade. They're in business. They'll understand a good business deal."

Nguyen looked suspicious. "What you mean 'deal'?"

"I'm not sure yet. I need to think about it and figure out a plan. But we still need to get word to them I want to meet with the leader of the pirates, and the sooner the better too. How do we do that, Captain?"

Nguyen looked long and hard at him. Then he turned around, released the handbrake, and floored the gas, spinning the rear wheels and throwing a rooster tail of sand into the air behind them. Without looking back at McQuaid, he replied through gritted teeth.

"I find out, Gunna'." Then he pointed at him. "You no find more trouble, heh?"   McQuaid nodded his head and responded with a resigned tone to his voice.

"Okay, Captain. We'll play it your way for now." However, his mind was chewing on the problem and it kept coming back to the same issue. What he needed was force superiority. Without that, the pirates would continue to feel empowered and come back to extract whatever blood, or payment, they wanted at a time of their choosing. His cargo business ran too lean to afford to pay for protection and even if he could afford it, it wasn't the way McQuaid handled that kind of problem.

They rode in silence the rest of the way to the hospital. Mattie was waiting for them and pacing near the front door. Nguyen pulled in next to her and parked. She walked over to McQuaid's side, holding her hand out to Kiko, who was already standing up to leap out of the jeep. She looked back to him with a smirk that didn't seem cheerful.

"Well? Did Captain Nguyen tell you he's planning on hauling Lijuan over to the jail, so he can use the rubber hose on her to get her to talk?" She looked over to Nguyen; smiling sweetly.

"We came to a meeting of the minds," McQuaid replied, wanting to appear gracious and dial down some of the tension between the three of them. "I'm going to speak with her first and see if I can get her to open up to me. With any luck, she'll be able to tell us something useful and I'll encourage her to be open and frank with the police chief as well." He swung his legs out of the seat and stood up next to her. "I could sure use a cold beer first, before I have to do all that talking though." He turned his head to look at her so Nguyen couldn't see and waggled his eyebrows at her. Mattie picked up on her cue without letting on and looked down at Kiko.

"I suppose you could use a Coca too, huh little girl?" Kiko nodded and started pulling her toward the store. McQuaid glanced back at Nguyen before he started following behind them.

"Be back real quick, Captain. Don't worry, we'll get everything worked out." Nguyen scowled after them, pulling his hat low over his eyes in frustration.

Kiko banged through the screen door first and was making a beeline for the ice chest, when she noticed two island women looking over the canned goods on the shelves, biding their time, while they waited for Mattie to return. She slowed to a respectable walk, still managing to get to the ice chest well ahead of McQuaid.

Mattie walked over to the two ladies and apologized for keeping them waiting. They started pulling cans off the shelf and talking together back and forth. Meanwhile, McQuaid joined Kiko, pulling a beer and Coke bottles out of the ice chest for the two of them. He popped both tops, handed her the Coke and ambled outside with his beer to flop down in one of the chairs on the front veranda. He took a long welcome pull from his beer, watching Kiko sit down on the steps with her Coke bottle.

Before long, the two island ladies walked out with straw baskets full of canned goods and meat wrapped in butcher paper, nodding and smiling to the two of them, before they turned and headed up the main street. Mattie walked out soon after, holding another bottle of soda and sank down in the chair next to McQuaid.

"So how was your trip, fly boy?" she asked. She wiped her arm across her forehead and then rolled the frosty bottle across her cheeks for some relief from the late afternoon heat. The sun had already dipped into the sea, drawing long shadows across the street. A hint of the evening sea breeze stirred her hair when she tilted her soda bottle back for a long drink. McQuaid pulled off his sweaty ball cap to get some air on the top of his head and gulped down another couple mouthfuls of his beer. He wiped his mouth with the back of his arm and slouched further back in his chair, crossing his long legs out in front of him.

"Well, the flight out and back was good. We did have some trouble in Manila though. Seems the pirates got there ahead of us and warned our buyers away." He glanced sidelong at Kiko, well aware her little ears were catching every word. Mattie sat up and leaned closer to him.

"That's somewhat disappointing," she offered in careful response, keeping her voice low. "Do you think we'll need to do anything about that, Richard?"

"Well, we managed to sell everything we brought over to some of the boat people and I filled your shopping list all right. Baacay should start bringing stuff over in the jeep before too long. As far as the rest of it, they seemed upset we knocked off the pirate leader's brother in the yacht attack. They're planning on a little retribution; or so they say." He casually finished off the rest of his beer and set the empty down next to him by his chair. Mattie hesitated to respond. Then she stood up and walked over to Kiko.

"Okay, little girl, time to get you in for your bath now." Kiko started to protest, but Mattie was firm with her, taking her Coke bottle and motioning for her to stand up and follow her inside. After some more whining she got to her feet, took Mattie's hand, and shuffle-walked behind her toward the door. Mattie gave McQuaid a "to be continued" look on the way by him and proceeded to herd Kiko inside.

McQuaid leaned back even farther in his chair, his hands clasped behind his head, watching the shadows drawing the night over the dusty street out front. The subtle evening breeze smelled of trees, dust on the street, and overheated metal. A small grove of palms trailed back into the jungle from behind a couple shotgun houses facing the store from across the street. Birds were settling into their swaying fronds for the evening. He could hear their fan leaves swishing and the heavy palm branches making a clacking noise above the hiss of the air currents passing through. The background sounds of nightlife had begun. Crickets, a few parrots in the distance, and even a screeching monkey or two, were testament to the island's bedding down after the end of a long day.

He knew he should be getting over to the hospital to talk with Lijuan, before Nguyen lost all patience. But he also needed to let Mattie know they were in danger. Much of his plan was still in the formative stages. Until he had checked in with a few friends needed to pull off the little operation he had in mind, any details would have to come later, when he had more to share. But Mattie was a sound backstop for him and he had no idea how long they had before the pirates decided to spring their own little plan on them. They'd need to be ready and he wasn't sure how much they could rely on Nguyen for protection. He feared it would be very little. At last, Mattie walked outside and sat down next to him again. Her face appeared composed, but he detected an unnatural quiet to her manner.

"So what's the score, Richard? Is this going to be bloody war all over again?" He could just make out her face in the fading light. Her voice sounded strained and worried. She brushed the hair back from her face and took another drink of her soda while she waited for him to tell her the worst of it.

Heaving a long sigh, he started in.

"The usual buyers Rajan had lined up in Manila told me they were warned by the pirate leader they couldn't buy from us. They said the pirate leader's brother was killed in the attack and he was going to come for me and my friends and kill all of us." He paused to see if Mattie needed to jump in. She remained quiet and very still, so he continued. "Nguyen says I should buy them off. Everything out here has a price, of course. But I don't think, even if we did pay them off, we'd buy much time from further harassment. They're criminals, Mattie. If they sense weakness, they'll keep coming back, until we don't have anything left, or we fight them to a standstill. The problem is, Nguyen doesn't know where they are and there is little doubt they know where to find us. He's afraid to tangle with them. He says there are too many of them and only three police on Lubang. I have to hand it to him there. He's not much of threat."

Mattie leaned forward to see his face in the dying light.

"Richard, we have money and we could offer to transport some contraband if they need us to. How are we supposed to fight back against them? Maybe Nguyen's right. If we pay them off, they might leave us alone." She said this last feigning conviction and watched for his reaction; waiting for reassurance.

He remained silent, just looking at her.

"You're not planning on paying them off are you?" she asked, her voice trailing off and resigned.

"That never works, Mattie," he replied, trying to keep his words gentle. "We need to find out where they're vulnerable and keep safe until we can formulate a plan to attack them, before they can get to us. It's the only way."

"Attack them with what, Richard? Cans of soup and luncheon meat?" she flared back. Mattie seldom raised her voice and bit back any further response, looking away, anger and frustration still distorting her features. He watched her sitting there in the dark. He knew she was strong and like him, she never backed away from a fair fight. But they weren't going to be able to fight fair this time.

She raised her soda to her lips and drank a slow few sips, taking the time to compose herself. When at last she turned back to face him, he could tell the pluck of her British upbringing had regained the upper hand on her emotions. "Sorry for that unseemly outburst. You were saying?"

"You're right to feel angry. I'm angry too. But it's too late to duck our heads and hope this all blows over. They're coming for us, Mattie. And we have too much to lose."

"I know, Richard. I guess I'm just scared, that's all."

He found her hand and squeezed it.

"Me too. But we might be able to come out of this on top if we use our heads." He began laying out his plan, with slow and methodical deliberation.

Mattie listened to him until he finished without interruption. After a moment's pause, she reached forward and placed her other hand on his arm, looking at him but no longer able to see his face.

"What do you think our chances are?" she asked.

"I think we could even the odds if we bloody their noses first. They might just cut their losses and run."

"And if they don't?"

"Then we're no worse off than we are now. If they think we're weak, they can just overwhelm us any time they choose. If we show them we'll fight, it should at least slow them down. I have connections through the Marine Corps and we could get some help from the Philippine military. They don't want criminals running drugs through the islands either. We need to marshal available resources and take the fight to the pirates, before they can strike at us. Mattie, one thing I learned in the Marines is people beat themselves before the enemy fires the first shot. There is no place in the world you can stay safe forever. Someday, you'll always have to decide whether you stand up and fight, or lie down and hope they show mercy."

She leaned back, not moving for a long time. Then, at last, she stood with her hands on her hips and the lighted windows revealed a glint of defiance in her eyes.

"Count me in, Marine. Nobody's taking what we've built away from us without a fight – not today anyway."

Chapter Six
Lubang Village Hospital, Lubang Island, the Philippines

McQuaid walked back to the hospital, still thinking about his conversation with Mattie. He knew she was scared, but she amazed him with her determination. Level headed and always careful to weigh her options, he didn't expect her to be adamant about taking a stand. Over the years, he had come to appreciate a certain iron in her though. Losing both her parents and then her husband was enough to take the stuffing out of most people. It hadn't been easy carving out a livelihood on a small island in the post-war Philippines either. With the now added responsibility of helping him raise Kiko, he couldn't guess at what she imagined the consequences might be, standing up to local criminals who thumbed their noses at the thin-spread law enforcement in the region.

They had avoided problems with them to this point by not presenting themselves as a worthy target. He and Mattie were both well aware of the drug trade running out of Hong Kong and other more obscure Chinese ports to supply buyers in Manila, which served as a waypoint to broader South Seas markets. But up until the recent confrontation with the pirates looting the foundered yacht, their paths seldom crossed. Without the death of their leader's brother on his hands, McQuaid Air Cargo might well have co-existed with the pirates, unnoticed for some time to come. That had all changed now.

When the British were driven out of Hong Kong by the Japanese during the war, the balance of power in the region shifted. Control of these new territories in China, including the island of Hong Kong, were previous spoils of war under the Treaty of Nanjing and ceded to the British after they defeated China in the Opium Wars. Their subsequent establishment of a British colony at Hong Kong, along with a fleet of British warships patrolling the South China Sea since 1842, created extended powers of sovereignty and order of the empire to the region. Pirating and general criminal activity was quelled wherever it threatened British interests.

Since the war, however, pirating had reemerged as a prevalent criminal enterprise. For the most part it remained unchallenged and had flourished. The presence of the American Navy at Subic Bay and even more U.S. military stationed on the air base at Clark Field were reassuring. But their powers were defused in matters of civil authority, again giving the pirates a crack in law enforcement they were all too happy to exploit. As long as U.S. personnel and interests were undisturbed, they were ignored and seen as a problem for the Philippine government and military. However, they were ill equipped and disordered since the war and riddled with corruption in their ranks. This produced a widespread, every-man-for-himself mentality and grew worse beyond the main island of Luzon.

McQuaid reached the front steps of the hospital, clearing them in one bound, and walked through the double screened doors into the front reception area. He was struck by the strong odor of alcohol and chlorine bleach, in general use in the tropics, for all manner of disinfectant cleaning. He nodded to the older Filipino nurse sitting at the front desk and pulled his over-chewed cigar out of his mouth, looking around for a trash can to toss it into.

"Evening, Isabella. Is the Doc around?" She smiled and stood up, reaching out to gingerly take his cigar with two fingers and then deposit it in her trash behind the desk, like a disease-infected bug.

"He in back. He wait for you, Gunna'. Go now and see," she said, gesturing toward the door behind her on the right. McQuaid leaned over the desk and pecked her on the cheek.

"Thanks, dear. You're looking fabulous as usual," he gushed, before she swatted him, giggling, and motioned him to go back without further embarrassing her. He winked at her nevertheless and ducked under a good-natured roundhouse. When he passed through the door, he spied the Doc striding toward him with clipboard in hand and a customary frown on his face. Doc ran the hospital like a Swiss watch, but things were never quite up to standards for him. *It must be a Brit thing*, McQuaid mused to himself. McCawley's eyebrows shot up above his wire-rimmed glasses when he spotted McQuaid.

"Thought you'd be here over an hour ago," he growled.

"How's she doing, Doc?" McQuaid asked, intending to be more conversational than anything. He didn't expect her to be laid up with physical injuries, as much as struggling with extreme shock from witnessing people around her being murdered. She was a young girl and he knew strong men who caved in after experiencing death under extreme circumstances like that. Whether or not they were her family, it would have been terrifying for her.

"She's in good shape for the most part. But she's not too keen on Nguyen." McCawley ran his hand through his thinning gray hair. "Can't imagine why that might be, can you? I mean considering how cheerful and compassionate a fellow he is. Come on. Let's go look in on her."

McQuaid followed him toward the curtained off partition nearest them. He pulled the drape back enough to admit them both into the small cubicle, where Lijuan lay propped up in bed. She was awake and watching them as they came in. They had bathed her and she appeared much healthier than the last time he'd seen her. A tense smile crossed her face when McQuaid moved to her bedside and took her hand.

"You're looking much better, Lijuan," he said, smiling down at her. Her face was framed by glossy, straight, jet black hair that might fall to her waist if she were standing. McQuaid figured her to be in her late twenties and even without makeup, she was striking in a classic oriental way. Full red lips parted around her smile, revealing straight white teeth. Dark eyes the color of obsidian glass watched him, waiting and apprehensive. Her eyes and nose both looked red, as if she'd been crying. Her hand, in his now, was warm but unresponsive. She was waiting for him to disclose his true purpose for this visit and was revealing nothing of her thoughts until he did so.

McQuaid pulled a chair over to her bedside and felt Doc McCawley move away behind him, drawing the curtain closed to afford them some privacy. He looked at her from eyelevel now, offering a warm and compassionate smile. The smile was genuine and not intended just to be disarming. He meant it. In his mind, she was an innocent young girl, caught up in an unexpected and terrible tragedy. Leaning forward, so as not to alarm her, he squeezed her hand.

"How are you feeling? Much better I hope."

Despite her condition, she remained poised and appraised him with care, studying his face, perhaps trying to decipher a deeper meaning behind the question. After a long pause, she seemed satisfied he could be trusted.

"I am much better now, thanks to you. I am very grateful, Mister McQuaid." Her voice was sweet and melodic, the words coming out with perfect diction and a strong hint of an English accent. "The doctor says I can go home tomorrow.

But I'm not sure where that might be at the moment." Her dark eyes welled up and she pulled her hand back from his, to grab a tissue by the bedside.

"We'll figure all that out together. No need to worry about it just yet though," McQuaid said, his voice soothing. He hoped she wouldn't fall apart on him. "I need to talk with you a little first, however. We don't know much about you and the police chief told me you weren't carrying any papers. Did you leave them on the boat somewhere?" he asked, his expression remaining hopeful. With an abrupt move, she turned away and brought her hand to her mouth.

"I don't have any papers," she replied.

McQuaid had a suspicion she might say that. He scooted his chair closer to speak to her again in a lower voice.

"They weren't your parents were they?" he asked, trying to be gentle.

She didn't move, her still face averted from his. He had lots of questions, but he knew he needed to be careful. If he spooked her, she might clam up and he would lose her to Nguyen's harsher methods, with little chance to discover what actual events took place on the yacht. McQuaid needed her to trust him enough to volunteer the truth. After a long pause, she turned back toward him, tears streaming down her cheeks and squeezed from eyes that were mere slits above deformed and quivering lips.

"They were just trying to help me," she got out at last. "They thought I was a refugee, trying to escape from Hong Kong and get to the Americans to defect. I didn't mean for them to get hurt. That wasn't supposed to happen." She covered her eyes now, crying unashamed, and her body heaving as she tried to catch her breath between ragged sobs. McQuaid stayed quiet and patient. His mind was working, dropping the odd shaped pieces of her story into place. He feared this was going to be far worse than he had imagined.

After a few moments, she pulled herself together, wiping her eyes and blowing her nose before looking back at him. When he remained silent, just watching her, she started in again. "Don't you see? I caused their deaths! They didn't know anything. They were just trying to protect me. They thought the pirates were bounty hunters looking for me." She slashed at her cheek with the heel of her hand, wiping away her tears in a sudden angry motion. "They were stupid, but they were kind to me. They didn't know I was just using them the whole time." McQuaid continued to listen without interrupting and keeping his expression neutral. "Do you see why I don't deserve to live? I am a heartless and unworthy person." This last was thrown back at him over her shoulder. She turned her body away from him, curled into a ball, and hid her face in her pillow.

McQuaid decided there was no better time than now.

"Who loaded the drugs on the boat? Did you?" he asked, his voice low and even. She didn't move. He tried a different tact, since she also wasn't denying anything. "Did the pirates know about the drugs before they came aboard?"

Lijuan lay very still. After almost thirty seconds, without another word from McQuaid, she rolled back over and faced him clear eyed and seemed determined to get something off her chest.

"I thought the drugs were going to be offloaded in Manila. That's where we were headed. But Grant wasn't taking the current into effect and we drifted way too far west before he saw the lights onshore. He changed course, but we were already in shallow water and he hit some rocks or something under the water." She sat up and clasped her knees to her chest. "He must have damaged the propeller shafts and put a hole in the hull below the waterline. We started drifting further west, out of control and taking on water. Alicia, Grant's wife, began calling for help on the radio, while Grant and I bailed water. The pumps couldn't keep up with it, even with both of us bailing. I thought we were going to sink."

"The pirates heard her radio calls?" McQuaid asked, trying to be helpful.

"They must have. It was very sudden. Alicia started screaming we were being attacked. Grant grabbed his rifle and ran up on deck to try and protect us. But they had a machine gun on the front of their boat. I was standing on the ladder from below and could see above the deck. They shot them both, Mister McQuaid. There wasn't anything I could do." Her mouth screwed up again and big tears rolled down her cheeks. She kept her eyes closed, as if to avoid seeing that horrible scene again. Dropping her face to her knees, she hid her face from him and continued snuffling.

"Didn't the pirates see you?" McQuaid tried filling in the awkward silence. "Did they hear you on the radio talking to Mattie?" She kept her head buried against her legs and rolled her forehead back and forth across her knees.

"I didn't know whether they saw me, or heard me. They just seemed to be in a hurry to get the bundles of drugs up from below and onto their boat. I think they could see we were sinking and were worried the drugs might be lost." She rolled her face toward him. "Some of the bundles were already ruined and floating around in the water below decks. They might have gotten out most of the ones that were still dry."

"How did the pirates know the drug cargo was on board?" McQuaid pressed again, trying to make the question seem innocent. She stared at him, her face still lying sideways on her knees, and then rolled her head back and forth at him. "You don't know, or you don't want to say?" McQuaid asked her, careful to keep any hint of a sharp tone from his voice. She just gave him a blank stare. Then a light came into her eyes and she seemed to come to some conclusion.

"They must have known somehow. Maybe they had been waiting for us in port and when we didn't show up, they decided to come looking for us." Lijuan paused and frowned at him. "I think they wanted me alive," she said.

McQuaid was puzzled.

"Why would they want you?" he asked, but already figuring they may have seen her as a valuable commodity for sale to the slave trade. That would explain why they ignored her until they'd recovered as much of the drug cargo as they could. It would have been a great day of salvage for them, had he not spoiled their plans by blazing away at them from the Goose.

She was staring back at him still, her eyes vacant, looking through him, at something only she could see. Then she turned her head to gaze straight ahead at the end of the bed, with an expression of resolve.

"They must have known they were going to take me back. I was supposed to make sure the drug cargo was delivered and in return they would give me my papers in Manila. I planned to make my way to the American Air Force base and turn myself in to them." She rested her chin on her knees, pensive and still looking away, as if she could see beyond the curtain partition. "They were probably going to take me back to Madam Chin. If the whole cargo wasn't delivered, she would make me come back and complete my contract." She turned her face toward him and looked into his eyes. "She would need to use me to make up her losses. That is only right."

McQuaid stared back at her.

"Who is Madam Chin and what sort of contract did you have with her?"

She looked back at him with a patient smile.

"You Americans are so naive. Where do you think all those party girls come from, when you sail into port looking for a good time? China is not like your America. Young girls in China are not valuable unless they are pretty and their families can sell them into the pleasure trade." She flopped back on the bed and looked at the ceiling, one arm thrown across her forehead. "My family sold me and my sister to Madam Chin when we were just children. We were the fortunate ones. She took care of us, fed us, and raised us to be clever young ladies. We were trained for pleasure, not hard labor like those unlucky enough to be born ugly. And even they were lucky their parents didn't just kill them right after they were born. There is no honor in being female in China. That is only for the males." She looked over at him again, raising her eyebrows. "Does this shock you, Mr. McQuaid?" Her voice was soft and compassionate.

McQuaid did know something about the Chinese pleasure guilds and that officials generally turned a blind eye toward the widespread selling of young girls as indentured slaves into prostitution. Pleasure palaces, which included specially outfitted barges moored near the larger ports, in both Japan and China, had been all the rage during and after WWII. The practice may have even started in Japan. But China was renowned for their callous treatment of women. The floating pleasure palaces, referred to as "flower boats" and brothels, flourished around Hong Kong, putting great demand on the need for pretty young women whose families were all too willing to sell them into slavery. McQuaid had never actually met one of these women, however. As he looked back at Lijuan, he couldn't imagine what misery and degradation she had endured in her young life. He sat forward and took her hand.

"Lijuan, I can't let the pirates take you back to Madam Chin. You are welcome to stay with us, but we need to deal with some problems first." She was watching him, wary now, and didn't offer any immediate comment. "The pirates will come looking for me too, not just you. They want to kill me, in return for killing their leader's brother when we attacked them yesterday." Lijuan jerked up straight, her face tight with alarm.

"You have to hide! You cannot let them find you. They are very bad men, Mr. McQuaid." She reached forward with her other hand and grasped his arm. It felt tiny and cool against his skin. "I could not live with myself if one more kind person is harmed because of me." She took his hand and held it against her face and closed her eyes tight; perhaps to blot out the horror of the continuing nightmare for which she felt responsible. McQuaid moved her hand to the other one and held them both in his.

"I'm more concerned with you right now. I'm capable of taking care of myself. So we need to deal with you for the moment." She moved her hands to her chest, holding his palm flat against her. He could feel her heart racing.

"Okay, what can I do?" she asked at last, her eyes wide and imploring.

"First, you will have to tell Captain Nguyen all of this. Make sure and inform him the two people on the yacht were never meant to be harmed and the drug shipment did not belong to you. He'll still want to put you in jail, however. But that may be the safest place right now. I have to drive up to the village of Looc first thing tomorrow, repair my other plane I left up there, and fly it back here to Lubang."

He retrieved his hand, but moved over to sit down next to her on the bed, keeping his voice very low. "I think I can bargain with the pirates in return for some expensive medical supplies I have on that plane. That will buy me time to talk to some old friends who can help me deal with them later – once and for all."

She began shaking her head and started to protest. McQuaid put his finger against her lips to quiet her. "Lijuan, I need you to listen to me. I can't be in both places at once and I have no idea how soon the pirates are going to come looking for me. I not only have to worry about you, but also Mattie and our little girl Kiko now too. I can't help everyone at the same time. You have to help me, by staying safe until I get back tomorrow night."

He paused, watching her. She was trembling with fright and who knew what other desperate apprehensions burdening her soul. Her lips started quivering again and he could see she was teetering on the edge. He pulled her to his chest, one of his bear paw hands gently holding her head against him and let her put her arms around him. He needed her to draw strength from him and do one more difficult thing he would have to ask of her.

He rested his chin on the top of her head while she clung to him, a mixture of emotions washing over him, holding her frail body against his. The fragrance of orange blossom soap in her soft warm hair filled his head and he could feel her ragged breathing against him. She was a beautiful young woman, an actual damsel in distress. McQuaid could have laughed at the melodrama of seeing himself as some sort of white knight, coming to her rescue. However, he had become just that. She was managing to get under his skin already and he knew he was vulnerable to feeling responsible for her.

The Chinese believe that if someone saves your life, you are forever responsible for them. Or maybe it was the other way around. He wasn't sure, but the last thing he needed was this young girl in the middle of his life right now. He barely knew her, but what he did know drove a stake into the core of him. She was a pawn in the hands of thieves and murderers. They had made her into a criminal already by association and now her life was in danger too. Somebody had to put a stop to it. With solemn determination, he concluded he was the only one who could.

It was almost nine o'clock in the evening before McQuaid left the hospital. He had filled Doc McCawley in on the plan and though he wasn't at all happy about it, he admitted they didn't have much choice. The heat inside the hospital had been bearable, with all the fans blowing full blast. By contrast, the cooler night breeze outside was refreshing, seeking out the sweat on his back and scalp, like cool, seductive fingers caressing the hot damp skin.

He was heading back to the store to relate his discussion with Lijuan to Mattie. He didn't relish the thought of telling her, how their already dire circumstances had become even more precarious. Lijuan understood he'd have to tell Captain Nguyen her whole story. And that Nguyen would come to the hospital and interrogate her; just to make sure their stories matched. And then he would have to arrest her.

McQuaid also impressed on her the need to play up to Nguyen's ego, to be nice to him and get him to like her, even to feel protective of her. Now that he knew she was a professional at seducing men, he had little doubt she could work her wiles on the police chief. As much as he hated to think about it, he needed her to make Nguyen believe keeping her around might offer some personal advantage to him. But only just enough, so he would be more motivated to sequester her if the pirates showed up.

He knew Nguyen well enough not to trust him if he was outgunned and intimidated, or if he thought he might profit from her somehow. But he might not know Lijuan could be worth a great deal of money to the pirates. There was no assurance they'd pay anything at all to get her back. But the police chief wouldn't want to risk a fight, so he'd be better off just hiding her and pleading ignorance as to her whereabouts.

McQuaid would further suggest he tell them she was with him on the way to Looc village if he was pressured. If they didn't know she was in his jail, he might be able to get out to Looc and back without major calamity if they happened to show up while he was away. He'd also realized taking Nguyen with him to help him out if needed in Looc, was out of the question now.

So he'd need to drive up there before dawn and get back as soon as possible. But he also needed to meet with Chief Mahutra while he was in Looc. There was still the matter of the Japanese soldiers threatening his village and their hostage. He wasn't sure if they'd need to use some of the medical supplies in the C-47 or not. But they might. He also knew he'd have to get most of those supplies back to Lubang, if he decided to take Mattie and Nguyen's advice to bargain with the pirates. That would be a tricky bit of negotiation, even with some of the expensive pharmaceutical drugs in his cargo. He hated to think how long it would take him to make up his losses on a shipment he had hoped would instead be quite profitable. Now wasn't the time to worry about that, however.

Dead brother or not, their leader had to be concerned with profits if he was to bargain for their entire band. If he had to choose between killing McQuaid and making tens of thousands of U.S. dollars reselling medical supplies, he might just go for it. He also knew he couldn't trust him not to double back on their bargain later. It was personal when it involved him killing a family member. But it might buy him some needed time to line up a few things that could tip the balance back in his favor.

As he approached Mattie's store, he noticed Nguyen's white police jeep out front and then the small red eye of a glowing cigarette hovering around ethereally above the chairs

102

on the front veranda. McQuaid figured he'd be hanging around, waiting to hear about his talk with Lijuan. At least he wouldn't have to chase him down to get his plan into action.

As he walked up the steps, he could see Mattie through the lighted windows inside the store, her back to him, restocking shelves from the supplies Baacay had brought over from the Goose. He headed over to the veranda and could just make out Nguyen's dim outline in the shadows. Nguyen reached over and removed his Aussie hat from the other chair to allow McQuaid to sit down beside him.

"Ho, Gunna', what you say? How Lijuan tonight? Hoping much bedda," he crooned, his gold tooth flashing in the light from the windows.

McQuaid took the offered chair and flopped down beside him. Nguyen shook a cigarette out from his pack and offered one to him, but he declined of course. The police chief knew he didn't smoke and fished out the smoke for himself instead, lighting it off the already burning one in his hand. Nguyen sat waiting for McQuaid to answer him.

"She's much better," he responded at last. "I think she's ready to talk with you now."

"Oh, now she want talk wit me, heh? Why she not talk before, Gunna'? Mebbe she hide from police? What you say?" He took a long drag off his cigarette, illuminating his face in a demonic, reddish glow. McQuaid ignored the unveiled sarcasm and looked over his shoulder to make sure Mattie was still busy inside the store. Turning back around, he leaned closer to Nguyen to ensure they wouldn't be overheard and started in.

"She knew about the drugs and was supposed to keep an eye on them until they made port in Manila. The supplier in Hong Kong held her papers, to make sure she would keep her end of the bargain. But the boat ran aground and the whole plan went bad. The boat owners didn't know anything about the drugs. She told them she was trying to make it to Manila and turn herself in to the Americans as a Chinese defector. The pirates were supposed to meet her in port and unload the drug shipment in secret, while the boat owners were ashore. In return for her help, they were supposed to give her papers back so she could prove to the Americans she was a Chinese immigrant." Nguyen sat absorbed in the story, watching him from the growing cloud of cigarette smoke. "When they ran aground, the boat started sinking and ruined most of the drugs.

The pirates must have heard their distress calls and hurried out from the port to intercept them."

"Why she hide from pirates?" Nguyen asked. The question was an astute one.

"She thought they were going to kill her for losing a good part of the shipment. But I'm not sure she even knew if they were the right people she planned to meet in Manila; especially after they shot the older man and his wife."

Nguyen sat digesting that and then leaned forward.

"Why pirates not kill her? Dey kill udders." It was another good question and one McQuaid had also wanted to better understand. So he was ready with an answer.

"She thinks they wanted to take her alive and return her to someone named Madam Chin, who runs one of the floating pleasure palace boats in Hong Kong harbor." Nguyen sat back in his chair with a strange expression on his face and McQuaid could see him looking out over the street in front, lost in thought. "You recognize the name?" McQuaid asked, when he didn't return his attention to their conversation. Nguyen hesitated before answering him.

"Madam Chin is great lady in Hong Kong," he said under his breath, as if he was afraid of being overheard repeating her name in the wrong crowd. "She is rich; berry powerful," he said, pointing his finger at McQuaid to emphasize this point. He began again. "So, she buy drugs for ship to Manila. Lijuan belong to Madam Chin. Dis' not good. She want Lijuan back. Mebbe pirates work for Madam Chin. Mebbe not." He was almost muttering to himself by this point, trying to work it all out in his head.

McQuaid responded with a dismissive wave of his hand.

"Listen, Captain, Lijuan is a young, innocent girl, who thought she was buying her freedom from slavery as a prostitute. She was just watching over the drug delivery. There wasn't anything she could to do about the pirates killing those two on the boat either. That hadn't been in the original plan."

Nguyen mopped his face with a handkerchief and expelled a loud puff of air through his lips.

"Mebbe pirates come back for her. Mebbe dey want kill you; take Lijuan back to Madam Chin." He shook his head in dismay. "Dis bad problem, Gunna'." He pointed his finger at McQuaid and began again, raising his voice in frustration. "Dis your problem. You make berry big mess here, Gunna'.

You big war hero, save girl, but kill big pirate...now big mess for all Lubang people." McQuaid started to say something in response, but Nguyen wasn't finished and waved him off. He held up three fingers and pushed them at McQuaid, as if he needed him to count them. "Lubang have three policeman," he said, his voice husky with growing anger. "Dez pirates have many men – many guns. Dey come to Lubang, look for you. How do I stop pirates with three policeman, Gunna'?" He stood up and began pacing back and forth, his hand rubbing the back of his neck, the glowing stub of his cigarette dangling forgotten from his lips.

McQuaid wasn't sure if he intended to finish the sentence, but moved to stand up and offer a reply. Before either could continue, Mattie opened the screen door and strode out onto the veranda, eyeing them both, first one, then the other.

"Hello, boys. Mind if I join your little soiree out here?" She cast a suspicious glance in McQuaid's direction. "Didn't know you were back from the hospital yet, Richard. How's Lijuan doing?" Lifting her eyes toward Nguyen, she gauged his reaction. The police chief seemed to notice his cigarette was about to burn his lip, snatched it from his mouth, and flicked it out on the street. He watched it bounce a couple times, amidst a small shower of sparks, fixated on it, as if he had never seen anything quite like that before. Mattie figured he was stalling and looked over at McQuaid again. "Well?"

"Lijuan is fine. But we've got a few new problems to deal with," he said without elaborating. He preferred to discuss things in greater detail without Nguyen around. "The police chief and I need to work out a few things. It seems Lijuan was somehow involved with drug running from the yacht." Mattie had been holding the screen door open, but let it go with a loud bang. Nguyen flinched. McQuaid continued. "She was just supposed keep an eye on the drug shipment until they made it to Manila. She wasn't involved in the buying or selling and had no idea the pirates would show up and shoot the older man and woman." Mattie just stared at him. "They weren't her parents. She was just trying to get to Manila to defect from China. They thought they were helping her escape from China."

"What are you planning to do with her, Captain?" Mattie asked, her voice quiet and strained.

Before he could answer, McQuaid interrupted.

"I really don't see that Captain Nguyen has much choice in all this, Mattie." He hurried to continue, ignoring a growing frown on her face. "Lijuan agreed to ride shotgun on the drug shipment and even if she couldn't have prevented the shootings, that alone makes her a responsible party in their deaths. Captain Nguyen is bound by law to at least hold her until after he's had the chance to conduct a thorough investigation. Right, Captain Nguyen?" With inner satisfaction, he noticed Nguyen appeared to be, at the very least, puzzled if not outright shocked McQuaid was suggesting he put Lijuan in jail. He recovered his poise however and staked his claim for the benefit of both of them.

"Dat true, Gunna'. You say Lijuan know 'bout drugs. She know pirates take drugs from boat in Manila. Lijuan break law here. She go in jail here," he said, gesturing toward the police station, expounding on his obligation for local law enforcement. With that, he marched off the veranda to his jeep, pausing for dramatic effect before he hopped in. "I go see Doc. He say Lijuan not sick. I talk Lijuan now too. No more wait, Gunna'." Then he turned and jumped into his jeep and sped off toward the hospital, before either of them could consider trying to slow him down.

Mattie was staring a hole in the side of McQuaid's head. It was plain to see she wasn't happy about him siding with Nguyen and was waiting for an explanation. McQuaid motioned her over to sit down next to him, but she remained standing, restraining herself with great difficulty, while waiting to hear his story.

"Well? What the hell was that all about, Richard? If I didn't know better, I'd guess Nguyen paid you off!" McQuaid waited for her to wind down, indulging the predictable effect his misdirection had produced. She noticed him waiting and heaved a sigh, then slumped down in the chair next to him. "Like I said – if I didn't know better. Okay, I'll bite. What's the real story?"

McQuaid grabbed a fresh cigar out of his pocket and rolled it around between his fingers, considering his words with care before he spoke.

"I need Nguyen to put Lijuan in his jail for the time being, to keep her safe; at least for the next day or two. It's not my preference as you can imagine." The light from the windows reflected a look of derision on his face. "You know I have to drive up to Looc tomorrow and bring back the other plane. The timing couldn't be much worse, but those Jap soldiers might see it as a bargaining chip, or worse, a military target." He shrugged, leaning forward in his chair and lowered his voice. "The pirates are the real wild card here. I can't take the chance they might drop in unannounced sometime while I'm gone and drag Lijuan off to God knows where, as some sort of hostage, to flush me out in the open." He looked at her, his eyes softening. "Mattie, they want me more than her. But they must know, if they take her, it forces my hand and I can't let that happen. There are too many of them for me to fight by myself." She placed her hand on his knee, leaning closer to better see his face.

"Richard, if they want Lijuan, you can't expect Nguyen to put up much of a fight."

"I know, but they'll want to steer clear of any police here, so they won't go looking for Nguyen. They won't know she's in his jail unless he tells them. I briefed the Doc to say he released her and doesn't know where she went, if anyone goes nosing around the hospital. I'll be gone a good part of the day though." He ran his hands over the top of his head, feeling the cool dampness from the heat of the night. "In truth, I'm more worried about you and Kiko."

Mattie sat up with a loud sigh.

"Look, we can take care of ourselves. We'll head into the jungle if they get that close. They don't know the area around town and there are lots of places we can hide. I've got several guns and I'm a good shot too – if I need to be." McQuaid was silent for a moment, thinking that one over. He put his hand over hers and squeezed.

"I know you can take care of yourself, kid. I just don't want to put you in that position. I can't take you with me because I don't know the situation in Looc. Hell, I could be jumping into the frying pan there too, for all I know."

Mattie stood up and paced back and forth a few times, pondering a response. He gave her the space and waited. After a spell, she stopped and replied with strong resolve.

"You've got to get the plane back. We can't afford to lose those medical supplies. I'd suggest you take Lijuan with you, but she'd be less help than Kiko and me. At least I can shoot."

"I thought of that too. I think she's better off locked up. If Nguyen makes himself scarce, she'll be okay. There's no profit in harming her. And she says she belongs to Madam

Chin in Hong Kong anyway. She seems to be the supply end of their drug business."

Mattie had just turned to renew her pacing and did an abrupt about-face.

"Madam Ching? THE Madam Ching?" McQuaid was puzzled.

"I think her name is Chin – you know her?"

"I know *about* her," she said. Her voice sounded strained. "Bloody hell, Richard, everybody around these islands knows about her. She's the most notorious pirate queen in all of Chinese history."

"You don't mean Madam Ching, the 18th century pirate queen? Hell, she's been dead well over a hundred years, Mattie," McQuaid smirked. "And there are a lot of Chins in China, kid."

"Madam Ching is very famous and revered by some in this part of the world. She had a son and much later, he had a daughter. In point of fact, Madam Ching, or Ching Shih by her real name, died in 1844. She was almost seventy. But her son's granddaughter was rumored to have taken over the family flower boat business and she'd probably be in her sixties by now. That's where Madam Ching started her career you know – as a prostitute on one of the Cantonese floating brothels." Mattie sat down again next to McQuaid, slumping in her chair, and leaned her head back against the wall. "She was so feared, she was the only pirate the Chinese emperor allowed to retire, with the stipulation that she would disband her fleet and give up that life forever."

McQuaid scratched his chin after contemplating her words.

"Pirate queen, drug running, and Madame of Hong Kong brothels? Really?"

Mattie's eyes had wandered out into the night, as if trying to peer back in time, seeking those events that had unfolded so long ago. Coming back to herself, she returned her eyes to McQuaid's and leaned forward to make sure she had his full attention.

"Richard, I think this one who calls herself Madam Chin, could be Ching Shih's great granddaughter and has assumed more than a part of the pirate queen's legacy in China's pleasure trade. I think she's leading the pirates again as well."

McQuaid thought this over for a moment.

"Well if that's true, she could have a stake in the opium and heroin trade. That requires a network of buyers, drug runners, sellers, and enforcers. And it's probably a lot more profitable and less effort to manage a drug trade business than plundering ships on the high seas these days." He rubbed the stubble on his chin. "If my memory of history serves me, Madam Ching commanded thousands of pirate ships and over eighty thousand men at the peak of her reign." He locked eyes with Mattie. "If it's her great granddaughter and she has connections to that old pirate network, I wonder how big her pirate legion is today."

Mattie just stared at him. She reached over and put her hand over his, leaning a weary head against his shoulder and closed her eyes. McQuaid's stomach twisted. He wondered if he had kicked over a hornet's nest.

Chapter Seven
Looc Village, Lubang Island, the Philippines

It was still dark when McQuaid started for Looc the following morning. Mattie had packed some sandwiches along with a thermos of iced coffee for the trip – even though Looc wasn't really that far. Nothing on the island was that far. And the mountain route was shorter than the coast road, but it could be perilous, with steep and deep rutted stretches, winding upward from the lowlands in a series of hairpin turns.

He felt bad sneaking out on Kiko, but this wasn't the right trip for her. He'd left Baacay behind for the same reason. It wouldn't be a mission for civilians. He had both Thompson machine guns upfront with him, several full clips of ammo, and a wooden box with a dozen grenades stowed behind the front seats. He wasn't expecting trouble, but Marines were trained to plan for the worst.

A thunderstorm had passed over them in the night, leaving the reddish dirt road more muddy and treacherous than usual. The rain had topped off the potholes with water and made the larger ones impossible to determine whether he dared risk an axle driving through them. He took the walkie-talkie with him and had instructed Mattie to keep in close contact with Nguyen and to report anything suspicious to both of them without delay. His best bet was to reach the airplane by mid-morning, change the fuel pump, and get airborne as soon as possible – then hightail it back to Lubang. But he also needed to head over to the village and discuss the situation concerning the alleged attack at Looc by Japanese soldiers with Chief Mahutra. There were formalities involved whenever they got together, which couldn't be rushed. Besides, he and Mahutra were friends. It would be good to see him again under any circumstances.

The air was dead still, dank, and misty. Even before dawn, the valley was warm and muggy. When the sun came up, the sweltering heat of the day would be merciless until he got up into the mountains. Better to get an early start whenever you had to travel by land in the tropics. He knew macaws and white face monkeys watched him from the heavy foliage on either side of the muddy road, which cleaved the jungle and allowed him to pass with a scant few feet to either side. He could hear the unmistakable baritone mating calls of howler monkeys, deeper in the trees. It was a good sign there weren't any humans about, or other predators that might cause them to fall silent.

While he manhandled the jeep around precarious turns and axle bending potholes in the road, his ominous last words to Mattie still rang in his mind: *I wonder how big her pirate legion is today.* Had he made them a target in his rush to heroics and masculine bravado? McQuaid had seldom been panicked, even in battle. But he had no fighter plane to fight back with now. It left him feeling naked and vulnerable. His accustomed singular focus on solving split second air combat problems didn't leave much time for fear. Flying made him feel like he had more control of his destiny. Air battles were fought by hardened men and expert aviators who accepted the risks of battle.

This time, however, he was risking the lives of people he wasn't sure how to protect. And the pirates could exploit his numerous vulnerabilities at their leisure. It was very unnerving for a man who believed in Achillean powers of righteousness, which bestowed upon warriors the ability to slay dragons, no matter the odds against them. At an intellectual level, he knew this to be silly and juvenile. Nevertheless, he submitted to this innate virtue that drove honorable men to fight futile battles, in wars so much bigger than themselves. The Marines and militaries the world over relied on this essential esprit de corps and drilled it into the psyche of every individual soldier. Still, he knew he needed more than physical strength, or any force of will he could muster, in order to defy the odds against him. What he needed was some kind of force multiplier or leverage against the pirates.

The sun was almost a quarter of the way through the day when he crested the last hill on the road to Looc and could see down the road into the valley below. The jungle fell away to his right, giving way to swaying grasses and stands of trees on the slopes of the savanna. He wiped the sweat from his forehead and out of his eyes to peer through his binoculars at the green expanse of the lowlands, ending at the island coastline, along the azure sea. A few miles distant, lazy wisps of smoke rose from cooking fires in Looc. Panning to the right, he spied the far end of the dirt strip between him and the village.

He was relieved to see the C-47 was still parked where he'd left it and didn't appear damaged. Continuing to pivot right, he surveyed the land to the southwest, all the way back up to the jungle's edge, bordering the steep incline into the mountains. All appeared quiet. Breathing a sigh of relief, he'd almost lowered his binoculars when he spotted a brief flash of light in the tree line, several hundred yards from the end of the airstrip. Something had reflected sunlight in an area where there shouldn't be anything manmade. He couldn't make out the source, but it seemed somebody else might also be watching his plane.

McQuaid dropped the binoculars on the seat, put the jeep in reverse, backed up off the road into the underbrush, and killed the engine. Pulling a canvas rucksack from the rear bed, he loaded half a dozen grenades, several extra clips of ammo and a spare canteen of water into it and secured the straps. He grabbed some face-black from one of his many coverall pockets and darkened his face and hands, then double-checked his .45 was loaded with a round chambered. Heaving the pack onto his back, he slung both Thompsons on his shoulders and melted into the jungle.

After only twenty paces or so, it was if he had entered another world. The rainforest enfolded him in its clammy, warm embrace. Earthy smells of spongy fungus and loam underfoot permeated the sweet fragrance of exotic flowers and woody scents of the moss-covered trees overhead. An occasional current of air hissed through the fluttering leaves around him and felt like a warm breath. Epiphytes hung from low hanging tree limbs and vines, splashing them with brilliant colors from red, orange, and yellow flowers, twisted through the dark and verdant foliage.

Mosquitoes, always a nuisance in the tropics, welled up in lacy clouds from the thick underbrush with each step he took. He hurried his pace to keep them from lighting on him as best he could. But he also wanted to reach the stand of trees overlooking the airfield in time to get a clear view of his quarry, before he was spotted flanking him.

It took almost an hour, but he determined the distance seemed right to allow him to get the best position to come in from behind whoever was keeping his plane under surveillance. As he neared the edge of the jungle, he could begin to see the open fields beyond and realized he had only underestimated the distance by about a hundred yards. He stopped long enough to allow his eyes to readjust from the dim forest interior and began moving along a lateral line again to approach from the rear. After some adjustment, he had the right angle to start edging closer to see what sort of threat he might be dealing with.

Once he exited the rainforest, there would be but a few rocks and shrubs between him and the stand of trees where he had spotted the flash of light. He dropped to one knee just before he emerged from the tree line and raised his binoculars to his eyes again. Twisting the focus knob with care, he saw the figure of a man materialize in front of him, a little over two hundred yards away. The man sat hunched down behind some rocks in the stand of trees, and was also using binoculars to watch the airfield below. So far, it didn't appear the man had detected him. McQuaid began moving forward, staying crouched and careful to keep the remaining cover between them.

After almost a hundred yards, he stopped and dropped behind some bushes around a small boulder. He glassed the figure ahead of him again. The man wore a uniform and had a rifle resting against a rock to his right within easy reach. Focusing in on him again, McQuaid could see he was a smaller, thin Asian man, wearing a Japanese uniform. The uniform was tattered and frayed with makeshift patches sewn in numerous places. His rifle looked to be a standard infantry issue, bolt action Arisaka. Watching to make sure the man was still looking toward the airfield he advanced another fifty yards. Dropping behind a small group of bushes, he eased his binoculars up again.

The man had turned away from the airfield now and sat facing him. But he seemed intent on pulling something out of a small pouch and then began eating. McQuaid was still a fair distance away and well hidden, so he wasn't worried about being spotted. He continued to study the soldier, and determined he was quite young, maybe in his early twenties, bearded, dirty, and emaciated looking. So the rumors were true. There were Japanese holdouts from the war still hiding out on Lubang.

He looked to the right and left to see how many others might be with him and was relieved to see there wasn't anyone else around. Could he be a lookout, or maybe a sniper? His weapon wasn't right for long distance shooting though. The C-47 was at least six, maybe even seven hundred yards away from the end of the runway, which might be another couple hundred yards away from the soldier's overlook. Not much of a threat with an open iron-sighted rifle and an effective range of three to four hundred yards max.

The man finished eating and turned around again, facing away to look back down the valley toward the airfield. McQuaid jumped up, ran another fifty yards, and dropped down behind a rock with an old mossy dead tree lying across in front of it. Moving with great care, he eased up to take another peek at the man, who was now within a stone's toss away. McQuaid worked one of the Thompsons off his shoulder and stuck the muzzle around the rock in front of him. He flipped the lever on the side of the action from full automatic to single shot and moved behind the rear sight to get a bead on the man, who still had his back to him. The shot wouldn't be a difficult one.

His finger moved to the trigger, but he stopped short of applying enough pressure to fire. McQuaid, though a fighter pilot and more accustomed to killing at a distance, wasn't squeamish about shooting an enemy. However, the war had been over for years and the man in front of him wasn't much of a man at all. But, he also wasn't stupid enough to let appearances fool him when dealing with a Japanese soldier, who were notorious for fanaticism and self-sacrifice. Shooting someone in the back wasn't a great option for him either, even though it would be much safer for him. So he belayed the shot and observed the man while deliberating his next move.

It occurred to him, even if he seemed to be alone, Chief Mahutra's runners had told Mattie there had been several Japanese soldiers in the village. A shot might alert the rest of them and he didn't relish the thought of being surrounded and outnumbered, so he waited. As he watched him, another thought came to mind. The man might soon be relieved by another soldier, who could appear behind him where he was vulnerable. He rolled over and surveyed the line of trees along the jungle threshold. There was nothing so far. But he decided he couldn't afford to wait any longer. The sun was getting higher and he needed to get that plane back to Lubang. He turned back around and watched the soldier in front him, while thinking about a strategy. There was one thing he could do, albeit a dangerous plan that required split second execution.

Laying both Thompsons to the side, he drew out his .45 automatic, making sure to double check a round was chambered and the hammer cocked. He rose up to his knees, watching the soldier ahead of him for the right moment and then stepped around the rock and began to run toward him in a crouch, making his approach as quick and soundless as possible. He almost made it.

The man either heard something, or sensed someone coming up behind him, and turned around to look back over his shoulder. His eyes went wide and his mouth dropped open in shock when he saw the big Marine bearing down on him from less than a few yards away. He recovered quickly though, grabbed for his rifle and raced to bring the muzzle around in time, just as McQuaid reached him. But instead of shooting him, like anybody but a damn fool should have, McQuaid lowered his head and tackled him, driving his shoulder into the man's gut and ramming him against the rock in back of him, like a pile driver.

The man let out a sharp yell, which was cut off by the whoosh of any remaining air out of his lungs when McQuaid's shoulder slammed into his sternum. He could feel the soldier's thin frame buckle under the assault of a two-hundred pound body in midflight, like he'd been hit by an oak log. The man went down without another sound and the rifle dropped from his hands before he could get off a shot. McQuaid bounded to his feet, the .45 extended in his right hand, ready to shoot him if he moved so much as a hair in his direction. But there was no need for concern. The man laid sprawled out, face up, his eyes open and staring and mouth hanging slack, with blood and spittle drooling from his lower lip. He might have killed him for all he knew.

McQuaid holstered his weapon and felt for a pulse, then expelled a sudden rush of air in relief, realizing he'd been holding his breath. The man was still alive, but wouldn't be any sort of threat again for some time. McQuaid reached down and retrieved the man's rifle, then pulled a long bayonet from a scabbard on his hip, before he relaxed and dropped to slump down beside him. Working the bolt on the Arisaka several times, he realized the young soldier only had three rounds in his rifle. He rolled him over, but found no cartridge belt or extra ammo in the knapsack he was carrying with him. Besides some water, he had a small bag of rice and a handful or two of dried berries, maybe enough to feed a squirrel.

McQuaid squinted up at the late morning sun and mouthed a thank you to whatever higher power might have chosen to smile down on him this day. He would otherwise have carried the remorse of killing this hapless young man for the rest of his life.

Using the laces from the soldier's boots, he tied both his hands behind his back and his ankles together. Grabbing the Arisaka and the man's bayonet, he ran back to where he'd left his own weapons and dropped these down beside them. After rechecking the tree line once more and looking all around on either side of the uphill slope, to make sure they were still alone, he dropped his binoculars down by his other gear, turned and began to jog back to the jeep.

He made it back winded and drenched in sweat, but satisfied he had made good time. Starting it up, he pulled the jeep back onto the rutted road, easing it over the hill slowly, again looking around with care for any sign of other soldiers. There was nothing but the expanse of dark jungle sloping up to his right and the long winding dirt road leading down into the valley below.

Driving the jeep back, he stopped to pick up his gear and then again to retrieve the bound and still unconscious soldier lying where he'd left him. Once he was secured in the passenger seat, he drove back onto the road and started down for the airfield.

The airfield wasn't much more than a large clearing, with a short, bumpy dirt strip for a runway. He veered off the road to drive up the runway toward the plane, checking for any new obstructions and deeper potholes along its length. But, since the runway was seldom used and on level ground, the weather hadn't really affected it much. It had always been rough and too short, but had served him well in a pinch.

After checking on the soldier one more time to make sure he wasn't dead, just unconscious, he grabbed his tool bag out of the back, along with the replacement fuel pump, and set to work. The job was straightforward and before long he was back in the jeep, bouncing along on the road to Looc. Checking his watch, he figured it was just coming up on noon, so assuming his conversation with Chief Mahutra didn't go too long, he should be back to the field and maybe even in the air, by two or three o'clock. He glanced over at the soldier again and wondered how the village might respond to him bringing back one of the Japanese raiders who'd made off with a tribal daughter.

McQuaid envisioned one of three possible scenarios. An ideal outcome would be to bring the man back to Lubang with him for questioning, in the hope of discovering the whereabouts of any remaining soldiers. But he might also be best used as a hostage, in trade for the village girl they had kidnapped. The remaining option wasn't anywhere near as desirable. It was possible the villagers would just kill him on sight. He would need to rely on the good sense and steady leadership of Chief Mahutra and hope he would prevent that from happening. In general, the islanders felt they still had a serious score to settle with the Japanese and this one had added another personal grievance to their tally.

Mahutra was chief of one of the largest villages on the island. Looc had grown to be a major fishing village, through generations of the Visayan people and their tribal leaders, since the Philippines were colonized by the Spanish and converted to Christianity in the late 1500's. Mahutra's father had been a wise old man who had sent his son to the University of Santo Tomas in Manila for a Western education before the war broke out. Juan Salas Mahutra became chief just before the end of the war, when his father was killed in a Japanese strafing attack on their village in retribution for aiding downed American pilots. Juan Salas had been on a native outrigger banca boat off the southern tip of Mindoro Island, fishing, as well as passing secret reports on Japanese ship movements through the area to U.S. naval intelligence agents. Through them, he later learned of his father's death and returned to his village to bury him and take over as chief.

McQuaid had met Mahutra during the war, when some of Mahutra's villagers fished him out of the sea after his fighter plane's engine overheated and he'd been forced to ditch in the bay near Looc. When brought ashore, he was met by Chief Mahutra, who amazed him with his warmth and surprising grasp of naval campaign strategies employed by both the allies and Japanese in their battle for the Philippines. He also spoke excellent English and while McQuaid waited for transport back to his squadron, he and the chief had become friends. Smiling to himself, he remembered that it was Mahutra who played a major role in his decision to remain on Lubang Island after the war.

They'd been sitting together overlooking the beach, near sundown, when McQuaid told the chief about being an orphan and even though he had a loving adopted family, he wasn't sure whether he wanted to return to their farm after military service and take up his previous life again. McQuaid was torn by feelings of guilt. His decision was divided between a sense of duty to return and give back something to his foster family in return for all they had done for him, and a strange pull on his spirit to begin a new life on the islands.

They were smoking cigars, watching a magnificent island sunset and drinking a delicious brandy Mahutra had acquired a taste for while living as a student at university in Manila. The chief had dragged out one of his prized bottles of Gran Duque de Alba Solera, Gran Reserva, and related its colorful history, from the conquest of Spain by the Moors in the 8th century all the way to the present. The brandy and other famous wines of the region in Cadiz were produced by the Catholic monks of the Jerez region, and it survived even the Muslim invaders, who couldn't drink them for religious reasons.

"The Moors took alcohol from wines and brandies of Spain to make perfume. They need much perfume." He made a face, holding his nose, and McQuaid laughed, imagining the rank body odor of the Muslim invaders. "This brandy very special, Captain. It was survivor of all who conquer Spain for hundreds of years." He fixed McQuaid with a solemn expression. "Like heart of my people. We survive many who conquer these islands. Must keep spirit strong in my people always. You must keep your spirit strong too, Captain, and listen to hear your own voice here." Mahutra leaned over to him and placed his hand over his heart.

McQuaid nodded back, appreciating what the chief was trying to tell him. They sipped brandy and smoked the chief's cigars in reflective solitude, listening to the surf and the last calls of seabirds, until the ocean was dark and their faces were lit by the glow of campfires along the beach.

Mahutra was only a few years older than McQuaid, but he was deep in ways the younger man was still trying to comprehend. Mahutra hadn't forgotten his friend's quandary and continued weighing his thoughts for some time, while darkness settled around them. He seemed to appreciate the struggle in his soul over the right path to an uncertain future. Then, in his quiet way and manner of intuition, he took his cigar from his mouth and looked over at McQuaid to ask that he consider a simple, yet profound question.

"Why don't you follow heart, Captain McQuaid, not feet? Where the heart is strong, the feet must always return."

His recollections of that time, several years past now, were interrupted when the man next to him started rolling his head around and his eyes fell on McQuaid and grew wide with alarm. He began to struggle with his bindings and almost threw himself out of the side of the jeep from his lurching back and forth. McQuaid pulled his pistol out of the holster with grave deliberation, aimed it at the man's head, and thumbed back the hammer. Turning his eyes from the road, he regarded the man with a chilling expression of determined malice.

"Don't do anything stupid, kid. You're not going anywhere. Sit back and just enjoy the ride." Whether the man understood English, or took his meaning from the large bore muzzle of the .45 automatic a mere inch away from his brain, he settled back and fixed sullen eyes straight ahead.

Satisfied, McQuaid released the hammer, shoved the pistol back in his holster, and returned his hand to the wheel. He wasn't in the mood for theatrics right now and preferred to drive the rest of the road to Looc in peace. War or no war, this man was his prisoner and he aimed to make sure he wouldn't be going back to preying on him, or the locals anymore – one way or the other.

They wound around the last corner and over a slight rise, to see the village of Looc sprawling out before them. Corrugated tin roofed and bamboo shacks squatted among stands of tall coconut palms, bending in the wind off the breakers from the white sandy beach beyond. It was a view of paradise he never grew tired of seeing and he was grinning from ear to ear by the time they arrived in the center of the village. Young men and children ran alongside, waving them on, laughing and grabbing onto the sides of the jeep to catch a ride in with him. Their mood changed when they realized he had a Japanese soldier sitting next to him. They ran up next to the passenger side and began hitting the man with sticks, jeering and tearing at his uniform; trying to drag him from the jeep. McQuaid waved them back and swerved to keep from running over them, while blocking them from getting hold of his prisoner.

He was relieved to see Mahutra standing in front of the village main house, his arms folded across his chest and dark eyes gauging the pandemonium headed his way. The chief wore his traditional Piña fabric shirt and a colorful pair of shorts. His coarse, jet-black hair was shoulder length and he held it off his face with a crimson scarf tied around his forehead. As they ground to a halt next to him, Mahutra stepped forward and extended his hand to McQuaid, his coffee brown eyes warm in welcome, while he made a point of avoiding any notice of the enemy sitting next to him. The men running alongside the jeep fell back to a respectable distance and grew quiet in the presence of their chief.

"It is good to see you again, Captain McQuaid. As always, you bring me the most interesting gifts," he remarked, his composure unflappable, despite the odious presence of the Japanese soldier. He continued to disregard the man's existence, which couldn't be easy considering the young soldier had moved over almost onto McQuaid's lap to keep from being yanked out by the angry villagers. McQuaid grabbed the chief's outstretched hand and swung his legs out of the jeep to stand in front of him. Mahutra, just an inch or so shorter than McQuaid, reached up and clasped his shoulders in a warrior's embrace, his big white teeth splitting his dark face from ear to ear.

"Welcome my friend," he said, with a warmth that was palpable to all those around them. "Let us retire to my house, out of the heat, and hear of your latest adventures." His eyes flicked toward the man next to him. "Shall we bring your dog, or chain him to a post outside?" The smile remained, but the eyes changed enough for McQuaid to discern the disgust concealed behind his outward good nature.

"We should bring him with us to keep him from shitting himself, or annoying the rest of your people," he responded. "Besides," he pulled cigars and a flask from one of his zipper pockets, "I've brought you more traditional gifts."

The chief's eyes widened and though McQuaid hadn't thought it possible, his grin became even bigger; whereupon he wrapped an arm about his friend's shoulders and turned him toward his house to lead the way. The chief gave a subtle hand signal to a couple of his men and the Japanese soldier was dragged from the jeep and carried toward the house like a trussed pig.

The main house was a large shack; a nice shack, but nonetheless, a typical island plank and bamboo affair under a slanted, corrugated tin roof. McQuaid was somewhat puzzled when he noticed there were real glass windows in the front now, facing the village square, and a door with a modern handle on it. These were new additions since the last time he had been in the village a few months back. They walked up one step to the wooden post and bamboo railed veranda and Mahutra reached out to open the door for him, motioning him inside.

Before he even stepped through the door, McQuaid felt a waft of cool air hit him in the face. He noticed electric lights and a standing hi-fi radio and record player cabinet against one wall. The chief's wife, Elisa, stood just inside to greet him, smiling and bowing several times, while she motioned for them to enter. She was a dark-haired beauty, with braided blue-black hair hanging to her waist and tied back with ribbon and sea shells. Her smile was warm, with perfect white teeth against rich latte-brown skin. She wore a colorful silk sarong that fell, full length, to the polished, bamboo wood floor.

"Welcome to our home again, Captain McQuaid, suh. May I bring you cold beer?" Her smile turned impish and she winked at him.

McQuaid bowed back to her and steepled his hands to his forehead in an island gesture of appreciation and thanks. She nodded her head back to him and turned to scamper off into the back room, through a beaded doorway. McQuaid turned to Mahutra with both eyebrows raised in surprise.

"Cold beer? You have cold beer?" He didn't need to feign disbelief. In truth, he was very surprised and curious about how the interior also appeared to be so cool and far less humid, compared to the street outside. He noticed a large ceiling fan whirring overhead, pushing a downdraft of even cooler air around them. Mahutra just grinned and waved him over to a low platform strewn with bright-colored sitting cushions. He turned and said something in his native tongue to the men holding the Japanese soldier behind them in the open doorway. They nodded and dragged the prisoner back outside, closing the door behind them.

McQuaid sat down on some of the nearest cushions and allowed a worried look toward the door.

"You're not planning on putting him in the pot for dinner are you, Chief?" He was kidding, but kept a wary eye on Mahutra as he took a seat next to him and pulled a low teak wood table between them before he spoke.

"We are civilized here now, Captain. We don't eat our captives so much anymore." He grinned, but McQuaid wondered how long ago "anymore" might have been. "Besides," he continued, it is not for me to decide such things.

122

He is your prisoner. I would ask what you want we do with him." Slipping off his sandals, he pulled his legs under him, before looking up for a response.

McQuaid unlaced his boots and set them off to the side, using the time to contemplate his answer. After settling himself, he replied.

"Maybe we should keep him alive to trade back to the other soldiers, in return for the girl from your village. Or I could take him back to Lubang and hand him over to Captain Nguyen for questioning. I'd like to find out how many other Japanese soldiers are on the island." He looked up as Elisa walked back into the room and knelt beside them to set two beer bottles down in front of the men. She smiled and backed away, then disappeared into the back room again. McQuaid resisted the urge to reach for his beer, while he waited for Mahutra to answer. But the chief smiled and motioned for him to drink first.

The bottle felt chilled and though not icy cold, it was cold enough and tasted like ambrosia on his parched throat. After a couple long, exquisite pulls on the bottle, he realized he had almost emptied it and regarded the chief with a sheepish expression. He needn't have worried. The chief was grinning again.

"Tastes good, eh, Captain McQuaid?" Then he laughed heartily and reached for his own bottle, upending it and almost draining his as well. McQuaid watched with approval and then leaned forward with keen interest.

"So what's the story here, Chief? It feels like you have some sort of chilled air coming in here from somewhere and if you have electricity for lights, maybe you have an electric icebox too?"

Mahutra didn't answer right away and was acting mischievous. Instead, he emitted a loud belch in appreciation. He waved to McQuaid to finish up his beer and pulled out the cigars he had given him on the way in, handing one over to McQuaid and sticking the other one in the side of his mouth.

Elisa appeared at once and held out a thin burning stick of wood to light his cigar. The chief puffed away on it until he was surrounded by a cloud of gray-blue smoke, then waved her over to McQuaid to light his cigar too. McQuaid obliged and they were soon reclined on their cushions, enjoying their smokes like two college buddies. They were from worlds apart, but shared the chief's hospitality as men who enjoyed each other's company a great deal. Without warning, Chief Mahutra jumped to his feet and snatched the cigar from his mouth.

"Come, Captain. Let me show you how civilized we are now. Come, come," he motioned for McQuaid to follow, as he made toward the far room in back, his bare heels thudding on the wooden floor. They passed through a small kitchen area where Elisa was standing over an open coal cooking fire in a rock stove. She smiled and bowed to them as they passed her on their way through to the outside and down another couple steps at the rear of the house.

Once outside, McQuaid was assailed by the pungent odor of rotten eggs. He turned to the chief and made a face.

"Smells like shit, huh?" Mahutra asked in sympathy. "It is sulfur dioxide," he explained, moving around in back of him. He pointed to the small Curtis electric compressor pump against the back wall of the shack, with copper chiller tubing running up and disappearing inside near the roof. "Has small gas leak and smells like fart. Not to worry. It is harmless. Pump compress gas in pipes; make them cold," he said, clenching his fists and then pointed up to the tubes disappearing under the roofline. "Fan blows air down through pipes under roof; cools house." Then he pointed to a long rubber belt connected to a pulley system, leading to a small gasoline engine. It wasn't running at the moment, so he continued tracing a line with his finger, from another spinning rubber pulley belt, which ran several feet over to a gear on the underside of a tall wooden tower. There was a windmill on the top spinning at a furious rate in the brisk ocean breeze. He had mounted a small electric generator in between, which McQuaid could see was providing the electricity to the cooling pump and the lights in the rest of the house.

"So, when the wind blows, you use the windmill to run the generator here and at night the gasoline motor," McQuaid reported with a trace of awe in his voice. It was an impressive set-up.

"And to pump fresh water from well to sink in house too," Mahutra added with pride. "I also have refrigerator, not icebox in kitchen. See, did I not tell you we are civilized here now?" He clapped McQuaid on the back and pushed him toward the house again. "Come, my friend. We sit inside. Too hot out here in sun."

They both turned and trooped back into the house, where Elisa was waiting to hand them both a fresh bottle of beer on their way to the front room. They flopped down on the pillows again and the chief glanced over at McQuaid with an expression that suggested a change of subject.

"So, Captain McQuaid, we both have big problems, no?"

McQuaid grinned around his cigar.

"We do indeed, Chief. I think I can help you with your Japanese problem though." Mahutra raised an eyebrow, but waited for him to continue. "My prisoner could be used in trade to get your village daughter back. But if that doesn't work, I can use some of the medical supplies out of my plane at the airfield to buy her back." He puffed on his cigar to get the tip glowing again. The cloud of smoke was swirled around by the overhead fan.

Mahutra was puffing on his cigar, thinking over this generous proposal for a moment before he responded. Then, appearing to come to a decision, he removed his cigar and leaned closer. His face suggested a more serious tone than before.

"You have bigger problem, my friend. We talk about your problem first," he replied, his eyes turning kind and compassionate.

McQuaid looked at him sideways.

"Meaning my problem with the pirates?" He was surprised the chief knew about that already. Word on the island traveled fast. He shouldn't have been surprised. Mahutra was known and well respected throughout the Mindoro Islands. His already broad network had been strengthened by his intelligence work with the American and Philippine underground during the war. McQuaid was quite aware, very little went on within a hundred miles the chief didn't know about.

Mahutra held up his beer bottle to offer a toast.

"You are my friend, Captain, but you make fierce enemies, almost as fast as you make life friends. I wish for you many more great adventures. We will share some of them together," he intoned with conviction. They clinked their bottles together and each took a long pull of beer, before slamming their bottles down with a ceremonial bang afterwards. After a slight pause, the chief aimed an index finger at the window looking out toward the coastline. "I know where pirate leader has camp," Chief Mahutra declared.

McQuaid removed his cigar from between his teeth.

"Can you tell me where and how many?" He had hoped Mahutra knew something about the whereabouts of the pirates and their strength in numbers. The chief nodded and stood up to walk over to a chest under one of the windows. After sorting through some papers, he came up with a map and unrolled it on the floor, placing his sandals and McQuaid's boots on the corners to hold it flat. A piece of ash from his cigar broke off and fell into the center. But instead of brushing it away, he pinched a piece of it between thumb and forefinger and placed it on the coastline of the west side of Mindoro Island, a much larger island less than twenty miles southeast of Lubang Island.

He put his finger on Looc and traced a route east, from the village, out to the bay, down through the Verde Island Passage, then southwest through the Mindoro Strait between their two islands, and west, down along the coast of Mindoro Island.

"Pirates go to this village, Mamburao, here in valley between mountains, up Mamburao River. River comes out into Sulu Sea, along west coast of Mindoro Island." He pointed to the river mouth. "Pirate boats go fast up river into jungle. Hide here, here, and here." He jabbed various inland spots along the river, placing little piles of ash on each one to mark them. McQuaid recognized the map as a U.S. Hydrographic Office chart of the Philippines, used by Navy intelligence during the war. It included terrain elevations and sea soundings around the islands.

McQuaid could see the areas of the island where they had bases, were picked for good reason. It was remote and rugged terrain. They had easy access to the sea from the serpentine river egress and ingress to their bases. He was looking closely at the sounding numbers along the coastline. There were reefs and a lot of shallow water. The river looked shallow as well.

"How many pirates are at these bases, Chief?" Mahutra sat upright and rather than answer, began rolling up his map. McQuaid looked up at him, puzzled. "You don't know, or you won't say?" he asked.

The chief just stood up and walked over to return the map to the chest without a word. When he returned, he sat down across from McQuaid again and looked past his head at something far in the distance only he could see. He smiled back at his friend and took another sip of his beer, then wiped his mouth with the back of his hand before answering.

"We are fishermen in this village, Captain McQuaid. We make nets to catch right size fish, with holes in nets big enough to let small fish out. Small fish too much work. So we let them go. Sometimes we catch very big Botete and throw back. You know Botete?" He held his hands up on both sides of his mouth, with fingers sticking out sideways and puffed out his cheeks like balloons. McQuaid laughed.

"You mean a puffer fish?'

"Yah, that's right; puffer fish. You know why we throw back?"

"They're poisonous, right?" Mahutra grinned and pointed back at him.

"Right! They kill you, if don't know secret how to cook them. Japaners eat them. They crazy, but they know secret." He clamped his teeth around his cigar and waited for his friend's response.

McQuaid thought about it for a moment and then shrugged back at him.

"I don't know what you're getting at, Chief."

Mahutra removed the cigar from his mouth and cocked his head to peer at his friend with amusement.

"Pirates fishermen too, Captain. They find right fish and don't bother fish too small, or fish too dangerous." He pointed his cigar at him. "You right size fish for pirates now. Before you shoot pirate brother, you were small fish. They don't bother you, if you not bother them. You need be poison fish now my friend – like Botete." The chief appeared content he had made his point and settled back, crossing his arms and began puffing away again.

McQuaid was still confused as to what his point was exactly.

"You're saying I need to be like a poisonous fish to them. Then they won't bother me anymore?"

Mahutra nodded through the swirling cloud of cigar smoke.

McQuaid pondered his words. He knew there was great homespun logic in there somewhere. How could he become poisonous to the pirates? The chief was right about not being noticed, before he shot up the pirate boat and killed their leader's brother. His fear was that now, no matter what he did, they would continue their relentless pursuit until they somehow settled the matter. How was he supposed to become more dangerous to them? He would never win a war of attrition. There were probably too many of them. So how could he become poisonous enough, so they would decide to stay away from him?

Elisa shuffled back in with a tray of food and more beers. She knelt and placed woven straw platters in front of them, heaped with portions of grilled chicken, steamed vegetables and rice. She beamed at McQuaid and motioned for him to dig in. Then she steepled her hands to her forehead, bowed and scampered back to the kitchen area. It smelled delicious and the big Marine had no problem doing it justice. He realized he had barely eaten all day.

He and the chief talked around mouthfuls of food and beer, about happenings in his village, fishing, and the weather. It was apparent he was waiting for McQuaid to work through his cryptic recommendation and come to some final revelation. Once they finished and Elisa had reappeared to whisk away their plates and empty bottles, he fixed Mahutra with a look of earnest.

"I think you should send some men over to the plane with me and let me give you some medical supplies to bargain with. Between them and the Jap prisoner, you should be able to get the girl back okay. I need to fly the plane back to Lubang as soon as possible. I would hate for the pirates to show up there while I'm away."

The chief just nodded back to him, his face a mask of serious contemplation.

"These soldiers are not big problem, Captain. We fight soldiers many times. These men stay in mountains and hide. They are crazy, but not stupid. We will give them food. I will bring this dog of a soldier back to them for return of our village daughter. We will not worry about these small problems." He rocked forward and clasped his knees to sit upright facing him. "Pirates are big problem, Captain McQuaid. I will help. We have guns, bows, and spears. My men will travel to Lubang village. Be there by morning and watch for pirates. We are good friends, Captain McQuaid. You Americans save my islands, save my people. I will help you now."

128

McQuaid was just starting tell him how much he appreciated his friendship and help, when there was a commotion at the door. They both stood and the chief strode over, flinging it open, to see two of his men there, pointing at McQuaid's jeep. They said something to the chief, who turned back to him to translate.

"They say radio in your car is talking."

McQuaid ran out the door and jogged down to the jeep to grab the handset off the walkie-talkie. He got there in time to hear another static filled transmission, which was barely intelligible. The village was at near maximum range of the radio and he wasn't getting a very clear signal. He could tell it was a man's voice.

"Gunna', you...come in store...Mattie no...look Kiko...you come. Gunna'...come." He turned the range receiver dial, to try to improve the signal and then pushed the mike button to talk.

"McQuaid here, what's happening, over?" The chief had moved up to stand beside him and hear what the problem was. McQuaid had a sinking feeling in his gut.

"Gunna', Baacay here. You come...to..." The rest of the message was a long hiss of static. He turned to the chief.

"I've got to get to the plane, Chief. It sounds like trouble."

The chief waved to a few of his men and spoke in rapid fire to them. They turned and sprinted off in different directions. Then he gave McQuaid a knowing look and placed his hand on the younger man's shoulder.

"You go. My men bring guns; go with you in plane. Go now, Captain McQuaid. Talk again soon."

They shook hands and he climbed into the jeep. No further words between them were necessary. His men reappeared with their rifles and jumped in the rear bed, as he started the motor and jammed it in gear, tearing away in a cloud of dust toward the airfield.

Chapter Eight
Lubang Village General Store, Lubang Island, the Philippines

Baacay was hysterical when Doc McCawley found him sitting next to Mattie on the floor of the General Store, holding her hand and sobbing. He had heard gunshots and run most of the way from the hospital. He was shocked to see the screen door nearly ripped off its hinges and dirty gray smoke drifting outside from somewhere inside the store. There had been a blaze in the back, but Baacay brought over a fire bottle from the airfield and extinguished it by the time he arrived. A cloud of dust that smelled like baking soda still hung in the air, with streaks of white powder all over the walls and the sundry goods shelves. There were no flames visible at present, so he turned his attention back to the drama unfolding on the floor in front of him.

Mattie lay on her back, one leg under the other, with her arms in supine position and a spreading pool of blood under her that soaked her white shirt bright red. Her eyes were open and staring, but she didn't appear to be conscious. McCawley was a seasoned trauma doctor, who wasted no time getting to work. He grabbed Baacay by the arm and shook him.

"Baacay, listen to me," he yelled sternly. "Run back to the hospital, get my nurses and medical bags, and drive them back here in the hospital truck. Get going man!"

Baacay bobbed his head and bolted out the door toward the hospital.

Turning back to his patient, Doc could see two gunshot wounds to her chest and what looked like it might be a stab wound, very near her heart, just to the right of the sternum. It didn't look good and she was losing a lot of blood.

"Oh, Mattie, what have they done to you, girl?" he asked under his breath. Checking her pulse, he was relieved to feel one, though it was weak. At least they had missed her heart. He stripped off her shirt and applied it as a compress to the two bullet holes high and to the left side of her chest. He put his ear against her, to listen to her breathing and heard a slight rattling noise. She was hemorrhaging into her left lung by the sound of it. Holding the compress against her, he rolled her to one side, to see if the bullets had passed through her and was relieved to see they had, without leaving extraordinary exit wounds. McCawley was trying to lay her flat again, when Mattie started convulsing and coughing up blood. She came to for a moment and recognized him leaning over her.

"James!" she gasped, with tears flowing. "They shot me and I think they might have taken Kiko. They were looking for Richard. I couldn't get to my gun in time to..." She began coughing again and bright red blood and sputum splattered his shirt and white jacket.

"Quiet now, old girl. I've got you. You did all you could, I'm sure. We'll find Kiko. Don't worry about her. I need you to lie there and remain calm now, so I can take care of you." She was clutching his hand and staring into his face, but then nodded her head and lay back flat on the floorboards. Doc was wondering where the hell Baacay and his nurses were. He needed plasma, bandages, and several other medical supplies he started sorting in his head and he needed them right away. All he could do in the meantime was elevate her head, keep pressure on her wounds, and hope her heart or breathing didn't stop.

A vehicle slid to a stop in the gravel outside and he heard boots on the front porch. But it was Nguyen who burst through the door, his eyes wide and pistol drawn. Doc motioned him over.

"Captain, I need your help with her right away. She's been shot and she's losing a lot of blood." Nguyen holstered his gun and dropped to the floor beside them.

"What you need, Doc?"

"Get your arms around behind her shoulders and lift her. Not too far and be gentle. I don't want to put too much pressure on her chest. Just raise her up enough so she can breathe easier and keep her lungs from filling with blood."

Nguyen understood and reached behind her, throwing his leg around to prop her up and hold her against his side. Doc was glad to see he was battle trained and not panicked. "That's good Captain. Now hold her there, so I can get a compress against the wounds on her back as well. I need to squeeze her wounds without putting too much pressure on her lungs."

Nguyen returned a quick nod. He used his free hand to rip open off his police uniform blouse and handed it to Doc to use for a compress bandage.

"Where Gunna'?" he asked.

"He drove out to Looc this morning to bring back the other plane. I'm hoping he'll be able to get back here later this evening. We need to get her over to the hospital." He gave a hopeful glance past Nguyen out the door. But there still was no sign of the hospital truck. What the hell was taking them so long?

"Captain Nguyen, I need you to hold her while I look around and see if I can find some bandages and alcohol around here somewhere."

Nguyen understood and took over applying pressure to the compresses, while Doc stood up and began rummaging around in the back of the store.

"Who burn store, shoot Mattie? Where Kiko?" He looked around him with concern.

"She didn't exactly say, but I suspect it was a few of the pirates. She said they were looking for McQuaid. He stamped on some smoldering papers and pulled one of the overturned stands of wooden shelves out, to keep it away from the embers. Then he spotted a roll of bandages, iodine, and some alcohol and snatched them up. He also found a couple rolls of tape and gathered them up as well.

"Where Kiko?" Nguyen repeated.

"Mattie thinks they might have taken her," McCawley replied.

Mattie began coughing again and he ran back over to help hold her up. He heard the hospital truck screech to a stop outside. Baacay and his two nurses rushed in the door, carrying medical bags and supplies. One of the nurses took over for Nguyen and McCawley started firing orders off to the other one. He looked over at Baacay.

"You and the police chief need to retrieve the stretcher from the truck and bring it in here. We need to get her to the hospital as soon as possible."

Both Baacay and Nguyen ran outside and brought the stretcher in, laying it down beside her. They lifted Mattie just enough to slide it under her and then hauled her quickly out to the truck. Doc McCawley told Nguyen to drive and turned to Baacay, as he started the engine to pull away.

"Get on the radio and see if you can find McQuaid. We need him back here straight away. Can you handle that?" Baacay nodded and ran back behind the bar to the shortwave set to comply. He turned to watch the truck spin around in a cloud of dust and gravel and tear away toward the hospital.

Baacay said a few muted words of prayer for Mattie and to keep little Kiko safe. But his heart was heavy and wrenched with fear when he saw the bloody smear on the plank floor in front of him.

Baacay wasn't able to raise McQuaid at first, but at last he heard some popping and hissing between words, that sounded like it was him. Then he heard him say "I'm coming" and slumped back against his chair, relieved he had accomplished something to help. It lifted his spirits to know Gunner McQuaid was on his way. McQuaid was his hero and he knew in his gut, he would make the pirates pay for this. He clenched his fists and slammed them on the desk holding the shortwave radio.

"Dey will pay!"

At the other end of the island, McQuaid was holding the brakes on the C-47, while he ran both engines up to full power. His cargo was light and even with the five armed men from the village strapped to seats in back, the plane was far from overloaded. But it was hot, there was no headwind, not even a light breeze, and the runway was short. They would need every inch of it, with flaps, to make it over the trees at the far end. He watched the two tachometers wind up to their redlines, the vibration building to a loud rattling, the controls shuttering under his hands. Finally, he released the brakes and the aircraft leaped forward, anxious to devour the runway ahead.

The C-47, also fondly referred to as a Gooney Bird by her aircrews during the war, was a lumbering but reliable workhorse. She began to rise off her tail wheel, bringing the nose down, so McQuaid could see over the instrument panel. It already seemed as if the dirt strip ahead of him wasn't going to be long enough. His eyes flicked down to his airspeed indicator and he had to resist the urge to pull back on the yoke. The airspeed gauge showed seventy mph and he knew he needed ninety, probably more like ninety-five, on a hot day without wind. He could see the end of the strip rushing towards him. He might be able to cheat twenty yards or so, beyond the strip, as it was flat ground, but that required an even steeper climb to clear the trees.

The cigar clamped in his teeth was almost bitten through now and he cursed around it at the stubborn progress of the needle on the airspeed gauge.

"C'mon, damn you, c'mon..." The end of the runway rushed under him - eighty mph! Pulling back on the yoke, the Gooney Bird clawed for the sky. "C'mon, baby, you can do it." The rumbling wheel noise stopped and they were airborne. Rocks and scrub brush flashed beneath them, as he yanked the gear lever up and listened for the whine of the electric motors, hauling the wheels into their wells in the engine nacelles.

He kept the backpressure on the yoke – not too much – eighty-five mph, the trees were eye level coming right at him; eighty-eight, ninety, ninety-five! At the last possible second, he pulled back hard and felt branches tearing at the metal skin under him, scraping the length of the aircraft, grappling for a hold that might drag them back to earth. But they couldn't quite get a grip on her and McQuaid expelled a long-held breath as the treetops swept beneath them.

He started a slow bank to the right, to the north, pulled the flap lever up and monitored the vertical speed until they achieved a decent rate of climb. Glancing to the right, he watched the turquoise sea breaking in large white-frothed waves onto the beach at Looc village. His eyes were drawn to a looming dark squall line of rain clouds spreading out in an ominous wall along the southeast horizon. A jagged flash of lightning lit up the dark sea under the low and angry storm front. Though it appeared to be heading toward them, he knew they could make Lubang airport. But without a doubt, a nasty weather system was bearing down on them. Dialing in the radio at the General Store, he pressed the mike button.

"McQuaid to base, over." He got an immediate answer back – loud and clear.

"Gunna', dis Baacay here, over." He sounded tense.

"Baacay, what's going on there? Where's Mattie, over?" There was a long pause. He was just about to repeat his question.

"Dis bad here, Gunna'. Mattie no here; Kiko no here. Pirates come. Dey shoot Mattie, mebbe take Kiko..."

McQuaid mashed the mike button again, in a futile attempt to try and talk over Baacay's continuing transmission. "When did this happen? Where's Mattie now?" he asked, shouting.

"...Doc take her in truck. She hurt bad, Gunna', over," he finished, unaware he'd been interrupted.

McQuaid, took a breath to slow down and collect his thoughts. He began again.

"When did this happen, Baacay and where is Kiko, over?" Again a long pause.

"Mebbe one hour. I hear guns shoot. Drive jeep from airport; find Mattie on floor in store. Store on fire. Put out fire and try help Mattie..."

He was beginning to ramble, holding the transmit button down, not allowing for a pause so McQuaid could get in a response. All he could do was wait for him to finish. "...dey shoot her, Gunna. No find Kiko. Mebbe Pirates take Kiko. Don't know...over."

At last he heard the click, signaling he'd let up on the mike switch at the other end.

"Baacay, listen to me. Just answer my questions and then let up on your mike button so we can talk back and forth, over."

Baacay rogered and clicked the mike back.

"Okay, good. Now, have you seen Captain Nguyen since the attack, over?"

Baacay told him Nguyen had helped Doc take Mattie over in the truck to hospital.

"Okay, here's what I need you to do. Find Nguyen and tell him I'm about half an hour out and I'm bringing some of Chief Mahutra's men with me. They have guns and can help us against the pirates. But I need Nguyen to meet me at the airport with his men and have him bring rifles with him, over."

"Okay, Gunna'. I go find Captain, meet you at airport, with mo' men and guns, over."

"Good job, Baacay. I'll see you soon then. McQuaid out."

He slammed the mike down on its hook and ran his hand over the top of his head, massaging the base of his skull to relieve some of the tension. It was hard to tell from Baacay's description of events, how bad Mattie had been hurt. His stomach clenched when he heard she had been shot. And Kiko missing too was even worse news still. The knot in his gut twisted tighter.

"Dammit! How did they know when to attack?" he wondered aloud.

Just then, a shear wind leading the storm front slammed the aircraft from one side and he had to fight the controls to keep from losing altitude. He was already staying low under the growing overcast, so he didn't have altitude to spare. His eyes flicked to the weather again – it was getting uglier by the minute.

After what seemed like an eternity, battling wind gusts and downdrafts, he could make out the tower beacon at Lubang Airport. They would be down in less than fifteen minutes. He'd need to get both the Goose and the Gooney Bird in the hangar until the storm blew over. That was going to slow him down getting over to the hospital to check on Mattie and start looking for Kiko. He refrained from hazarding a guess at where Kiko might be at the moment. She was a survivor though. A slight ray of hope flashed into his mind. Maybe she got away and was hiding in the jungle. Kiko knew plenty of little hidey-holes in the vicinity. It was possible Mattie told her to run when she spotted the pirates. She might have escaped and would wait for things to calm down before she reappeared. He sure hoped so.

The Gooney Bird was beginning to buck again in the air turbulence. But he was already making his final approach to the east-facing runway, heading into a strong onshore wind, with gusts that rocked the wings. The wind fought him all the way, but he succeeded in getting her on the ground without mishap and taxied up to the hangar to shut down. He was relieved to see Baacay was already waiting for him, with the hangar doors rolled back. He had hooked their small tug up to the Goose and dragged her inside already. He noticed Nguyen was sitting in one of the police jeeps off to the side. He had both deputies with him and they appeared to be carrying rifles. Good – at least something was going according to plan.

The propellers were still freewheeling when he jumped out of the side hatch with Chief Mahutra's men. He yelled over to Baacay to bring the tug, but he was already on it. So he turned back to speak to Nguyen, who had marched over and appeared more agitated than usual.

"What's the story, Captain?" For once he didn't start off with his usual cowboy attitude. *Things must be mighty screwed up,* he thought to himself.

"Baacay find Mattie in store, lying on floor shot in chest – mebbe two times. She at hospital now. Doc is taking care for her. Doc say you need get there now. He say you need fly Mattie to American base tonight. He say she need big hospital."

McQuaid glanced up at the sky behind the police chief and frowned. Nguyen turned to look too. Then looked back around at McQuaid; concerned. "Storm bad, no?"

McQuaid just nodded, running different storm-running scenarios through his head. It wasn't going to be good any way you sliced it. He looked back at Nguyen.

"Have you seen any of the pirates? And what do you know about Kiko?" He prepared himself for the worse.

"We see no pirates, Gunna'. Baacay say dey shoot Mattie, mebbe take Kiko. But we not see anybody. Mebbe dey go back to boats." A number of different emotions seemed to be playing across his face; fear was one of them.

McQuaid turned around and motioned for Baacay to hold on pushing the Gooney Bird in the hangar and waved him over. He took the smaller man by the shoulders and looked him square in the eyes.

"I need you to stay here with Mahutra's men, Baacay." When he started to protest, McQuaid held his hand up and cut him off. With a patience he wasn't feeling at the moment, he explained what he wanted him to do. "Somebody has to stay here and protect the aircraft. I need the Gooney Bird to fly Mattie to the hospital at Clark. We can't take the chance the pirates might come back and damage them. Do you understand?"

Baacay nodded. "I stay here, keep pirates away fom planes. You go Gunna. I stay here." He looked up at him with a sober and determined look in his eyes.

McQuaid hesitated for a second, then smiled and patted him on the shoulder. "Thank you, Baacay. I know I can depend on you."

And he knew he could. He believed Baacay would lay down his life if necessary to save Mattie, probably the same for him as well. Turning back to Nguyen, he grabbed him by the arm and started jogging toward the jeep.

"C'mon, Captain. We better get this show on the road, or it's going to be a real short flight!"

Doc McCawley was sweating under the bright surgery lights. He worked with efficient determination, putting his affection for the patient out of his mind as much as possible. His rubber-gloved fingers were deep inside Mattie's chest cavity, trying to find the damaged, bleeding ends of veins and making repairs to organ damage from the two bullets that had torn through one of her lungs, just missing her heart. He had provisioned the hospital well, with a good stock of plasma, pharmaceuticals, oxygen, resuscitators, and quality surgery tools. His nurses were trained by him and worked well together as a team. Their training paid off in spades during difficult trauma surgeries like this.

Mattie was anesthetized, covered in sheets, and strewn with bloody gauze. She had lost a lot of blood and though the plasma helped keep her heart pumping, she would soon be struggling to get enough oxygen to her tissues with a reduced red blood cell count. What she needed was whole blood and that was something he didn't have.

He noticed the concern in the eyes of his nurses over their masks. They knew he was fighting against time and maybe losing. Pushing away his own fear, he wiped his sweaty brow with a sleeve and continued to probe around the clamps they were using to pinch off known bleeders. He was searching for an elusive source of the blood squirting into the chest cavity from somewhere beneath her left lung. Mattie's ribs and the various steel forceps in his way were making his job almost impossible. The other nurse was administering oxygen and keeping a careful eye on her breathing and pulse. He used a retractor to lift the lung up and back, enough to allow the nurse to dab the area again with gauze, so he could see where the blood was puddling up from. At last, he spotted the culprit.

"Got it. Clamp!" The shiny steel implement was slapped into his open palm with authority. A small part of his mind reveled in the thrill of conquest only a surgeon could appreciate. He reached in with a delicate touch and pinched off the offending bleeder. The nurse mopped the area again and this time, no blood welled up, as it had persisted in doing up to this point. She looked over at McCawley and even with just her eyes showing, he could see the relief and a smile pushing up the edges of her mask. Now they got back to the routine business, stitching the rips and holes in tissue and torn veins, removing clamps and testing for leaks. McCawley doused the area with liberal doses of sulfa powder to limit infection as they worked.

Mattie had been shot twice by hard tipped rifle bullets. She was very fortunate they went through her without much distortion, or mushrooming. There was plenty of damage done, but if they had hit bone or more vital organs, she would not have even made it to the table with the location of her wounds. It was plain to see someone had also run her through with a sword, maybe thinking to finish her off. The blade had nicked her heart, but the wound was superficial and they stitched it closed without much trouble. All in all, she had been very fortunate. But McCawley knew chest trauma created other dangers he was ill equipped to deal with in an outpost hospital. Among other things, she needed whole blood and lots of it. If he had more time, he could blood-type her and maybe find a donor on the island somewhere, but what she really needed was a full hospital, with whole blood reserves and a crack combat surgical team capable of handling anything he might have missed. As adept as he was at field surgery, he knew he was a hack compared to full med school trained surgeons, who would view his repairs as a humane form of butchery. Still, if the patient lived, he knew he'd spared her the alternative.

An hour later, he parted the surgical suite curtains and emerged, stripping off his mask and gloves. McQuaid and Nguyen stood waiting for him, their faces drawn and anxious. He beamed a doctor's "all's well" smile at them.

"She made it, gentlemen. But she's not out of the woods yet. We still need to get her over to Clark Air Base without delay. She's being stabilized with plasma, but she needs whole blood and a better staff of doctors than we can provide here, I'm afraid." McQuaid stepped forward to shake his hand.

"I knew if she had any chance, you'd be able to save her, Doc," he said, his eyes telling McCawley everything words could never express. Under normal circumstances, McCawley was a man who never lacked for words. But he just nodded and turned back toward the operating room.

"We'll get her ready for you, Richard," he offered over his shoulder. Then he paused and twisted around to cast a disparaging look in his direction. "I hope I can trust you to keep her in one piece and deliver her to the hospital on Clark, the same way I gave her to you." He smirked at McQuaid and then he was gone. No answer had been expected.

Twenty minutes later, they brought Mattie out the front on a stretcher and loaded her in the covered truck bed for the trip to the airport. One of his nurses would fly along to take care of her on the flight over. McCawley stood watching them from the top step of the hospital veranda.

A sudden flash of lightning and a cannon shot of thunder shook the building, followed by a torrential downpour. McCawley stepped back under the overhang, looking up with concern. He had been so busy indoors with the operation he hadn't noticed the weather creeping in on them. McQuaid glanced over and saw the concern on his face. He slogged back through the growing puddles and up the steps to reassure him.

"Don't worry, Doc. We're in my house now. I'll get her there." Water streamed off his face and his flight coverall was drenched. Brick red mud was splattered up to his waist, from the rain splashing up from the muddy roadbed. His eyes, however, were steel gray and evoked a determination almost unbearable in intensity. McCawley was reassured.

"I know you will, Richard. Fly safe and take care of yourself." He took his stethoscope from around his neck and jammed it in his white coat pocket. "Keep me posted."

"I will. See you later, Doc," he offered back. Then he ran down to the truck and hopped in the passenger side. Nguyen ground the gears and pulled away and they soon disappeared in the blinding downpour.

Chapter Nine
The Fánróng Fùqíang, off Mindoro Island, the
Philippines

Jiang Xian Hui stood rocking back and forth on seasoned sea legs, arms folded, glowering down at the small petulant child before him. She just sat there at his feet, her arms tied in front of her, dark eyes blazing up at him. There was a red welt becoming a nasty bruise on her face, where he had backhanded her when she refused to answer his questions. She seemed anything but cowed.

"Do you know who I am, child?" he asked again, his voice measured, but portending further violence if she failed to give him what he wanted. Instead of shrinking back, Kiko gathered her legs under her and rose to her knees, and then, with what looked to be a painful but determined change in posture, she struggled to her feet. Unblinking, her eyes smoldered, never leaving his face, while her expression turned dark and feral. It was disquieting to watch this malevolent transformation come over her, even for a man comfortable with violence.

He stared back at her for a few moments longer, torn as to whether further punishment might change her willingness to cooperate with him. Above all else, he was a practical man and had not risen to leadership through brute force alone. Knowing when to bend or break another person's will was a lesson he had learned in blood over the years. This little girl was not afraid of him. Instinct told him she would not give in to what he needed by force alone; and he was a man who trusted his instincts. He would need a lever to budge her. His decision made, he turned on his heel and walked out of the cabin, taking care to lock the door behind him and click off the lights.

Jiang emerged into the passageway outside the cabin, and was at once thrown full-faced against the bulkhead, as the ship pitched with sudden violence in the turbulent seas. He had to brace himself several times, while he made his way up the ladder well to the bridge to confer with his helmsman.

The Fánróng Fùqíang was, from outward appearances, a common, seven hundred ton coastal trader, running trade goods between ports on the South China Sea. Her rusting blue hull paint, along with salt weathered rigging above the waterline, belied modern, powerful twin diesel engines in the engine room below.

She was equipped to run light and fast, her real cargo being high-value contraband, stored in a clever series of clandestine inner hull partitions. She traveled with a loose gaggle of innocent looking working fishing boats, which were anything but. They served as lookouts, diversionary assets, and if necessary, enforcement for the mother ship. However, with the impending storm her flotilla had run to safe harbors, for she alone had the profile necessary to weather the near gale force winds, driving ten to twelve foot seas.

The Fánróng Fùqíang was making for the southwest shore of Mindoro Island, having just passed through the Verde Island Strait, allowing them southern passage around Lubang Island. Waves crashed over her bow as she cut through the crests and rode the steep sides down the troughs, to bottom out and climb the dark wall of water again on the far side. They hoped to see calmer seas soon, when they put the island between her and the storm blowing in from the east-southeast. With luck, they could reach the mouth of the Mamburao River in a couple hours.

Despite her ocean-going profile, she drafted shallower than one might assume and was able to navigate a good way upriver before having to evade grounding. Their upriver base allowed for docking the ship, warehousing, and redistribution of contraband by smaller boats to other jungle outposts farther upstream. From there, the smuggling routes melted into the dense rain forest, to reemerge at covert rendezvous points anywhere along the miles of unpatrolled beaches.

Jiang appeared on the bridge from below and made his way over to stand next to his helmsman, peering out at the storm through the cockpit windows. The wind howled and moaned around them like demon witches, while the furious wipers worked to keep the driving rain from obscuring her bow. Jiang flung his long black hair braid around to his back and conversed in singsong Cantonese with the man, both of them gesturing back and forth out at the storm. After a last frowning glance out the windows, he looked down at the binnacle containing the helm compass and clock. Taking note of their course line and the time, he strode over to the chart table to plot their forward progress again. He needed to make sure they were passing well outside a series of treacherous reefs guarding the western shoreline. Once they were back safe at their base again, he would have the time to further contemplate the fate of his bothersome hostage.

Jiang felt he had at least exacted some revenge for the murder of his brother from this crazy man running McQuaid Air Cargo. He reasoned he had dealt him a serious blow by killing the woman in the General Store, whom he knew to be his business partner, good friend, and perhaps even his lover. Still, only a madman would attack one of his heavily armed fast-boats with a cargo airplane, even allowing for the clever use of machine guns fired out the windows at them.

With such a man, he felt he needed some extra insurance and the little girl was the perfect foil to keep him at bay. At best, he could sell her into the pleasure trade. She was about the right age, but they'd have to break her spirit first. He didn't enjoy torture, especially on children, but business was business. At worst, he could make her disappear when the time was right. Not much profit in that, but another alternative would be to trade her back to McQuaid for a good sum of money – so much better to receive a handsome sum in return for one's trouble.

He smiled to himself as he moved the calipers, using five nautical mile increments between plots along their course line to his base. These were all idle suppositions of course. His orders had been clear. She was to be delivered unharmed and he was resolved to complete the transaction for his prearranged fee. If nothing else, Jiang was a man of his word.

Meanwhile, Kiko stood in the dark below, where the pirate leader had left her. Born in a fishing village, she had spent many hours on small fishing boats as a little girl and so wasn't bothered by the pitching deck. Her eyes were swollen and red, not from crying, but from a burning fury growing in her young body. Years before, she had been helpless watching her father and then her mother butchered at the hands of wicked men. It seemed her fate was repeating itself now with her adopted parents. The injustice of it was like a flaming torch, threatening to consume her mind and body.

Earlier that day, when the pirates had burst into the Lubang store, she was in the little kitchen in back stacking dry goods in the pantry for Mattie. She had heard the screen door bang open and then Mattie screaming. She had poked her head out of the kitchen door, just in time to see two strange men grab Mattie by the arms and a Chinese looking man, with a long black braid, lifting a rifle. His black eyes were cold and cruel. He pointed the gun at Mattie and then calmly shot her once, the sound of the shot deafening in the small space. Then he worked the bolt to rack another round into the chamber and fired again. Kiko was horrified to see Mattie lurch backward with each gunshot and blood spray from the two red holes that sprang out of the back of her white blouse. Her head dropped to her chest and she sank to her knees, as Kiko's little fists went to her mouth to scream. But she had no air in her lungs and couldn't make a sound.

The pirates dropped Mattie's arms, watching her fall backward like a sack, while her head slammed onto the wooden plank floor with a sharp thud. The pirate leader walked over to look down at her and pulled a short sword out of a scabbard at his belt. He paused, watching her face without emotion, and then shoved the blade deep into her chest near her heart. She saw Mattie's head lift up in pain, her mouth open, eyes wide and then she slumped back, her head lolling lifeless to one side.

It was then the pirate noticed Kiko standing a short distance away. Their eyes met; hers in fear, his widening and then narrowing to sinister slits. He motioned to one of his men. She tried to run, but they caught her with ease and twisted her arms behind her, until she cried out in pain. They tied her hands and dragged her out of the store into the street. She watched as one of the pirates tossed a lit torch into the store and turned to rejoin them as flames leaped up against the far wall.

They trotted her down the main street to the bay, where they had a small, fast-looking boat tied up to the pier. Within minutes, they were gone, speeding out of the bay toward a group of other small boats, with a large merchant ship at anchor in the midst of them. She was hauled aboard without ceremony and stashed below in a small dark cabin. Soon after, she heard the metallic clanking noise of the anchor being raised and the throaty roar of diesel engines. And then, with a sinking heart, she felt the ship get under way. Her world was falling apart. Mattie was dead, maybe Gunner and Baacay too. All the people who were important in her life were gone once again.

Standing now frozen in despair, she stared at her feet, unable to make them out in the dim light, not really even caring. Her mouth hung open and a string of drool dripped down the front her shirt. She had to pee and without any hesitation, let it flow out of her. A puddle of urine spread beneath her onto the deck. Slumping to the floor, she sat in her own filth. It just didn't matter.

A half an hour or so later, the pirate leader unlocked the door and turned on the lights. Her head still hung to her chest. The man walked over and squatted down next to her to look her in the face. When she failed to acknowledge him, he grabbed her by the hair and yanked her head back to face him. He said something in a language she didn't understand. She just looked straight ahead, her eyes downcast and glazed. The man spoke to her again, this time in Tagalog.

"What are you, an animal? You sit in your own piss like a swine?" She didn't look up, or acknowledge him. "Who is working with this McQuaid?" he shouted. "What did Lijuan, the young girl from the boat, tell him about us? Tell me what you know if you want to live!"

Kiko continued to stare at the deck, uncaring. He let her head go and backhanded her with a sharp crack across the left side of her face, knocking her backward onto the deck. The shock of the pain snapped her out of her apathy. But she didn't cry out. A small trickle of blood dripped to the deck from her split lip. Taking no notice of this, she rolled to her side and levered herself up, looking at him from under her brow. A strange light came into her face, her lips curled back from her teeth; her eyes became gleaming slits. It was a maniacal look, bordering on the paranormal, and seemed as if a demon had possessed her and was about to lash out at him.

Jiang straightened up and took a quick step back, in part from surprise, but also because he feared she might leap forward and tear at his bare legs with her teeth. She was still struggling, determined to get to her feet, as if she meant to charge him. He reached down, grabbed her by the hair again, and shook her like a rag doll.

"I can kill you and no one will ever find your body. No one will come for you. I alone decide your fate, little girl." He wrenched her face close to his and hissed in her ear. "You will tell me what I want to know child. There is no hope for you now, only pain."

Chapter Ten
Clark AFB Hospital, Luzon Island, the Philippines

McQuaid sat at the end of the runway, engines running; steeling himself for what he knew would be a perilous takeoff. The starboard engine temp gauge was indicating a little high, but he tapped the glass with his finger and was relieved to see the needle drop back into normal range.

Baacay was in the right seat and one of Doc's nurses belted in next to Mattie, who they had tied down to a cot in the rear with cargo straps. They had unloaded the medical supplies in the hangar and left Mahutra's men and Nguyen to hold off any further attacks. *A lot less likely now with this weather*, he thought to himself. He watched the wind whipping sheets of water against the plane while he deliberated. The wipers couldn't keep up with the deluge and just slung water back and forth, obscuring all but dim shapes beyond the windshield. The runway lights were smudges against the pitch-black sky and his landing lights only made things worse. The beam was reflected back into his eyes from the gleaming curtain of driving rain.

He sat there, weighing the chances of even being able to stay on the runway long enough to get airborne. Besides, not being able to see down the runway more than a few feet ahead, there was a chance that with so much rain being sucked into the engine intakes, they might stall. Losing power on takeoff was sure to be fatal. He looked over at Baacay, who sat staring out the windshield. It wasn't hard to see he was afraid; but trusting his hero to get them through somehow. McQuaid thought about what McCawley had told him. Mattie would almost certainly die if they couldn't get her to a hospital for a blood transfusion. Even if he were able to take off, he didn't know how bad the storm was ahead and whether he would be able to stay under it, or have to climb through to get on top.

A jagged bolt of lightning lit up the rain pounding the runway around them, followed by an ear-splitting clap of thunder. The flash of light revealed he had maybe a five to eight hundred foot ceiling under the rain clouds beyond the end of the runway. It was anyone's guess whether it would get any better, or worse, out over the bay. He could see the lighthouse beam at the point, flashing through the rain to the north from the harbor mouth. That was at least a good sign.

But there were too many unknowns. He came to a decision and reached under the instrument panel, pulled the parking brake and then punched the intercom button.

"Baacay, I want you to take the nurse in back and get out." Baacay began to protest at once. But McQuaid held up his hand and jerked his thumb toward the back. "I can't risk any more lives here. Mattie is done for if I can't get her to the hospital at Clark. So I'm going to risk it, but by myself."

Baacay looked at him, his eyes wide in surprise for a moment and then replied.

"I tell nurse go. I stay with, Gunna'," he pleaded. But McQuaid just shook his head.

"Baacay, I know you're brave, but I can't let you go with me. You can't do anything to help and if something goes wrong, you'd be killed for no good reason. I can't let you do that. Mattie and I will get through somehow. Don't worry; but we're going alone." Baacay started to say something, but McQuaid just pulled his headset jack out and motioned him to the rear. They sat staring at each other for a moment, each knowing it might be the last time.

McQuaid winked at him, smiling, and motioned him back again with his head. Then snapped off a quick salute and turned away to face forward, trying to ignore him while he stared out at the runway.

Baacay gave a deep sigh in resignation and pulled his headset off. He slid out of the co-pilot's seat and disappeared into the aft cabin. After a few minutes, McQuaid felt the pressure change in the cockpit as the cargo door was opened and a moment later, he heard Baacay slam it and dog it shut. He gave him a few more seconds to clear the area, then straightened himself in his seat, yanked his seat harness tight and pulled the bill of his ball cap low over his eyes. He grabbed a cigar out of his zipper pocket and clamped it between his teeth.

"May as well bet the farm on this one," he muttered to himself around the cigar, and advanced the throttles to full. He could just make out the edges of the runway in the glare of the landing lights, as the Gooney Bird began to pick up speed. He could feel the wheels mushing through the pooling water on the concrete. The engines were roaring now and so far, they were running without missing. The tail wheel lifted off, dropping the nose, so he could see a little better, but it was still impossible to discern much beyond ten to fifteen feet ahead.

His eyes flicked back and forth between the runway and the airspeed indicator.

She was lighter after dropping her cargo, but the heavy humidity and rain decreased lift for the wings. So, he would need even more airspeed than usual to get off and without being able to see the end of the runway, it was more about guessing how much he had left. The airspeed gauge seemed to take forever to reach seventy-five mph, but he was still looking for a minimum of eighty-five. His visibility had dropped to zero now and he kept his fear in check through force of will alone, trying not to think about the low buildings and a small stand of trees somewhere beyond the end of the runway threshold.

The right main wheel dropped off the right side of the runway and he felt the Goose lurch and yaw to that side, as the tire started to bog down in the mud. He stood on the left rudder pedal to correct and pulled back on the yoke. It was time to fly, even if he didn't have all the airspeed he wanted. A moment later, the wheel noise stopped and he could see the vertical airspeed indicator begin to come alive, as the airplane started a shallow climb off the runway. Yanking the gear lever up, he was relieved to make it off the ground in one piece.

There had been some nasty wind gusts during his takeoff roll and he compensated with rudders as needed. Once he was clear of the runway however, the plane was immediately buffeted and battered right and left. He had to muscle the controls to hold his course and climb. The black bottoms of the clouds descended down toward him at an alarming rate, just as the harbor lights passed beneath them. He'd only made it to six hundred feet when his visibility dropped to zero and the buffeting got much worse.

He eased the throttles back and pushed the nose down a few degrees, watching as the altimeter paused and then started to wind back down. At six hundred feet, he came back out under the clouds and could see the landing lights reflecting off the ocean water on the bay ahead. It might be a good idea to keep them on for the duration. He wished he knew how thick the cloud cover was, but dared not risk climbing blind up into a possible thundercloud with shear winds that could tear them apart. Staying under the clouds would make for a rocky ride, but at least he had some visibility ahead and could see the water below, if he kept his landing lights on. The aircraft was bouncing around and on occasion would hit a pocket of turbulence that produced violent bucking up.

Mattie was sedated in the back, but he thought he heard her moaning a couple times, after some bad jolts. He just gritted his teeth and pressed on. But the rain was getting worse rather than better. Blinding flashes of lightning seared his vision and were becoming more frequent, along with sharp claps of thunder. But at least they appeared to be more off the right side, than in front of them.

After about twenty minutes, he was tiring from fighting the controls and figured he had another ten to twenty minutes before he would have no choice but to start climbing, to clear the ridgeline near Mount Samat Peak. He didn't relish the thought of heading into even worse conditions, but it had to be done. Then his eye was drawn to the cylinder head temperature gauge for his right engine. The needle was moving upward, out of the green. So far the engines had missed a few times when the rain was bad, but had calmed down again and stayed steady. Losing an engine at night, in a heavy thunderstorm near the mountains, was the last thing he needed right about now. He kept a closer eye on the gauge and throttled back some, to put as little strain on the engine as possible.

After another ten minutes, some blurs he hoped were lights came into view ahead. That meant he was nearing the Luzon coastline and it was now or never if he was going to clear the mountains. He pushed both throttles forward and eased back on the control yoke, watching the needle on the altimeter begin to wind upward. He glanced down at the lights one more time, trying to discern any detail he could use to gauge his exact position and spotted the lighthouse beam on Manila Bay, just before the dark ceiling closed in over them. That was a relief anyway. They were very close to where he knew they needed to be.

Now at only a thousand feet and climbing, he knew he needed to have at least fifteen hundred feet below him to make it over the ridgeline. The plane was beginning to buck again as he fought the controls. He'd dialed in the radio beacon at Clark before taking off and was keeping an eye on the direction finder gauge as he continued to climb. So far, the needle hadn't moved but he needed almost a direct line of sight to the beacon before it would register and he was still behind the mountains at this altitude.

While he was figuring how much more they needed to climb, the starboard engine sputtered a few times and his eyes dropped to the temperature gauge again. It was half way into the red. He could make it on one engine, but then he wouldn't have any margin of safety left if the other engine started acting up. He retarded the throttle on the right engine, while increasing left throttle and compensating with rudders, as the aircraft yawed to the right. The cylinder head temperature on number two engine continued to climb and it started missing again. If he kept on like this, it could seize up on him.

There was no other option, so he pulled the right engine throttle all the way back and feathered the prop, then switched off the fuel to that side. His airspeed began to fall off, but he stabilized everything and continued a shallow climb, now passing through twelve hundred feet. Then he was relieved to see the RDF needle snap to the left and pointing dead ahead to line up with Clark's beacon. He had been holding his breath and let it out with a sudden whoosh – only twenty to thirty miles more. He dialed in Clark's tower frequency between bumps and keyed his mike.

"Clark Tower, this is McQuaid Air Cargo, just clearing Samat Peak to the southeast. I'm a C-47 emergency flight with one engine feathered, about thirty miles out, requesting straight in clearance to land, over."

It was a moment or two before Clark tower responded. They probably weren't expecting any air traffic in this storm.

"Clark tower to McQuaid Air Cargo, roger. State the nature of your emergency, over." A sudden violent wind shear slammed the aircraft down fifty feet or more and he was in a fight for his life to regain control before they plowed into the mountain ahead. The landing lights began to reflect off trees and rocks. On one engine, it was all he could do to keep the aircraft from sinking anymore and not stall, much less regain the lost altitude. He simply didn't have the airspeed to escape the mountains, now reaching up to engulf them.

He slammed the left throttle to the stop and eased carefully back on the yoke, praying they would get out from under the column of air in time. Then he saw the trees rising up to meet them, their dripping wet branches beckoning him into death's embrace.

Another man would have panicked and covered his face, in a futile brace for impact. But McQuaid wasn't that man and instead, he yanked down a notch of flaps; then pulled hard on the yoke. The flaps should provide more lift at lower airspeed. The nose came up, but he felt the beginning buffeting of the controls and their usual tautness, turned to a mushy feel that spelled the early signs of a stall. In a few seconds, the aircraft would just stop flying and spin out of control into the trees and rocks below, becoming a tangled fireball of metal and burning fuel. He let up the back pressure on the yoke just enough to try and keep the airspeed up; willing the airplane to climb.

"C'mon, old girl. We can do this. Just give me a few more feet and I'll get you home." Time slowed and in a corner of his mind, he heard Clark tower calling back on the radio for a response. He noticed an outcropping of rock sliding by, outside the left side window, with trees at eye level to the cockpit and a ghostly steel radio tower appeared out of the rain to his right, its red beacon lights blinking, leering back at them.

Branches slapped and clawed the underside of the fuselage and then the co-pilot's windshield exploded inward with a loud bang, as something struck it from out of the darkness. A gale wind blew in through the large hole, whirling papers and debris around and blinding him for a moment. He forced his eyes straight ahead and kept his hands steady on the controls. Somewhere, deep within, a feeling of calm settled over him. It seemed like he could see himself from the outside, sitting there, steering his aircraft through a narrow corridor of escape, surrounded by chaos. As he watched, he could see flashes of lightning from the storm reflecting off the wet fuselage and ethereal static charges that glowed and snapped from the wingtips as they passed over the jagged terrain.

He knew that somehow it would all come out just as it was supposed to, as if all his movements had been choreographed beforehand. During the war, in combat, there were other occasions when this prescient out-of-body awareness had taken him over. It was disturbing and yet somehow comforting to know he had this gift; it kept him safe. And then, just as suddenly as it had begun, the Gooney Bird slipped over the ridge and the buffeting stopped.

He could see the blur of lights around the overcast in the valley floor ahead. With a gentle push, he moved the yoke forward and felt the wings bite into the air once more. The controls firmed up again under his hands and time returned to normal. His airspeed gauge was winding back up with the nose pointing lower now, as he rode the mountain downslope toward the farmlands below.

"McQuaid Air Cargo, please say again your position, over." Shaking off his reverie, he reached down and grabbed the mike off the hook.

"McQuaid Air Cargo here. Sorry, I got a little busy there for a moment. Just cleared the Samat Peak ridgeline and..." he glanced down at the instrument panel again, "...I'm currently at thirteen hundred feet, over." He had to shout over the wind, roaring in through the missing co-pilot's windshield.

"McQuaid Air Cargo, roger, we have you on radar now. Please state the nature of your emergency, over."

"I have a gunshot wounded female British citizen on board from the hospital in Lubang who requires immediate emergency medical assistance, over." He hoped Mattie was still okay in back, after all the battering they had taken on the flight over. There was no way he could check on her until they landed.

"McQuaid Air Cargo, we understand and will have an ambulance waiting for you on the apron. Be advised, weather conditions over the field are poor, the ceiling is nine hundred to a thousand feet and descending, with driving rain. Make straight in for runway two. Wind is out of one-eight-five degrees at fifteen knots, gusts to twenty-five; altimeter pressure at the field is 24.55. Please advise when you can see the tower beacon light."

He rogered the tower, set his altimeter to field pressure, and settled down to prepare for landing. With a little more luck, the left engine would get them down safe.

He was still in the soup, on instruments, glancing up every few seconds, straining to see any evidence of ground lights, or clearing. Nearing a thousand feet, the blackness began turning gray, but still, nothing to offer a clue as to whether he was right side up, or down. His mind was screaming at him to roll his wings level. Without his instruments to guide him, he knew from experience, vertigo was making his inner sense of orientation completely unreliable and would kill them if he didn't fight the impulse to try and level his wings. Maybe his instruments had been damaged. Everything seemed all wrong! *Steady on. Stay focused,* he reminded himself. *Keep a slow, stable descent going.*

"McQuaid Air Cargo, we have you at fifteen miles northwest of the field and nine hundred fifty feet. Can you see the tower beacon yet?"

"Clark Tower, negative; not yet." In fact, he couldn't see anything and driving rain was pouring in through the missing right windshield, creating a small pool of water that sloshed back and forth across the cockpit floor, soaking his boots and socks. He hoped it wouldn't seep through the floorboards and short out anything vital while he was trying to land. He gave a wry shake of his head. It just kept getting better.

Finally, he popped out under the clouds and could pick out the tower beacon and runway lights through the rain, dead ahead and to the left. He banked left, to line up on the runway; throttled back on his remaining engine, and dropped his gear and flaps. The rest of the landing was a welcome routine. After taxiing over to the closest hangars, he saw the dark green truck with a white-encircled red cross pull up next to him while he was shutting down. They had a fire truck sitting nearby as well. He unbuckled and moved back to kneel down next to Mattie and was surprised to see her eyes open, looking up at him.

"How's it going, fly boy?" she croaked. She saw the concern on his face and closed her eyes, smiling. "Looks like I finally have you worried." He just smiled back and patted her hand.

"They've got the ambulance waiting for you outside, Mattie. I'll ride with you over to the hospital and make sure they don't take anything out you'll need later."

She sneered back at him, without opening her eyes. He brushed matted, sweaty bangs back from her face and then moved over to open the door to the let the medics in. There were two medics and a doctor waiting, who climbed up the crew ladder and took charge of her. He stepped back and watched them work.

After a quick flurry of activity, the medics unstrapped her stretcher and hauled her out to the ambulance. The doctor, a young medical corps lieutenant, paused to speak with McQuaid.

"What's the story with her, sir?" he asked, looking for rank on his flight coverall epaulets. McQuaid handed him the medical records McCawley had given him earlier.

"I'm not in the service anymore, Doctor...Winford," he read off the man's nametag, stitched onto his white coat. "Name's McQuaid, Richard McQuaid, and I run McQuaid Air Cargo out of Lubang Island. She's Mattie Adams and owns the village store there. She was attacked by pirates. They kidnapped our little girl, shot Mattie, and left her for dead. Doc McCawley, who runs the hospital on the island, patched her up as best he could, but she needs a blood transfusion."

The young doctor glanced out at the ambulance to watch the medics tying her stretcher down inside the vehicle. Sheets of rain swept back and forth across the tarmac and drummed on the aircraft roof over their heads. He returned his eyes to McQuaid, appraising him, as if he wasn't quite sure what to make of his explanation.

"She was shot by pirates?" he asked, his tone incredulous. McQuaid just nodded, watching him back, his mouth a thin line. "I've heard stories, but didn't realize they would be so bold as to attack any of the towns, even on one of the smaller islands like Lubang. What were they after, do you know?" he asked.

"They were after me," McQuaid answered. He turned to climb down the crew ladder and jumped in the back of the ambulance with Mattie.

Chapter Eleven
Clark AFB Hospital Mess, Luzon Island, the
Philippines

McQuaid paced outside surgery for over two hours while doctors gave her whole blood, took x-rays, checked for any internal bleeding, and finally trundled her off to the ward for recovery. Earlier, he had called over to base ops to request someone from maintenance look over the Gooney Bird and give him an estimate on repairs. He was sure it wouldn't be cheap. However, he was more worried about Mattie at the moment. One of the surgeons, a balding Army Major, Dennehy, finally emerged through the swinging surgery doors to meet with McQuaid and fill him in on the prognosis.

"You're Richard McQuaid?" he asked walking toward him with his hand outstretched. McQuaid, nodding, took his hand and scanned his face for any sign of alarm. The surgeon noticed he was looking a little pale and moved to reassure him. "Don't worry. She came through just fine; a little worse for wear, but she'll be okay. Do you know who did the initial surgery on her?" he asked, raising reddish bushy eyebrows above his pale blue eyes.

"Doctor James McCawley," McQuaid replied, without elaborating, thinking it strange to use Doc's first name. He almost didn't remember it. People on Lubang always just called him Doc. "He runs the Lubang hospital."

The Major offered a slight nod in return.

"Well, you can tell Doctor McCawley he did a fine job on her surgery. He saved her life, you know. And you can tell him for me, if he ever wants a field combat surgery job with the U.S. Army, I'll pull whatever strings I need to get him in." He beamed back at McQuaid.

"I'll tell him, Major. He'd really appreciate that coming from you."

"Henry's the name, Mister McQuaid. Friends call me Hank. I hope you will." He reached into his pocket and fished out a pack of Lucky Strikes, then shook one out, offering it to him.

"Sorry, Hank. I don't smoke cigarettes, but I do enjoy a fine cigar on occasion," he chuckled.

"Do you now?" the doctor mused, flicking a Zippo lighter open and lighting his smoke. He inhaled and then blew the smoke out with relish. "Join me for a cup of Joe then," he said, pulling a flask out of his pocket. "I have a little stiffener here for us." He clapped McQuaid on the back. "You look like you could use some. I hear from the fellas over at base ops, you pulled off a fancy piece of flying to get your patient over here in that thunderstorm." McQuaid noticed the pocket on his white coat had wings embroidered over his name. "Care to fill an old pilot in? Don't get out much anymore and I could use a good war story." He winked at McQuaid and led him over to the mess area of the hospital to grab some coffee.

"Not much to tell, Hank. Really. I needed to get her here and flying through the thunderstorm was the only way to go." He got in line behind him and grabbed a large white mug off the rack next to a couple big steel coffee urns. He glanced around, noticing several tables with chairs and what looked like a few medical staff sitting around in quiet conversations. Hank finished pouring a dark black cup of coffee and turned back to look at him skeptically.

"Sounds kinda humble for an ex-Marine fighter pilot, if you ask me."

"How'd you figure that one out, Hank? I've been out for a while now."

"Seems we've got a few friends in common. One of them told me to hold you down until he could get over here to talk with you. You know a Major Wilmouth?" Dennehy cocked an eye at him to gauge his reaction.

"I sure do," he replied, breaking into a grin. "But I thought he was back on Guam by now."

Dennehy motioned him over to one of the tables and they both sat down. Hank slouched down in his chair and took a quick sip of coffee before he answered.

"Yeah, he would have been, but they needed to pull an ignition harness on his Corsair. Said his engine was missing and he suspected electrical. He'll be out of here in another week – if he's lucky. Parts are harder to come by these days. Says he knows you from the war?" He watched McQuaid over the rim of his cup. "You guys were in the same squadron together in '45?"

"Yeah. Actually, we traded off as wingmen flying off the Essex in support of the Luzon campaign near the end there." He jerked his thumb back over his right shoulder. "We strafed the shit out of this base a number of times when the Japs held it during the occupation of Manila."

160

The Major nodded and reached over to pour some whiskey out of his flask into McQuaid's cup and then into his own.

McQuaid continued, "I got out right after that and decided to stick around for a while, running an air cargo service here in the islands." He took a sip of his "doctored" coffee, wincing as the alcohol burned going down. It was a good burn though. He watched Hank take a sip of his, without as much as a twitch. Must have used less in his cup, or he was used to extra gas in his Joe.

"How's the cargo business going for you?"

"Not too bad, actually. Extra costs, like what I'm going to need to spend to fix that airplane out there, kinda hurt though." He smiled, bemused by what could end up being a considerable unbudgeted sum against his maintenance expenses.

Dennehy slouched down in his seat even further and hooked his hands behind his head, sighting down his nose at him.

"What's the story with the pirates? I heard the woman you brought in had been shot by pirates?"

"Right – I'm fairly sure that's the way it went. I wasn't around to see what happened exactly, but that's what my maintenance man told me. They shot her and left her for dead. She's a tough bird though." He took a sip of coffee, letting the liquor do its work to relax his nerves. His muscles were still knotted up from tension and fighting the controls on the flight over. He paused, watching the other man gazing at him behind pensive eyes.

His cigarette had been growing ash in his hand and must have started getting warm. He looked down at it, and then flicked it at the ashtray on the table. It went straight in, as if he was used to making shots like that. Taking a last drag on what was left, he stubbed out the butt and looked back over at McQuaid with some concern.

"The doc who met you out at the airplane told me you mentioned they shot her to get to you. That right?" A cloud passed over McQuaid's face and his cheeks flushed. He was thinking about how he could make a long story short, when he spotted Jake Wilmouth rounding the corner down the hallway, heading their way at full throttle. His face lit up and Dennehy turned around in his chair to see who he was looking at.

"Gunner, I can't leave you alone for five minutes without you dismantling good airplanes and practically putting the entire base around here on alert!" he boomed.

Heads swiveled around to see who was disturbing the otherwise calm atmosphere in the mess.

McQuaid just laughed, shaking his head and getting to his feet. Jake noticed the Major and stuck out his hand on his way by and it was pumped by Dennehy in return. "Thanks for taking care of my pal's woman, Hank." He looked back and forth between them with hands on hips. "I see you two have met." He gave McQuaid a pointed look. "The doc's a good man to know with the kind of trouble you get into, Gunner." They all laughed.

"How about I grab some coffee and pull up a chair with you gents – if you don't mind?" he asked, but no one presumed he was planning on taking "no" for an answer. It wasn't long before he plopped down beside them with a fresh mug of coffee and looked back and forth at them. "Well, what'd I miss?" Hank just waggled the flask at him and he quickly lowered his cup for fueling. "Oh, absolutely! Don't mind if I do and thanks for offering," he grinned. He waited, while Dennehy poured in a liberal dose and then looked over at McQuaid with eyebrows raised. "Well? How's Mattie?" he asked, more serious now. McQuaid took a deep breath and blew it out before answering.

"Major Dennehy, er Hank, tells me she pulled through just fine. I think we got lucky, if you ask me."

Dennehy chimed in to offer a few details.

"She's lost a lot of blood, but assuming there isn't any infection from her surgery at the hospital on Lubang, she should be much better in a few days."

"Damn, McQuaid. What the hell went on over there? Word around here is she was attacked by pirates." His face was drawn with concern.

"Word travels fast I see," McQuaid replied back evenly and taking a slow sip of coffee, while he waited for Jake to launch into his usual unabridged monologue.

"Roger that, Gunner. But, it's hard to keep a secret like that when you practically crash landed your airplane in the middle of a gawd-awful storm, with the runways on the base all closed due to weather, I might add." He took a quick breath and reloaded. "Running on one engine, with tree branches sticking out of the engine air intakes and every other orifice."

He leaned forward for effect. "Did you decide to stop and do a little pruning in the forest on the way over here, Gunner? And then of course there's the little issue of the bullet riddled English woman, evidently shot by some unsavory types with guns, and oh, did I mention swords?" He stopped for a quick breath and McQuaid decided he needed to wedge in there before he really got wound up.

"Listen, Snake. I've got enough problems without you lining up a bunch of curiosity seekers for me to deal with. I need to get my plane fixed and Mattie back to the island with as little fuss as possible around here." Wilmouth remained unfazed.

"Looks like your plan ain't workin' so well, twinkle-toes. And for the record, I didn't tell anybody anything other than Hank here – who happens to be an old friend and was naturally curious to know how his patient got two bullet holes and a stab wound in her chest." McQuaid just looked at him. "Maybe you'd like to let your buddy Snake in on the action, just in case you might need the Calvary next time." He stared back him, hoping he'd take the hint.

McQuaid sighed and looked over at Dennehy.

"You say he's a friend of yours too?" The Major raised his hands in self-defense.

"We're not related, if you were worried about that."

McQuaid noticed a couple medics at the table next to them were trying their best to appear like they weren't eavesdropping. He sighed again in resignation.

"Okay, here's the short version. Apparently, I riled up the local buccaneers when I shot up their pirate boat while they were busy attacking a private launch offshore of Cabra Island; murdering the owners. We killed a couple of them. One happened to be the brother of the bunch and now they're after my head."

Wilmouth just looked at him.

"Shot their boat up with what?" he asked, looking confused. McQuaid ran his hand over his head and glanced around, feeling even more sheepish. The next table over was silent in rapt attention.

"Well," he lowered his voice a bit, "I flew the Lubang police chief out there with me and we sort of strafed their boat with the Goose." Everyone was staring at him now.

"The Goose? Your flying boat?" Jake asked, somewhat bewildered. "What'd you use for bullets, goose shit?"

That broke up the medics at the next table. McQuaid glared at them and they both shut up, turning back around to feign conversation with each other. McQuaid knew he was on total defense now. His foolish exploits were now up for ridicule with the toughest crowd around – fellow aviators – who called "bullshit" on anything that smelled suspicious, or too audacious – if that was even possible with fighter pilots. McQuaid cinched his tale up even tighter, just in case.

"Not exactly," he began again. "We took a couple of my Thompson submachine guns and I fired one out of the pilot's window, while the police chief shot his out of the co-pilot's window. We got in two runs before they tucked tail and ran. Which is a good thing, because they had a mounted .30 cal. on the deck and were popping off at us the whole time." Both Majors had their mouths hanging open by this point; not sure how to respond. "Anyway, I was over on the south side of the island, earlier today, trying to help the Looc village chief get one of the tribe's daughters back from some Japanese hold-outs who attacked the village and took her hostage. Meanwhile, I guess, the pirates attacked the general store on Lubang and shot Mattie because they couldn't find me." He stood up to get some more coffee, but Wilmouth's hand shot out and grabbed him by the arm.

"Hold on a moment there, Tonto. There are Japanese soldiers still on Lubang?" He looked shocked.

"Yep, 'fraid so. And I grabbed one as a prisoner to take over to the village to help the chief use for a hostage trade." He sat back down figuring they weren't about to give him any quarter at this point. He was right. Jake put both hands up to his eyes and rubbed them and then looked over at Major Dennehy.

"Did I not warn you about him?" He pointed in McQuaid's direction. "He doesn't just get into trouble, he invents it where there isn't quite enough to go around already." Dennehy just offered an empathetic nod in return. Wilmouth looked back at McQuaid. "Anything else?" he asked.

"Yeah, Kiko's missing." He looked at Jake bitterly. "I think the pirates took her." This bit of unexpected news wiped the smirk off his friend's face.

"They took Kiko?" he asked, his eyes narrowing and his mouth set in a harsh line. "Are you sure?"

"Not certain – but almost." McQuaid was slapping his empty mug against his open palm in frustration. "The worst thing is, I don't know what they would do with her. She's just an innocent little girl, Jake." His eyes were downcast and he stood up again to refill his coffee cup. The two men sat mute and motionless, as did the two men at the table next to them. Just then, an orderly entered the mess and walked over to Major Dennehy.

"Sir, your patient is awake and asking for someone named McQuaid." Dennehy stood up, slurped down the rest of his coffee, and nodded his head.

"Thanks, Lieutenant. I'll bring him along with me." The orderly turned and walked off. McQuaid sat his cup down next to the coffee urn and moved back to the table. Dennehy looked over at him. "Let's go see how she's doing, son."

Jake stood too and caught McQuaid's questioning look with compassion.

"I've got a few things to do still, Gunner. If you like, we can meet up later at the 'O' Club." McQuaid just nodded back to him.

Major Dennehy led the way out of the mess. Jake hung back, watching, as his friend walked away. He knew McQuaid could use his help. He just wasn't sure yet what he really had to offer. But he'd give whatever he had and find whatever he was lacking. He'd be there on Gunner's wing no matter what.

They had Mattie propped up on a couple pillows with IV bottles of whole blood hanging on stands next to her bed. Her hair was all matted down and she was pale, groggy, and exhausted looking, but nonetheless awake. She looked over at McQuaid when he and Major Dennehy walked in. A slow smile of relief crossed her face and she turned her head to see him better. McQuaid moved over to her bedside and took her hand.

"How're you feeling, Mattie?" he asked, at once feeling foolish. She shot him a pained expression. He blushed. "Sorry. Pretty dumb question, huh?" She smiled, her eyes crinkling at the corners.

"Well, I'm not quite ready to go dancing. But with all these pain killers they have in me, I could probably fake it, as long as you don't mind they didn't exactly dress me up either."

He laughed and turned around to grab a chair; pulling it over to her bedside.

"How're you doing, Richard?" She looked up at him with a brave face, but a tear ran down her cheek and dripped onto her pillow. He leaned forward and wiped away another tear, just as it was getting started.

"I'm okay." She nodded.

"Thank you for getting me here. One of the orderlies told me it was quite a ride and they were amazed we made it at all. I guess they don't know you very well, huh?" She started to laugh, but winced instead.

He brushed sweaty locks of hair back from her face and kissed her on the forehead.

"It wasn't that big a deal, kid. Just a little breezy and kinda rainy." She snorted in reply and he laughed, self-conscious in spite of himself. "Okay, it was a bit hairy. But the Gooney Bird is almost as tough as you. I couldn't have done it without her." She smirked up at him.

"So, I should thank your airplane, right?"

He felt a gentle hand on his shoulder and looked back at Major Dennehy smiling down at him. He looked over at Mattie as well.

"Hate to break this up, boys and girls, but somebody needs their beauty rest."

Mattie stuck her tongue out at him, but McQuaid could tell it was halfhearted. Her eyes were starting to get heavy.

"Do you know who he's talking about, Richard?" she asked, her voice sleepy and distant now. Then her eyes closed and he just sat there for a minute or so longer looking down at her face and holding her hand.

He was glad she hadn't asked about Kiko, another benefit of the drugs. Finally, he stood up and looked back at Dennehy, with a predictable question on his face.

"Don't worry, McQuaid, she'll be all right. She just needs rest now and we want to keep an eye out for any infection. So far, so good. Why don't you get some rest? You look like you could use some. Come back in the morning." He squeezed his shoulder and turned around to walk out.

"Doc," he called after him. Dennehy paused and turned to look back at him. "Thanks," he said. The word sounded way too simple for how he felt.

Major Dennehy smiled and acknowledged all that remained unspoken with a quick bob of his head. Then he walked out, lifting some papers up from a folder and already working his way over to another patient.

McQuaid looked back at Mattie. She seemed to be resting and comfortable now, but he knew she was lucky to be alive. It was embarrassing to hear her praise for him delivering her to the hospital in one piece. She'd also been attacked because of him in the first place. He rubbed his hands over his face in frustration and decided he needed to get busy before he started feeling sorry for himself. Heading for the door he was trying to decide what he should do first and settled on checking in with maintenance on his aircraft.

They had dragged the Gooney Bird into one of the hangars near the flight line, out of the rain. The overhead lights were on and there were a couple maintenance ladders pulled up to the wings. He was surprised to see a mechanic hanging out of an access panel under the right engine cowling. It was after 2100 hours and he really hadn't expected anyone to be working on aircraft that late. He ducked under the wing and looked up at the man standing on a stepladder with a flashlight in one hand and a wrench in the other. The mechanic saw him and kneeled down out of the access port.

"Can I help you?" he asked without much enthusiasm. His eyes scanned his flight coverall looking for some rank.

"This is my bird and I just wanted to check on the damage. How's she looking to you, Sergeant?" He had noticed the man's stripes right away. The man replied with newfound respect.

"Well, if you're the pilot, my hat's off to you, mister," he said.

"Oh?"

"Yep. I'm not sure how you were able to get this crate here at all, much less in one piece." He began to reel off a number of damage items, finishing off with: "And the port engine would have quit on you if you hadn't gotten her down quickly." He motioned to one of the ladders under the other wing. "It seems you broke one of the oil lines with a branch that punched through the engine nacelle." He looked back at McQuaid. "How low were you flying anyways – if you don't mind my asking?" The man was probably in his early thirties, thin, with blonde hair, and not intending to be judgmental as

167

much as curious. He pulled a rag out of his pocket and wiped his hands, while he waited for McQuaid to fill him in.

"I guess I just barely made it over the south ridge line of Samat Peak on one engine. The other one overheated and I had to shut it down." The man just nodded.

"Looks like you were loaded light. Under normal circumstances, one engine should have gotten you over without too much of a problem. These Gooney Birds are made to bring you home."

Watching his face, McQuaid could tell he was a fan of the aircraft. He looked back up at the engine over his head, figuring if it had overheated, they'd need to overhaul it. That wasn't going to be cheap. He commented back somewhat absent mindedly to the mechanic.

"A wind-shear pushed me down into the mountain. I damn near didn't get over the ridge at all. I guess we got lucky, huh?" He was looking under the wing and feeling along the fuselage, running his hands over deep gouges and pulled out some leaves caught in a couple of the control surfaces at the trailing edge of the wing. The man next to him hadn't replied, so he glanced over at him, curious about the sudden silence. He was staring at him. "Something wrong, Sergeant?"

The man paused before answering.

"You might want to come back and take a look at this," he replied. He waved his flashlight toward the rear of the plane and turned to walk toward the tail. McQuaid followed him, watching, as he crouched down and shined his light into an open access panel, just forward of the tail wheel. He moved aside so McQuaid could see inside.

"You were a lot luckier than you know, mister," he said, his voice low and strained.   McQuaid could see one of the control cable pulleys had torn loose from its attachment bracket and the steel strands of the elevator cable were cut and sticking out at all angles, like a bad haircut. It appeared there were just two thin strands left keeping the cable from separating all together. A cold sliver of ice lodged in his stomach. If that cable had broken, he would have lost all vertical control of the aircraft. Fighting the controls in the storm had put tremendous strain on the cable pulleys. This one had ripped loose and the jagged sheet metal had turned into a saw, hacking back and forth across the cable, almost severing it. He sat back on his heels, looking over at the other man, who was watching his face for a reaction.

168

"That was a close one then, wasn't it?"

The other man nodded, stood up, and started walking back toward the front of the aircraft. He turned around to McQuaid in mid stride. "Well, the starboard engine and that cable seem to be the worst of it. The port engine looks to be fine. It hadn't started to overheat, even with the oil tank down to under ten gallons. Shutting down the starboard motor may have saved it, by using all the remaining oil for the port engine." He picked up a clipboard and glanced over his inspection notes. "I should be able to work up an estimate for you by tomorrow morning sometime, Mister McQuaid. You might want to check in with the maintenance chief later. That's Master Chief Barrows. You can usually find him in the maintenance office." He pointed off to the left at a door in the far corner of the hangar.

"Thanks, Sergeant. I appreciate all your help on this." He shook the man's hand and decided to head over to the 'O' Club for something to eat and to meet up with Jake. He was just the man he needed to go over the rough battle plan he'd been working on in his head. Chief Mahutra had told him he needed to appear poisonous to the pirates. What better way to be poisonous, than with a Snake? He chuckled to himself.

Chapter Twelve
The "O" Club, Clark AFB, the Philippines

Fortunately, the rain had let up a little by the time he hitched a ride over to the 'O' Club from maintenance. As he walked into the darkened entry, he could hear the voice of Lena Horne, crooning to the strains of Stormy Weather. He smiled to himself. How appropriate in so many ways. A curvaceous woman at the reservations podium looked him up and down as he approached the dining room entry. He realized his flight coveralls were out of place for the dinner crowd and decided he'd be better off in the bar.

"You look like you've been pulling a few long-nighters, sweetie," she cooed at him, arching dark eyebrows over striking green eyes. Her lipstick glistened bright red, like the sequined cocktail dress she was wearing, and her lips curled up into a brilliant white smile. She brushed back a lock of thick dark hair and gave him a suggestive wink. He laughed and walked over to put in a note with her to watch out for Jake when he arrived. Looking down at his rumpled, stained coverall, he responded with a sheepish smile.

"Well, ma'am, I probably do look a bit frayed around the edges." The 'O' Club liked to put smashing women up front to better lure the fly boys in. It was good clean fun and another executive perk for homesick military officers. She countered with a provocative grin.

"Honey, you look like you're just about all edges," she drawled, her eyes twinkling. He laughed outright at this. "I prefer you call me Lillie, instead of 'ma'am'. What's your name, sugar?"

He leaned an elbow on the maître d' stand and met her flirtatious stare. He was no Jake Wilmouth, but he could hold his own.

"Name's Richard McQuaid. Nice to meet you, Lillie. I'm supposed to meet a Major Jake Wilmouth here. Maybe you could let him know I'm in the bar if he comes in?" He looked down at his clothes with pointed concern. "I'm really not dressed for the dining room tonight." She looked him up and down again, taking her time, lips pursed, eyes approving, in spite of his apology.

"Maybe not this dining room, sugar." The point of her pink tongue lingered in the corner of her mouth. She gazed into his eyes and leaned closer, cocking her hips. "But not to worry," she breathed, fingering his collar with bright painted red nails, "your Major friend is already in the dining room waiting for you." She gestured behind her, with just her head, never taking her eyes from his. "And if you're uncomfortable in those clothes, maybe you'd like to leave them out here with me, before you head in."

McQuaid could see Jake, seated at a far table. He had spotted him already and was waving him in.

"Well, so he is," McQuaid replied and winked back at Lillie. "Thank you kindly, ma'am. I wish I could take you up on that very generous offer, but I really don't have anything on under this," he said, running his coverall zipper up and down to his waist a couple times, exposing matted chest hair and leering back at her. She flushed and giggled, then slapped his arm and waved him past her.

Wilmouth was dressed in a cream colored collared shirt and natty cashmere sport coat. He grinned at McQuaid as he approached.

"Clearly, they don't let you out much," he quipped, then scooted over in the booth to let him slide in. He already had what appeared to be a scotch and water on the table in front of him, down to almost half a tank already. "Get you a drink started, my man? I see you met Lillie," he said, his eyes wandering toward the door. "I think she likes you, Gunner," he breathed, patting his hand.

"She likes everybody, Snake," he said and then smiled upward, as one of the club's devastating cocktail waitresses greased to a stop at their table and leaned over to drop a drink napkin down in front of him. He was very relieved to see it wasn't Jewel from the night before. She looked down at him and smiled, feigning shy, batting dark heavily mascaraed eyes at him. She looked Chinese and reminded him a lot of Lijuan.

"May I get you drink, suh?" she breathed, her voice soft and sweet. Wilmouth had his chin on his hand, watching her amorously, batting his eyes at her in return. She looked at him sideways and smiled back. "You too, suh?" Jake just held up two fingers and continued gazing back at her, his eyes dreamy. McQuaid ordered the same as Jake and they both watched, entranced, as she moved back toward the dimness of the lounge room. Her body seemed to glide rather than walk on perfect high-heeled legs. Blue-black hair knotted in a long ponytail swished back and forth across an outstanding rear, above a wasp waist over a tight black skirt.

"You know, Gunner," Jake got out at last. "God is really quite the joker." McQuaid waited, but realized he was supposed to pick up his cue.

"Yeah?"

"Damn straight. There are never enough of those to go around for us poor saps and if you get lucky enough to land a really terrific woman like that, they start changing into your mother the day after you get married." He heaved a loud sigh, took a long pull of his drink, and then turned to face McQuaid growing more serious. "But on to other delightful guy stuff. Son, you have managed to get yourself into quite the major league shit storm. It's a damn good thing you have old Jake around when you need a good shit-proof umbrella, huh? Admit it, old man." He poked him in the shoulder, grinning with that now familiar evil glint in his eye.

McQuaid nodded, admitting to himself that his friend was right. There had been times when Jake had literally saved his life in combat. But this was different. It could cost Jake his career if they screwed up. Risking your life in combat for your wingman came with the territory.

"I'll give you that one, Jake. I do need some help. We have to assume the pirates have Kiko, so I have a plan to get her back in one piece and those pirates off my back. That is, if you're up for some off-op action." He looked over at him, ready with a wave-off and an apology if he gave him even the slightest sign he'd stepped over the line. "This won't be a cake walk and you need to drop me like a hot rock if you don't like the sound of what I'm going to tell you."

"Since when has it ever been easy with you, Gunner? I've pulled your fanny out of the fire so many times now, it's starting feel routine. Fill me in and I'll be the judge of whether this sounds any tougher than usual."

Their drinks arrived and they both placed food orders before McQuaid was able to launch into it. To his credit, Jake listened without interrupting; on occasion taking what looked like it might be a bracing gulp of scotch, but his attention remained riveted on the plan as McQuaid went over each point. Their food arrived and they ate without a pause in the briefing. Finally, McQuaid sat back and slugged down the last of his drink.

"Well?"

He waited for Jake to chip in, not sure how he would respond to the bolder mission elements. Jake seemed to be digesting it all with careful deliberation and held up a finger to him to let him know he needed a moment to respond. At long last, he leaned forward to offer his critique, which was, by all appearances, to be delivered with unusual seriousness.

"First of all," he began, "you are one crazy bastard, Gunner." McQuaid's heart sank. "But," he held up his hand in response to the disappointed reaction on his friend's face, "it's a damn fine battle plan." He looked around the room to make sure no one was close enough to overhear. "I need to bring Doc Dennehy in on this."

"Why? He's a surgeon at the hospital. What good would he be in this operation?" Jake expected his reaction.

"He's also the base Flight Surgeon and very tight with the Wing Commander, Colonel Macy. We'll need top line sign-off to pull off this little caper of yours, Gunner." He looked over at his friend with a warning. "I'm in, but I'm also still in the Marine Corps, my friend – which means, I could tell you I will be there for you, right up to the time I get orders to be elsewhere, and probably at some crucial point of this mission." He sat back and let McQuaid chew on that for a moment.

"What's in it for Macy then, except maybe a court martial?" McQuaid was skeptical and already thinking he may have to go to plan B. Of course, he'd need to develop one first. But Jake was on top of it.

"Macy and the base commander aren't unaware of what's going on around here you know, sport. They get reports of the drug running and know the pirates and unsavory privateers around the Philippines are bold and operating with impunity from local authorities. The government forces here are still in tatters, or corrupt. There are plenty of bad guys exploiting this huge gap in law enforcement." He paused to down the last of his drink and held up two fingers to the roving cocktail waitress, who gave him the high-sign back. He continued. "The Philippine government wants the U.S. military to intervene, but our official operational posture is not to get embroiled in local squabbles, or civilian police actions."

"So how could the Air Force justify what amounts to a local smack-down of smalltime criminal activity, which is offshore and more under the purview of the Navy anyway?"

Jake leaned forward again and jabbed the table with his finger to emphasize his point.

"Because it's not smalltime at all and it isn't even just local. Listen, Gunner, the Chinese are using this break in hostilities to further their own agenda. And that is, to turn a blind eye at the least, but at the worst, maybe even sponsoring a growing drug running and slave trade operation. Intelligence...," he paused, skewering him with a hard look. "I'm going to tell you something confidential now." He arched an eyebrow at McQuaid making it plain he was waiting him out. McQuaid sighed.

"Don't worry. I'll keep it under my hat."

"Okay," Jake continued, "so one of the reasons I'm back and forth from here to Guam, is Pacific Command is very concerned the Chinese are maneuvering to dilute our power base here. They see our winning the war and putting bases in the Pacific around the Chinese mainland as a threat to the future of their national security. We think they are encouraging widespread criminal activity along the trade routes between the Philippines and Indonesia as a sort of catalyst, or provocation, for them to grow a stronger navy and air force in what they are claiming is self-defense. No one can refute their right to protect maritime commercial interests in the region." Jake paused again to let this sink in a bit.

The light began to dawn on McQuaid. He nodded his head now.

"So what they really want to do is offset our military monopoly, without seeming to be aggressive, at a time when they are weakest."

"Correct. Before Pearl, we pulled their collective butts out of the frying pan when Japan was rolling through Manchuria, enjoying total air superiority against a fledgling Chinese air force. In the summer of '41, we had a secret American fighter group based in China, on the Chinese payroll, to shoot down Japanese bombers, which were the leading element for an all-out invasion of the Chinese mainland. If you'll recall, the Japanese needed China to secure natural resources they didn't have and Roosevelt had already been blockading Japan's trade routes, hoping to starve them out of the Axis Powers supporting Hitler."

McQuaid was nodding again. He remembered hearing about recruiting efforts, for pilots around the fleet who wanted to be part of a covert mercenary force. Thinking back, he realized it had to have been sanctioned and organized at higher levels than they were told.

"Wasn't the 14th Air Force sent over there to protect the Burma Road? I remember the Japanese were trying to pinch off that supply route, to choke off Chinese resistance to their invasion. So, there was an earlier American group over there operating covertly?" Jake nodded.

"Yep. Right up to the attack on Pearl in December. Then the gloves came off, so they just folded that group into the 14th Air Force. They racked up an impressive number of Japanese air kills, saving millions of innocent civilians and won the adoration of the Chinese."

"That's right. I remember now. The 14th Air Force came in later, after Pearl. They nicknamed the original volunteer group the Flying Tigers. Even though the Chinese were grateful to us then, now they're probably worried about a shift in the balance of power in the Pacific surrounding them." Jake gave him a quick thumbs up.

"You've got it now, my boy." But McQuaid was still puzzled.

"How does this all boil down to attacking local pirates, way out in the Mindoro Islands here?" Jake smiled back at him.

"Simple. We've been looking for some justification to squelch these incursions in and around the region, without creating an international incident. This might be perfect. It's close to Clark, so we'd have local air assets to call on, and we'd send a message to China that the U.S. is starting to push back. I need to run this up the channel and see if I can get approval to organize a strike team to back up your rescue efforts. Your job is to be the bait and get a substantial showing of the pirate fleet in one place. If they've got Kiko, we'll get her back, mop up some local hoods, and send word back to the Chinese authorities that our military is beginning to crack down on a growing threat to U.S. interests in the area."

McQuaid was elated and shocked at the same time. He could never have imagined this turn of events. But, he narrowed his eyes back at Jake.

"This operation can't be more important than getting Kiko back safely, Jake. We need to have that understanding up front. Everything else is secondary to me. I'm a patriot as much as you are, but if Kiko gets hurt, this whole thing will be for nothing in my book." Jake responded with a scornful look.

"Gunner, I've always had your wing. That's not going to change. Let me get clearance for this op, but I'll insist you and I create the battle plan. We'll make sure Kiko is back safe in our hands before we move against the pirates. Deal?" He held out his hand.

McQuaid looked him in the eyes, trusting him, but understanding Jake's motivations might sway his best intentions. He didn't have much choice, however. Without his help, he was outmanned and reduced to cannon fodder at a time and place of the pirate's choosing. He reached out and clasped his hand.

"Deal."

Chapter Thirteen
Room 11B, Clark AFB Hospital, the Philippines

Jake had put him up with him in his billet for the night and McQuaid fell into his rack exhausted, fully clothed. The next morning Jake was already gone, so he grabbed a quick shower and a change of clothes out of his away bag. After a cup of coffee in the hospital cafeteria, or mess, as he was more accustomed to calling it, he stopped in to check on Mattie. She was awake, propped up with pillows, and poking at some breakfast on a tray in front her.

She looked up and beamed as soon as she saw him. He had stopped and grabbed some daisies growing near the front sidewalk to the hospital on the way over. The sun was out and cheerful rays of sunlight streamed in from windows outside her room lighting her face. She had been bathed and looked much better than when he saw her last, though he could tell she was still out of it on pain killers.

"Richard!" She held out her hand for him to sit by her, as he moved over to the bed. "I'm so glad to see you!" She probably was happy to see him, but the meds made her more gleeful than she should have been, more like she hadn't seen him in months, rather than just hours. He sat down beside her and handed her the flowers. As women do, she started looking around for something to put them in right away, settling on her water glass. She stuck in the flowers and fluffed them around for effect. McQuaid realized it was the little feminine things she did, that touched him about her.

"You're looking much more chipper this morning, kid," he replied, leaning over and kissing her on the forehead. She looked up at him, feigning amazement.

"Well, I'm still feeling sort of punchy on all the pain killers, but I guess I should plan on getting wounded more often. You've kissed me twice now in less than twenty-four hours." Her face turned impish. "A girl could begin to get ideas." McQuaid gazed back at her unabashed.

"I've missed you," he responded, his tone simple and direct. She squinted back at him.

"I've seen you every day for the last three years, McQuaid. Why is now so special?" He realized he had backed himself into a corner, but squeezed her hand and tried to find the right words.

"Mattie, we've been through a lot over the years. But I never thought I might lose you, so I guess..." He was struggling. She had him on the ropes and knew it.

"...I took you for granted; decided I couldn't live without you; want you to be the mother of my children..." she prompted helpfully and then in spite of herself, burst out laughing. He laughed with her. It felt good and natural to be there kidding around with each other again. He leaned over and kissed her on the lips, being gentle but firm, holding the kiss as she responded, sliding her arm around his neck and pulling him closer. He could feel her breath in his mouth and her fingers caressing his neck, the fresh smell of her hair and skin. Pulling away to look into her eyes, he could see they were glistening and her mouth was trembling.

A wave of emotion broke over him, bringing unexpected clarity to his feelings for her. He realized how close he had been to losing this woman, whom he had come to know with great intimacy over the years in every way but a physical one. He brought her hand up and kissed it, then enfolded it in both of his. She watched him, her expression apprehensive; perhaps fearful of breaking the spell.

"What I meant to say, was, I realize I'll need to take better care of you. I can't run the air cargo business without you and when I'm not flying, delivering cargo all over the islands, you're the first one I look for when I get back. I want to share more of myself with you, not just the business. I..." She didn't let him finish and pulled his face down to hers, nose to nose, gazing into his eyes with a look he had never seen before. She placed her finger against his lips.

"Richard, ever since I first met you, I knew you were a dangerous man for me." She rubbed her nose against his, watching his eyes watch hers, trailing her finger tips down the side of his face. Then she became self-conscious and dropped her eyes. "After Frank was killed, I went into hiding. I buried myself with him, out here, in the middle of nowhere. I didn't expect, or even want anyone else in my life for the longest time – until you came along. I just didn't think we had much of a chance. I knew someone had hurt you and you were hiding too."

She stopped talking, looking back at his face and then down at his hands. He was watching her back. He knew he needed to be patient when a woman was pouring her heart out;

showing herself to be so vulnerable. After a moment of gathering her thoughts, she pressed forward.

"I want to be there for you, as I always have. But, I need more from you. Kiko and I need more from you." Suddenly, her eyes grew wide and she gripped his face, pushing him back, to see his expression. "Oh my God, Richard, where is Kiko?" He sat up straight and heaved a sigh. She watched his face; fearful now. "Did something happen to her? Tell me. I can handle it," she whispered. He drew back a little more, thinking about how to phrase his response.

"She's missing," he replied, knowing the best answer was the most direct one. "Baacay told me when he found you, Kiko was gone. We don't know if she ran and hid, or the pirates took her. We looked everywhere. But I promise you we'll find her." He stated this with intensity. Mattie had put her hand to her mouth. Tears welled up and were falling down her cheeks. He reached over and cupped her face with his hand. "Mattie, we don't know anything yet. I'm working on getting a search party together. If the pirates took her, they will want to use her to bargain for me." Or, kill her to get back at me, he thought, more honest with himself than he wanted to be with Mattie at present. She regained her composure and clutched his hand.

"We've got to find her, Richard. She's just a little girl, who's already been hurt so badly. If the pirates have her, she'll be terrified." She started to lean forward and grunted with pain. Then fell back on her pillows in frustration.

"We'll find her. I promise you that. You'll be fine here. You need to take care of yourself now and get plenty of rest. I'm meeting with some of the military on the base. I think they'll be able to help. As soon as I know more, I'll come back and fill you in on the plan. But right now, all I know is I need to get you well and my airplane repaired. I shouldn't be long though." She was watching him, assessing his words, but then clenched her fists and slammed them on the bed by her side and glared back at him.

"I feel so damned helpless right now! I should be flying back with you. And I need to get back and run the store at some point too." He patted her shoulder and tried to soothe her.

"There'll be plenty of time for all that. Your job right now is to get better. I have to go, but I'll check back in with you later today. I'll speak to your doctors and see how long before you can travel again." Her face softened as she looked into his eyes.

"Thank you. Please hurry back." He squeezed her hand again and stood up to leave. "And Richard?" She bit her lower lip before continuing.

"Yes Mattie?" She seemed to have second thoughts and just shook her head. He nodded. "Okay then. I'll see you later today." He motioned to her breakfast tray. "Eat." She grinned back and he headed out into the hallway and over to the nurses' station. He spotted one of her doctors and walked up to him. The man recognized him and closed the patient folder he was reading to step forward and shake his hand.

"Mister McQuaid? We met at your plane when you dropped off your patient. I'm Doctor Winford."

"Yes, I remember. Thanks for taking care of Mattie for me, Doc. And I was wondering. Do you know how long it might be before she can travel? I'd like to get her back over to Lubang as soon as possible." Winford nodded his head.

"Sure. Well, I would think she might be strong enough to travel in a day or so. We're still watching for signs of infection, but she seems to be doing fine so far. Where are you staying?"

"I'm at the officer's billet and staying with a Major Wilmouth."

"Okay. We'll get word to you as soon as we know more, but you should plan on at least one more day," he replied. "Her stitched wounds will be sore, but she'll need to start moving around anyway. We'll keep her on some medication to help with the pain."

"Thanks, Doc." He shook the man's hand and headed out to make his way over to the maintenance office to speak with Chief Barrows about their progress on the Gooney Bird. It was only a half mile or so over to the hangars and it felt good to get back out in the sunshine.

A couple sleek and muscular looking fighters flew over in loose formation; the distinctive throaty sound of their engines caused a slight pang in his heart, even after a few years away from them. He recognized them as Navy F4U Corsairs – maybe part of Jake Wilmouth's flight, still over from Guam. He stood and watched them turn back toward the field. Flashes of sun glinted off their canopies as they dropped their wheels to land at the far end of the runway.

He missed flying high performance fighters. Flying was flying, but so was driving, until you drove a race car. He wondered if his decision to attack the pirate boat, which had brought everyone nothing but misery so far, was some misplaced, nostalgic attempt to relive his more swashbuckling years as a fighter jock.

Brooding still, he crossed the hangar parking lot and walked through the outside door and then in through another one marked Maintenance. Chief Barrows was sitting behind a battered wooden desk, barrel chested and gruff looking; a dark mat of chest hair growing out the top of a crisp tan day-uniform – just like you'd expect a Master Chief to look. He walked over toward the desk as the chief looked up, then scowled at him out of a dark jowled four o'clock shadow, which couldn't be more than a few hours old.

"You must be the infamous *Gunner* McQuaid," he growled without preamble. "I'm glad you finally wandered over. I've been going over your maintenance records here." McQuaid had a sinking feeling and prepared himself for the worst. He stepped forward and offered his hand.

"Guilty as charged, Chief." Barrows barely looked up and just wrapped a huge paw around his hand. He expected a crushing grip. Instead, the man's hand was comfortably firm, but his palm felt like coarse grain sand paper. The chief raised large wiry and unkempt eyebrows that almost touched the low hairline of his military buzz cut.

"Well McQuaid, we'll have you fixed up in no time and on your way." He smiled back at him like a large bull orangutan might smile – after he noticed you'd just stolen his last banana. But McQuaid was puzzled.

"How's that, Chief? I didn't even get to look at the estimate yet." Barrows just leaned back in his chair, which groaned under the strain and gazed back at him with what might have been uncommon patience; brown goatish eyes almost hidden under the heavy brows.

"You're the fellow that was in here yesterday, trading in a bad fuel pump, aren't you?" he growled again. Then fished a pack of unfiltered Chesterfields out of his pocket. He offered one to McQuaid, who waved it aside with thanks.

"Yep, that was me." Barrows busied himself lighting the cigarette, then looked up at him again, with a too pleasant expression, through an impressive cloud of blue smoke.

"Major Wilmouth's friend right?" It almost seemed like a trick question.

"That's right." Satisfied at last it seemed, Barrows stood up, stubbed out his just-lit cigarette, grabbed his sheaf of papers and strolled out the office door, motioning him to follow. They walked out to the airplane still sitting where he'd left it, but he noticed a shiny new engine on a wooden stand under the wing and two mechanics working on pulling the old one. He also noticed another maintenance ladder beside the cockpit and new glass installed in the co-pilot's window. The chief waved a paw at the airplane and began reeling off what they'd done to it so far. McQuaid was amazed.

"Chief, I don't mean to sound anything but grateful, but how the heck did all this get done so fast and without so much as a signature from me?" Barrows stopped in his tracks and fixed McQuaid with a withering glare. Master Chiefs have perfected this paint-blistering look over the many years; doubtless beginning when the rank was first created.

"Son, I've got orders to get this airplane back in the green by the end of today and military aircraft up my ass, waiting to get into maintenance. How you plan on paying for it isn't really my problem. Now unless you think you need to sign something, we're going to just continue on until we're done – as ordered."

"Can I ask by whose orders, Chief Barrows?" He could feel his temperature rising. Even an ex-Captain deserved some consideration. Barrows glowered at him and pressed his lips together again, before answering.

"Of course you can, Mister McQuaid," he replied in a slow, tight cadence, like he was ordering a firing squad to take aim. "These orders came down directly from Wing Commander Macy. I think you might want to quiz your friend, Major Wilmouth, if you have any further questions." He raised his eyebrows all the way to his dark salt and pepper hairline, but his mouth remained a thin straight line. McQuaid didn't need to be hit over the head with the hint. Nevertheless, he tried to keep things amicable. A Master Chief was a force to be reckoned with, either for, or against you. "For", was always the smarter option.

"Thanks, Chief. I'm sure everything's in order. I want you to know I really appreciate all this, even though I still don't know what I did to deserve it." Barrows just looked back at him expressionless.

"That's makes two of us son." He shook his head, turned on his heel and walked back to the lair of his office without so much as a glance back.

Later that day, McQuaid was walking back toward the hospital after a late lunch alone. A Military Police jeep pulled to the curb ahead of him and Jake Wilmouth hopped out, with a quick salute to the enlisted at the wheel. He matched stride with McQuaid and handed him a small manila envelope.

"What's this, Jake?" He unwound the thread clasp and pulled out what looked like a maintenance invoice for repairs to his airplane. Jake kept pace with him, waiting for him to finish reading. As he got to the bottom tally, he stopped in his tracks with a sudden knot in his stomach. The bill added up to more than he had made on all his cargo hops in the last eight months. He groaned and looked up at the sky. Whereupon, Jake just reached over and pointed at one of the check boxes near the bottom. McQuaid looked at where his finger was and did a double-take. It was marked: Paid in Full. He looked over at Jake, not comprehending what he was looking at.

"You paid for this?" Jake frowned back at him; clearly pained.

"No you idiot. Does that look like the kind of money I could ever lay my hands on?" He pointed to the checked box again and tapped his finger on the signature and title below a line marked: Authorization. He recognized the name Jonathan Macy, Colonel. McQuaid looked back up at Jake in wonder, who, by now was grinning back at him like a fool.

"The US Air Force paid my bill? How'd you pull this one off, 'Marine' Major Wilmouth?" he asked, with emphasis on "Marine". Looking at his friend, who was doing everything he could to look chaste and innocent as a choirboy, he realized there was much about Jake Wilmouth he still didn't know. The man seemed to have gained tremendous clout, since the last time they flew together. "Did you marry his sister when I wasn't looking, Snake?" Wilmouth just guffawed and motioned for him to keep walking. He looked around to see if anyone was in earshot. It seemed to be a new found habit of his.

"I spent most of the morning in Macy's office, outlining the situation we discussed. He liked the general plan, got on the phone with the base commander and briefed him while I was still sitting there. I also recommended they pay for your repairs, since naturally, you were going to need your plane to carry out the mission."

"Naturally." He looked down at the five figure number in the total column again and then back at him; incredulous. "Jake, who the hell are you?" They began walking again, McQuaid just continuing to shake his head in amazement.

"Yeah, there's that. I figured you'd need to know a little about my operation here, but all I can tell you is, I'm working with Navy Intelligence on special detachment concerning the matter we discussed last night over dinner." He smirked and held his arms out, as if to embrace McQuaid. "Quite aside from the fact that you're the closest thing I have to a brother and if I was a woman, I'd probably already have thrown myself at you, in tribute to your godlike physique and..." McQuaid punched him in the shoulder.

"Knock it off and answer me straight, will you for once?" Jake shrugged and began again in a more sober tone.

"Here's the scoop in a nutshell, chum. Your problem actually came at the right time for what we see as the need for a series of shots fired across the bow of the Chinese, so to speak. Navy Intel is continuing to see unusual activity and new military incursions into our theater of ops around the China Sea. The Chinese are maintaining their ignorance, so diplomacy isn't working and Intel thinks it's time we get proactive. The fact that this involves a local civilian rescue of a child, which the military can claim was the reason for moving against the pirates in Philippine waters, not to mention the fact they've already killed two other British civilians in their previous drug running incident, begs for a reasonable response. This will be a measured military interdiction against these dangerous criminals, at the request of local Philippine government officials."

"Did local Philippine government officials actually make this request?" McQuaid was beginning to wonder if there was anything Jake couldn't pull off at this point.

"Yes, in a manner of speaking," he replied with cryptic persuasion. McQuaid wasn't so sure he wanted to know the details about that.

"And they understand this is a rescue of a child, first and foremost?" he asked instead.

"Absolutely. And that's why you're going to help me formulate the plan to get her to safety first, so we can move against the pirates without putting her at risk. What we need to find out is, are they in fact holding her prisoner? If so, where they're holding her and then we finalize a plan to rescue her." They had both stopped walking now and McQuaid was standing with hands on hips, now more concerned than ever before. This was beginning to sound like a major operation. He knew from experience, the more complex something was, the more uncertain the outcome. But Jake was continuing to explain. "Once we're sure she's safe, we execute the second part of the plan, which is to spank the pirates hard and make sure they run home to Momma squealing about how we're ruining all their fun. We have some suspects, but we need to know who Momma is, back in China, so we want to make sure to follow the message back to the source." McQuaid started walking again and was thinking about that. Jake noticed he had gone quiet. "What's the matter, Gunner?"

"I think I might know who Momma is and this could be a lot bigger than you think, Snake. Ever heard of Madam Chin?" Jake shook his head. "She runs the Flower Boat business back in Hong Kong." Jake looked pensive and commented back, after giving that a few moments thought.

"We know prostitution drives the demand for young girls, who are enslaved to the business and they depend on drug money to buy off police and politicians – even the British. Do you know this Madam Chin?"

"Not at all. But I've heard she might be at the root of the pirate run drug smuggling business throughout the islands here. It's a hell of a business angle if you think about it. She's already cornered the market on prostitution along Hong Kong harbor. And she may also rule a sizable drug cartel; quite possibly through an old pirate network handed down through the years from her great grandmother, who in the mid 1700's was the most powerful woman pirate in Chinese history." It was Jake's turn to be amazed. McQuaid continued. "Only now, instead of pillaging booty on the high seas, they traffic drugs and women slaves back and forth between mainland China and the islands in and around the China Sea." Jake had stopped and was staring at him now.

"That sounds like the old opium trade routes, Gunner. Ironically, back then it used to be the British who were the drug dealers, trading opium to China in return for tea; both highly prized commodities of the old British East India Company. But when China outlawed the sale of opium, confiscating tons of the drugs at the docks and even tossing merchants in prison, there was hell to pay. The short version of that story resulted in the Opium Wars between Britain and China in the 1800's, where the Chinese were soundly defeated and had to make huge land and trade concessions to the British Crown. They were humiliated and abused by the British Empire for over a hundred years."

"That's right! That's how the British got Hong Kong," McQuaid responded. They were both staring at each other in sudden revelation. "The pieces are beginning to fall into place here. Seems like they might still have an old score to settle with us Westerners; particularly our British allies. It strikes me as a fitting bit of Chinese revenge, to secretly profit from a drug and prostitution cartel, using a former centuries old pirate ring to do their bidding – right under the noses of the British Magistrate of Hong Kong. And use it as a shrewd lever against the US power base in the Philippines to boot." Jake was shaking his head at this crafty bit of subterfuge.

"Clever bastards. I'll pass this along through our network to the British in Hong Kong, who undoubtedly know a lot more about their China history than we do. They can probably bring some pressure to bear at that end too. What was the older pirate woman's name again, Gunner?"

"I think it was Ching Shih. Mattie knows all about her. I guess everyone in this part of the world knows about her. They called her Madam Ching, in Canton, where I guess she came from originally. At the peak of her reign, she had almost 2000 ships under her command and near 80,000 men." Jake whistled, staring at him. "The Chinese and Portuguese, even the British couldn't defeat her, so they struck this deal. She got to retire with all her spoils, if she promised to disband her fleet and never to return to pirating again."

"Maybe she didn't really get out, Gunner." McQuaid shook his head.

"No, she got out alright. It seems she died a very wealthy and proper woman in the mid 1800's. But she had a son, who later had a daughter. She would be in her sixties right about now. Madam Chin, running the pleasure boat business in Hong Kong, might be the granddaughter, or even great granddaughter. And Ching Shih began her career as a prostitute on the Canton Flower Boats."

"Sounds like the old girl figured out a cunning way to pass along her legacy. We need to find out a lot more about this Madam Chin." He pulled a pencil out of his pocket and scribbled some notes on the back of McQuaid's maintenance bill. "I need to get this down. Colonel Macy's not going to believe it."

"Okay, but Jake, we don't have any time to lose here. I've got to get back to Lubang and out to see Chief Mahutra."

"Who's Chief Mahutra?"

"Juan Salas Mahutra is the chief of the village of Looc, down by Golo Island, near the southern end of Lubang Island. That's where I was when the pirates attacked Mattie. By the way, Chief Mahutra used to work with Navy intelligence, spying on Japanese ship movements during the war. His claim to fame was spotting the heavy Japanese task force coming around Mindoro Island, leading up to the Battle of Leyte Gulf."

"One of the largest naval battles in the Pacific. I remember. We were tipped off to Admiral Kurita's battle group trying to sneak in the back door, to divert Admiral Halsey's naval support away from General MacArthur's invasion of Leyte Island. The Japs knew if they failed to avert the loss of Leyte, the Philippines would be lost, cutting off their last remaining supply routes. They would lose the war. Somebody alerted the allies Kurita was making a break through the Mindoro Strait and they had submarines waiting to meet them. They decimated his task force and turned the tide for the allies. That was your guy Mahutra?

"That was him."

"You've got some heavy weights in your corner too, Gunner – impressive!"

"Yep and he's still got the best intelligence network around the Mindoro Islands. Based on what he's already told me, we think the pirates may have a base somewhere along the Mamburao River, on Mindoro Island. He can help us snoop out their defenses; also, if and where they've taken Kiko. Then we'll know what we're up against. I'm glad you got them working on my airplane right away, Snake. I'll need it."

"What about Mattie?"

"She's safer here and besides, she needs continued hospital care for a day or two more at the least. I'm on my way over to see her now." Jake brightened up at this last.

"Well, lead on Macduff," he said doffing his hat. "I'd love to meet the little woman whom I suspect is likely the better business half of McQuaid Air Cargo." McQuaid looked pained; then smiled back at him.

"Actually, she's a little more important to me than that." He cocked a knowing eyebrow at his friend.

"What? Have you been holding back on me, old son? Now I'm really intrigued. C'mon, Gunner me boy. I want to get acquainted with the woman who could bring down the great Perseus, melting his heart, if not his golden wings." He moved ahead of McQuaid, skipping backwards and tapping his chest with a silly grin on his face."

They arrived at the hospital a few minutes later and were waved on in by one of the nurses. McQuaid walked in first, with Jake in close trail position. Mattie looked like she was asleep, so they pulled up short and began padding back out, as quiet as possible, when her eyes fluttered and she looked over at him. Her mouth turned up in a groggy, but cheerful smile.

"Hello, Richard. I was just having the most wonderful, narcotics induced dream." She noticed Jake skulking about behind him, his cap in hand, looking like he was dying for an introduction.

"Who's your friend there," she asked, blushing, as she realized she wasn't looking her best for guest visits. Now she was wide awake and brushed her hair back from her eyes, appearing self-conscious. "I'm sorry, I must look a mess," she said, as she tried pulling herself to a sitting position. McQuaid moved over to hold her down.

"At ease there, kid. No need to get too formal with my old wingman here." Jake stepped forward and reached down to grasp her hand.

"Jake, meet Mattie Adams. Mattie, meet Major Jake Wilmouth." They both exchanged pleasantries.

"I had no idea Richard had such handsome friends," she replied. Jake grinned and gave her a quick wink. "Did he bring you over here to check me out?" McQuaid frowned down at her.

"Actually mam, I insisted he bring me over to meet you." He gave her a warm smile; then turned to cast a wicked look at McQuaid, making him nervous about what his old wingman might come out with next. "I figured anyone this one falls for must be special. You know, back in the squadron during the war, his incredibly poor luck with women was legendary. But you'd be hard pressed to find a better man to hang your future on." McQuaid was stunned at the praise. Mattie just smiled back at him and squeezed his hand.

"Thank you, Major Wilmouth. You say you think he's...'fallen' for me?" Her eyebrows raised up at him, suggesting some obscure misstep. "So, you two have been talking about me behind my back I take it?" Wilmouth's smile froze and his face turned bright pink. By his expression, it was obvious he was thinking: *could it be the big lug hadn't actually said anything to her yet?* He started to stammer, but Mattie took pity on him, patting his hand and grinned back at him. "Fear not, Major Wilmouth, our secret is safe." She laughed and he laughed back with her, nervous and not quite sure still if he'd stepped in it or not. McQuaid moved in to rescue him.

"He's not really in the know yet, Mattie. I just mentioned to him today that I was growing very fond of you, quite aside from..."

"Fond?" Mattie's face was now a study in practiced innocence. "Is that like, man-speak for, buddies?" McQuaid shot her a hard look. "Richard, I fear we're putting your friend on the spot here. But I appreciate you sharing that you are "fond" of me, as of course, I too am quite fond of you." She shifted her gaze back to Jake, who looked like he could use a parachute. "Major, I hate to change the subject on you when we were already having such a gripping conversation, but, there is actually one thing you can help me with. Do you have any news about Kiko? Richard and I are her guardians and he told me he is working with the military to try to get a rescue party together. We think she's been kidnapped by the same pirates who tried to kill me." Jake pounced on this opportunity to get his foot out of his mouth and looked relieved to return to a subject he felt more qualified to address.

"Yes mam. In fact we are working out a very comprehensive search and rescue plan with higher command here at Clark Air Base. The pirates have killed two other people, severely wounded you and are possibly holding Kiko, your ward, but she's also a young native island child. The US military is always sensitive to helping the locals near our air bases. We're not positive, but it's possible they've taken her. The military will be assisting the Philippine authorities in this effort, but I can assure you, everyone is taking this very seriously and we'll do everything we can to return her safely."

"Thank you Major. We appreciate your help." She felt the need for a little levity and so looked past him to McQuaid. "Well Richard, even though he's the only friend of yours I've ever met, I approve." Jake turned to look at him too and gave him a thumbs-up with a silly grin.

"What'd I tell you, Gunner?" He reached over and squeezed Mattie's arm, giving her a wink and a dazzling Jake Wilmouth patented lady-killer smile.

"A lot of things – and a few I wish I hadn't told you. Which question are you referring to?" Wilmouth looked hurt.

"I told you she'd go for me, didn't I?" he asked brightly. Mattie slapped him on the arm and laughed.

"We didn't cover that one this time, Snake." He sighed at Mattie. "But for the record, women pretty much all do. He's widely hated for that by the way." Mattie patted him on the arm again and smiled at both of them, her eyes twinkling.

"Snake?" she inquired, looking bemused at Jake. "I presume that's some sort of goofy, male bonding term of endearment?"

"Just a radio call sign we used in the military, mam. Like Gunner here. Old habits die hard. And, speaking of his old habits..."

McQuaid grabbed Jake's arm and began steering him toward the door.

"Well, Major Wilmouth was just leaving, so say good-bye Mattie."

"Bye, Snake." She laughed, as he waggled his fingers back at her and blew her a kiss.

"Be right back," McQuaid tossed her way, as he was helping Jake disappear out the door. They walked down the hall to the mess together. "We've got a lot of work to do Snake. What do you need from me to get this plan formalized? I still have to get back to Lubang and find out where they might be holding Kiko. Of course, there's always the possibility she's reappeared after hiding out somewhere and the whole rescue thing becomes moot. Then what?" They had arrived at the coffee urns and he grabbed a fresh mug off the rack, handing another one over to Jake.

"What we need, is to flesh out the operation along with any contingencies, like for instance, that Kiko isn't a hostage. However, that still leaves you as the man the pirates especially want to meet." He grinned back at him/ McQuaid slapped the cup into his open palm.

"So, in any case, I'll need to be the tip of the spear." Jake had moved around him and began pouring coffee into his mug. He nodded and then waved him to one of the open tables, looking around first to select one without anyone near enough to eavesdrop. They sprawled in their chairs and Jake took a quick slurp of coffee before answering.

"You're the only one that can smoke them out, Gunner. They really want a piece of your hide buddy." He watched him over the rim of his cup. McQuaid, gazed back at him, weighing the implications. Jake pressed on. "So, I say we rough out our plan here, double check it for weak spots and then get in to see Macy as soon as possible. Once that's done, you need to hightail it back to Lubang and figure out the scoop on Kiko. If she's there, we switch to our alternate plan. If not, you get with your contact Chief Mahutra and reconnoiter where they're holding her and then figure out a way to get them to trade her back." McQuaid was nodding. "The key here is to get a sizable group of them out in the open, so I can lead an attack to put some serious hurt on them." He offered a mirthless smile. "I know that sounds too simple, but it's a start to a plan, right?"

McQuaid stared out the windows of the mess at the bustling airfield beyond, thinking of the hundreds of ways their plan could go wrong. Jake waited, stirring some sugar into his coffee to bide his time. Finally, McQuaid turned back to him with a look of determined resolve.

"Alright then. Let's get started. I'll let Mattie know the score and be right back so we can get to work." He stood to leave, noticing Jake smiling up at him. He stopped, raising an eyebrow back at Jake. "What?"

"I like her Gunner. She's a real trooper," he said. He was being sincere. "Tell her we'll get Kiko back."

"Thanks Snake. That means a lot. See you in a few then."

Chapter Fourteen
Aircraft Maintenance Hangar, Clark AFB, the Philippines

Later, after many cups of coffee, sandwiches and sheaves of papers, Jake slapped his pencil down and sat back in his chair. McQuaid was still laboring over their scribbling, circles, lines and arrows, racking his brain to see if they'd missed anything.

"This should work, Gunner. What do you think?" After a few more seconds, McQuaid tore his eyes from the pages and looked up at Jake. He nodded his head and laid his pencil down as well. "Okay. I'll get this typed up and over to Macy for preliminary approval." McQuaid looked skeptical.

"Think he'll buy it?" Jake leaned his chair way back and stretched his arms over his shoulders to scratch the back of his head with both hands. He regarded the ceiling tiles for a spell while he gave the question full consideration. After a moment or two, he rocked his chair forward again and stabbed their pile of papers with his index finger.

"What makes this work for us is timing. The top brass are already looking for solutions to security threats in the area without diplomatic complications. The fact that we can paint this as a combat training exercise, which results in a co-incidental humanitarian rescue of a local island child from real bad-guys, along with the broader strategic value and all with minimal asset and diplomatic risk to the U.S. military makes it a winner." He pulled a sheet out of the stack and tapped one of the paragraph headings.

"See this? The Operational Objective is twofold: "Aggressor training and close combat support, in a joint exercise with the Philippine Navy". If we do it right, we minimize risk on our side, get you and Kiko back, if she's a hostage and score a strategic win against an advancing Chinese backed insurgency around the Philippines." He sat back again. "Ultimately, we're being the good neighbor, helping the Philippine government with local security training they sorely need, while reaffirming enforcement of the neutral zone around our military bases in the region." He gave McQuaid a ruthless grin. "Can you imagine the looks on their sorry faces when they think they've suckered you in for the kill, making you walk the plank, or whatever pirates do to the poor bastards who royally piss them off and then suddenly, they realize they're surrounded by a massive military task force from both air and sea?" He was standing now, grinning like a loon and waving his arms around in his excitement. McQuaid was less thrilled.

"Lucky me, huh? But I have to hand it to you, Jake. I can't think of any other way to leverage that kind of firepower. It's brilliant. Now, go sell it to the old man and let me know, if he bites, so I can start setting up a timetable from Lubang. Meanwhile, I've got an airplane to check on."

They shoved off in different directions. Jake headed for operations and McQuaid steered toward the maintenance hangars. He checked his watch and cocked an eye at the sun. It was early afternoon and any trace of the storm from the day before had cleared out. The air was hot and muggy, but clear and refreshed by the rain, with a light, but welcome breeze on his face. It was a gorgeous day to fly – assuming of course everything checked out from maintenance. He was still amazed Jake had gotten his repairs paid for. If it weren't for the uncertainty over Kiko, he would have been elated.

He found Master Chief Barrows out in the hangar conferring with one of his mechanics. The Gooney Bird wasn't anywhere in sight, so he headed over his way. Barrows spotted McQuaid walking toward him and strolled over to meet him halfway. He pulled a well-worn, unlit corn cob pipe out of his mouth in order to speak with him. It appeared he saved his cigarettes for inside the office, or outside the hangar. Open flames were forbidden anywhere around aircraft.

"Mister McQuaid, I was just about to send someone over to the hospital to let you know your airplane is ready and sitting out on the apron." He waved his pipe stem toward the hangar doors. His voice seemed less gravelly than usual. "I suggest you fly it around the base a few times and test everything out before you head back home."

"Thanks, Chief. I'll do that." He did indeed seem less gruff and if McQuaid didn't know better, he'd have thought he was a kinder version of himself compared to the day before. Barrows glanced down at his clipboard to read some items off to him.

"We pulled a couple cylinders on the left engine, just to make sure there wasn't any evidence of overheating and everything looks good." He paused and squinted back at McQuaid. "How's your lady friend?" he asked sticking his pipe back in his mouth, his eyes appraising him. McQuaid smiled back.

"She's looking better already, Chief. Thank you." Barrows just nodded his head. There seemed to be something else on his mind. He consulted his clipboard, flipped the papers up and down a couple times and then pulled his pipe out of his mouth again.

"I got the lowdown on you from operations this morning, McQuaid. Ex-Marine fighter pilot, fought in several battles off the coast of Luzon here," he continued, his voice solemn, waving his pipe stem toward the north end of the island. His eyes became distant. "We came ashore with the Army Rangers and fought our way inland; all the way to Manila. Lost a lot of good men, but we rescued the American survivors of the march to Balanga." He paused and watched one of his mechanics pull the cowling off an airplane at the other end of the hangar.

"The Bataan death march survivors? You were here?" McQuaid was impressed.

"Yeah," he replied, his voice growing husky. "The Army Rangers surprised the Japs at Camp Cabanatuan, before they could execute 'em. That was the first POW camp we liberated. They had to know we were coming and we only hoped we could get to them before the bastards started killing off the only witnesses to their bloody war crimes." He spat these last few words out, as if they were bile on his tongue. McQuaid remained silent and let him talk. He had heard the stories, of course, but this man had been there; on the ground. Barrows continued.

"The Rangers attacked the camp at night, surprising the Japs before they knew what hit 'em. We were backing them up and got there right after." He gave McQuaid a sharp look, as if he expected him to tell him to stop. But he just motioned him to continue, sensing the chief needed to tell this story. Barrows tucked his clipboard under his arm, pulled out a pocket knife and seemed intent on scraping around inside the bowl of his pipe.

"The place stunk like shit, blood and rotting corpses. It was god damned awful. But I'll never forget their faces. Some of them couldn't walk and crawled up to us, hugging our legs, McQuaid. They had been proud American soldiers – like you and me. God knows the hell they'd been through, just to survive until we got there. I laid my rifle down and held a couple of them like children, while they bawled their eyes out." Tears welled up in the grizzled chief's eyes. "We found out later the Japs had told them they were planning to line them up and shoot them all the next day. Those men thought it was their last night to live. Instead, we got 'em all back." He wiped his eyes unashamed. "From there we marched to Camp O'Donnell, just up the road from here and then on to San Fernando. It was much the same at all the camps." He looked down at his clipboard again, not really seeing it and then back up to McQuaid's face. "Anyway, I heard you were one of the Marine pilots who provided air support for us, especially once we got to Manila. We sure appreciated you guys clearing the way for us." McQuaid nodded his head.

"It wasn't so bad for us at Manila, Chief. We had air superiority by then. The tough part was taking this air base back from the Japanese air force. We lost a few of our own here." Barrows nodded, sharing a moment of commiseration with him.

"Well, I heard what you did for that woman from Lubang. That was plenty scrappy of you, flying through that storm to get her to the hospital here and all." He knocked his pipe out on his hand and pocketed the scrapings, folded his pocket knife and rubbed the back of his neck, looking around to see if anyone was within earshot. "Anyway McQuaid, I just wanted to apologize for being kinda rough on you yesterday."

"Forget it, Chief. Thanks for fixing my airplane." Barrows just touched the stem of his pipe to his forehead in a mock salute and turned to walk back to his office, waving his arm back at him.

"Just get that damned thing off my apron as soon as you can, McQuaid. I've got important military aircraft to maintain around here you know." The gravel was back in his voice again. McQuaid smiled to himself, watching him go.

He walked out to the Gooney Bird, glad to see her sitting there basking in the warm afternoon sun. He finished his pre-flight, making sure they'd topped off oil and fuel. After starting up, the tower cleared him taxi to the active runway for a few turns around the flight pattern and some landings. The test flight was to make sure there weren't any lurking problems after such extensive maintenance. The airplane's performance was flawless and the starboard engine hummed along in harmony with its twin. He reminded himself to go easy on the new engine to break it in.

He climbed to five thousand feet and did some slow turns with the windows open to feel the warm fresh air blowing into the cockpit. The view was awe inspiring after the cleansing rain. A cloudless panorama of bright green hills met the speckled sunlit ocean in the distance and then joined with the endless cobalt blue sky. It seemed he was all alone, high above, admiring the simple beauty of this land which had once been the scene of such violence and atrocity toward fellow human beings.

He thought about Chief Barrow's war experiences here; the tens of thousands of American soldiers lost, their blood soaked into the land and beaches of these islands, so far from their homes and families. And the massacre of hundreds of thousands of innocent Filipino civilians during the last desperate days of the Japanese occupation of Manila. The Japanese had lost three times as many men as the allies. It was almost too horrible to imagine. He remembered the fresh young faces of the boys he had flown with – just becoming men – who never saw their homes, or their loved ones again. He heaved a deep sigh, thinking about that last day when he watched his best friend, Jerry Alder, desperately trying to escape from his dying fighter plane as it tumbled toward the sea. So senseless and cruel are we humans, he thought, shaking his head in sadness. If there was a God, he could only hope he would forgive the survivors of their terrible sins against each other and help them heal their deeper wounds; forever buried with their memories.

He pulled his thoughts back inside the cockpit and back to the present. The controls under his hands felt firm, with all the normal vibrations, telling him his airplane was alive and well again. Looking down at his panel gauges, he could see deep into the body and heart of the Gooney Bird. She was ready and so was he, for yet another battle that lay ahead of them.

Chapter Fifteen
Air Wing Operations, Clark AFB, the Philippines

He was tying down later, when Jake pulled up in one of the flight line jeeps. His hand was draped over the steering wheel, with one leg hanging out. McQuaid noted he was wearing a fresh pressed Khaki uniform and spit-polished, black "low quarter" dress shoes. The oak leaf insignia on his collar and the silver wings over his left breast pocket reflected the sun above his "fruit salad", or rows of bright colored citation ribbons. He wore dark green aviator sunglasses, but his tanned face was split with a wide grin. He raised two fingers off the wheel to greet McQuaid as he walked over to hop in.

"A magnificent day to be an aviator, eh Gunner? How's she flying?"

"They took good care of her here, Snake. They even puttied over and repainted the gouges on the fuselage. I can't tell you how much I appreciate you doing all this for me." Jake just smiled back at him, shoving the jeep in gear and wheeling about to head off the flight line.

"You can buy me a beer later, Kemosabe. Right now we've got a meeting with Wing Commander Macy. He wants to look you in the eye and see if you have the stones to pull off this little stunt without getting me killed, or more importantly, embarrassing him and the entire 13th Air Force." He looked over at McQuaid, his eyes hidden behind his sunglasses, but his mouth was turned up in a lopsided smirk. "No pressure right?" He laughed at McQuaid's look of dismay and turned his attention back to the flight line gate in time to snap off a crisp salute to the gate guard as they passed through.

Wing Operations was housed in the base administrative building, with typical institutional pea green painted walls and dark mirrored linoleum floors that smelled of over waxing. It was close enough to the flight line for convenience, but far enough away for desk-job types to engage in normal conversations, without having to yell over the roar of high performance aircraft. Most of the important administrative staff, though, were pilots, many still active and as a group, accustomed to a more relaxed practice of military formalities.

McQuaid was used to stodgier Navy and Marine air operations and protocols compared to this newly minted, US

Air Force. Every branch of the military had a feel to it. But this group seemed very different. Even though comprised of former members of Army aviation, prior to forming the USAF in 1947, there was a definite sense of re-genesis to the place. Everything looked and smelled military, but it all seemed somehow fresher.

Previously, the Navy, Marines and Army all had individual air groups, whose missions were for direct support of Marine invasions and/or Army infantry on the ground. However, as long range strategic bombing proved itself in the overall military arsenal, it was determined that a separate, all independent air service branch was needed; not just for the bombers and their crews, but also for air defense of those bombers.

In essence then, the new Air Force was comprised of bomber wings, cargo and personnel transport planes and their own fighter aircraft support groups. They could be called upon to back up select ground operations and often were, but their primary mission was to take the fight to the enemy; well in advance of committing any ground troops. An all-air fighting force, both offensive and defensive aircraft, dedicated in support of each other, was a new military concept. However, it proved devastating in practice when a short air campaign resulted in atomic bombs obliterating Hiroshima and Nagasaki; forcing Japan's surrender within days of those attacks.

The new Air Force was intended to act as a strategic deterrent to war, while protecting U.S. interests anywhere on the globe. The implication to future challengers of U.S. military superiority was hardly a subtle one however, given this big-stick of atomic weapons. With this backdrop, it should have come as no surprise to McQuaid the new air force was created by independent thinkers, savvy in congressional trench warfare for budget appropriation; experts at wrestling dollars away from the tight fists of their more conventional counterparts. They were brash and determined to lead the pack in military hierarchy, taking on the toughest missions and creating an aura of supremacy around those who fought from the sky, over those who battled on the ground.

Wing Commander Macy's office was on the main floor of the building and guarded by his aide, a 2nd Lieutenant Winter, who sat outside in an adjoining office. He looked up from a typewriter he was clacking away on, as Major

Wilmouth walked into the outer office door and approached his desk. He stood and snapped a perfect salute, which was returned by Wilmouth; though not quite as snappy in a subtle display of the status of higher rank.

"May I help you sir?" he asked, his eyes cool; sizing up the two of them in a practiced manner, which was courteous, but implied he was empowered by the Colonel to fend off anything that wasn't official and already on his calendar. Jake knew the drill.

"Major Wilmouth and Mister Richard McQuaid, head of McQuaid Air Cargo, here at the request of Colonel Macy."

Lieutenant Matthew Winter had been expecting them of course, but nonetheless looked down to confer with his day planner and confirm they were indeed legitimate, standing on ceremony, which led McQuaid to assume he hadn't worked for the Colonel long enough to become comfortable in his position. He found their names however and waved them over to a couple office chairs, while he buzzed his boss to let him know they had arrived.

After a brief pause, the man was stunned to see Macy open his office door and walk out to greet them in person. McQuaid was also impressed and more than a little puzzled. This would have never happened in the Marine Corps chain of command. Macy was a full "bird" Colonel; damn near royalty, but it seemed he felt the need to greet them both in an uncharacteristic and informal fashion. Wilmouth didn't seem surprised and offered a routine salute to his superior, which Macy returned, almost as a casual afterthought and then reached out to shake his hand.

He was a good looking man, about even height with McQuaid, thin and broad shouldered, with dark eyes and hair and graying only somewhat at the temples. His tailored tan "daily" uniform was immaculate, with knife edged creases and a silver eagle on the collar. Silver wings were pinned over the left breast pocket; which was further emblazoned with rows of brightly colored combat ribbons. McQuaid was impressed. If ever there was a stereo type for a wing commander, Macy looked every bit the ringer.

"Hello again, Major," he said to Wilmouth and waved him past to hold out his hand to McQuaid. "Mister McQuaid, I presume?" His manner was brisk, but without any sense of pomp. "Major Wilmouth has told me some fascinating stories about you." He raised an eyebrow, as if to suggest a few might have even been north of "fascinating". McQuaid resisted the urge to look to Wilmouth for clues. Instead, he stepped forward and returned the Colonel's handshake.

"Nice to meet you Colonel Macy. I trust I'll be able to back up any elaborate claims the Major may have made to you thus far." The Colonel chuckled and flicked a look in Wilmouth's direction, suggesting he had indeed shared a colorful story or two at McQuaid's expense.

"Well, I especially wanted to commend you for your brilliant amphibious air assault on some of our more nefarious local criminals. I'm dying for some details on that maneuver." He winked. McQuaid's grin froze in place. He was hoping to save that story for much later, but he supposed Jake needed to let Macy in on why the pirates had taken a special interest in him. Macy grew more serious. "It was a deplorable display of their emboldened operations in our local waters. Such a brazen attack, killing those people in cold blood, leads me to believe they weren't expecting any consequences from law enforcement. It's only a shame you didn't arrive on the scene a little sooner." He waved them to a couple chairs at a small round conference table, closing the door behind them.

He flipped open a silver embossed cigarette box, offering them smokes, which the two men refused. Macy didn't smoke either, so he put the box away and grabbed some glasses and a bottle of scotch off the bar area next to them; another privilege of rank.

"Drink?" he asked, splashing a liberal dose into each of their glasses; assuming "yes". He began again, once they were settled around the table. "Major Wilmouth reported that your attack on the pirates and killing a couple of them, may have created a few more problems for you than you were prepared for. Do you mind talking me through your situation?" He took a drink of his scotch, watching McQuaid over the rim of his glass. McQuaid gauged his response. A concise synopsis is what he'd be looking for. He glanced down at his glass, turning it around on the table with his fingers, while he pondered the right words. Then looked back up at Macy and began an unemotional, military style operational debrief.

"Right. So, a small group of pirates attacked a foundering private yacht out of Hong Kong, twenty-five miles offshore of Lubang Island, which had been radioing for emergency assistance. They were taking on water and both engines had failed. The Lubang police chief picked up the call and asked me for assistance. I was en route; flying him out there, when we learned pirates were attacking them. We spotted the yacht from the air and determined the pirates had a deck mounted, .30 caliber machine gun and had already wounded, or killed two people already; one down on the deck and the other floating nearby in the water. There was a young girl hanging onto a line in the water, we believed was still in danger, so I instructed Captain Nguyen to help me use a couple of Thompson submachine guns I keep on board my aircraft, to shoot back at the pirates during a couple low passes. We were able to scare them off, killing a couple of them in the process. We rescued the girl and later discovered she had been a party to loading the yacht with some packages of drugs, unbeknownst to the owners, which the pirates managed to get away with. The police chief took her into custody." McQuaid paused for effect at this point in the story.

Macy appeared spellbound, as did Wilmouth, though he had already heard this story once before. Macy set his glass down before responding.

"And you have some evidence there is a connection between Hong Kong and the pirates running drugs in and around these islands?" McQuaid had expected the question.

"The young woman locked up in the hoosegow in Lubang City told me she works for a Madam Chin in Hong Kong. She's the supply end of the drug smuggling operation. She was supposed to make her connection at the harbor in Manila and the people she was meeting were local pirates. I'm not sure if they're part of the same group we shot up raiding the yacht. But I believe it's probable." Macy nodded.

"These pirates came back later looking for you and shot your partner in your business and took a child hostage; your ward I believe?"

"That's right. Mattie Adams is still over at the base hospital recovering from her wounds. Kiko is an adopted Filipino island girl, about nine years old. Her parents were killed by the Japanese, so Ms. Adams and I became her guardians. She's missing now and we presume she was kidnapped by the pirates."

"And you believe they'll use her to get to you?"

"I do. Apparently, one of the pirates we killed was the brother of the leader of this pirate band. I was told there's a price on my head now." Macy nodded his head again, seeming to be deliberating on a number of other questions. He looked over at Wilmouth.

"And you think this pirate band is part of a bigger operation in the Philippines, Major?"

"Yes sir. As you know, the recently created Central Intelligence Agency has been accumulating reports in the Indo-China theater of operations, which reveal an extended Chinese network of operatives are acting as insurgents in and around the China Sea. Their mission appears to be to capitalize on the gap in hostilities in the region, to enable drug and slave smuggling cartels for a share of the profits, as well as to create an appearance of lawlessness they will be forced to police. It's meant to be a ruse; managing regional instability and criminal activity to substantiate the need for escalating a military buildup. In this way they could pose a threat to U.S. operations around China, without appearing to be hostile. It's quite clever when you think about it. Diplomatically they're covered and we would appear weak, or even imperialistic if we push back. After all, the Chinese were our allies during the war." Macy rubbed his chin and leaned toward McQuaid.

"It seems we should be better neighbors, gentlemen. The Philippine government has already asked for our help. Perhaps the Chinese government would also appreciate our taking some initiative in reducing some of this criminal activity in their vicinity. Wouldn't you agree Mister McQuaid?" McQuaid eyed him with growing appreciation. The subtle implication was crystal clear.

"Colonel, I do believe the pirates are acting as if they are immune to local law and civil authorities here in the islands and they continue to grow even bolder in their incursions. If they are indeed backed by China, they will be well armed; as I've already observed. I would expect considerable resistance." Wilmouth looked over at Macy, to add his assessment.

"Colonel, we have the opportunity here to look like white hats, so long as our intelligence hand is kept behind our backs. If you'll allow me to conduct the joint operation with the Philippine Navy, I outlined to you earlier, we can keep this localized. But timing is essential. I could get you the orders, but we could lose the element of surprise, which would elevate our risk factors. The Air Force chain of command would be slow and subject to many more eyes than we'd prefer on this at the moment. If you are willing to authorize the operation, I can keep you covered at our end without a lot of questions."

McQuaid realized at that moment, Macy was being handled by Jake. The Colonel might outrank him, but Wilmouth had some sort of leverage here. Macy might object, but he had the feeling it wouldn't be favorable for his career. He sat back in his chair, watching his former wingman converse with the Wing Commander of Clark AFB, recognizing the body language and subtle gestures of power. It was unsettling to realize how much he didn't know about his old friend.

"McQuaid, can you flush these pirates out in the open?" Macy was looking at him again.

"As long as I can be sure Kiko won't be in the line of fire – yes." Macy considered that for a moment.

"What do you suggest?" Wilmouth jumped in once more.

"We have a local intelligence asset who can find out if they're holding her and where, Colonel. Assuming they want to trade her for McQuaid, he can help set up the location for the exchange. Once she's safe, we can deal with the pirates without restraint and in concert with the Philippine Navy." This seemed to satisfy Macy.

"Alright gentlemen. I'll set this up and co-ordinate with the Philippine military officials. Major Wilmouth, beyond the clearance you asked for, is there anything else you need for this "training exercise"?

"Nothing we haven't already covered Colonel. We'll use my flight's aircraft and pilots. I'll be the flight leader. Once the little girl's safe, the only person we need to worry about is my old buddy Richard here. But he's a fellow Marine and I am his ex-wingman after all." He grinned over at McQuaid. He made it sound so easy. But they all knew the odds were subject to chance and at best, were an informed guess. Macy stood up and McQuaid knew it was time to leave. There was a knock at the door and Lieutenant Winter ducked his head in.

"Colonel, the hospital is calling." He paused.

"Yes? Just put it through to my desk Matt. Major Wilmouth and Mister McQuaid were just leaving."

"The call is for Mister McQuaid, Colonel." He looked apologetic, but concerned. "I think it's important."

The call was from Mattie's Doctor. She had taken a sudden turn for the worse. Jake ran him over to the hospital in his jeep and they walked in together. Doctor Dennehy just happened to be on rounds and waved them over. One look at his face and McQuaid knew it wasn't good.

"Mister McQuaid, I'm afraid our optimism was premature. Ms. Adams started running a high fever a couple hours ago, with subsequent bouts of vomiting and convulsions. We think it's a post-surgery infection, but we're not really sure why yet. We've had her on a high dose of Penicillin, but it seems she's not responding very well."

"Can I see her?"

"Of course. Keep it brief though. Between the high fever and the drugs we've got her on, she's probably feeling pretty crappy." He looked over at Major Wilmouth. "Sorry, Major. I think one visitor is plenty." Wilmouth nodded. He figured McQuaid would want to be alone with her anyway. McQuaid gave him a quick look, but he just waved him on.

"Go. I'll be out here waiting. We can talk later."

Mattie was lying on her side, facing away from him when he pushed through the curtain next to her bed. He noticed a new bottle of saline water and another smaller bottle had been hung on stands, their drip lines disappearing into both her arms. Her hair was matted and sweaty looking and her hospital smock was soaked through. He moved around to the other side to face her, pulling a chair over to sit down close to her bed. Her face was red splotched, hot and flushed looking. He reached out to hold her hand, noticing how hot and damp it felt. She opened her eyes to bare slits and looked at him. They too were red and swollen. He was shocked at how much her condition had changed in just the few hours since he'd seen her last. He squeezed her hand, smiled and leaned over to speak to her.

"Mattie, I heard you weren't feeling very well and came right over." She just stared at him, her eyes appearing to have difficulty focusing. He reached over to the stand near her bed for a cloth he spotted, soaking in a bowl of water. He rung it out and mopped her face.

"Thanks for coming, Richard." Her voice was low and croaky. "That feels good." He felt her give his hand a slight squeeze in return. "I probably don't look so good, huh?" She closed her eyes, squeezing out a tear which ran down her cheek. He wiped her eyes with the damp cloth. "I hurt so bad

Richard. What's happening to me?" He leaned close and put his face against her hot cheek.

"Don't worry kid. The doctors think you have some infection from the surgery. They're taking good care of you and you'll be back in the pink in no time." He hoped he sounded convincing. She dropped his hand and reached up to touch his face.

"Richard?"

"Yes Mattie?"

"Have you found Kiko? Is she okay?" He sat back to better see her face.

"I'm flying back to Lubang as soon as I leave here. I'll find out what's going on with her. Hopefully Baacay will bring her out to meet me at the airfield and our worries will be for nothing. But if the pirates do have her, Major Wilmouth and I worked out a plan with the military here, to rescue her. I should only be gone a couple days and then I can fill you in on everything. You just need to work on getting better." She gave him a slow, weak nod in response. "Jake's a real friend Mattie. He's been a huge help. We can do this." She opened her eyes a little and her lips turned up in a weak smile.

"Snake?"

"Yeah." He chuckled.

"I like him Richard. I'm glad he wants to help." She paused and looked into his eyes for a moment before speaking again. "Please get her back safely Richard. Don't worry about me. You can't do anything more for me here. Just stay safe and get Kiko back." Her eyes closed again. "Everything will be okay," she whispered. He brushed the hair back off her forehead and gave her a gentle kiss. She seemed to know he was there, but had drifted off. He put the cloth back in the bowl and made his way out of the room. Letting her sleep seemed to be the best he could do for her at present. He looked back at her before he went through the door. She seemed so sick and frail. His heart felt heavy and it was all he could do to turn his back and leave her. But he had another urgent mission and she was right. There was nothing more he could do for her here.

Jake was standing out in the lobby area, still talking to Major Dennehy. They both turned to look at him and he had to compose himself before walking over to them. Jake was the first to speak and by his expression, he was plenty worried.

"How's she doing Gunner?"

"She's very weak Jake, and says she hurts real bad. I only spoke to her for a few minutes. She wanted to know about Kiko, so I told her I was flying back to Lubang to find out what happened to her. I don't know what else I can do." Dennehy laid his hand on his shoulder.

"Son, there's nothing else you can do. We're taking good care of her and with a little luck, the Penicillin will do its job."

"What happened Doc? She looked really good the last time I saw her. Now she looks like she's on death's doorstep. Is she going to be okay?" Dennehy looked down at her patient folder, scanning over the notes and nodded his head.

"We know she has an infection. It's just not clear where exactly, or how bad it is. Doctor McCawley did a fine job with her surgery and indicated he took ample precautions to avoid infection. But she had wounds to her heart and left lung, in addition to the deep penetrating wounds to her chest cavity. That's a lot of trauma for one body."

"Doc, is she going to make it?" he asked, his voice rising. He watched the doctor's face for any sign he might be holding back on him. Dennehy looked up at him with concern, but appeared sincere.

"We can't heal her, Mister McQuaid. All we can do is help her body out with that part. She seems to be in good health otherwise and we're treating her with the latest and best antibiotic we have. The next twenty-four hours will be critical. Chances are good she'll recover."

"But what are the odds here?" Dennehy paused, looking away for a moment to consider his answer. When he returned his gaze to McQuaid, his eyes and voice displayed conviction.

"If her fever breaks over the next twenty-four hours, she should pull through just fine."

"And if not?" Dennehy gave him his best consoling physician's look.

"Then, I'd say she's got less than a fifty-fifty chance." McQuaid stared at him for a moment, mulling this over in his mind. Jake was watching him.

"We've beat those odds before. Just give her all you've got, Doc. I'm betting on Mattie. She's the toughest bird I know. The best thing I can do for her, is get our little girl back." He glanced over at Jake. "Snake, how do you feel about taking a little hop over to Lubang with me?" Jake grinned back – relieved at the change of subject.

"You need to ask?"

McQuaid thanked the Major and they made their way out of the hospital and jumped back in the jeep for the ride back over to the flight line. On the way, McQuaid outlined his next moves and they decided Jake would fly on his wing, instead of the right seat of the Gooney Bird. That way, he'd be able to get back to Clark without depending on McQuaid having to ferry him over later. Besides, at some point, Jake needed to huddle with his fellow pilots from Guam to plot out their part in the operation.

Chapter Sixteen
Lubang Village Polis Station, Lubang Island, the
Philippines

Jake dropped him off at his cargo plane and then drove over to operations to file the flight plan for the both of them. He needed to make sure the Air Force knew he was providing a one man fighter escort back to Lubang. Within an hour, he met McQuaid at the Gooney Bird, wearing his flight gear and under thirty minutes later, they were flying over the same ridge line McQuaid had barely cleared a couple nights before. They leveled off at six thousand feet and McQuaid looked out the cockpit window to watch Jake's blue, gull winged fighter easing up abreast of his left wing. They had selected a private channel and he heard a metallic click in his headset, as Jake checked in with him. There was no need for radio formalities, without anyone else on the same channel with them.

"Feels a little like the good old days, eh Gunner?" He could see Jake grinning back at him in the cockpit of his fighter. He grinned back. It did bring back some good memories. "Remember? We used to wow them with that two ship barrel roll, in perfect formation?" He laughed. Of course he remembered. It was their signature aerobatic maneuver, requiring hours of practice and nerves of steel, especially when the two of them were in tight; just a few inches separating their wing tips.

"Yeah, but I don't think this old girl has those kind of moves in her, Snake. Let me strap on one of those Corsairs again and we'll give it go. Any chance you might pull a few more strings and get me a couple hours stick-time in one some time? You seem to have some kind of Voodoo magic going for yourself these days old buddy."

"I'm sure we could come up with a good excuse to get you back into a sportier model if you like. What do mean Voodoo? You referring to my usual Snake charming act?"

"Macy's no snake, partner. I got the feeling you had some altitude on him." There was a longer pause before Jake came back with an answer.

"I think I know what you're gettin' at Gunner. We'll have to take that up over a few beers sometime. That is, if I decide to tell you at all; you being a civilian now." It was clear he was eluding to the intelligence mission he had going.

McQuaid knew better than to press; not on the radio. The airwaves were never truly private.

"Fair enough. By the way, I notice you've left out any talk about a girl back in Guam the last couple days. Anybody clever enough to get their hooks in you yet?" He looked back over to see if he could make out his expression. He noticed he was laughing, before he keyed the mike back to respond.

"Maybe one or two. It's hard to keep track." It was McQuaid's turn to laugh. That rang true. Whereas he preferred to be selective and stick to one bird at a time, Jake liked taking them on by the flock. He tried to imagine a single woman who could run Jake Wilmouth to ground.

"You ever see Gwen around over on Guam?" He wished he hadn't said it almost as soon as it came out of his mouth. Why stir up old memories; especially painful ones? It had been over three years since he spoke to her last. But that nightmare he'd had a few nights ago, dredged her up again and he was curious. There was a long pause before Jake answered.

"Now there's a name I haven't heard in a while. You still have a little flame going for her?"

"No, that's definitely over. I just wonder how she's doing from time to time. That's all."

"What about you and Mattie? She seems like more your type, if you ask me." McQuaid paused to think about that. Gwen was his type too. But Mattie was different. There was something about her he couldn't quite put his finger on. She had sort of sneaked up on him. Gwen was young love, fireworks and lust. Mattie seemed more dialed into him somehow; like they fit together in a way he'd never experienced before and she'd proven she would be there for him, no matter what. It was comforting to know she was always there. She had become an essential part of him and his life, without him realizing it was happening.

A knot of fear that had been growing in his stomach started twisting in his gut again. He was concerned about Mattie and now about Kiko too. He could see her little face, looking up at him, laughing and reaching out to hold his hand. What if they couldn't find her? He'd matured quite a bit since he and Gwen had parted ways. It dawned on him, that without having established anything more formal, he had a family to worry about now. And his family was in serious jeopardy.

"Hello, anybody home over there? I'm not boring you, am I?" Deep in thought, he had left Jake to himself too long.

"Sorry. I was just thinking about Mattie and Kiko. You remember I told you I was an orphan as a child?"

"Of course I do. Why?"

"Well, I think I found my family Jake. Mattie and Kiko are my family now, and I'm beginning to fear I might lose them."

"That's not going to happen, Gunner. Not if I have anything to say about it. And I usually do, right?"

"Yeah. I've noticed. I'm being serious now. There's no way I could do this without you Jake. But neither of us has any control over Mattie getting well. And if the pirates do have Kiko, I can't get it out of my mind that they might just kill her to get even with me. An eye for an eye seems like it might be more their style. There is nothing either of us can do if it all goes bad." The knot in his gut twisted tighter just thinking about it. An even deeper well of pain, filled with the loss of his friend Jerry, then Gwen and the other faces of people he'd gotten close to and lost during the war, began pulling his mind toward a dark abyss. He clenched his teeth and forced the images away. He couldn't let it happen to the people he cared about. Jake seemed to sense his despair.

"Gunner, listen to your old buddy for minute. First of all, Dennehy is the best damn surgeon in the South Pacific. If he says Mattie should pull through, you can write that down in ink. And whether or not the pirates are part of a bigger operation, or just looking out for themselves, they'd have to be stupid to think killing Kiko would settle the score with you. A better bet would be to use her to get at you directly. Taking you out of action permanently, is much better insurance against any further retribution. Like I told you before, you're the bait we need to get them out in the open." McQuaid considered that for a moment. Jake might be right. If the pirates did have her, their odds were certain to be much better if they used Kiko to get him to surrender to them – unarmed and helpless – right where they wanted him.

"It makes sense, Jake. We're just a few minutes out of Lubang airport now. So, let's hope we find her there and we don't have to worry about any of this." Jake double clicked his mike to acknowledge him, as McQuaid started pulling back his throttles to begin his descent. They made their final approach and touched down fifteen minutes later.

As he was turning off the runway to taxi over to the hangar, he noticed Baacay walking out of their cargo office to meet them. He hung his arm out the cockpit window and waved Jake's plane over to a parking spot where they tied down the Goose, when it wasn't in the hangar. Baacay had the cargo door open and was working his way up to the cockpit, before his props had come to rest. He pulled off his headset and climbed into the back to meet him. Baacay was glad to see him, but his face looked long and drawn.

"Ho, Gunna. So happy you back. How Mattie?" He seemed braced for the worst; wringing his hands. McQuaid clasped him by the shoulder and offered him a warm smile in return.

"She's still in the hospital at Clark airbase. Don't worry; they're taking good care of her now." Baacay seemed more relieved. McQuaid felt it best to hold back on any further details until he knew more himself. For now, it would suffice that he knew she had made it to the hospital in one piece and was alive. He turned his attention to the more pressing subject. "Baacay, have you seen Kiko?" The man's face dissolved into grief, then fear, all in a matter of seconds.

"Kiko no here, Gunna'. Pirates take. 'Dis berry bad, Gunna'. You talk Chief Mahutra. He know pirates take Kiko!" He wiped his eyes, but looked pathetic. McQuaid reached out and put his arm around the younger man.

"Come on, Baacay. Let's get this airplane tied down and then we'll talk to the chief. Is he here in town?" Baacay had moved ahead of him now and jumped out onto the tarmac. He looked back up at McQuaid, as he climbed down the short crew ladder.

"Yah. Chief Mahutra go see Lijuan. Talk to Nguyen." Just then he looked over and spotted Jake ambling over toward them. Jake reached over to shake Baacay's hand.

"Hello Baacay. Good to see you again," he offered, overlooking his lack of composure. Baacay was glad to see him again as well, but wasn't able to muster more than a slight smile in return.

"Ho, missar Snake." Jake, laughed slapping him on the back.

"You remembered!" Baacay nodded and then excused himself to start setting chocks under the wheels of the Gooney Bird. Jake turned to McQuaid.

"Well? What's the story, Gunner?"

"It's not good," he replied, rubbing the back of his neck, where the tension was building into a pounding headache. "Chief Mahutra's here, over at the jail, talking to Lijuan. She's the girl we rescued from the pirates." Jake nodded, remembering their earlier discussion. "The police chief, Captain Nguyen has her locked up for her own protection. Not sure why Mahutra's over there, but we should drive over and see." McQuaid led the way and they both hopped into the company jeep. It was a short drive and within in a few minutes, they were walking up the steps to the police station.

It was a plain affair, white washed concrete block, with "Polis" painted in black block letters over the door frame and steel rebar over the dirty glass windows. McQuaid was surprised to hear shouting from inside. He recognized Nguyen's voice and when they walked through the door, they could see him and Chief Mahutra standing toe-to-toe, both red faced and looking like they were about ready to come to blows. He closed the door behind him and Jake, with a louder bang than usual. The two men both stopped to look over at the intrusion. It may have defused the atmosphere enough to prevent mayhem from ensuing. McQuaid nodded to Mahutra and then directed his attention to Captain Nguyen.

"Captain Nguyen, I see you and Chief Mahutra have met. I hope we're not intruding, but my friend Major Wilmouth and I need to speak with Chief Mahutra, when you two are finished discussing," he let the verb sort of dangle for a moment, then continued, "whatever it is you're discussing." Meanwhile, Jake was giving them both his best military recruiting poster smile. They both regarded him with blank stares, not sure how to shift gears from almost thrashing each other, to making small talk with the two Americans. Mahutra, perhaps the better poised of the two, smiled and stepped forward to clasp arms with Jake.

"I am happy to meet you Major. A friend of Captain McQuaid is also a friend of myself." His eyes clicked to McQuaid's, without changing his smile in the least. "We should go out from here, where we will not be further annoyed by this strutting peacock of a policeman." He made a point of ignoring Nguyen, whose face had begun to take on the appearance of an overheated teapot about to whistle.

Jake peeked over the chief's shoulder at Nguyen; offering him an innocent grin and a slight finger wave good-bye; which seemed to annoy Nguyen even more, if that was possible. McQuaid gave him a polite nod of acknowledgement as well and walked out the door to wait for Mahutra to join him. Mahutra kept his back to the jail, while moving a short distance away, so they could speak without being overheard.

"What's brought you here, Chief?" McQuaid was anxious to get to the point. Mahutra glanced back to make sure they weren't being observed. It wasn't hard to see he was still angry over something concerning his conversation with Nguyen. He gestured over his shoulder at the jail.

"That policeman is big problem. He does not want me talk to his prisoner. I told him I need only few minutes quiet talking with her and he can come back. Say he does not want her talking with me about drugs and pirates. Why is he worried about this Lijuan person, Captain McQuaid?"

"I couldn't say, Chief. Why did you want to talk with her?"

"My apologies first, Captain. I have heard about your friend Mattie from my men. I hope she is okay. Baacay told me you took her to hospital. He also told me Kiko is not in village. Say pirates took her. I have news about Kiko and want to ask Lijuan about pirates. I want to find out what she know." McQuaid was becoming impatient.

"What news do you have about Kiko, Chief?" His voice was strained and he was hard pressed to contain his concern. The chief reached out and took his arm.

"I send many men to look for Kiko, Captain. Pirates take her to place I show you on map, near Mamburao River. They keep her there."

"Is she alive?" McQuaid was afraid to hope.

"She is alive, Captain McQuaid. My men have seen her. Say she looks well." McQuaid had been holding his breath.

"That's great news, Chief!" He turned to Jake. "Their main base is near the mouth of the Mamburao River, on Mindoro Island, probably fifty miles southeast of here." Jake had been taking it all in.

"So far so good then. Maybe we could have Chief Mahutra, get word to them we want to negotiate for her release. We need to get them out in the open water and away from their base." McQuaid was nodding back at him. He turned to Mahutra with the obvious question.

"Chief, can your men get word to the pirates? We could meet them out in the bay somewhere and make the exchange." Mahutra appeared confused.

"Exchange for what, Captain?" McQuaid realized he hadn't brought the chief up to speed on their plan.

"We plan to use me in trade for Kiko. They want me anyway, not her. Once we make the trade, Major Wilmouth plans to attack them from the air. We will also have Philippine Navy boats waiting to surround them, once he disables their gun boats." The chief looked even more concerned now and it was McQuaid's turn to be puzzled. "You don't like the plan, Chief?" Mahutra waved his hands at this.

"Good plan, Captain McQuaid. But no good for you. Pirates take Kiko away. Also take other island girls. My men say they do not know where. I want to talk with Lijuan. Find out where pirates take Kiko. But policeman is no help. I know of this man Nguyen for long time. He is always pig's ass, but we help each other on this island many years. I don't know why he does not now let me speak to Lijuan. I think Lijuan can know where pirates take Kiko." McQuaid could feel his blood beginning to boil. He'd just about had it with Nguyen already. This was the final straw for him. He brushed past Mahutra and was starting toward the jail, when he felt Jake's hand on his shoulder.

"Hold on there, Wild Bill. Before you go storming in there, maybe we should figure out why Nguyen is so reluctant to cooperate here. What's his angle anyway?" McQuaid stopped and looked back at him.

"Angle?" Jake looked over at Mahutra.

"Chief, did you tell the police chief you knew the pirates were holding Kiko hostage?" The chief nodded his head in response. "So he knew why you wanted to talk to Lijuan?"

"I tell him pirates have her for prisoner. Tell him I want to know where pirates take Kiko." McQuaid was watching their exchange and began shaking his head as if to clear his thoughts.

"What are you driving at Snake?" Jake was rubbing his chin and seemed lost in thought. Then, he looked from Mahutra back to McQuaid.

"Something you told me that night in the club over dinner. You were wondering how the pirates knew when to strike; on the only day you were away at Chief Mahutra's village." McQuaid was confused.

"Right, but if they were tipped off, why would they attack looking for me, if they knew I wasn't going to be there?" Jake looked a little unsure of his answer, but decided to spell out his suspicion nonetheless.

"What if they weren't looking for you at all? As a matter of fact, what if they wanted to make sure you wouldn't be around?" McQuaid stared at him for a moment and then his blood ran cold. He turned away, hiding an expression which would alarm anyone who knew him. It all clicked into place. His hand moved to his holster, but he had not strapped his .45 back on his hip, when he got out of the Gooney Bird at the airport. Both Jake and Chief Mahutra noticed the gesture and sensed their friend was near a tipping point; where violence was sure to win over reason. *Nguyen had been behind it all the whole time.* McQuaid was gritting his teeth.

"The bastard set me up!" he bellowed. He's been working with the pirates all along. He knew if they killed Mattie and took Kiko, I'd go after them. I guess he figured they'd knock me off and he'd be rid of me for good. I never figured him for being that cold blooded." Jake laid a gentle hand on his shoulder.

"Gunner, listen to me. We don't know anything yet for sure. But there is more than a chance the police chief's in their pocket somehow. This is just typical small town mob influence. We know the pirates have been buying off Philippine military officials; why not the local sheriffs?" It was all making sense to McQuaid now. He and Nguyen had always been "friendly" adversaries. He just thought it had been a personality conflict. Chief Mahutra wasn't convinced.

"Why do pirates need police chief here on Lubang? Pirates have base on Mindoro Island. They smuggle drugs from there. Lubang is very small island." Jake had already thought that through.

"Because of you, Chief. You're the reason they needed to have insurance on Lubang." McQuaid was speechless and just stared at him; wondering what in the world he was talking about. "Look, we need to go over a few things and this isn't the best place for an intelligence briefing. Do you have anywhere we can go that's a little more private?" McQuaid shrugged and pointed back toward the airfield.

"Sure. I have an office in the hangar. I've got a bottle of scotch over there too." Jake grinned at him.

"Let's bust it on over there then. We're just standing around here burning the little daylight we have left!"

Chapter Seventeen
McQuaid Cargo Office, Lubang Island Airfield, the
Philippines

McQuaid drove them back to the hangar, where they could all sit in the office there and talk in private. Jake had turned around in his seat on the way over, filling the chief in on him being with the Marines, based on Guam, but flying over with a small group of pilots for some training with the Air Force at Clark. The chief listened with great interest and then asked him why the Marines were training with the Air Force, when they were supposed to be part of the Navy.

Jake glanced over and met McQuaid's eye, appearing impressed with this local tribal chief's understanding of their military services organization. Continuing, he related to the chief, he was on special assignment and that the Navy, Marine Corps and the Air Force, were partners in the Pacific theater of operations now, since the war had ended.

Mahutra nodded and asked if Jake was also working with the Navy in Subic Bay. Jake shook his head and explained the Marines were traditionally part of the Navy but, with its own separate chain of command and were now more of an expeditionary force. Once the war ended, their role had changed from direct naval support, to include their own detached mission profile; one that involved training for quick-action deployment onto land from the sea and now from the air as well. He used his hands to demonstrate how the Marines were landed from Navy ships to capture and secure enemy beaches, like they did on Luzon, to clear the way for Army infantry, which was a far larger division of American ground forces. The chief seemed to take it all in with ease and then asked another excellent question.

"Where are your enemy beaches you will capture for Army now, Major Wilmouth?" It was a loaded question and one which gave Jake brief pause to look closer at Mahutra, who from outward appearance seemed benign and just curious. McQuaid couldn't help chuckling to himself. He was watching Jake being out-maneuvered by someone who still wore feathers and magic amulets, but knew enough to inquire whether the Marines might now be considered irrelevant after WWII. The two fellow Marines had commiserated earlier about how this was already becoming a political football in Washington. Even at the Joint Chiefs level, the fat

221

appropriations for Marine Corps budgets were being questioned as lavish indulgence without a clear mission purpose. Jake was smiling back at the chief, like someone who was determined to remain gracious, after stepping in dog poop.

McQuaid was all too aware, that while Mahutra couldn't be more pro-American, he was nevertheless a proud Filipino and part of an island nation where history had proven them vulnerable to invasion from the sea on all sides. They had already been conquered by several foreign empires; the Portuguese, then the Spanish and during WWII, by the Japanese.

But he and the chief had also argued over the Battle of Manila in 1899, when the Americans first arrived after having annexed the Philippine islands, as part of their spoils from victory in the Spanish-American war. Thousands of Filipino dissidents were killed by American troops under orders to put down local revolutionaries, who had been fighting the Spanish for independence and were now forced to fight the Americans instead. Portrayed as American atrocities against the Philippine nation, they became part of the history of the islands her people endured and came to forgive; but never forget.

McQuaid believed Jake had only meant to fill the brief drive from the police station to the airfield, with some casual banter. Since he'd been informed of the chief's intelligence role during the Battle of Leyte Gulf, he had wanted to connect with him; for various reasons. What he hadn't expected, was to stumble into a topic of great political debate and unrest for Filipinos, which was hard to repress, in spite of their deep appreciation for America liberating them from the brutality of the Japanese occupation.

Jake was bright enough to sense he had stepped in something with the chief; he just wasn't sure what and turned to McQuaid for backup. McQuaid had spent many hours and bottles of beer, in debate with Mahutra, over the tempestuous Philippine-American history and relations. So, he reached over and patted Jake on the shoulder to reassure him.

"The chief and I have often explored the many joys and conflicts between Americans and the Filipino people Jake. And you have no idea what a rogue he can be when he wants to argue politics." He flung an evil look back at Mahutra, watching as the chief allowed a sly smile to creep across his stern demeanor. Jake noticed it too and much relieved, grinned back at him. The chief reacted by laughing uproariously and clapping both hands on the back of Jake's shoulders, in a show of affection. Jake just shook his head and turned around to face the front for the remainder of the ride over.

McQuaid, laughing now as well, realized how good it felt to let loose, for even a few moments respite from the relentless foreboding that had been creeping into his bones. And then the guilt slipped in again – like a knife. The pirates were holding Kiko prisoner, still alive he hoped and if she was, she would also be terrified. Mattie was fighting for her life, in a hospital bed among strangers. And he was here, far away from both of them; laughing as if life were gay and carefree for him.

Without realizing it, he had slammed the steering wheel with his fist and transformed his face into a mask of despair. Out of the corner of his eye, he could see Jake staring at him. Mahutra was also watching. He pulled the jeep over and stopped.

"Sorry guys. I'm just feeling a little sorry for myself over here. Two people I care about are in grave danger because of me and I can't shake the feeling I'm running out of time." The chief leaned forward in his seat and put his hand on his shoulder.

"You are a warrior and will always sail the deep waters my friend. So much safer to sit on the shore, around a warm fire with the rest of our families." McQuaid knew he was right. Even though he had remained on Lubang after the war, with the intent of leading a simpler, less violent life, crossing paths with the pirates had once again thrust him into the familiar role of an aggressor. He had reminded Mattie he couldn't just walk away from a fight that last night they sat together on the veranda in front of the General Store.

In a strange way, just his presence on Lubang had set him on an inexorable collision course with regional power brokers and thugs. Once a warrior, there was never a comfortable refuge somebody like McQuaid could escape to and overlook such things. Someone had to stand up to them. Heaving a sigh of resignation, he realized he needed to accept his role in all of this; something both Jake and Chief Mahutra had already deemed him worthy of, without passing judgment on the possibility of so many horrible outcomes. It didn't make it easier, it just made things clearer. He offered a silent nod to Mahutra, letting him know he understood and appreciated the deeper implications of his words and gunned the jeep forward again.

As they pulled up in front of the McQuaid Air Cargo office, an anxious Baacay trotted out to meet them. He looked to McQuaid for hope and a word of consolation. But the big Marine had no good news for him and just shook his head. They all filed into the cargo office and after settling everyone around the small table, with small bamboo chairs and a couple cargo boxes to sit on, McQuaid grabbed his bottle of scotch and some "clean enough" glasses and poured everyone a liberal first round. Jake stood up and holding his glass high, intoned a solemn toast.

"To stout ships and friendships, may they carry us through the hell of any storm, or bring the storm to any hell!"

They all clinked glasses and downed them in one shot. McQuaid poured a second round and turned back to Jake, who had regained his seat and appeared ready to get on with the briefing. First however, Jake held up his hand and asked Baacay if he would walk over to his aircraft and fetch a duffel bag he'd brought over with him from Clark. Baacay jumped up to comply. As soon as he was out of earshot, McQuaid looked over at him and snarled.

"Well? Tell me why I shouldn't just drive over to Nguyen's office and shoot the bastard?" Jake gestured with his thumb toward the chief, ignoring McQuaid's outburst.

"Our friend here, is a deep U.S. military intelligence agent." He looked over at Mahutra with a knowing smile. "I did a little checking on you, Chief. Not only are you still assisting the U.S. in the region, you also have questionable ties to the intelligence bureau for the Philippine Naval Patrol; possibly all the way up to Commodore Andrada." Mahutra busied himself with his drink, devoid of expression. Jake pressed on. "Chief Mahutra and Andrada know each other through mutual friends from the Escuela Nautica de Manila, where Andrada attended, prior to becoming one of their most decorated Philippine naval officers. Incidentally, he also attended and graduated from West Point in Annapolis, where he became friends with many prominent up-and-coming new U.S. naval officers." Jake took a breath and a quick sip of his scotch before continuing.

"Chief Mahutra's father, the previous Looc tribal chief, enrolled him in the University of Santo Tomas, but, through what I would characterize as a series of strange coincidences, other acquaintances in Manila introduced him and Andrada to each other. When the Japanese defeated the allies in the Philippines and Manila was captured, everything moved underground and it was Andrada who recommended the chief to one of General MacArthur's staff. That's how he was recruited into US Navy Intelligence. He did a fine job for us there and may have even helped us win the war in the Philippines – as we already discussed Gunner." Chief Mahutra was smiling now.

"You are well informed Major," he replied. His tone was warm, but sounded somehow more official. "Understandably, you would also know about Baacay then?" McQuaid's head whipped around.

"What about Baacay?" he asked, lowering his voice to a harsh whisper. Jake had been watching Baacay out the window, as he climbed up the crew ladder into the cockpit of his fighter. He looked back to McQuaid.

"Unfortunately, Baacay is an unwitting agent for the pirates based on Mindoro Island. He talks to the fishermen in the harbor, some of which aren't just fishing for fish. The pirates have a rather sophisticated network of spies set up between Luzon, Mindoro and Palawan. A number of them also hang around in Lubang harbor. Some of Baacay's fishermen friends, report on everything that goes on around here. That includes information on McQuaid Air Cargo and I suspect, probably as a safety check, on what Nguyen might be up to as well." He paused, allowing McQuaid to digest some of this. McQuaid looked thunderstruck. He could feel his face flush, as he considered how close he had been with Baacay the last few years. Had he been betraying him all this time too? It was Mahutra's turn at bat.

"Captain, you need not worry about Baacay. He is very loyal to you. He would never tell the pirates anything you would not want them to know. But he does not know his friends, which he thinks are only simple fisherman, are paid by the pirates to talk to him and then to report back what he discussed with them." McQuaid was also looking out the window now, with new found interest, observing Baacay as he climbed back down the crew ladder, carrying Major Wilmouth's duffel bag over his shoulder. He also noted to himself, that Chief Mahutra's English had made a remarkable improvement over the space of the last few minutes. He made a face and wondered what other surprises about his friends were in store for him.

"That's why you sent Baacay out to get your flight bag, eh Snake?"

"Exactly. He doesn't need to know about any of this – especially anything to do with his complicity in their plans. First of all, it would devastate him if he knew he was hurting you and Mattie somehow and secondly, it would ruin him for our purposes." McQuaid's eyes narrowed.

"What purposes?" Jake slugged back the rest of his drink and leaned forward to explain.

"First things first. The pirates know all about Mahutra and his intelligence work here for our military. That's why they needed Nguyen in their pocket. They control Lubang and you through Nguyen's eyes and ears. Baacay is just a dupe. He doesn't know anything about the pirates." He waved away McQuaid's attempt to refill his glass and continued. "I'm not even sure how deep Nguyen is in with them for that matter." Mahutra's ears seemed to perk up at that. McQuaid too was curious.

"What do you mean by that?"

"I'm saying, I don't really know deeply entrenched Nguyen is with them at this point. That's why I didn't think it would be the right thing for you to barge in on him, on the assumption he's in any position of control here. We need to find out where they've taken Kiko before we let Nguyen know his cover is blown." McQuaid nodded.

"Makes sense; and Baacay?" Mahutra leaned in.

"Captain McQuaid, you must not let Baacay know he is talking to the pirates when he speaks to the fishermen, or to Captain Nguyen. Better that he not know anything about this. We need Nguyen's help to find Kiko. If the pirates do not know that we have found out about Nguyen and Baacay, we control information to them. If we control their information, we control them." Jake was nodding at this last. Just then Baacay walked back into the office and handed the duffel bag over to him.

"Thanks, Baacay. Much appreciated," he said, meaning it and smiling back at the man. They all smiled at Baacay, as he returned to his seat and finished off his drink with a flourish. McQuaid was feeling uncomfortable with his next move. He wasn't exactly sure how to proceed. They needed to find out where the pirates were taking Kiko,

Mahutra wanted to speak to Lijuan and he still wasn't sure what she could tell him. They needed to get past Nguyen without tipping him off and none of this could be discussed in front of Baacay now, who was looking around at them, maybe wondering why no one was talking anymore. He came to a decision.

"Baacay, I need you to stay here while I take Major Wilmouth and Chief Mahutra over to meet with Captain Nguyen at the police station. We'll round up the chief's men and send them over to help you guard our hangar and aircraft. With the pirates still around somewhere, I don't want to take any chances. Do you understand?" Baacay nodded his head.

"Yes Gunna. I wait here." He jumped up and walked over to the corner, behind McQuaid's desk and picked up the rifle leaning against the wall. "I watch airplane. No pirate touch airplane, Gunna. No worry." He looked around at the men sitting at the table, brandishing the rifle in both hands. "No worry, I watch out 'fo airplane." Looking at the determination on his face, no one in the room doubted he would. McQuaid stood and motioned them outside.

"Let's go. We'll stop over at the General Store first. I need to see what needs to be done there. Baacay told me he put the fire out before too much damage had been done. I hope he's right." Jake and Mahutra rose from their chairs and they all trooped outside to pile into the jeep. As they drove away, McQuaid looked back in the rear view mirror and saw Baacay standing outside the cargo office, looking after them, the rifle cradled in his arms. He felt like he was deserting him.

Mahutra, who was in the front seat this time, leaned over to McQuaid, so he could talk over the engine noise and the wind.

"I have my men in front of store and at the hospital; also at docks. If the pirates come back, they will fight them. But I must return to my village." Jake had leaned forward from the jump seat in back, to better hear their conversation.

"What are you hoping to get from talking to this girl Lijuan, Chief?" Mahutra turned sideways to speak to him and so that McQuaid could hear as well. He hesitated and seemed to weigh his words with care.

"She might know where we can find the leader of this group of pirates here in the islands. Maybe the Mamburao River pirates are taking the girl there." McQuaid glanced over at him.

227

"Where would that be, Chief?" Mahutra looked back at the road behind them, his expression wistful and sad. He rested his arm on McQuaid's seat back to steady himself against the jeep bouncing over bumps in the road.

"Their leader is not here in the Philippines, Captain. Pirates take these girls to China to sell. They make a lot of money from young girls."

"She's only nine years old, Chief! Are you saying they might sell her into prostitution?" He was horrified just thinking about it. Mahutra's response wasn't to be reassuring.

"They also take much younger girls Captain. These are not good people. Do not expect them to be kind. They only care for profit." His eyes were hard, his mouth set in a grim, straight line. Making money on the weak, through drugs and prostitution, was an ancient and sordid reality for many poorer Far Eastern countries. And while Mahutra was also aware this vile disease had been exported to the tranquil islands of the Philippines, he despised his island brothers, who desecrated their rich heritage with such a livelihood. He felt great sorrow for McQuaid. These were matters he himself couldn't bear to comprehend. It was hard for him to imagine how an idealistic man, from a great country like America, might view such things. He had only met Kiko once, but he knew of many other pretty and innocent young island girls, who had been stolen from their families and sold to the flesh merchants. Worse still, some were even traded by their parents for a fee. Mahutra resisted the urge to spit out the bitter taste this left in his mouth.

They arrived in front of the General Store. McQuaid turned off the motor and was just sitting there, looking out at the fire blackened windows over the veranda and broken front door. He had not been back here since the day before the attack. Two of Mahutra's men were sitting on the veranda chairs, their rifles at their sides, watching them. He swung his legs out of the jeep and walked inside. Chief Mahutra moved over to speak with his men, while Jake followed him into the store.

He pushed the shattered remains of the screen door aside and stepped inside, his boots crunching the glass from the broken windows underfoot. He was assaulted by the smell of rotten meat and a metallic stench of dried blood, he recognized from his days in the hospital on Guam. He could see where Mattie had lain, wounded and bleeding. There were brown stained, bloody bandages and a dried puddle of old blood on the plank wood floor. His eyes moved up and around, taking in the blackened walls on the right and the ruined meat cases, under a cloud of black flies, buzzing around brownish lumps of poultry and pork left in the broken glass display cases. It was sickening to see how the place had deteriorated. But he was grateful to Mahutra's men for keeping looters away. The rest of the store's goods were still on the shelves. He realized Jake had moved up to stand beside him.

"It's not as bad as I feared it might be Gunner. We can put this place back together without too much trouble." McQuaid remained silent, just needing to put these images away in a place where he could deal with the rage, without losing control and driving over to murder Nguyen in cold blood. He heard Chief Mahutra step inside behind them, his feet crunching the broken glass in the doorway.

"Captain, we need to talk about how we will deal with this policeman." He was right and McQuaid decided he'd seen enough already. He turned around to face Mahutra. "We need to speak with this girl Lijuan. We need to know where the pirates take young girls. You have to find Kiko before she is lost." Those last few words felt like a knife in his gut. The chief was right. They were wasting time here. It was useless to stand around looking at something they could fix later. Jake put his hand on his shoulder.

"Gunner, I have an idea how we might want to handle the situation with Nguyen." McQuaid looked over at him, his eyes smoldering; the rest of his face an emotionless mask. Mahutra stopped to listen as well. "Something else you should know about Nguyen might help us out here. He's not from the Philippines. He's Vietnamese. Intel on this Jiang guy, the local pirate leader, says he's Chinese." McQuaid was listening, but nothing Jake has said so far sounded in the least bit helpful.

"Why does Nguyen being Vietnamese make any difference?" he asked. Mahutra leaned forward to speak.

"People of Vietnam do not like the Chinese, Captain. Long ago, China had a very bad war with Vietnam. The Chinese made them slaves, raped their women and stole their children. Many people from both countries were killed when the people of Vietnam's hate for China become very great. Much more blood was lost, but finally Vietnam became free again. This was long ago, but people of Vietnam still do not trust Chinese. The Philippines has always been a friendly country to Vietnam. But then many Chinese pirates came here and killed island people again. Before the Spanish came, Chinese pirates burned Manila and killed many people from the Philippines. Maybe this policeman, Nguyen, does not like Chinese." Suddenly, McQuaid was very interested.

"You might have something there. One thing I know about Nguyen, he likes to play for the winning team. Right now, with the U.S. military pulling back and the Philippine military looking weak, the pirates may seem to him like they have the upper hand." Jake was nodding his head.

"He may not like working with the pirates either. It just might seem to him like he doesn't have much choice. What he may not realize is, the Philippines have become a major U.S. strategic investment. While he probably doesn't see a lot of change here on Lubang yet, the Philippines as a nation and now a major ally of the U.S., is going to be in our spotlight for the Pacific region. If he really wants to be on the winning team, he needs to switch sides now, before he's identified as a co-conspirator with the Chinese, by aiding these pirates." McQuaid was thinking hard about previous conversations with Nguyen. It occurred to him the man might indeed be a reluctant ally for the pirates. And if Nguyen was a native Vietnamese, with a cultural aversion to becoming a minion to people he may have grown up hating..." A light bulb went off in McQuaid's head.

"Okay, this is how we're going to do this." He outlined a plan to deal with Nguyen and get him to let them talk to Lijuan. If the pirates were working for Madam Chin, she might know where to look for Kiko. He would need Jake to share some of their intelligence on China's insurgency to him and their ulterior motives to thwart a strong, unchecked American presence in the region. Jake might be reluctant to divulge any intelligence with a known conspirator for the enemy. But everything he knew about Nguyen, suggested he was very pro-American. It would be a troubling alliance for him, if he knew it would make him a traitor to the U.S. The real story could be more like what Jake had alluded to as local racketeering and violence Nguyen had knuckled under to and accepted payoffs for; as the easier way out. If Nguyen was just looking out for himself, McQuaid was the best one to turn him. There was one thing he knew about Nguyen for sure. If the man had any secret desire, it was to be like his American heroes – a sheriff from the Old West, not a pirate.

Chapter Eighteen
The Fánróng Fùqiang, in the South China Sea

Kiko was lying on a thin, grimy, sweat soaked mattress, her arms shackled above and behind her head. Her ankles were also shackled and chained to the deck fitting in front of her. She was blindfolded, but could hear the whispering and moans of a number of other girls around her, also being held captive in the muggy and fetid hold of the Fánróng Fùqiang. They had been herded aboard in the night, at a dock along a muddy river, somewhere in the Philippine islands. With just a brief glimpse around before they blindfolded her, she wasn't able to recognize anything and so had no idea where they were starting from.

Within hours, the engines were started and she had felt the ship moving into rougher water. At this point in time, it seemed to her like they had been under way for several days now. Once a day, they were given water, some brackish fish soup and were allowed to use one of the ship's heads. So far, they had been fed three times. Otherwise, they were left shivering in the dark, not from cold, but from the terror of an uncertain and ominous future awaiting them.

Some of the girls were crying and sounded very young. The older ones tried to sooth them and keep them quiet. If their cries grew too desperate, one of the ship's crew came down to shout at them. Once already, she had heard screaming and the sounds of them beating one of the offenders, until they fell silent again. This had continued to be the routine for quite a while, along with the rhythmic rising and falling of the hull against the waves, the loud throbbing of the diesel engines and all too often, horrible retching noises from the girls who were seasick.

Kiko had withdrawn to her private world; a place of dark numbness, which protected her from falling prey to hope for a better future. It was a familiar world she had first retreated to after the death of her parents. It was better not to think, or feel; not to care whether she lived or died. Gunner had found her in this world and coaxed her back to the light. After a long while, she came to accept that he cared for her and wouldn't abandon her again if she was bad, or he just grew tired of her.

When he first introduced her to Mattie, she was terrified she might not want to share her with Gunner and

231

would make him send her away. But Mattie surprised her by treating her like her own child. She taught her how to read, to count and even gave her clothes of her own, she didn't have to share with younger children. Mattie spent patient hours with her in the kitchen, teaching her to cook and tend to duties around the store. Gunner taught her to help him with his cargo business and soon she realized he even depended on her help. She felt important in her new job.

Despite her misgivings, Kiko came to trust and even enjoy their company. Over the last few years, it didn't seem to hurt as much when she thought about her parents. She even began to hope she might be happy again someday. Now, they were both gone and she was alone once more; in her dark place again. It would not be her destiny to be happy. But she would find a way to hurt these men. Gunner had taught her things she could use and she would be clever and patient. They would not know she would kill them, until it was too late. She smiled to herself. Soon she would be dead too, but first they would pay for hurting Mattie and Gunner and these whimpering girls around her. She needed to stay strong for all of them. The thought of standing over the lifeless bodies of her tormentors someday, filled her with a resolve that was white hot.

Her dark deliberations were interrupted by a change in their vessel's motion and sounds. The ship had moved into calmer waters and the engines were throttled back. After another long period of time, the engines were reduced to idle, and then the propellers were reversed. She felt and heard a loud bump and the engine noise ceased. Wherever they were traveling to, they had arrived. Soon she heard the crew unchaining the girls nearest to the exit. They were shouting at them and dragging them outside. When they came for her, she didn't resist, or make a sound of complaint, even when she fell, banging her bare legs several times, trying to climb the steep metal ladder to the upper deck. At least it was cooler above. It was raining and the raindrops felt delicious on her burning skin. Her eyes were still blindfolded, but she couldn't see any light around the edges; so she thought it might still be night time.

They were being pulled along and she had to run to keep up on her shorter legs. There were fish smells of a harbor now, distant bells, men laughing and she thought she detected the muffled sound of music in the background. Voices and bodies were jammed together and once again she was pushed down to lie on a wooden floor with the others. A door banged shut, the voices faded and she was left to wonder what would happen next. One of the younger girls began crying next to her. She reached over and pulled her against her; shushing her, urging her to be quiet. The girl held onto her, snuffling and whining a little, but soon quieted down and fell asleep from exhaustion.

A fragrant scent of Gardenia wafted in from somewhere, penetrating the acrid smell of sweat and sour stench of unwashed bodies. The music she had heard earlier seemed louder now. Her hands were still bound in front of her, but she managed to work her blindfold up enough to peer under it, hoping to see something of the room they were in. But without windows, it was pitch black inside. Kiko allowed her mind to drift back into her darkness. There was nothing more to do for the present, but wait.

The man across from the docks lowered his binoculars and jotted a quick note in a small pocket ledger. He glanced at his watch and continued: "...coastal trader, blue hull, docked at Hoi Wan Road, Pier 18, 21:09 hours. Cargo included twenty-five females, led ashore bound and blindfolded. Ship under Chinese flag, name on stern, Fánróng Fùqíang." He pocketed the book and pen and stuck an ornate, Calabash pipe back in his mouth; drawing in the smoke, thoughtfully considering events unfolding on the pier across from him. Satisfied nothing more remarkable was to ensue, he removed his pipe again, struck the bowl on the heel of his boot and then stepped on the still glowing dottle. Pulling his dark sea coat collars up to the brim of his Fedora against the rain, he merged with the shadows and was gone.

Jiang Xian Hui was sitting at a hand carved, teak wood table, logging his delivery of human cargo, on a manifest receipt. He used a fine tipped brush, dipped in black ink, to scribe the Chinese characters next to a simple sketch of each girl they had transported on the Fánróng Fùqíang. There were twenty-five of these thumb-nail sketches, listed down the left side of the long page, each sketch bordered by a thin lined square, with the girl's name underneath. Jiang was describing their physical condition at time of delivery, along with any notes on special skills, personality, even hair and skin blemishes.

He took pride in his skill at penning the delicate Chinese characters, and the fine detail of his work. These descriptions would later be transcribed into personal files on each of the females. Every step of their training, room and board would be documented, along with daily costs. Some would be resold for immediate profit at underground auctions, where potential buyers could poke and prod them at their leisure, weighing their bid against future profits.

The lucky ones would be purchased as concubines, for finer Chinese households. There, they would perform traditional duties as a "second wife" and provide sexual favors for one man. Others, not so lucky, or pretty, were sold into the trade and forced to grind out repayment in the many flower boats and brothels around Aberdeen Harbor. These ranged from tawdry little tenement like affairs, just off the waterfront, to the multi-deck floating hotels, some of which were so lavishly appointed, they could almost be considered elegant.

It made no difference to Jiang where they ended up, so long as he received payment in full in the next day or so and could head back out to sea without mishap. He was nearing the end of his report, when a door opened to the right, admitting an older woman, wearing a regal, red and gold embroidered Dragon Robe. The rich silk fabric hung floor-length, just brushing the dark mahogany floor. Her jet black hair was grey streaked and drawn up in a tight coiffure, retained with fine carved ivory forks sticking out on either side of her head. Though her make-up heavy and colorful, it was tasteful and belied her true age, which she liked to suggest was somewhere south of fifty. She glided into the room to stand next to Jiang, allowing one of her manicured hands to protrude from oversized sleeves and rest on his shoulder. Blood red nails, over an inch long, flicked his thick black braid back and forth. He turned in his seat to look at her and she regarded him with a wolfish smile, through ruby colored lips.

"What lovelies have you brought me this time my dear Jiang?" A delicate scent of Gardenia blossoms filled the room around her. She was taller than the average Chinese female and appeared thin, but the blousy cut of her robe obscured her shape, as it was designed to do. Jiang paused, watching her expression, never quite knowing how to interpret her often mercurial emotions. He sighed, laid his writing brush down and leaned back, rubbing his eyes. "You must be very tired after your long trip," she responded, her voice soothing. The long ruby nails clicked as she began massaging his shoulder, seeking out the knotted muscles with an artisan's skill. He leaned into her hand closing his eyes.

"I brought you twenty-five lovely young girls, Năinai." He hesitated. "And some of the money from the opium you had that wretched girl bring over to sell in Manila." The hand rubbing his shoulder paused. He opened his eyes and turned to look up at her. Her eyes were hooded, the smile cooler and frozen in place. "The boat was sunk before it reached Manila. We retrieved most of the packages of opium, but some were ruined in the water." She stood back from him now, her face becoming stern with a heavy lined eyebrow raised.

"How does a boat sink itself? Can you explain this?" She had put her sleeves together, her hands now hidden within the shiny red material. Her head was tilted back and she was looking down her nose at Jiang, lips pressed together, dark eyes flashing. He knew she would not be patient enough to allow him a full explanation.

"There were problems," he began.

Kiko's eyes fluttered open in the dark room, as she heard muffled sounds of a shrill voice shouting, somewhere on the other side of the door. Then a man's voice began yelling back. She could not make out what they were saying, but there was little doubt, a war of words had erupted inside the building. There were more shouts and then sounds of what might be glass breaking. The loud voices continued, back and forth between the man and woman. There was a deafening thud; then a deathly silence. She waited, but all remained quiet. The other girls in the darkened room began to whisper. They were sure someone had just been murdered.

An explosion of light and sound ensued, as the door in front of her was flung open. A dark silhouette was framed in the doorway. As Kiko's eyes readjusted, she began to make out some details of the foreboding shape of a person standing there, in a scarlet robe, the red reflected in the flashing eyes, bared teeth and white horns sticking out of an oversized head. She gasped as she realized she must be looking at a demon. The other girls began to scream. The shape of doom glided into the room, the fearsome horned head swiveling back and forth, as if it was searching out a victim.

"Where is this girl? Bring her to me!" The voice was loud and shrill in the small room. Kiko could see everyone around her shrinking back from this demonic presence, each fearing they might be the girl she was demanding be brought to her. Jiang moved up behind her and turned on an overhead light. The loathsome shape resolved into an elegant lady, clad in beautiful red silk robes, the horns became exquisite ivory combs, constraining a mound of shiny black hair, wound into a bun on top of her head. Though it was now revealed she was no devil, she looked almost as frightful, with snarling red lips, flashing black eyes and inch long, blood red claws.

Kiko was still holding the smaller girl against her, but her back was pressed against the far wall, so she had nowhere to go. Jiang had moved up to stand next to this woman in red and was scowling down at her. There was no mystery now, which girl it was she wanted. As their eyes met, it seemed as if she were looking into her soul and would soon suck the life out of her. Then the woman's expression changed and she smiled down at her. The smile made her even more afraid. She did not appear happy in the least.

"So, you are the pathetic little treasure I have taken in trade?" Kiko had no idea what she was talking about. But she met her glare with ferocity. The woman looked back at Jiang in surprise. "She is not a tame little creature. Might she be too costly to train?" Jiang just stared down at her, stroking the long goatish beard at his chin.

"She may indeed be too wild. However, it was never my intention to sell her." He looked back at the woman he called Năinai, or Grandmother. But everyone else around Aberdeen Harbor, referred to her as Madam Chin. "She is my tool of revenge," he replied, his voice harsh. She gave him a sideways glance and offered a scornful laugh in return.

"For what? That worthless dog of a half-brother of yours? He came from my loins and I don't even mourn his death, Jiang!" She gazed back down at Kiko, her expression one of mild curiosity, looking up and down the length of her, as if to appraise her by the pound. Thus far, neither of them had acknowledged Kiko as a person, or even seemed to care whether she understood what they were talking about. In fact, she did not understand a word of their conversation in Chinese. However, she recognized by their faces, that neither the pirate leader, nor this older woman felt anything for her but contempt; as if they were deliberating over a piece of meat, which they were concerned might have spoiled.

"What do you know of the whereabouts of Lijuan?" she asked him. Jiang hesitated and then motioned for them to go back inside the building. He wasn't sure whether Kiko could understand them or not and preferred to discuss the matter out of her earshot. So far, his experience with her left him wondering how devious she might turn out to be. As they left the room, his eye caught hers and a curious look crossed his face. They returned to the room where Jiang had been finishing his delivery receipt, before he made his reply.

"I am told she was moved from the hospital and is now safe in the care of our man on Lubang." Madam Chin was growing impatient.

"Why did you not return my property to me, along with the rest of them? She has failed her assignment and I want her back! She needs to be punished and make up her losses." Jiang had already prepared to answer that.

"I did what I could with the time I had. I thought it was important to deliver this shipment and return what money I could from the sale of the remaining opium." He swept his arm back to point at the door of room they had left. "She is a hostage and with her I control this big American called McQuaid, who has complicated our operations around Lubang." Madam Chin was listening, trying to remain patient while she waited for the answer to her question and noticing Jiang was growing more agitated. "Our friends in the Philippine military tell me he planned to attack us with fighter planes from the military base on Luzon, to get this little girl back. The commander of the American base was to coordinate with the Philippine Navy in this raid. It seemed prudent, considering all we have at stake, to speak with you before I took any further action. Lijuan is safe for now."

Madam Chin felt a sliver of ice travel up her veins. This was becoming more disastrous than she had first imagined. This McQuaid person had powerful friends in the American military; the gods only knew where else. She had already been furious at Jiang for being so stupid as to attack the boat carrying the opium, which they had secreted aboard the unsuspecting pleasure craft under British flag. So long as the cargo remained hidden, their flag had reduced the risk of inspection and seizure.

As if attacking them wasn't bad enough, but allowing his brother to kill two British citizens in the process, was nothing short of gross incompetence. Now he had kidnapped this child of an American, with friends at high levels of the largest American military base in the Asian Pacific. Both the U.S. and Philippine military had been alerted to their activities now. The only thing keeping her from snatching the dagger hidden under her robe and stabbing Jiang in a merciless rage, was the knowledge that Lijuan and Jiang were the only two who could tie her to the incident.

Blood relative or not, Jiang was lucky she had not already ordered him garroted and thrown into the harbor with the sewage. She pretended to be listening to him prattle on. At the same time, she was deliberating on how best to eliminate both this child, he was foolish enough to take hostage, as well as Lijuan. She decided she needed Jiang for now, but she would have to consider what to do about him later. There were forces at work here Jiang could never know about. She had to contain things, before news of this reached Minister Li Peng, putting her own neck beneath the blade.

Chapter Nineteen
Lubang Island Jail, Lubang Village Polis Station, the Philippines

The sun was setting below the storm clouds over the mountains to the west like a sullen bloodshot eye. It had rained an hour or so before and the jeep splashed through deep puddles before coming to a stop in front of the Lubang Police Station. McQuaid set the brake and turned to Jake.

"Ready?" Jake nodded and patted the small valise he was holding. They walked up the steps together and into the entry hallway. They could see Cho, the other of Nguyen's two deputies, lounging in a wooden chair in front of the long front counter. His head swiveled as they came through the door and he stood up with admirable nonchalance and walked to the left out of sight around the corner of the hallway.

By the time they reached the front desk, the police chief was out of his small office and waiting for them, sans Aussie hat. The overhead lights reflected off his shiny dark scalp beneath the few remaining strands of hair left on his head. He stood behind the counter, hands on hips, already frowning. McQuaid figured they weren't going to have an easy time of this. Nguyen was plenty steamed when they last saw him earlier in the day and he didn't appear to have cooled down much. He watched them both in surly silence as they stopped in front of the counter. Cho had disappeared in back somewhere, leaving them alone. Perhaps he wanted to stay clear of the blast zone. McQuaid was the first one to break the ice.

"Captain Nguyen, I don't think you ever got to meet my friend Major Wilmouth here. He cocked his head toward Jake, who smiled and gave him a quick wave. Nguyen's dark and hooded eyes clicked in his general direction and then right back to McQuaid. He removed his hands from his hips and crossed his arms, making it plain he was in no mood for any sort of friendly reception. McQuaid set his jaw, grinding his teeth and was about ready to go off script when he felt Jake's elbow against his ribs. He cleared his throat and began again with what they had rehearsed.

"Captain, I came to apologize for the earlier upset this afternoon. Chief Mahutra has been kind enough to help us guard Mattie's store and our airplanes from another possible attack, but I asked that he show you more respect, since you've also been working with us to protect the town against the pirates." Nguyen's arms moved behind his back and he rocked back and forth on his shoes a couple times before answering.

"No pirates attack Lubang befor' you shoot pirate boat, kill brodder of pirate chief. Dis' quiet town Gunna. No need guard for pirates. You make big problem for me and Lubang people. Dis' chief of Looc village, he yor friend. He tell me I am big problem." He pulled one arm from behind his back and waved his index finger back and forth in front of their faces. "I am not big problem here, Gunna'. You make problem for me." He retracted his arm and it joined the other one behind his back again. McQuaid nodded his agreement.

"You're right, Captain Nguyen. I know I've caused a lot of problems. I didn't intend to do that. I only tried to protect those people out on the yacht. They were defenseless and that young girl Lijuan's life was in danger too. If you had been in my place, knowing how you are sworn to protect people around here, I believe you might have done the honorable thing; same as me." Nguyen blinked a couple times, finding little to disagree with in that logic. McQuaid continued. "It's like the Old West in my country out here, Captain. You are the only Sheriff around. I know that can be a tough job, especially when the nearest help is all the way over on Luzon. We've pulled together in tough times before. I've helped you and you've helped me. That's the way we do things out here. That's the way it should be." Nguyen looked like he might be starting to thaw.

"You right, Gunna. We help people in islands. People need strong law, good police. But you no listen to me. You become problem now Gunna. Dis' no good. Need one police. You are not police Gunna. You need listen when I say no kill pirates! Lubang need you fly planes, help island people, help me, help Mattie in store. Dis' what you need do here Gunna." McQuaid held out his hand.

"Captain, I'm truly sorry to have caused you all these problems. Please accept my apology. I need your help now too." Nguyen grimaced, looked from McQuaid to Jake and then back to the hand held out to him. With what seemed like great reluctance, he took his arm from behind his back, reached forward and shook his hand. McQuaid gave him a warm smile in return. "Thanks, Captain. I hope we'll be able to get back to normal here again soon." Nguyen stepped forward to the counter, placing his hands on it, both palms down, shoulders sagging and looked back at McQuaid with a troubled look on his face.

"Gunna, I have berry important question. I ask Doc from hospital 'bout Mattie. He tells me, he not heard from big hospital. What you know 'bout Mattie from big hospital?" His shoulders seemed to sag even more, "Have more questions. Where is Kiko? We no find Kiko in Lubang Village. Chief from Looc village say pirates take Kiko. Dis true?" McQuaid had never seen Nguyen on the verge of grief. It surprised him. He looked as though he had been covering it with anger over the quarrel with him. Jake had been right, there was indeed a more sensitive man under all that showboating. He crossed his fingers, hoping he was right about the rest of it too.

"The doctors at Clark hospital fixed Mattie's wounds, Captain. She's alive and we hope she'll be much better soon. I spoke to her before I left. She's worried about Kiko too. Mahutra's men have seen Kiko at the pirate base on the Mamburao River. He told me she was alive, but then they took her somewhere else and we don't know where. We need to find her, Captain. I'm afraid they might hurt her to get back at me." Nguyen had been listening closely and when he heard this last, he clenched his teeth and narrowed his eyes until they almost closed. He turned away, reaching up with his right hand to smooth back the fine hair on his head. Then glanced back toward the door to the cells in the rear of the office, appearing to be wrestling with something. When he returned his eyes to McQuaid, he was defensive again.

"What you do, Gunna? You kill more pirates now? Try get Kiko back?" He seemed to be working himself up to a lather again, but they could tell there was more going on under the surface. Jake took this as his cue to step in with his part of their two man show.

"Captain Nguyen, I work for U.S. military intelligence here in the Pacific. We have information which leads us to believe China is behind a secret operation to intentionally cause trouble in the Philippines and Indonesia. Among other things, they are financing drug and slave running operations around the islands. Their goal is to keep local governments and our military busy fighting a lot of small battles with provocateurs and insurgents, while they quietly build up their military in response to what they are claiming is growing criminal violence in the region." Nguyen looked confused.

"I do not understand...provoc..." he couldn't pronounce the word. McQuaid took over.

"Provocateurs are people secretly working for the government of one country, who cause trouble for the military and police of another country, distracting and confusing them. China is behind the pirates and other anti-government forces in and around the Philippines, Captain."

"Why they do dis?" It was Jake's turn at bat again.

"They want the Americans out, so they can gain more control over countries in Southeast Asia and the surrounding island groups, while their economies are still weak from the war and government officials more open to corruption. We're in their way." A storm cloud seemed to pass over Nguyen's face. But he remained silent, mulling this information over in his head. Jake pressed on. "This pirate leader, whose brother was killed, he's Chinese and is believed to be working for Madam Chin. The Chinese government is secretly working through her large network of pirates, smugglers and spies, controlling them through her, without revealing who is really behind it all." Nguyen's eyes narrowed, but he seemed to be tracking with him.

"But Americans big heroes for island people, kill Japanese, win war, give island people money to fix Manila." They had anticipated Nguyen might believe he was just taking harmless payoffs, like other law enforcement officials scattered around the islands, who at this point in time, were unsupervised by higher authority in Manila. Jake continued.

"Captain, the Chinese want people here to believe the Americans are trying to hold onto the Philippines and make them seem like bullies if they tried to prevent a Chinese military buildup. This country was granted independence by the US right after the end of the war, so we're not really trying to hold onto these islands. But the government and military here was so devastated by the Japanese, they've asked for our help while they rebuild. They've agreed to let us keep a number of military bases here for a while longer. So our military at Clark Air Force Base and the naval base at Subic Bay, will be acting on behalf of and with the full support of the independent Republic of the Philippines, when they start clamping down on the pirate's drug and slave running activities and other corruption in the region."

It was time for McQuaid to drive the final nail home. Jake handed him the map he had already pulled out of his valise, which presented a graphic illustration of Chinese covert activities around Southeast Asia. He smoothed it out on the counter in front of Nguyen and pointed to the big red arrows, sweeping out from the Chinese mainland into the Philippines and Indonesia. There was another big red arrow from China into Vietnam and Cambodia.

"These are the areas the Chinese have sent their intelligence agents into." He made sure Nguyen noticed the Cambodia and Vietnam areas. "But we've begun exposing their activities to these country's government officials, so they know who is really behind all the trouble they're having to deal with. The pirates around the Philippine islands are just another bunch of criminals the Chinese have backed to help them accomplish their long term goals." Jake jumped in again.

"What the pirates don't realize, of course, is they are doomed if the Chinese are able to gain total control. They would be the first ones put on the list for imprisonment, or worse, right alongside of this Madam Chin. Historically, the Chinese tend to rule harshly, allowing little or no personal freedoms." He swept his hand across the map. "The reason China is so big, is because they've conquered all these countries here: Mongolia, Tibet and in the recent past, even Vietnam, on the peninsula here." Nguyen seemed to notice the arrows into Vietnam, Cambodia and Thailand for the first time.

"Vietnam not Chinese," he pointed out.

"That's true. But the Chinese fought a bloody war with Vietnam in the past and enslaved the Vietnamese people. The Vietnamese fought back heroically and eventually, they were driven back out. Now the French are in their way, much like we're blocking them here in the Philippines. And they would have taken India too, but the British got there ahead of them." They needed to bring all this back to the point of their meeting with him. It was still Jake's turn. "In most cases, China has taken over all these weaker countries and has rarely been defeated, unless a foreign power blocked their progress. As you mentioned, Captain Nguyen, Vietnam is an unusual example of a smaller country fighting back and winning against overwhelming Chinese imperialism. But now, they are working behind the scenes in Vietnam and Cambodia again, using the same tactics at play here; backing criminals and rebels working to overthrow those governments, while secretly under the control and direction of the Chinese." He paused, taking a step back to allow Nguyen to look over the maps with renewed interest. After a few moment's scrutiny, the police chief looked up and his narrowed gaze passed back and forth between the two of them.

"Why you tell me 'dis?" he asked, staring at McQuaid now. He leaned forward and addressed Nguyen with renewed passion.

"I told you we need your help, Captain. The pirates have Kiko and we have to find her soon, before they hurt her, or worse. But we need to get to her before the Chinese realize we're on to them. If we don't, they'll cover their tracks by eliminating anyone who could be traced back to the Chinese leaders running the show. That means everyone in the chain, from Madam Chin all the way down." Nguyen just stared at him, his eyes focused on somewhere else in his mind. He seemed to come to a decision, straightened up and crossed his arms over his chest.

"What you need from me, Gunna?" McQuaid exhaled a long held breath.

"We can start by talking to Lijuan, to see where we can find Madam Chin. Chief Mahutra thinks they might be taking her there. If we get to her ahead of them, we might be able to take her back, before she is hidden away and lost to us, somewhere in the miles of waterfront around Hong Kong." Nguyen nodded, as if he had come to the same conclusion.

"I help you, but you kill no more pirates, Gunna," he announced. He looked over at Jake. "I need help from American soldiers here. Pirates come back, dey look for me and hurt island people in Lubang. Pirates come look for Lijuan. She will not tell dem I keep her all time in jail. 'Dis must happen for sure. What you say?" Jake was ready for this.

"Captain, I promise you our military will be here to protect the town and keep the pirates from taking Lijuan out of your custody. You are the Sheriff of all Lubang's territory. Just tell me what you need for us to do to help you." It seemed to McQuaid, as if Nguyen stood a little straighter. He turned around and yelled something in Tagalog. His Deputy, Cho, reappeared as if by magic. He must have been just on the other side of the rear office door, waiting for the signal.

He handed the police chief a ring of keys, then wandered out around the counter and down the hall. They heard the door to the front of the police station open and close. Nguyen motioned for them to follow him into the back and he led the way through the back office door, into an area where they had two small jail cells. Lijuan was sitting on a cot in the first cell, watching them as they walked over. McQuaid smiled at her while he waited for Nguyen to open the lock and let them in. Nguyen looked in at her as he opened the door.

"You have visitor, Lijuan," he said to her, as if that weren't obvious. She stood up, smoothing her clothing and brushing her hair back out of her eyes, looking back at the men without expression. She seemed suspicious as she sized up Major Wilmouth, whom she hadn't seen before, wearing a military uniform. Nguyen stood to the side and let them in, but made no move to leave them alone with her. McQuaid expected this however.

"Hello again Lijuan. You look much better than the last time we spoke." She smiled back, nodding her head in return. McQuaid continued, turning toward Jake to introduce him. "This is my friend, Major Jake Wilmouth. He and I flew together in the war." Jake stepped forward to shake her hand, surprised at what a beautiful young girl she was, but also noting she was quite nervous. That wasn't surprising however, considering she was facing three strange men, all with different agendas for her.

"Pleased to meet you," he offered in simple reply. He intended to follow Gunner's lead on this one. McQuaid noticed Nguyen out of the corner of his eye, wary and watching them both. She did look better since McQuaid had seen her in the hospital a couple days before. But he could see the worry on her face. Still, he was relieved to see she didn't appear to be any worse the wear from interrogations she may have endured from Nguyen. He came right to the point, not sure how much patience he could expect from the police chief.

"Lijuan, we wanted to talk with you about a little girl the pirates have taken, named Kiko. You might have noticed her when we first brought you to the hospital." Lijuan's expression remained neutral. "She's a local island girl and only nine years old. Mattie Adams and I, she's my partner in our air cargo business, adopted her after the Japanese attacked her village and killed her family a number of years back. They have taken her somewhere, along with another group of young girls and we're hoping you might know where." He paused, waiting for a reaction.

Lijuan's eyes flicked toward Nguyen and then back to the two Americans. She had been holding her arms stiff against her sides. She moved one hand up to brush her hair back from her eyes, but thus far, wasn't offering any sign she could help. McQuaid wondered how much she knew and what she might have been instructed to hide. He turned to Nguyen in frustration and asked that he step out into the office with him. The police chief frowned at him, but went along without protest. McQuaid spoke to him just outside the door, his voice as low as possible.

"Captain Nguyen, could we have a few moments alone with Lijuan? She's clearly scared to talk with you around. I'm not sure why, but I promise you, anything she tells us that could be of benefit to you, I will let you know. I really only want to get information from her about Kiko." Nguyen surprised him by offering no resistance. He pointed back the way they'd come.

"You talk Lijuan for five minutes Gunna. No more. I come back five minutes. Dis' girl my problem. I help you find Kiko; help Mattie. You remember I help you Gunna." He looked at McQuaid with eyebrows raised in expectation of something more; meaning some quid pro quo. McQuaid nodded in understanding.

"Don't worry, Captain. We'll back you up if it comes to that. Personally, I think you'll be the least of anyone's worries, pirates or otherwise." They were just about ready to head back in, when they heard peals of laughter coming from the jail. He and Nguyen looked at each, puzzled. They pushed their way back in to find Lijuan doubled over on the cot, laughing, watching Jake strutting back and forth in front of the bars of her cell. He was hunched forward, his hat pulled low over his eyes, hands hovering over his hips like a gunslinger, eyes squinting, lips puckered; as if he were concentrating on something, or someone in the distance. McQuaid had to stifle a laugh.

As soon as Jake realized they had returned, he straightened up, whipped his hat off and offered an award winning performance of an innocent man, caught in the act of doing nothing. Nguyen was confused, looking from him to Lijuan and back. When no one seemed to find any of Jake's antics unusual, he just wandered back out front to his office, shaking his head. Lijuan had her hand over her mouth, trying not to burst out laughing again. Jake was smiling back at her, as if they had been sharing a funny secret together. Then he turned back to McQuaid, his eyebrows arched, his hands on his hips, as if he were daring him to accuse him of the obvious. Lijuan pointed at him and busted out laughing again in spite of herself. The look on Jake's face made McQuaid laugh too.

"What?" Jake asked, feigning ridiculous innocence. "You've never seen my shootout at the OK Corral impression before?" He did a fast draw with his right hand, index finger and thumb in the shape of a pistol. He finished by blowing on his finger, as if it was the overheated barrel of a six shooter. Then he grinned at McQuaid, like the caricature of a sappy cartoon hero.

"Really? That's what that was? For a moment there, I could have sworn you were making fun of Captain Nguyen." Jake feigned distress at the injustice of being stabbed by his trusted friend.

"Now you know me better than that, Gunner! Would I stand here, an officer and a gentleman, poking fun at a duly elected peace officer, in his own police station?" But McQuaid wouldn't bite. Jake looked over at Lijuan and grinned again. "Well, I got her to laugh at least, didn't I?" Indeed he had. Lijuan stood up, composing herself and walked over to McQuaid.

"Your friend is very funny," she said, her smile more distant now. "Thank you for coming back for me, Mister McQuaid." She looked at him, her face solemn. "Captain Nguyen has not hurt me, but he told me not to talk about pirates, or the drugs with anyone but him. I think he is worried they will come back for me and he will not be able to stop them." McQuaid was thinking, all else considered, that might be the last thing he was worried about. Lijuan continued, looking back and forth at both of them. "I can tell you where to find Madam Chin. They take island girls to her for sale in Hong Kong. But they keep new girls in many places. Only Madam Chin knows for sure where they take them." Jake was considering this.

"Lijuan, how many brothels does Madam Chin control in Hong Kong?" She paused to think about that for a moment.

"She owns many buildings and boats in Hong Kong. It is a very large city Major. She also owns other places where men come for women, in other cities in China." McQuaid felt the knot in his gut tighten again, along with a familiar sinking feeling of despair seeping into his bones. He caught Jake's eye. They didn't have to say anything. It was all beginning to appear hopeless. Lijuan could see they were at a loss to know what to do next. "I am sorry I cannot be more help to you Mister McQuaid. I have made you a lot of trouble. You should give me back to the pirates. They will return me to Madam Chin. I will look for Kiko and try to contact you later." Her almond eyes welled up with tears as she looked up at him, her face distorted with emotion, distraught over the helpless state of their situation. It was an astounding and selfless sacrifice for her to make. McQuaid was touched. He pulled her against his chest, his hand against the back of her head. She put her arms around him, hiding her face, sobbing.

"It's not your fault Lijuan," he replied, keeping his voice soft, resting his chin on the top of her head. "If anyone, I'm the one to blame here." Jake caught his attention and he turned to look at him.

"Gunner, I just thought of something. You remember I told you we would put feelers out to the British in Hong Kong?" McQuaid nodded. "They might be able to help us. If anyone knows what goes on along the waterfront there, they should know." Lijuan pulled away from him, looking over at Jake, her tear streaked face distorted in alarm. She shook her head at him.

"Madam Chin pays British government men in Hong Kong much money. They will not help you find her." McQuaid mulled over this new twist. Since the war, the British had regained control and the administration of Hong Kong. If money was to be made, there would plenty of room for corruption in their ranks. Paying for protection was a time honored business practice in every country. But there had to be others who played by the rules. He needed to get to Hong Kong and scout out the situation first hand.

"Jake, I'm going to head into Hong Kong myself. I need to find this Madam Chin and I'll do whatever I have to do to locate Kiko and get her back. If you have contacts there, it could cut down the time I'd spend trying to do it all on my own. Jake looked at him askance for a moment, then frowned and shook his head at him.

"Gunner, you can't just drop in on Madam Chin, on her turf, surrounded by all her goons. Even if you could find her, why should she just turn Kiko over to you?" Lijuan put her hand up to his face.

"Mister McQuaid, you must listen to your friend," she said, imploring him to be sensible. "Madam Chin has many men who protect her and her property. She is wise and powerful. She will have you killed before you can find her. She has many eyes and ears in Hong Kong. You are only one man. This is a very bad idea." She dropped her hand, but continued looking into his eyes, hoping he would see the truth of what she was saying to him. He was listening, but his frustration with not being able to do anything had been growing too. Without any doubt, there was nothing he could do about finding Kiko here on Lubang. And McQuaid was not the kind of man to stand around waiting. He turned back to Jake.

"I've got to head over to Clark, no matter what and check on Mattie. But then I plan on flying into Hong Kong. I don't expect you to go with me Snake. That's way out of your jurisdiction and I imagine the Marine Corps would frown on you getting involved in any way." Jake just looked at him, but he could see in his eyes he was right. He looked back at Lijuan. "Do me one favor, if you can. If Captain Nguyen asks you where I've gone, just tell him, since we don't know where to find Kiko, I told you I'm flying back to Clark hospital to take care of Mattie. Will you do that for me Lijuan?" She nodded her head without hesitation. "Good. Thank you for your help." He took her small hand in his, leaned down and kissed her on the forehead. She closed her eyes, a tear running down her face.

"Good bye Mister McQuaid. I will pray for you," she said, almost whispering the last few words. He smiled back, patting her hand. He looked over at Jake.

"Ready?" They spoke to Nguyen on the way out, letting him know Lijuan had not been as much help as he'd hoped.

"We're heading back to Clark Air Force Base tonight. I need to check on Mattie. She'll want to know we still haven't located Kiko." Nguyen was sitting behind his desk and leaned back in his chair upon hearing they were leaving Lubang.

"Lijuan no help you find Kiko?" He seemed concerned.

"She says there are many places she could be in Hong Kong. There is no way she could know which place they might take her." Nguyen just looked back, like he was thinking that over. "What are you planning to do with Lijuan, Captain?" Nguyen scowled and looked down at the papers he had been reading on his desk; then met McQuaid's eyes again.

"I need take Lijuan to police in Manila. Dey send me letter to bring her about dead people on 'dis boat. Dey British people from Hong Kong. British police from Hong Kong want talk with her. She know 'bout drugs and pirates. Mebbe she work for pirates too." He ran his hand over the top of his head, wiping away the beaded sweat in frustration. "Dey put her in jail in Manila for judge in Manila. Not in Lubang." Nguyen seemed angry. But McQuaid didn't have the time or patience to deal with this anymore. Time was running out for Kiko and he was worried about Mattie too.

"Thanks for your help, Captain. I'll be back in a few days. I'll stay in touch with Baacay by radio." Nguyen just nodded, his eyes following them as he and Jake made their way out into the early evening. It had started to rain again. *Great*, he thought, *another night flight back to Clark in a storm*. But looking up at the sky, it just looked dark, without the usual wind and thunder. At least that was in his favor.

He and Jake didn't speak much on the way back to the hangar. Baacay met them and McQuaid told him they still didn't have any word on where to find Kiko. It was best to keep his flight to Hong Kong a secret from him too; for now. He would be taking the Goose, so he left Jake to keep Baacay busy, while he made sure he still had extra clips for the Thompson submachine guns and enough grenades stowed aboard. He also checked to make sure the raft was still secured in the rear area, before he walked back to the cargo office. Baacay and Jake looked up as he came through the door.

"Okay, it looks like I'll take the Goose over to Clark this time. That engine they put in seemed a little rough. They installed it, so I want them to look it over just in case." Jake nodded.

"Sounds like a plan. I'll fly over with you. I've got to get back to work and my guys are probably wondering what happened to me by now." He stood up, grabbed his duffel bag and shook Baacay's hand. "Hope we see each other again real soon." Baacay smiled, nodding back at him and they walked out to the airplanes together. He helped Major Wilmouth into his fighter and then stood by with a fire bottle, while he cranked the engine, a cloud of smoke pouring out of the exhaust stacks of the big Pratt & Whitney radial engine, as the eighteen cylinders lit off, one after the other. Jake gave him a thumbs-up, once the big three bladed prop was spinning and the deep throated engine rumbling, at a low rpm idle. He wheeled the fire bottle over for the fire watch on McQuaid's start-up. But he was still standing outside the rear cargo hatch waiting for him. He put his arm around the smaller man, pulling him over to the side away from the Corsair's engine noise to talk with him.

"Baacay, I'm not sure how soon we'll be able to bring Mattie home from the hospital on Clark, but I need you hire a couple friends and fix all the damage to the store. I don't want Mattie to see it like it is right now. Do you understand?" Baacay shook his head with great enthusiasm, but then looked worried as an afterthought. McQuaid smiled back at him, anticipating his concern. "Don't worry; she's a very tough lady. She'll be okay. I don't know how soon I'll be able to return, so just do whatever you need to do to get it all ready for her." Baacay grinned back at him.

"You no worry Gunna'. I fix store. Open fo' people in Lubang. Mattie show me how take care of store. I make sure Nguyen pay fo' beer too!" He grinned again. McQuaid laughed with him, then pulled an envelope out of his back pocket and handed it to him.

"There should be enough money in here to pay for repairs and to restock all the shelves with anything we lost in the fire. If you need something from the marketplace in Manila, get Rajan on the radio and have him bring it over in his boat." Baacay nodded, taking the envelope and putting it into the deep front pocket of his shorts. "One last thing – Chief Mahutra told me he's leaving some of his men in town to help you guard the hangar and the store while I'm away. I wrote down a telephone number for Major Wilmouth's office on the envelope for you too. If the pirates come back, get on the radio to Rajan and have him call him at that number on Clark Air Force Base. He'll send help if you need it. So you should be okay until I can get back." Baacay nodded. "I'm depending on you. You're the boss while I'm away Baacay."

"We be okay Gunna'. You no worry. Tell Mattie, she no worry. I take care of store and watch airplane." McQuaid could tell he would do all that and more. He winked back at him and squeezed his shoulder. Then jumped into the Goose and slammed the cargo door after him.

Chapter Twenty
Clark AFB Hospital, Luzon Island, the Philippines

The rain had become a deluge by the time they got off the runway, so they climbed to get through the storm clouds and on top to clearer air. McQuaid had the throttles almost against the stops. He kept one eye on the instruments and the other looking out the windshield, hoping soon to see stars ahead, instead of an endless blur of water and blackness. Jake was ahead of him somewhere, a few miles ahead by now, flying the much faster Corsair. At seven thousand feet, they were still climbing, with zero visibility.

"Gunner, you still okay back there?" They were both busy just flying the airplanes, but it was good to hear a familiar voice.

"Yeah, I just passed through seven thousand. How's it look up ahead Snake?" McQuaid reached up and pulled the engine mixture handles back another notch, leaning the fuel a little more, as the air grew thinner in the higher altitude. It wasn't an exact science and with the thicker humidity in the rain clouds even less so. He could just tell by the engine sound when the fuel to air mixture was out of whack.

"I'm already through ten thousand now. The rain's starting to lighten up. I'd give it another thousand feet or so and I should be on top." The Goose was much slower and the Corsair was turbo-charged, in addition to being much lighter, with a far superior power to weight ratio. So he expected Jake to punch through the clouds a lot faster than him. Sure enough, before long he was back on the radio with him. "Okay Gunner, I just popped out of the soup at eleven thousand six hundred feet. I'm leveling off here and will throttle back to let you catch up." McQuaid just gave him two clicks on the mike to acknowledge.

About five minutes later, he was above the rain and popped through the clouds into a clear, bright starry night on top. The moon was near full and lit the cloud caps in breath taking whites and silvers against the jet black of night. He could see wide dark holes in the clouds beyond, so it appeared the worst of the weather was behind them. A few miles ahead, he could just make out the winking navigation lights on an aircraft; at about the same altitude. That had to be Jake's Corsair.

253

"I'm on top now Snake, leveling off at a little over eleven thousand feet, heading zero-one-seven degrees. I think I have you spotted a few miles ahead of me, just about twelve o'clock." Jake clicked his mike and he noticed his navigation lights pause and reverse direction. He must have turned back to face him, and then flicked his landing lights off and on twice. That was a positive ID. "Okay, I see your landing lights. Stay there and I'll catch up with you in a couple minutes."

"Tally you Gunner. I'll swing back and form up with you on your left wing."

"That'll work. I'll stay level and maintain present course and altitude." Two clicks back in response. His lights got bigger and then he flashed by his right wing and out of sight, to circle around behind him. McQuaid figured they were almost to the Luzon coastline by his math. He already had the ADF for Clark dialed in and was also monitoring the Manila airport frequency too, just in case there was other traffic in the area. It would be hard to miss another airplane in the vicinity though. He could spot their navigation lights for over twenty miles all around him. There didn't seem to be anyone else around and Manila tower was quiet. Stormy weather kept everyone who didn't have to be in the air, huddled on the ground with the birds for the rest of the night. He could just see the radio tower lights blinking to the left and below, on the south slope of Samat Peak and another set of beacon lights against a majestic set of twin peaks poking through the blanket of clouds on the right. That would be Mount Mariveles, which guarded the entrance to Manila Bay. They'd be hugging the southeastern slope of Mount Samat, on a direct course line into Clark. Both mountains were old calderas; Mariveles being the younger of the two.

"Snugging up on your left here, Gunner." McQuaid glanced out the left cockpit window and could see the green nav-light winking at him from Jake's starboard wing tip. Red was left and green was right; same as ships.

"I see you Snake. I'll keep her steady." Soon they were in standard formation, flying along with each other at eye level. "Nice night over here don't you think?"

"Beautiful. And it appears to be clearing on the other side of the Bataan peninsula. We could probably start our descent in a few minutes. By the way, I've been meaning to tell you what a crazy idea this is." McQuaid was surprised it took him this long.

254

"You mean flying into Hong Kong by myself?"

"Yeah, that. If I could go with you I would, but that doesn't mean I'd want to. What are you hoping to gain? There are miles of waterfront around Hong Kong Island. They could be keeping her anywhere. And just because it's a British territory, doesn't mean they're all friendly."

"I know Snake. But I'm tired of sitting around trying to figure out what to do about it," he replied, finding it hard to keep the frustration out of his voice. There was a long pause before Jake came back.

"Listen, I know you how you feel. We're both Marines. Sometimes you have to fix bayonets, stop thinking so much and just charge the hill. That's great when you have the enemy surrounded and enough men to make it to the top, despite the casualties. But you're one guy, in a strange country, surrounded by millions of Chinese and a few scattered Brits. All I'm saying is, you need as much intel going in as you can get. A little cavalry to back you up wouldn't be such a bad idea either, sport." He was making sense of course, but McQuaid was in no mood to wait for reinforcements at this point. Still, maybe Jake had a card or two up his sleeve.

"What did you have in mind, Snake?" His voice was flat, hinting he had no real affection for the subject.

"Just give me a day to make contact with British intelligence in Hong Kong. If anyone knows about what goes on along the waterfront, they should. They seemed to know quite a bit about the Chinese government's clandestine operations concerning the pirates. If this Madam Chin is controlling smuggling networks on the ground, don't you think they'd have people keeping an eye on her?" McQuaid thought about that. It was a bright spot in his dimmer plans thus far. Maybe Jake was right. It sure would make life easier if he knew how to pinpoint where they might be holding Kiko. But Jake wasn't through. "And another thing, just because you've worked with Nguyen in the past and think you know him, doesn't mean I'd trust that guy as far as I could chuck that fat deputy of his. He may be setting you up as we speak."

"But he doesn't know I'm planning on flying into Hong Kong. He probably thinks I've given up." It even sounded lame to him. He could picture Jake shaking his head over there.

"We both know he's a lap dog. If he has anything he could share with the pirates to make himself look informed and valuable, he'll get word to them somehow. And Lijuan, I'm not sure what went on between you and her, but she seems too eager to please. Don't start thinking with your little head over there Marine." He was right about one thing, he didn't have any idea what went on between them; it was complicated. And it would be awkward to explain too. Jake was mostly black and white. Those were conversations Marines just didn't have with each other.

Besides all that, if the truth were told, he was attracted to her. Why wouldn't he be? She was young, exotic and beautiful. It was a classic set-up – for a big jar-headed Marine that is. He knew better. One thing he'd learned as an orphan, if it looks too good to be true, it probably is. And even if she were falling for him, she'd be bringing way more baggage than he was looking for. He'd already set his course in life with Mattie and Kiko now. Not only was Mattie the safer bet for him, she was far better tuned to his psyche. Maybe he even loved her. He had implied to her that he did. It felt good and unnerving at the same time. McQuaid didn't let people in.

Since he had last seen her, lying there burning up with fever, he had been afraid she might not make it. He'd bottled that fear up and stowed it away; out of sight. But panic was beginning to wrap its icy tendrils around his mind and body again; dragging him toward an old deep, dark abyss he had known as a child.

Mattie had become a warm and wonderful flame in his life. He had resisted her at first. It was so much easier to just soldier on, trudging straight ahead, avoiding encumbering entanglements. But Kiko had sneaked up on him. She had pried open his heart again. And Mattie slipped in that open door, right behind her. Now his worst fears could soon be realized. Jake had begun talking again, his voice pulling him back from this downward spiral.

"Another thing, Gunner. As imperative as it is for you to find Kiko, I think Mattie needs you more right now. At least until she gets back on her feet. You'd never forgive yourself if you went after Kiko and..." His voice trailed off.

"And she died alone, without me there to be with her?" he finished for him.

"Yeah, that's what I meant to say; maybe not so bluntly."

"And if I don't go after Kiko, to be with Mattie and I find out later I could have saved Kiko? I'd feel much better about that?" His anger and frustration came through loud and clear, even over the radio. Jake didn't answer.

The ADF beacon beeped, sounding off the Clark AFB Morse code identifier in his ear and he noticed the needle had snapped over to point out the correct bearing to the base from their present position. It was time to start their descent. He glanced left to make sure Jake was clear of his wing tip, then reached forward and pulled back the throttles, feeling the aircraft begin to slow and sink. He dialed in Clark's tower frequency and heard Jake already calling in their position and landing request. It was just as well. He didn't feel much like talking.

They landed without incident and even though the rain had stopped some time ago, the tires swished through standing water on the runway. By the time they hitched a ride to the hospital, it was almost eight o'clock. McQuaid was still quiet and brooding. Jake had filed their paperwork and ordered fuel by the time he jumped into the jeep next to him. He pulled a flask out of his flight jacket pocket, took a swig and handed it over to McQuaid.

"Here, I know Dennehy would approve. You look like you could use a dose." McQuaid took the flask and downed a decent snort of the hot, burning elixir. Indeed, it would have been doctor prescribed. He felt like he needed to brace himself to face what might lay ahead for him at the hospital. Whatever was happening, it would decide his next move and perhaps the rest of his life ahead. He was anxious to know which way it was going to be.

There was only one nurse at the nurse's station and she was on the phone. With Jake in trail, he continued down the hallway to Mattie's room and pushed open the door. The lights were off, but after his eyes adjusted to the near darkness, he realized her bed was empty and had been stripped. His first reaction was confusion, then panic, followed by anger, all in a split second. Jake stood beside him now, staring at the empty bed.

"Wouldn't someone let you know if she'd been discharged?" he asked. McQuaid reached up to rub his eyes with his forefinger and thumb, trying to imagine how she might have gotten better fast enough to have already been discharged. He suppressed a couple choice expletives in favor of pausing to consider other possibilities.

"Probably. I would think they'd let me know where she's been moved to in any case." Dire possibilities began to wedge their way into his more rational mind. He reached over to the wall and flipped on the lights, hoping there might be some clues somewhere in the room. But the room had been stripped of anything personal, like the bed. "Let's see if we can find someone who knows something. They may have tried to reach me somehow. But it's not like we were near a telephone or anything." Jake nodded in agreement.

They walked back out to the nursing station to speak with the duty nurse. She listened as McQuaid inquired about Mattie and after referring to her files and an active patient roster on her clipboard, let them know she didn't have any record of Mattie's release, or transfer – strange, to say the least. McQuaid asked the dreaded question, whether it was possible she had died and been removed from the room. The nurse again referred to her files and told them she had no evidence Mattie had even been a patient in that room, but if she had expired, they would have sent her records with the body to the morgue. Jake stepped forward to help.

"Mam, I'm Major Wilmouth, U.S. Marine Corps, here on temporary detached duty. Is Major Dennehy around? He's been an attending physician for Ms. Adams." She was trying to help and looked through the doctor schedules.

"I show Doctor Dennehy was on the schedule earlier today, but I don't have him attending the patient you're talking about." She looked back up at him from her file.

"Is there a way we can get in touch with Major Dennehy...?"

"Why don't you gentlemen wait in the mess and I'll call him? He just went off duty an hour ago and it's not too late at night." She gave them both her firm and professional smile. "I'll come and get you as soon as I know something more." McQuaid sighed, massaging the back of his neck, where the muscles were taut like cords.

"That would be terrific, mam. Thank you for your help." Jake gave her a dazzling smile and they headed off to the mess to wait. As they turned the corner, out of earshot, McQuaid couldn't contain himself any longer.

"What the hell was that all about?" His kept his voice low, but he was getting hotter and more worried by the minute. Jake was also at a loss to explain how they could have simply "lost" a patient. He was shaking his head as they rounded the last corner to the mess and recognized the back of Major Dennehy's head; his body hunched over one of the tables, facing away from the doorway.

"There's Dennehy now! Maybe we can finally get some answers." They headed over and circled around the table to face him. There, sitting across from him, was Mattie, in an unattractive hospital robe and slippers, but otherwise looking very much alive. She even appeared in surprising good health. She looked up at McQuaid and it seemed to him as if she lit up the entire room.

"Richard!" She tried to stand up and winced in pain. He moved around the table and took her into his arms. "Richard, god it's so good to see you!" He was worried about squeezing her, so he leaned over her and as gentle as possible, held her against his chest.

"Mattie, we didn't know what happened to you. We couldn't find you anywhere," he replied, his voice husky. By now Dennehy had pushed his chair back to stand up, turning to Jake with a confused look on his face.

"We sent word to you through the squadron. Didn't they reach you by radio?" He seemed put out by the lack of Air Force efficiency, implying Army efficiency, where he came from, would never have created such a problem.

"No one here could tell us where she was, or even that she'd been here at all Major," Jake replied back, sounding testy, despite his joy at seeing Mattie was okay. Dennehy's consternation was now even more pronounced. He pointed to a thick brown file folder lying on the table in front of them.

"I've got her patient folder right here, for you to take back to her doctor on Lubang. But they should have had her room transfer and outpatient info at the nurses station." He ran his hands over his face and then over his balding head in exasperation. McQuaid had pulled his chair over next to Mattie now; with his arm around her shoulders and waved his free hand back at Dennehy.

"Don't worry about it Doc. I'm just happy to see she's recovered." He looked back into her eyes now, deeper brown than usual and only inches away. "You are recovered, aren't you?" he asked, watching her as if he thought she might keel over. She just squeezed his hand, kissed him on the cheek and looked back at the doctor.

"I'm feeling much better, thanks to Major Dennehy. Don't worry, if it wasn't for all the stitches holding my chest together, I'd be doing cartwheels right about now." Dennehy gave her a little wave as he stepped back to allow them room together.

"Glad I could help, Ms. Adams. But I must say, you are one tough little cookie." He grinned back at her. "I have to get going kids." He looked down at Mattie with a doctor's frown. "I insist you need to spend one last night in that room I arranged for you, so I can get a final peek at you tomorrow before I sign your walking papers." He smiled down at her. "Just to make sure, young lady," he said, cupping her chin with his hand and looking into her eyes. "I think you'll find it's just what you need right now." He winked at her; making her blush. She nodded back to him and beamed at McQuaid.

"You can wait one more night before you send me back to the salt mines, can't you Richard?" He frowned back.

"Only, if you promise to clock in an hour early, every day for the next few years." They all laughed and Dennehy made a polite exit, allowing Jake to sit down in his chair opposite them. Mattie waited until Dennehy was out of sight and looked back and forth between the two of them.

"Well?" They knew she was referring to Kiko. She could tell by their faces the news wasn't going to be good. McQuaid sighed and pulled his arm around to place both hands on the table; pausing before launching into it. She was impatient. "Snake?" She looked to him, since McQuaid seemed to be at some loss for words. Jake, who was rarely at any loss for words, decided he needed to take the point.

"Well, it turns out the pirates snatched Kiko, like we feared." He leaned forward in his chair, eyeing McQuaid for a sign he should hand him the ball. McQuaid just motioned for him to continue. "We think they took her to Hong Kong, along with a group of other young girls from the islands." Mattie sat straight up.

"Hong Kong? Well at least she's alive. Why the hell would they take her all the way over there?" She pondered that for a second or two, before she arched her back around to look at McQuaid, her mouth hanging open; eyes wide with shock. "They took her to Madam Chin?" The table remained silent for a moment or two longer, as her revelation continued to unfold. "With other girls they plan on selling into prostitution?" Her voice was rising now, her face turning red with anger. "I will find that harpy and tear her eyes out if she harms Kiko in any way, if it's the last thing I do." McQuaid knew it would be useless to point out she was in no condition to do anything of the sort. But he had little doubt, looking at her face, if Madam Chin were in the room at the moment; she would be in the gravest peril of losing her eyesight, at the very least.

"Mattie, I'm leaving first thing tomorrow morning to fly over to Hong Kong. I'm staying there until I find her and can bring her back." Mattie was looking at him, her eyes still flashing daggers. Then, what he had just told her fully registered. Her face shifted from anger, to horror in the space of a few heartbeats. She grabbed his arm with a death grip.

"By yourself? Richard, you can't do that!" His expression remained frozen. She could see he had made his decision and nothing she could say would get through to him. She turned to Jake for support. "Major Wilmouth," she corrected herself, "Snake. Can't you talk some sense into him? I thought you were his friend!" Jake glowered back at McQuaid.

"There. See how you take advantage of my friendship? Now I'm the fall guy for your incredibly bad behavior." McQuaid shot him a pained look in return. Jake looked back at Mattie, shrugging his shoulders. "What can I do if he insists on charging into the fray with a toothpick for a spear?" He put his hand over hers. "If it's any consolation, my dear, he won't be going it alone."

"Really?" she asked. McQuaid raised his eyebrows. This was news to him as well.

"Absolutely. We have good relations with the British in Hong Kong of course. And the Chinese are very happy to have them back in charge of the islands, after their less than satisfying experience with the Japanese occupation. I've got contacts there with British military officials we can turn to for local assistance. So, I wouldn't worry about him having to be the Lone Ranger." McQuaid neglected to pose the question of loyalties to Madam Chin and payoffs to British bureaucrats, who might be more trouble than they were worth. He didn't want to create more concern for Mattie at this point. Jake was addressing him now. "You'll want to fly into the Royal Air Force base at Kai Tak. I want to arrange for someone I thought of to meet you there – an intelligence agent. He can help you navigate the sometimes murky waters between the RAF, the Crown Territories Districts administration and Chinese police officials. Locating Kiko will only be part of the problem we need to deal with. Getting her back and both of you out of

Hong Kong safely, avoiding a lot of unnecessary red tape, will be the real hat trick." He raised an eyebrow at McQuaid, intending to pass along a more sinister implication. "I need to get over to base ops tonight, and start getting communiques out, if you insist on tearing over there first thing tomorrow." McQuaid was reading his body language and knew they needed to cover a lot more in private.

"Did you want to get together tonight still?" he asked, thinking he meant they should do this right away. Jake waved that off.

"Not necessary. I've got a bunch of work to do and you'd just be sitting around, getting in the way, until I know more. We'll meet tomorrow, early AM." He looked over at Mattie with a smirk. "Besides, I'm thinking you might need to spend a little time with your business partner here. I'm sure you both have a lot of things you'll want to catch up on." He waggled his eyebrows at her. Mattie blushed and punched him in the arm.

"Now I know how you got that nickname, Snake." she countered, but smiled back at him, appreciating his consideration. He was indeed perceptive. She looked into McQuaid's eyes. "Do you mind walking me to my room, as long as you seem to have a little extra time ashore, sailor?" she asked, her voice low and breathy. She batted her eye lashes back at him for effect, managing to keep a straight face. McQuaid gave her a lascivious leer in return.

"Are ye shor' yore knowin' the dangers of cavortin' with the likes of a salty sea dog?" he growled, in his best imitation of Cap'n Kidd. Jake just rolled his eyes, but he seemed to achieve the intended effect on Mattie. She just reached up and pulled his face to hers, looking at him nose to nose, their eyes only an inch or so apart.

"Have no fear, sir. I'll go easy on you." With that, she closed her eyes and kissed him firmly on the lips, holding their kiss until she heard Jake, "harrumph" on the other side of the table. He scraped his chair as he got to his feet.

"Well kiddies, I'll just shove off; as long as you don't need me for anything else?" He waited, dangling the "anything else" for a moment or two. The kissing continued unabated, but both Mattie and McQuaid raised their hands and offered him a finger wave. Jake chuckled and made his way out of the mess and down the hall, already thinking about everything he needed to get done that night to keep his pal McQuaid's rear out of the fire tomorrow.

His mind's eye drifted back to the exotic vision of the Chinese cocktail waitress at the "O" Club from the night before. Hopeful for a moment, he checked his watch and then frowned; sighing in resignation. If Gunner only knew the sacrifices he made. He hailed a passing jeep outside the hospital and headed back to base ops to get to work. He needed to hurry if he was going to reach Laddie Dunross, at ASIO in Hong Kong tonight. Jake smiled to himself. This sort of caper was a perfect match for the big Aussie intelligence agent. He also had a healthy disrespect for the Brits running Hong Kong too. If anyone could help McQuaid tip-toe around that minefield, Laddie was the man for the job.

Mattie dragged McQuaid to her room, "ssh-ing" him along the way, as she peeked around corners to make sure they were slipping by hospital staff unobserved. They made it to her door at the end of a long hall in the convalescent wing of the hospital. She was giggling like a school girl and had backed against the closed door, pulling him against her, watching his face.

"Well, this is my room," she said shyly.

"So it is." He was smiling down at her, feeling the warmth of her body pressed against his. Some of her hair had been flung across her face, with all the running around and her brown eyes peeked out at him with a childish innocence. Her body smelled of soap and fresh skin. He brushed the hair away from her face and kissed her, then drew back to look at her again. She kept her eyes closed and her lips parted, then ran her tongue over them, savoring the taste of him. Seeming reluctant, she allowed her eyes to open again, peering deeply into his. He was waiting for her.

"Did you want to come in for a night cap or something?" she asked, drawing out the question; not sure how he would respond; hoping she had read him right; wanting him, but needing him to want her as much.

"You actually have booze in there?" he asked, gray eyes twinkling; his mouth turned up at one corner, taunting her. She smiled back, dropping her eyes with a mischievous look. She was enjoying the playful lustiness of the moment, but was aware of a hunger growing inside and their time remaining, precious.

"We could look around – maybe find something." She rolled her eyes to the side and caught her lower lip with her teeth, appearing to be deliberating their options with care. He leaned against her warmth, nuzzling her left ear with his lips and pulling the earlobe into his mouth. Mattie shivered, ducking her head and pulling away, feeling an electric shock travel down from her ear to her loins. She thrust her hips against him in reflex, feeling a hardness growing against her. Grabbing the front of his shirt, she pulled him closer, her lips against his face.

"McQuaid, if you don't take me inside and make love to me right now, I'm going to rip your clothes off out here in the hallway," she mouthed, in an insistent, but low, sultry voice. Her breath rushed out of her, as his lips moved to her ear again, feeling the rough stubble of his face against her skin.

"Are you sure we wouldn't pop some of your stitches?" he asked, chuckling, reaching down to pull the ties on her robe loose, and pressing himself closer still, feeling the heat of her body through the thin cotton gown. She gasped, fumbling behind her for the door handle.

"I don't think popping my stitches should be your biggest concern right now Marine," Her hand found the handle and the door gave way. Still clutching his shirt with her other hand, she drew him into the cool dark of the room, feeling her way to sit back on the narrow bed. Stripping off her robe, she flung it on the floor and began working his shirt over his head. The door had closed behind them, the only light in the room now, coming in under the sill from the hallway outside. They could just make each other out, as frantic, ghostly images. He moved away from her just long enough to drop his pants. She scooted back to lay back on the bed, drawing him down to her, feeling his hand sliding her gown up above her thighs. She stopped his hand.

"Just leave that on for now. I don't want all those ugly, scratchy bandages coming between us." He paused, not quite able to see details of her face, but placed a gentle hand against her cheek, reassuring and loving her.

"Are you sure we should be doing this so soon after...?"

"I'm so sure, Richard," she hissed. She put her hand over his, pulling his palm down to her lips, feeling him move on top of her and gasped as he joined with her. Tears came to her eyes, not from pain, but joy, as Mattie realized she was able to let him into her mind and body, without feeling the guilt of betraying Frank anymore. He had been the love of her life. No one but Frank had ever touched her this way. But she knew this man in ways she could have never known Frank.

Her hands were around the back of his neck, fingers splayed across his broad shoulders, pulling him deep inside and into her being. Tears ran down her cheeks, but she was smiling, happy, for the first time in many lonely years.

Chapter Twenty-One
Aberdeen Harbor, Hong Kong Island, China

It was still dark when McQuaid slipped out from under Mattie's arm and made his way to his heap of clothes next to the bed. The radium numbers on his watch displayed the time as just before five AM. He needed to get over to meet with Jake and also feared a nurse might be stopping in at any moment to check on Mattie. They'd been lucky so far. Or, on second thought, maybe Major Dennehy had done them the favor of keeping her off the schedule for hospital rounds for the night. After all, he was planning on discharging her later this morning anyway. He thought back to their conversation in the mess and remembered Dennehy telling her the room he had arranged for her was just what she needed right now; then winking at her. Smiling to himself, he realized they'd been in on this together. There was far more to this one than met the eye.

He glanced over at the silhouette on the bed and grinned. They'd been left alone to explore each other and indulge their passions in private. Later, they had lain together, Mattie's head on his shoulder, dragging her fingertips through the thick matte of hair on his chest, both of them content to enjoy their moment; leaving unspoken possibilities and fears for another time.

Unlike with Gwen, their lovemaking had lacked any sort of frenzy, or defined expectation. Mattie seemed to have a prescient sense for what he needed, moving his hands and body to hers, in sensual ways, guiding him with touch and soft sounds, which required no words. There was much they would need to discuss, as their lives were now even more intertwined than before. But he knew they would somehow find their way to face whatever the future presented them, together.

Finished dressing, he leaned over her sleeping form, just able to see her face under a pile of curly brown hair. Somewhere in the middle of the night, she had thrown the sheets off from the heat and he could see the bottom edge of her bandages under the hospital smock. The "unbecoming" nightgown was bunched up, well above her hips, exposing long tan legs and the curve of her hips and belly. She had drawn her legs up, lying on her side, knees together, her arms around a pillow and looked sound asleep.

It struck McQuaid, what a beautiful and mature woman she was. It baffled him how this could have somehow escaped him in the years they had worked together; never taking their relationship toward anything like this before. Why now, he wondered? He remembered their passion of a few hours ago and longed to climb back into bed, losing himself in her again. But he had to go. He reached down, gently brushing her hair back from her cheek and was about to plant a chaste kiss on her forehead before leaving. She stretched her arm back, sliding her hand around his neck and pulled his face down to hers.

"You're awake?" he asked, surprised, but glad he could talk with her before slipping out. She turned her face around, finding his lips, her eyes still closed.

"I've been awake for a while." She kissed him and lay back on the pillow, facing away from him again. He sat down on the bed next to her, pulling her gown down to a respectable length, but sliding his hand up along her thigh and over her stomach. His fingers glided over the soft fine down, below her navel, as it gave way to the coarser, thicker tuft between her legs. She smiled and turned to lay face up, opening her eyes to bare slits, regarding him with an impish smile. "Richard, do not tease me unless you have time to make things more interesting." He laughed, pulling his hand back and slapping her bare rear.

"I have to go."

"I know."

"I'll be careful."

"I know you will. But tell Snake, as much as I have come to adore him, I will have no choice but to hunt him down and kill him if anything happens to you." Her face was serious now; her eyes open all the way, looking into his. "Got it?" He gave her a slow, knowing nod in return, admiring that toughness in her again.

"Got it." He patted her thigh. "I'll let him know. He can get you set up with a room in the transit billets here on base for a day or so. I know Doc Dennehy wants to keep you close so he can check up on you one more time before we head back to Lubang. Jake can arrange a ride back to the island in case it takes me longer than a couple days in Hong Kong." She put her hand to his face again.

"Okay. Stop worrying about me. I'll be fine. Now get out of here so you can find Kiko and come back sooner. I can't run your sorry-ass cargo business and the store by myself you know." She winked at him and turned on her side again, closing her eyes and plumping her pillow under her head; pushing him off the bed with her rump. "My Doctor ordered me to rest. Certainly not to spend half the night horsing around with you, wasting precious beauty sleep," she murmured.

"Well, if it's doctor's orders, I guess I should leave." He stood up and leaned over to kiss her on the cheek; then made his way to the door, closing it behind him without looking back. It was just as well. The light from the hallway would have revealed the tears running down her face, wetting her pillow.

The dark eastern sky was just turning pink, as he pushed opened the door to operations. The building was ablaze with light however. Base ops was always open for business, though more sparsely staffed in the wee hours. He wasn't sure where to go, so he collared a three-striper and asked. The man pointed down the long, mirror polished linoleum hallway.

"Last door on the right, sir." He continued on without looking up and noticing McQuaid wasn't even military. He was young enough to call everyone older than him "Sir". Just as he was about to come up on the doorway to Jake's office, he appeared in front of him, barreling out of the office at full steam, sipping out of a large coffee cup while staring down at what looked like a long sheet of teletype paper. McQuaid had to swerve to keep from mowing him down.

"Gunner!" Jake motioned with his head for him to follow him, not even breaking stride. "Glad to see you're finally up. I'm just about finished lining up your little vacation." He glanced back to leer at him. "You and Mattie have a little time to yourselves last night?" McQuaid frowned back.

"Yes and thanks for asking." He had to lengthen his stride; just to stay up him. "By the way, she wanted me to pass along a message."

"Really?" He turned to look back over his shoulder at him, with genuine interest.

"Yeah. She told me to tell you if you get me killed, she's going to find you and put you out of your misery and guilt over screwing the pooch." Jake was shaking his head up and down in avid agreement, still not breaking stride. He arrived at a large, chrome coffee urn in the break room, pulling the spigot open to refill his cup, before he looked back at McQuaid.

"Well, tell her she should fear not, with me on the job. In fact, I've got some very good news for you this morning, old son. You can thank me later, if you ever have time to get over your smug self." He finished filling his cup and handed McQuaid a clean one. "Seriously though, I couldn't be happier for you and Mattie." He grinned back at him. In spite of his jaunty banter, he looked like he was tired from being up all night. McQuaid slapped him on the back.

"She was kidding. She says she adores you and I'm rather fond of you myself, you big lug. If I didn't know it would go right to your already oversized head, I'd tell you just how much we both appreciate all your hard work." Jake just winked, reaching for the sugar canister.

"Well, because I already know you are a pathetically broke cargo driver, I don't want you to worry when I tell you, what I'm about to present to you is worth a lot of money. And because the Marine Corps already provides me with an exorbitant paycheck, I won't even need to charge you for it." He handed him the Telex he was holding and began stirring in his sugar, watching him while he read.

"What is this?" Jake pointed to one of the heading lines farther down page.

"Skip over some of this stuff. I was communicating with several contacts in Hong Kong, over different issues. This line here, see where it says ASIO?"

"Yeah."

"That's Australian Secret Intelligence Organization. See this number and initials LD? That's Laddie Dunross. I met him in Guam right after the war."

"I thought you were talking to British Intelligence."

"I was; well both actually. The British and Australians have been working closely together in Southeast Asia since '42. The Aussies formed the Coast Watchers to secretly report on Japanese ship movements around the islands in the Pacific." McQuaid remembered.

"Yeah, Chief Mahutra told me he worked with the Coast Watchers."

"Right, so the Brits and the Aussie's have a large bureau in Hong Kong. I happen to know Laddie best and thought he might be a better contact for you over there. He's not all that keen on some of the bureaucratic corruption and payoffs running through the old guard in the administration either." He motioned for McQuaid to bring his coffee and they headed back to Jake's office for privacy. The office was small, but had a solid desk and a couple chairs. Jake closed the door after them. He sat on the edge of the desk, while McQuaid settled into a chair, sipping his coffee and looking over the Telex again.

"So what are these intelligence services working on in Hong Kong, since the war is over now?" He glanced up at Jake.

"War is never over, Gunner. It just goes underground again. We defeated the Axis Powers, but in the process, we empowered Russia and China. They are both huge anti-democratic regimes and are jockeying for position in Asia and the South Pacific islands." He reached behind him to fish a bottle out of his drawer, adding some "stiffener" to his coffee and offered some to McQuaid, who just shook his head. Jake looked back at him over the rim of his cup. He could see he was beginning to appear frustrated.

"Jake, I just need to get Kiko back and return to running my business with Mattie. This is starting to sound way above my pay grade. How does Madam Chin figure in to all of this?" Jake set his cup down and retrieved the Telex from him, scanning further down the page for reference.

"According to Laddie, Madam Chin is connected to the Chinese government through an intelligence operative, named Li Peng, she thinks is a corrupt local government official. They have a reciprocity agreement you'll find interesting. She provides drugs and fresh young girls for men of importance and power, who need to remain discreet and with, shall we say, refined tastes? Li Peng provides her a steady stream of well-heeled clients, money to buy drugs and "protection" from law enforcement. That includes British officials."

"The British are being paid off by the Chinese government?" McQuaid was astonished.

"Not THE British, but a few key players the Chinese have compromised through their vices. It gets better. Madam Chin also runs a large scale child slavery business – buying, or stealing young girls for prostitution. We knew that already. What I didn't know, was, certain Chinese and British government officials have their own private harems, maintained and replenished by this Chin woman. So now, you

have the three primary vices covered: payoffs, drugs and sex."
McQuaid was getting that knot back in his gut. How in the
world was he going to find Kiko and get her back?

"So it's a cesspool over there. I get it. Did your man
have any information on where we might find Kiko?" Jake
grinned around his coffee cup.

"In fact he did. According to this," he tapped the Telex
he was holding, "he observed a group of bound females taken
off a freighter in Aberdeen Harbor and delivered to a
warehouse along the docks, near the..." he referred back to the
sheet of paper, "...Lin Yao, a floating palace owned by Madam
Chin. It's not your usual flower boat brothel. Apparently this
one is an exclusive club for the wealthy and high level
officials only." He looked up at McQuaid again.

"What makes him think these might be the girls the
pirates brought over from the Philippines?" Jake read from the
Telex again.

"'Vessel name, Fánróng Fùqíang, blue hulled coastal
trader, 25 females offloaded at Hoi Wan Road, Pier 18.' That's
the same ship we are looking for, out of the Mumbarao River
pirate base. It sounds like that's our boy." McQuaid was
nodding now. At least they knew where she had last been seen
in Hong Kong – the pier at Hoi Wan Road. He took a drink of
hot black coffee, his mind a thousand miles away, on the dim,
dark waterfront along Aberdeen Harbor, wondering about
Kiko. He had been fearful for her, when he had no idea where
to look. Now, that fear was transforming into anger, as he
imagined her huddled among strangers, scared, tired and
hungry. He needed to get going.

"Okay Snake. How do I reach this Laddie Dunross?"
Jake sat down next to him and began his briefing.

The flight over would have been enjoyable, had it not
been for his worry for Kiko and the tension of impending
conflict. He held no illusions about Madam Chin just handing
Kiko over to him. Jake had also briefed him on the real reason
he selected Laddie as his connection. The man was former
AIB, the previous Australian Intelligence Bureau, which later
became the present ASIO. He had been a deep cover agent,
inserted in Hong Kong, right after the British were overrun in
January of 1941; just eighteen days after the attack on Pearl

Harbor. His mission had been to coordinate guerrilla activities with several Japanese resistance groups and to gather intelligence on the Japanese from Hong Kong, supplying the allies with much needed organizational and logistics info.

There were Japanese conspirators too however. Former members of the Hong Kong Police were recruited by the Kempeitai, a secret police arm of the Imperial Japanese Army, similar to the German SS; but even more brutal and feared, if that was possible. Laddie, who spoke several languages, including Japanese, Mandarin and Cantonese, was never sure who he could trust from one moment to the next.

However, there were other powerful forces at work in the area, older British merchant trading houses with roots in the opium trade dating back to the early 1800's. They conspired with the AIB and British Intelligence, anxious to protect their wealth and vast holdings in Asia; financing resistance groups and lending their own impressive spy network to the cause.

Laddie Dunross survived in a very dangerous shadow world of subterfuge and betrayal, completing his mission and lending great assistance in the final liberation of Hong Kong. If anyone knew how to help him get Kiko out safely, Jake believed it would be Laddie. McQuaid was looking forward to meeting him.

It was almost six hundred and fifty miles by air to Kai Tak Royal Air Force base and took him a little over four hours to get there from Clark. He was quite familiar with the area, having flown cargo back and forth to Manila from the New Territories, Kowloon and Hong Kong Island. Kai Tak was across from the island, bordering Victoria Bay next to Kowloon City. It was a brilliant sunny day, with only a few clouds on the horizon.

From about sixty miles out, he could see Victoria Peak in the distance on the left, the highest point on Hong Kong Island. Just ahead, the Dao island group was coming into view. The dark green mounds rose out of a royal blue sea, pointing the way to Tathong Channel; which led into the Victoria Bay harbor. At this point, he knew he was about twenty miles from Kai Tak and dialed in the tower radio frequency. A lovely British female voice greeted his approach request.

"McQuaid Air Cargo, good afternoon sir, I understand you are thirty-two kilometers southeast of the airfield. Proceed on course and give us a call back over Shek O Beach, just inside Tathong Channel, for further instruction. You may set your altimeter to the field pressure of 29.50 and the temperature here is currently twenty-five degrees centigrade." Shek O Beach was about midway up the Shek O Peninsula, the southeastern point of Hong Kong Island, bordering Tathong Channel. It would be easy to pick out, as a wide swath of bright white sandy beach.

"Kai Tak tower, McQuaid Air Cargo, roger." He was at seventy-five hundred feet and began throttling back for his descent. Leaning forward, he adjusted his altimeter gauge to Kai Tak field pressure. After a few more minutes, he spotted Shek O Beach on the left and called the tower back. He was given some course changes and directed to descend and maintain twenty-five hundred feet for the rest of his approach.

It was always a bit strange to realize the relatively small British Crown Territory below him, was such a distant and secluded British outpost. He could begin to see the bustling port around Victoria Harbor, with large lumbering gray British warships, a wide assortment of Chinese sailing vessels, from Hung'tous and Sanpans to Junks, all shapes and sizes, darting in and around the larger ships like gnats. Their white, gray and sometimes bright colored sails, looked like confetti scattered on the water from a distance. On any other occasion, flying into Kai Tak would a treat for him. Everyone spoke English and they were always cheerful. Today, he was more anxious about what might lie ahead.

On final approach, he lined up with Kai Tak's North/South runway; coming in low over Victoria Harbor. The Goose barely cleared the tall masts of some red sailed Junks and looking down, he could see flat bottomed barges, ferrying mounds of festive colored produce from Kowloon over to Hong Kong Island. He was low enough now and gliding at minimum rpm, so he could hear boat whistles and other typical bustling harbor noises, out through the open cockpit window. Some of the children aboard the boats were waving at him, with laughing upturned faces and he hung his arm out to wave back. It was so peaceful here now, but not so many years ago, the Japanese had sailed into this very harbor and slaughtered thousands of soldiers and civilians alike. He hoped these children would never have to experience such brutality in their lifetime.

After touching down, the tower directed him to taxi over to a row of hangars on the east side of the airfield, with

Squadron 88 stenciled on the side. He noticed several of the larger Sutherland Flying Boats parked at the far end, near a ramp into the water. There were also some sleek looking, Super Marine Spitfire fighter planes and an assortment of small, twin-seater training aircraft, tied down and chocked. He was looking for an open spot to park, when he spotted a drab green, British made, Austin utility truck, more affectionately known as a "Tilly", parked near the end of the row. The tall man leaning against it, was wearing a dark civilian long coat and a wide brim Fedora. That seemed to be a good bet for his welcoming committee. He taxied up next to the vehicle and made a sharp left turn, in order to line up with the other aircraft in the row and put the small truck under his left wing. The man was waiting for him when he opened the rear hatch and hopped down.

"Mr. McQuaid, I presume?" His accent was unmistakable – Australian, not British. He stepped forward to shake McQuaid's hand, wearing a wide grin under a brown handlebar mustache. He was a little taller and at least as broad shouldered as the American. His grip was sure and firm and though his eyes were gray, like his own and seemed cheerful, he detected a wariness in them, which was a bit off-putting. "Laddie Dunross is my name. I believe Major Wilmouth told you I would be meetin' you on your arrival?"

"Yes, thank you." The man looked past him into the Goose, to see if he needed help with luggage, or anything else. McQuaid turned and retrieved a long duffel bag, grabbing the strap and heaving it on to his shoulder.

"That's all you have?" McQuaid nodded and pulled the hatch shut after him.

"I've got everything I need in here." The man smiled back, then turned to lead the way to his vehicle.

"I'll give you a lift to my digs. We can talk about what's afoot when we get there. How was your flight over mate?"

"The usual. I've made this run back and forth a number of times. Summer weather can be a bit unpredictable, but it was great flying weather today. I have no complaints." They had arrived at his truck and he motioned for him to sling his duffel into the back, under a box frame canvas roof, mounted over the short truck bed. Typical for British territories, the driver was on the right, so McQuaid jumped in next to him, on the left side, noticing there were no military markings anywhere to be found on the vehicle.

His "digs" weren't at the airfield, for they made their way straight over to one of the exit gates. After satisfying the military gate guard with his papers, they were soon bumping along down the road, swerving around bicycles, and other assorted vehicles and pedestrians. Laddie had told him they were headed to the Star Ferry terminal and they would make the short trip over to Hong Kong Island by boat. The man seemed at ease and open to being engaged in conversation.

"Jake told me you've lived in Hong Kong since before the war." Laddie kept his eyes on the road.

"That's certainly right. I was in the service in New Guinea up to '39, livin' the good life, but got transferred to Hong Kong after the Jappers began pressin' their fight through Manchuria. We figured they'd be headin' our way south before long."

"I thought you were from Australia." Dunross glanced over his way, ready to offer a snide retort; then seemed to decide against it.

"I am Australian," he offered, in simple reply. McQuaid was confused.

"What did you mean by 'livin' the good life' in New Guinea then?" Dunross was nodding his head now, appearing to have sorted out how he led him off track.

"We trained in the jungles of New Guinea as members of the Coast Watchers. It was the farthest thing from the good life really; just yankin' your chain a bit there mate. It's the second largest island in the world, with the baddest jungles you'll ever want to know about; maybe only the Amazon could be worse. New Guinea is the last line of defense north of Australia. So we trained to live off the land and serve as forward observation units." His eyes looked as if he had returned to somewhere back there and he grew silent, for a few moments, before returning to himself. He looked back at McQuaid. "Sorry mate, what were you sayin'?"

"I think you answered me actually. How did you end up in Hong Kong of all places?" Dunross chuckled at that.

"Right. Well I happened to be good at larnin' languages. We had Chinese and Japper instructors, who lived with us. No one was allowed to speak English. A bloke had to larn quick, or be left behind. No books really. We had to live and breathe it all day, every day, until we got it." He turned to smile at McQuaid. "I guess I just picked it up faster than my mates. Anyway, they transferred me to Hong Kong, to train with British intelligence and planned on sendin' me into Manchuria to spy on the Jappers movin' west. That all changed the day after Pearl Harbor, when they attacked the RAF at Kai Tak airfield."

He turned a corner and down shifted to start down a long steep hill. They could see the ferry terminal ahead, with the sparkling blue harbor beyond.

"The British had their thumbs up their arses the whole time. Hong Kong was surrounded, once the Jappers took Canton near the end of '38. But the Brits couldn't decide whether to reinforce, or abandon the colony." He looked at McQuaid sardonically, a smirk on his face. "They didn't exactly need to read their bloody tea leaves to know they were comin'." McQuaid just nodded, reminiscing on his own frustrations with command decisions, leading to the attack on Pearl. It took no imagination to see Dunross wasn't a huge fan of the British.

They pulled into a parking lot along the wharf, next to the Hung Hom Star Ferry terminal. Dunross offered some large, colorful Chinese bills to a man tending the lot and with McQuaid's duffel bag in hand, they headed into the terminal to board the ferry. The Star Ferry was the only means to get from the mainland, at Kowloon, to Hong Kong Island, other than by Sanpan. Throngs of much shorter, dark headed Chinese pushed around them on all sides.

It was surprising they didn't have to wait long, in spite of having lost two ferries in their fleet to attack during the war. Faces reflecting all manner of lifestyle, were pressed hard against them, along with nervous livestock, as the boat filled to capacity; and then some. The trip cost almost nothing and McQuaid enjoyed watching the activity along shoreline of the island and the retreating mainland around Kowloon. A British Army transport plane roared low overhead and McQuaid followed it with his eyes, as it landed behind them at Kai Tak.

Dunross had another car waiting at Wan Chai terminal on the Hong Kong Island side and soon they were winding their way up into the hills from the harbor front. He couldn't keep track of the all the turns and street names, though many were English, like Harcourt, Connaught and Queen's Road; along the harbor. But then they turned onto a narrow, steep, upward winding road, called Pok Fu Lam, skirting the base of

Victoria Peak. The Peak, as the locals referred to the almost 2,000 foot mountain above them, overlooked a panoramic view of the harbor and islands to the south. Dunross noticed McQuaid craning his head out of the window, trying to see the top of The Peak.

"All the tall poppies live up that way," he said, jerking his thumb up toward the mountain. McQuaid looked back at him, puzzled. Dunross laughed. "You know the fat cats, full ticks and the like?" McQuaid nodded.

"You mean the ridiculously wealthy." Dunross grinned back.

"And the bitchy molls. That's high class whores to you Yank. And some of them are even females." He slapped McQuaid on the back, laughing at his own joke. "My digs are a bit more quaint, over near Aberdeen, just up the road a stretch." McQuaid laughed with him. Dunross was easy to like. Before long, they were winding through narrow cobbled streets overlooking a harbor below. Dunross pointed it out.

"That's Aberdeen Harbor. We'll head down there after we grab a bite and knock about what you have in mind for gettin' the little girl back." The southern facing Aberdeen Harbor, looked a great deal seedier than Victoria Harbor, on the north side of the island. He could see dilapidated warehouses and rafts of junks and multi-storied houseboats, tied together near the piers, along the shoreline. There were a few luxury yacht and high-masted sailing vessels anchored farther out in the bay; standing well clear of the riff-raff nearer the shoreline. Most of the wharf area looked somewhat foreboding.

They pulled through an archway, overhanging a narrow unpaved alleyway, skirting rain filled pot holes, around to the back of a weathered wood, rundown looking tenement building. Dunross led the way over to unlock the backdoor and they made their way into a comfortable looking apartment, with tasteful furnishings, nautical art and seascapes hanging on the walls. Dunross pointed out an overstuffed couch, with a coffee table and two large upholstered end chairs.

"Flop yourself down over there mate. I'll pour us a couple whiskeys. You feelin' hungry at all? I've got a bit of stew I could warm up."

"Sure. All of that sounds great." McQuaid threw his duffel down by the couch, but wandered around the room, looking at some of the titles of Dunross' books on wall shelves. He was amazed to find a number of classics, Melville, Keating, Hemmingway, Henry Lawson, a famous Australian author, among other more eclectic works. There were books on war, weapons and bound collections of letters written at Gettysburg. One collection of essays was by Thomas Jefferson and another by Abraham Lincoln. A well-worn book, which stood out from the rest, was entitled Plato's Republic. It seemed his host included old world philosophy among his varied reading interests. He called over to Dunross.

"Quite a collection of books you have here Laddie. Do you get time to read many of these?" Dunross answered without turning around, busy pouring their drinks.

"Most of them more than once. Does that surprise you mate?" McQuaid blushed. He hadn't meant to imply they were for show, or that his host wasn't intellectual enough for such heady reading.

"I guess it shouldn't," he replied. "They don't tend to let the stupid ones in to Intelligence, if you'll pardon the pun." Laddie was smiling, strolling over with their whiskeys in hand.

"One thing they drilled into us, was, it takes muscles and mind to make good agents. Your brain needs constant trainin'; just like your body." He had thrown his Fedora off at the door, along with his long coat, exposing a shoulder holstered pistol under his left arm. He handed him his drink and pointed to the book shelves. "There are a number of books in there I contributed to as well. You wouldn't recognize the authors, but intelligence work is a livin', constantly evolvin' science." McQuaid was impressed.

"So you're a writer too?" Dunross smirked and took a healthy slug of his whiskey before answering.

"Nah, I'm not much of a writer, Mr. McQuaid. But some of my methods found their way into the bibles of spy craft." McQuaid was watching him, waiting for him to elaborate, as he sipped his own drink. "Workin' in the Orient is a fascinatin' intersection of opposin' intellectual cultures and articulate violence. Hong Kong may be one of the few places on Earth, where you can become rich, or dead, with equal voracity mate." He motioned for McQuaid to follow him into a spacious kitchen off the main sitting room, where he started pulling together the stew he had mentioned earlier.

McQuaid was surprised at how well appointed everything seemed to be; anything expected of a modern kitchen. It wasn't luxurious, or elegant, but it reflected the refined tastes of its owner; like everything else about the apartment he had seen so far. Despite the shabby outward appearances, at street level, Laddie Dunross lived a life inside his house, much as he did outside; with artful deception.

After lunch they got down to business. Laddie had pulled out some charts and photographs of the harbor front area around Pier 18 at Hoi Wan Road. McQuaid was surprised to see they were very good quality aerial photos and looked brand new. He asked him about this.

"Well I figured we could use a few overhead shots of the warehouse and docks area, so I just borrowed one of 88 Squadron's Tiger Moths, those biplanes you saw parked next to their flyin' boats and nipped over for a couple quick shots after daybreak. Nothin' to it mate." McQuaid just looked back at him in continued amazement.

"You're a pilot too?" Laddie grinned back at him.

"I took a few lessons once." McQuaid nodded. He was sure that was an understatement. Dunross just winked back, but then was all business again, pointing to a long low building at Pier 18. "That's where they brought the ladies to. It looks like a warehouse, but it's much more actually." He moved his finger over to a large boat tied up at a dock on the end, which looked like one of the old Mississippi riverboats. The paddle wheel on the stern and twin smoke stacks were easy to make out. There were three decks, with a large pilot house on top. "This here is the boat they take all the mucky-mucks out on; cruisin' around the harbor and there ain't much that doesn't go on aboard that one." McQuaid was intrigued.

"It looks like an American riverboat."

"It's a copy for sure, but the Chinese have been usin' paddle boats up and down the Yangtze River, since before the eighth century. This bloody moll, you're referrin' to as Madam Chin, supplies that party boat, the Lin Yao, from this warehouse. It contains her administrative office, a holdin' area for these young girls she'll be trainin' as doxies and a storehouse for spirits, food and delicacies for the guests aboard the Lin Yao." He paused and looked at McQuaid with compassion. "Most of these young girls are virgins, Mr. McQuaid. One of the highest paid services aboard the Lin Yao is for defloration of virgins." McQuaid rubbed his eyes in frustration. He could feel a growing sense of rage, welling up inside him. He shot a haunted look at Dunross.

"We've got to get her out of there right away." Dunross looked back down at the photos.

"I quite agree. The trick will be to get in and out, without bringin' her henchmen down on our heads." He tapped the image of the riverboat on the photograph. "The Lin Yao sails every night at ten PM and doesn't return until just before dawn. Almost everyone at the warehouse will be on that boat tonight. They'll be leavin' the young girls, includin' Kiko, locked up in this storeroom here," he said, pointing to the room on the floor plan he'd sketched out. He raised his chin, motioning at McQuaid's duffel bag. "I presume you brought some of your own equipment there?" McQuaid nodded.

"Yes. I thought some of it might come in handy."

"Let's have a look then, shall we?" McQuaid walked over and knelt down to unfasten the straps and opened it up. Dunross joined him, pawing around inside to see. He pulled out one of the Thompsons; admiring it for a moment.

"A fine weapon. A bit on the noisy side however." He looked through the bag some more, unholstering and hefting McQuaid's heavy .45 automatic. "Very nice." Then he noticed the grenades. "Plannin' a bit of a celebration with these are you?" he quipped. McQuaid looked down at them and then returned Laddie's gaze.

"Only as a last resort." Dunross just cocked his head and stood up, satisfied he'd seen everything he needed to. He motioned for McQuaid to follow him and led the way through the kitchen, past another door to a larder in back, then over to the far wall and pulled a chord from a low hanging ceiling light. Looking around them, there wasn't anything to see other than sacks of grain, beans and well-ordered shelves of can goods. But Laddie placed his hand on the bare wall in front of them and pushed. There was a slight click, and a portion of the wall gave way to a hidden panel. He pulled this open and stepped inside, snapping on another light. McQuaid entered behind him and was stunned to see what looked like a well outfitted armory.

An assortment of guns, including automatic weapons, hung from large wall brackets. As he looked around in growing amazement, he made out several types of light, to heavy machine guns, smaller sub-machine guns, a wide variety of pistols, automatics and revolvers – even a bazooka. On shelves to the right, there were a number of grenades, what looked like packages of C2 plastic explosives, some land

281

mines and bazooka shells. Under the shelves were scores of metal ammo boxes of every known caliber. He looked back at Laddie with unreserved awe.

"You planning your own little war here, or just saving all this for a rainy day?" Dunross grinned and gazed around, admiring his collection.

"The right tool for the right job, I always say mate," he replied. McQuaid continued gawking at the incredible storehouse of ordnance on the walls around them. Dunross stepped past him to lift a small submachine gun off one of the brackets, racked the slide, checked to make sure it wasn't loaded and handed it to him. "This one should do the trick." McQuaid hefted it and sighted down the barrel, noting the ammo magazine was the stick type and stuck out of the top; opposite of the way his Thompson was loaded. The barrel was also unusually thick. Dunross anticipated his question and pointed to the barrel. "This here's a silencer and it has a thirty round stick magazine, as you can see."

"What is it?" McQuaid asked. He was somewhat surprised by his selection. It wasn't a very elegant looking gun. In fact, it appeared it had been made rather cheap in construction.

"This is called an Owen Gun. It's Australian made, for the record," he stated, not bragging. "It's the preferred weapon of many Commando military units. As you can see, it's quite light," he remarked, pointing out the heavy gauge wire shoulder stock, in place of a more common, bulkier wood and metal stock. "It's reliable, accurate at short range and with the silencer, very quiet. It's also a 9mm, so unlike your Thompson, you can hold it steady, without her jumpin' off your aim when shootin' it. It's meant to be fired from the hip in fact." McQuaid nodded, holding it at waist level now, two fisted, by both the front and rear hand grips. He was right. It would be easier to manage. "I think this might be a better close-quarters weapon for you mate." McQuaid agreed and liked the idea of the silencer. Even though he was used to his Thompson, he deferred to the man's experience, which he suspected was considerable, in the category of up-close-and-personal. Dunross pushed on another panel, on the wall to the left. It opened to reveal a set of stairs, heading down and out of sight.

He grabbed some stick magazines off one of the shelves and motioned McQuaid to bring the Owen Gun with

282

him. "C'mon. Let's give her a go." He led the way down the steps, turning on lights as they went, until they reached a long, low concrete-block room, with sand bags and targets at the far end. There was a small table at the front and Dunross laid the extra clips of ammo on it, took the sub-machine gun from McQuaid and snapped a loaded stick magazine into the top mounted receiver.

"So, Jake tells me you flew fighter planes together. Bein' a pilot myself, I can imagine that takes a fair bit of trainin'. Did either of you get yourselves into any ground action?" He busied himself with racking the slide on the weapon to arm it and then set the safety. The question came off as casual, but McQuaid knew he was fishing. Rookie pilots were a liability to everyone around them and had demanded constant vigilance to keep them from killing themselves and putting other's lives in jeopardy. He understood Laddie's underlying question and appreciated his unassuming manner in asking.

"Marines are all trained as infantry riflemen first, Laddie, whether they end up pilots or cooks. In fact, if you'll recall, pilots fought on the ground, alongside cooks and clerks during the Japanese invasion of Wake Island, right after they hit Pearl. Many of them died along side of their Marine brothers, with their winged anchors face down in the bloody sand." Dunross gave him a look that told him he'd made his point and then turned toward the sandbags at the far end of the room. Snapping the safety off his weapon and aiming down range at the targets, he held the gun at his hip and fired off a few rounds. It made a soft sputtering sound, rather than the loud, sharp crack of shots McQuaid was used to hearing with the Thompson. One of the targets bounced from the rounds hitting it. It was easy to see the man was a practiced shot. He tossed the Owen Gun over to McQuaid.

"Give 'er a try yourself."

McQuaid pointed the gun down range and squeezed the trigger, feeling the weapon jump in his hands, while noting with satisfaction, his rounds hit just in front and then up through the target. He knew to fire in bursts and after a little practice, he mastered aiming, firing and reloading the gun. After about an hour, they climbed back up the steps and into the weapons room again. Dunross spent a few minutes replenishing the spent magazines and pulled a silenced pistol off a rack, pocketing some extra ammo clips for it as well.

Soon, they were back in the sitting room, looking over the map and photos once more. Laddie was using his finger to retrace the outer walls of the warehouse.

"There are three doors into the buildin'; one entry for each side of the pier and one on the back side, facin' away from the docks." He moved his finger along the street, less than a block. "We'll park here after dark, and you'll walk over from the buildin' adjacent to the warehouse. I'll cover these two doors here, while you make your way in from the back." He pulled out his floor plan for the building and pointed to several internal rooms, marked Office, Storeroom and another Storeroom, closest to the door facing the pier. "This is where they keep the ladies. You'll need to get in there quietly, fish your girl out and meet me back here." He tapped his finger on the photo again. "We should be able to do this without much trouble. They won't be expectin' us, but things rarely go as planned. So you need to be on your guard and ready to improvise if you have to." He glanced up pointedly at McQuaid, making sure he agreed. McQuaid acknowledged him with a quick nod. "I've planned out much more complicated operations than this, but even though it looks straight forward, there is no accountin' for bad luck." He held up his index finger, to emphasize his final remarks. "Speed – that's the key mate. Get in, get the girl and get back out as quickly as you can. Load everyone into the car straight away and we're off, slick as a lizard's belly." He paused, waiting for McQuaid to respond and noticed he looked hesitant.

"We're doing this by ourselves? I thought a few more of your team might be joining us." Dunross leaned back with a wry smile.

"My team? Mister McQuaid, you do realize what we're doin' here is highly illegal? Hell, it's a bloody capital crime to even own a handgun in Hong Kong, much less stage an attack on one of our local citizens with machine guns. This is what we call a black operation; small, discreet and without alertin' local coppers – many of which are in the pocket of this Chin lady. From what Major Wilmouth told me, you were ready to come over here and charge in, guns blazin', all by your lonesome." McQuaid looked sheepish.

"Okay, I get it. I'm ready. Let's do this." Dunross clapped him on the shoulder and grinned.

•

"And Bob's your Uncle. How about another whiskey? We have quite a spell to wait before sundown and there's no time like the present."

Chapter Twenty-Two
Hoi Wan Road, Aberdeen Harbor, Hong Kong Island, China

Jiang Xian Hui walked through the staging area of the warehouse at Hoi Wan Road, on his way out to the pier. He was leaving Hong Kong and by nightfall, would be well on his way back to the Philippine Islands. The lights were on now and the young girls he had brought over were arranged on small straw mattresses along the walls. They were manacled, both hands and feet, each with food and water bowls between them, along with a waste bucket for peeing and defecating. The room stunk from sweat and overfilled buckets, but he was used to the smell. To Jiang, it was the smell of money and his money belt had received considerable fattening from this last delivery. As he walked between the rows of mattresses, the girls watched him, wary and shrinking back as he drew nearer to them – all except for one.

Jiang looked down at the pathetic rag of a girl, with the blazing black eyes, watching him back, like a ferret preparing to pounce on its prey. He paused at the foot of her mattress, studying her, more curious than concerned. He doubted he would ever see her again, but somewhere in his calloused soul, he found himself admiring the pluck of this child. She couldn't be more than ten years old and yet, she seemed to have the heart of a lion. Of course, she would be beaten into submission and cowed like the rest. But for now, it wasn't fear reflected back at him from those eyes.

He squatted down next to her; careful to keep his distance. Even though she was trussed and couldn't reach him, he wouldn't want to chance having to defend himself and maybe injuring her. She was no longer his merchandise and grandmother or not, Nǎinai would not tolerate anyone damaging her goods.

He noticed she hadn't eaten any of the rice and vegetables in her bowl like the others. Flies gathered on the remaining food and buzzed around her face, crawling into her eyes and over her mouth. But she didn't flinch, or make any move to dislodge them; she just continued staring at him; unblinking. Jiang pointed a finger at her face and spoke to her in Tagalog.

"I am leaving to return to your islands, little mouse. Nǎinai will be your mother now. She will teach you to be obedient and when I return, from killing your American pilot, I think I will sample you for myself." He grinned back at her, noticing her eyes change. He was gratified to see a look of fear cross her face, mistaking it for a concern for her own safety. In fact, this was the first Kiko had heard McQuaid might still be alive. Her concern was for his safety, not her own.

Watching this man in front of her, she memorized every detail of his face. She would find him again someday and somehow wipe that dirty smile from his face forever. She smiled back at him, warmed by the thought of him writhing in pain at her feet and noticed the look of consternation reflected back from him. Jiang was indeed puzzled by her expression. What crazy thought could produce a smile from this wretched little creature, at a time like this? He decided she had lost her mind. Maybe she wouldn't even survive her training to become a jìnǚ (whore). Sometimes, the only way to break one of these girls, was to beat them almost to death. After that, she might not be pretty enough to earn much on her back. He snorted. No matter – she wasn't his problem to worry about any longer.

He stood up and sneered down at her one last time, before turning and making his way out the door to the pier. It would be a long trip back to Lubang and he needed to hurry. Nǎinai would have his head if he failed his mission.

Kiko stared after him for a few moments longer before she was satisfied he was gone for good. In that moment, she realized if she was ever to fulfill her promise to kill him, she would need to survive herself. Looking around the room, she noticed many of the young girls regarded her with fear. It occurred to her how difficult it must be – to always be afraid. Since losing her parents to the Japanese and watching Mattie's vicious murder, right in front of her, there wasn't much left to scare her.

The future had become very gray and bleak to her, until this pirate leader had told her Gunner was still alive. If this was true, she needed to keep up her strength. He would need her to help him; now that Mattie was gone. The memory of her was hard to keep in her mind without a heavy heart and feeling like she might cry. Mattie and Gunner had become the most important people in her life and now with Mattie gone, she knew Gunner would need her help more than ever. She had to be ready.

Looking down at the fly covered bowl of rice and dirty brown vegetables, she knew she had to eat, even though the thought of it made her want to vomit. She reached into the bowl of food, scattering a cloud of flies and scooped up a mouthful of the sticky rice and vegetables with her grimy fingers. Careful to wash down each bite with water from the other bowl, she ate every morsel, with slow and deliberate resolve. Then she scooted back on the mattress to lean against the wall, hugging her knees. Gunner would come for her; she knew he would. He told her he would always come back.

A loud thump jarred her from these thoughts. The door leading into the interior of the building had opened and a short, fat little balding Chinese man marched in, wearing a black silk robe and what little hair he had at the back of his shiny pate, pulled into a long black braid. He had over-sized, cartoon-ish lips; like a small, underinflated red rubber inner tube, folded together under his nose. His hands were hidden within the long flowing sleeves of his robe. Standing just inside the doorway, he surveyed the room, his eyes dark and brooding; as if he was reviewing a small, pathetic herd of livestock. Walking between the rows of mattresses, he came to the first couple girls and barked something at them in a language Kiko couldn't understand, but sounded like the same language she had heard the pirates using. She knew they were somewhere in China and so imagined it was Chinese.

The girls also didn't understand him and he became agitated, flapping his arms around at them, pointing to their clothing and yelling, his inner tube lips opening to a full circle and then folding flat again. Kiko found them fascinating. The girls scrabbled backward on their mats, to get away from him, cowering, with their backs pressed against the wall. When they still didn't do, whatever he was trying to get them to understand, he marched over to the first one and yanked her to her feet by her hair.

She started screaming, so he slapped her hard across the face and then slammed her full force against the wall. The sound her head made, bouncing off the hard surface, was like the hollow sound of a ripe melon. Her eyes rolled back in her head and she slumped to her knees. But the man yanked her back upright and slapped her back and forth across the face again, splattering those nearest her with blood and flecks of spittle. When she remained unresponsive, he threw her face down on the plank wood floor in front of her mattress and strutted over to the next girl in line.

Meanwhile, another much skinnier man, holding a bucket of steaming soapy water and a long handled brush, scurried in through the door behind him. He dropped these beside the fallen girl, reached down and stripped off her filthy gray smock in one motion; casting it aside. He laid her out on the floor, face up and began scrubbing her limp body lengthwise with the scrub brush, dipping it back into the sudsy water after every few strokes. He pushed the brush between her legs and turning it sideways, forcing her legs apart and proceeded to scrub her genitals. Then he rolled her over and continued the same routine on her back, pushing soapy water between the cheeks of her buttocks. The coarse bristles of the brush left raw scratches on the more delicate areas of her body. Meanwhile, the fat little man with funny lips was yelling at the girl on the next mattress.

This time she understood what he wanted. She jumped up and stripped off her smock, then stood facing him, trembling, trying to hide her breasts and genitals with her arms. The man ignored her humiliation, reached over and yanked her arms down to her sides and continued on to the next girl. The skinny fellow arrived in front of her, motioned for her to stand on the plank floor in front of her mattress and proceeded to scrub her down as well. When it came time for Kiko's "bath" she had already stepped to the front of her mat and thrown off her smock. She stood waiting for the little fat man, her arms held stiff against at her sides. He looked at her without expression and moved around to the other side of the room.

They repeated their scrubbing with all the girls and then brought in a large wash pan of hot water and square bars of yellow laundry soap. The man demonstrated to them what he wanted next. They were to wet their hair from the wash pan, lathering their face and hair with the soap and then rinse. The girls proceeded to crowd around the one large pan of water and washed their hair and faces, trading the soap around to each other. A couple girls even washed each other's hair, trying not to scratch themselves with the sharp edges of their manacles. Another girl helped sit the unconscious girl upright, to help with her hair and face as well.

Finally, they all stood in the center of the room in a clot, shivering, looking around with trepidation at what might befall them next.

Meanwhile, the men had removed the bowls of food, dirty clothing and buckets of waste and the skinny man mopped up the excess water on the floor with rags and took away the wash pan, before leaving the room. A woman in a lime green blouse, with dark green silk pajama pants, wearing tall clogs, came in after them. She was older, with her long dark hair piled on top of her head with pins, looking as if she had been quite beautiful when younger. She set a large porcelain bowl of hair combs down at the front of the room and motioned for the girls to come and claim one and then return to the front of their mattresses. Then she gestured for them to comb out their wet hair, while she waited for them.

The girl who lay unconscious on the floor at her feet, began to stir and started moaning. She sat up rubbing her swollen face and began to cry. The woman squatted down next to her and brought her face to her breast, soothing her as she continued to sob, rocking back and forth with her. After a minute or so, she helped her to her feet and taking a comb from the bowl, she combed her hair back for her with gentle strokes; careful to avoid the large knot growing from the back of her scalp. When she was finished, she cupped the young girl's bruised face in her hand and regarded her with a warm compassionate smile, while wiping the tears from her cheeks.

Then, she stood up, looking back and forth, at each of the girls, making sure they had combed their hair and were looking presentable. Satisfied at last, she gave them a quick bow, retrieved her empty bowl and left the room. Her clogs made a gentle clopping sound as she vanished through the door and closed it behind her with a soft click.

For the next fifteen minutes or so, nothing happened. The girls were afraid to move and so stood where the lady who had brought them the combs left them, standing shivering in front of their mats. They began tentative whispering among themselves. The young girl to Kiko's right turned to her and gave her a timid smile. She was quite pretty and looked like she was also from the Philippines.

"My name is Lilibeth," she said in her native tongue, her voice low, so as not to be overheard. You were very nice to me before, but you are very scary. I hope you will be my friend." Kiko just looked at her for a moment, not knowing how to respond. The girl had a sweet smile and seemed to be about her age, maybe a year or two younger, with latte colored skin and eyes almost black, framed by long, thick curly brown hair. She was able to understand her, though her words had a strange accent to them. She decided she may as well talk to her.

"I am Kiko. What island are you from?" The girl smiled back, her teeth bright white. She looked around with a furtive glance before continuing.

"Do you know Palawan Island?" she asked. Kiko shook her head. "You must know Palawan. It is south of Mindoro Island. I am from a village called Taytay. Where are you from Kiko?" She looked back at her with a serious expression on her face. One of her eyes crossed in toward her nose and Kiko couldn't help but smile back at her. "Why do you laugh at me?" she asked, sounding hurt. Her eye turned in even closer to her nose.

Kiko put her hand to her mouth and giggled, in spite of herself. She didn't know why she was laughing. It just struck her as funny somehow. It seemed the most important thing in the world to Lilibeth, for Kiko to know her and where she was from, despite of all the danger they were in here. Kiko had a few passing friends in Lubang, but was always so busy with her job helping Gunner in his cargo business and Mattie at the store, she never seemed to have time for lasting friends. Now, she was being held prisoner, in a horrible place, far away from everywhere she had ever known and this young girl wanted to be her friend. For how long – minutes, hours only? It was hard to know how long any of them had left. But, maybe now was the best time for a friend.

"I am sorry, Lilibeth. I don't laugh at you. It is just your face; you looked so serious." She smiled again; trying to let her see she was grateful to have a friend in this wretched place. "I am from Lubang Island. It is near Luzon, across the sea from Manila, the capital city of the Philippines." Kiko knew this with complete certainty, as she had spent many hours with Gunner, poring over maps of the area and had flown into Manila on a number of occasions to buy goods for their store; like the last time she was there with Baacay and his brother Rajan.

She remembered the unggoy he had bought her. She missed that stuffed monkey and it brought tears to her now thinking about all the people she cared about she might never see again. But then she remembered – Gunner would be coming for her. He would find her and bring her home again. She realized Lilibeth was staring back at her. Kiko was about to tell her about Gunner, when the door at the end of the room opened again. The old woman she had first thought was the devil had returned.

She was wearing a dark, bright colored, floral patterned silk robe, with black silk pajama pants and tall, thick sandals. Her hair was up on top of her head again, held together with tall black combs this time. She moved into the room with a haughty air of elegance and majesty. Another, smaller girl followed, carrying a ledger book and a brush pen. She was much younger, maybe not much older than any of the girls in the room. Her hair was left long and flowing down the back of her oxblood colored robe and she was also wearing black pajama pants, with black leather slippers.

The young girl kept her eyes downcast and straight ahead, walking close behind the older woman, who had now arrived at the head of the line of naked young girls. The first girl's face was beginning to show her bruises now and the older woman looked at her face with disdain. Reaching out her hand, she turned her face to either side, then stood back to look at her breasts and then down the length of her body to her toes. She motioned for the girl to turn around and looked at her shoulders, back and buttocks. Turning to her assistant with the ledger book, she muttered a few words, which were transcribed. Then she moved along to the next girl, ignoring her uncontrollable shivering. It was part of her procedure. She wanted the girls to be cold, so she could better observe the shape of their breasts and nipples. After a thorough inspection, she moved to the next girl and the next, offering notes back to her assistant on each individual as she continued down the line.

As she moved closer to Kiko, an unmistakable fragrance of Gardenia preceded her. Kiko watched the woman with veiled curiosity while she inspected her friend Lilibeth, making her pirouette a couple times to ensure she saw everything. Lilibeth looked petrified. Not only was she shivering from the cold, but her knees were knocking together so hard, Kiko was afraid she might collapse. After whispering more dictated notes into the ledger, the woman's baleful eyes met Kiko's. Both females, regarded the other as if they were caged cobras, watching for an opening to strike. The woman moved over to stand in front of her. Kiko's emotions had hardened again, after opening herself up to Lilibeth, even enjoying herself for a brief period for the first time in many days. Now she felt the white hot flame of anger moving up from her belly to her eyes once more. Her brow was furrowed, mouth twisted in defiance, as her eyes blazed back at the woman before her.

Madam Chin wasn't bothered in the least by an uncivil and petulant child, but she did notice once again this one had a spirit she would need to break, if she could ever become useful. She had been sorting these girls into categories for appearance and possible issues needing attention in their training. Jiang had informed her this smaller child was the adopted daughter of the American Marine pilot and his former, now deceased, female companion. What was of more concern to her, were the risks she inherited, if this American discovered she had been brought to Hong Kong with the other girls.

Jiang had been given strict instructions on how imperative it was to kill this American before he discovered her whereabouts and used his military connections to contact the British. In spite of her many spies and purchased officials in police and city administration, it was inevitable there were those who would do anything to destroy her. They coveted her monopoly over the brothel trade around Aberdeen, even stretching beyond Victoria Harbor and Kowloon. If this American came to Hong Kong looking for his child, there would many who could aid him. She was as yet uncertain which would be the safer option – to simply make her disappear, or find a profitable use for her somewhere on the mainland, away from Hong Kong.

Under no illusion she might be easily trained as jìnǚ, she had been considering how to best dispose of this problem. The girl was very young; still under the age of pubescence. Perhaps it would be better to export her to the interior of China; far enough away this American could never find her trail. Still, there were those who would pay a great sum to copulate with a child. Obviously she would have to be drugged. This girl was too high spirited to submit to defloration. Yes, it would be much better to offer her as submissive and pliant to a client's every sexual deviance. Imagining more possibilities still, there was always the potential for even greater profit through extortion. She could think of a few important officials she might control without limitation, if she arranged to have photographs made of their decadence with a child. Her eyes glittered in anticipation. Yet, she risked much more by not taking extreme precautions – so much to consider.

Turning her back on Kiko now, she made her way to the other side of the room, continuing the inspection and categorizing of her wares. As the young girl with the ledger passed by, her eyes flicked sideways at Kiko. She may have imagined it, but it seemed to Kiko there had been an almost imperceptible smile. Then she turned and continued on the heels of Madam Chin, following her down the line of the last remaining girls.

When they had completed their work, the old woman walked out of the room, with her assistant running to keep up, leaving the door open behind them. Right after, the woman in green returned with a pile of clean smocks. She tossed them on the closest mattress and motioned for the girls to come over and put them on. Once she was satisfied they were clothed, she had them line up in front of their mattresses again. She beamed back at them, appearing genuine in her concern for their comfort. Then she steepled her hands below her chin and bowed before turning and leaving the room, closing the door behind her. The girls at once began their whispering again. Lilibeth sat down on her mattress and motioned for Kiko to join her. She leaned close to speak to her without being overheard.

"What will they do with us Kiko? This beautiful lady is very nice to us. I like her and hope she will take me home with her. But that old woman frightens me so. Do you think they will make us work in the fields, or cook and clean all day?" Kiko knew all too well what they wanted from them. She had overheard Gunner and Mattie talking about Madam Chin. She also remembered when the Japanese soldiers first came to their village. Her father had made her hide under their hut and promise not to make a sound, or come out until he called her.

Before the horror of watching the soldiers kill her father and mother, along with most of the other elders in the village, she had seen soldiers dragging women and young girls into the bushes. They laughed as they ripped their clothes from them, beating them with fists and hitting them with their rifle butts if they resisted, until their screaming subsided to whimpering; if they could even muster that.

Kiko knew from watching animals in the village, how they copulated with each other. Her mother had explained to her how their babies were born from such mating. She had watched from her hiding place, while the Japanese soldiers rutted with the village women like animals; sometimes one after the other, on the same person. It was shocking to see how they tormented and abused the girls, killing many of them in the process. She had hidden her eyes and clapped her hands over her ears, trying to shut out the screaming and sounds of laughter. This was what Madam Chin wanted from these girls. They would be sold like animals to men like them; to be mounted repeatedly, while they taunted and laughed at them. How could she explain this horror to innocent little Lilibeth?

"She will take the prettiest girls and sell them to men who have much money, but are old and fat. They will do what they want with our bodies, once they have paid her money." She looked at Lilibeth with haunted eyes, wishing she could think of something nicer to tell her. But she knew her words to be true. Lilibeth was looking back at her, eyes wide, as if she were about to scream, her lower lip quivering; her little hands balled into fists. Kiko reached over and put her arm around her shoulder. She held Lilibeth, sobbing against her shoulder and began to tell her about Gunner. He would come soon and bring them both back to safety.

On the other side of the door, at the far end of the warehouse, Madam Chin sat at the heavy wood table, deep in thought. She was tapping a long, red enameled finger nail against Jiang's manifest receipt, next to the entry for the little girl named Kiko. Thinking about her dilemma with this child, she could feel conflicting emotions of anger and fear, welling up inside her. She reasoned, if it were not for this American and the complexity of dangers he could bring with him, by way of the American military, she would have no compunction to having her drugged and offered at a premium to the many pedophiles among her clients, who would be glad to pay extra for sex with her. Such a proposition was of course the most sound business decision. But it was precisely because of this meddling from the American that she could foresee herself squandering such an opportunity for profit, by having her garroted and the body discarded somewhere they would never find it.

If the bumbling British, or Hong Kong police in her employ, were to somehow be coerced into demanding she return the child, she could then deny any knowledge of her existence. And without a body, they would be powerless to hold her for trial. But she had already spent a good sum to acquire this girl from Jiang. It would be very unprofitable to dispose of her, no matter how much safer to do so. The old woman's mind was spinning. What could she do to make a profit, with the least risk?

She pulled a small, silver and jeweled snuff box out of her sleeve, from the small pocket under her robe. Inside were pea sized balls of pure opium, rolled in honey and flakes of golden saffron. Digging one out with the end of her nail, she popped the delicacy into her mouth to chew, while she reconsidered her options.

A soft glow began to work its way up her spine, mushrooming into her brain, as the powerful drug swept through her bloodstream. She much preferred to eat opium, in the ancient way. The effects lasted longer and didn't foul her lungs by smoking it. Her thoughts became more round, the sharp edges of her problem turning to butter. All her puzzle pieces lay right there in front of her. She just needed to take the edge off her foreboding to see them more clearly. Her eyelids drooped, the heavy mascara on her lashes almost obscuring the gleam coming into her eyes, as a smile drew up the corners of her ruby lips.

A clever plan had begun to unfold on just what she must do. Not only would she earn even greater profit from her, but afterwards, she would also be rid of her forever. How clever and yet so simple. She pulled a servant's bell rope sash to the left of the table. There was one person she needed to make sure was aboard the Lin Yao tonight. She smiled to herself again. Yes, tonight would prove very profitable indeed.

There was a knock at the door and the short fat man with the red inner tube lips came in, bowing from the waist, before looking up at her for instructions. She hesitated an appropriate amount of time before acknowledging his presence. Then she looked over at him, her eyes sharp and flashing.

"Get word to Minister Li Peng. We have prepared a special guest for his entertainment on the Lin Yao tonight. Make sure the cameras are working and have plenty of film." She paused, collecting her thoughts. "And bring the young girl to me; the last one on the left. Go now." She dismissed him with a wave, watching as he bowed again and left, closing the door with care not to bang it behind him.

Alone now, with most of the details sorted out in her mind, she smiled, her face blissful, allowing the radiant glow to envelop her like a lover's warm embrace.

Chapter Twenty-Three
Hoi Wan Road, Aberdeen Harbor, Hong Kong Island, China

A golden sun had descended to the line of the sea, in the west over Aberdeen harbor. Long, deep purple shadows chased the dying light across the floor in the flat belonging to Laddie Dunross. He and McQuaid had spent several hours going over the finer details of their mission. They were ready and as prepared as they could be, given the intelligence Dunross had gathered, but wouldn't be leaving for a few more hours yet. Laddie had determined they should move in only after the Lin Yao had left her dock at ten pm. Most of the people in the warehouse would be going aboard, leaving only a couple people to keep an eye on things while they were away. McQuaid should be able to lift the locking bar on the inside of the back door, using the pry-tool Laddie had provided him, find the girl and make his way back out; before anyone knew he'd been there. With any luck, he'd be winging his way back to the Philippines well before dawn.

For the past half hour or so, they had been getting better acquainted with each other. Dunross was curious about the American's perspective on the war in the Pacific. McQuaid filled him in on some of the missions they flew with the task force off the northern coast of Luzon in '45. Laddie knew the historic overview of the campaign of course, but not the details. He was intrigued to hear about the battles he experienced from the cockpit of a Marine fighter plane. Jake had filled him in on how he and McQuaid were friends and flew together during the war, but he was also puzzled about why he chose to stay in the Philippines and not return to his family in America, like most other servicemen.

"My adopted father died just after I joined the Marine Corps and with me gone, my mother couldn't work the farm by herself. If it hadn't been for the war, I probably would have stayed and I'd still be a farmer there in Iowa today." McQuaid had slumped back into the couch, hands behind his head; his long legs stretched out and crossed in front of him. The next part of the story was more painful and he didn't often relate it to friends, much less strangers. But he and Laddie had already grown closer, as men in war often do. Laddie was patient; drawing him out and allowing him to unfold the story at his own pace.

"My mother sold the farm and moved into the city of Des Moines, Iowa. Iowa is part of our country's heartland; also called the bread basket of America. It's hundreds of square miles of nothing but wheat and corn. She wasn't really cut out for the city though and took up drinking. While I was in the hospital on Guam," he paused and looked over at Dunross. "Jake told you about my being wounded and having to convalesce for a few months at the hospital there?" Dunross just nodded in the affirmative. McQuaid continued. "Well, I couldn't exactly travel and one day I received a telegram from a hospital in Des Moines. My mother had passed away and I was the only next-of-kin they had listed for her. I had to send them a check for burial arrangements. But I never made it back to see her." McQuaid took a deep breath and let it out noisily. He looked over at Dunross. "I really had nothing to go back home to. That's why I decided to open my air cargo business after the war. I was hoping to live the good life myself; making enough money to afford to live on a tropical island. It seemed like a good idea at the time."

"Tough luck with your mum there, mate. Seems like you did alright flyin' cargo though and it is a tropical paradise there in the Philippines after all." His face appeared divided now, obscured by shadow on the one side and the sunset, reflected through the window glass, created a blade of orange light across the other. McQuaid could tell by the unblinking and distant look in his eyes, Dunross had touched on some painful memories of his own.

"How was it in Hong Kong during the war? That's if you don't mind me asking of course."

"Nothin' you'd care to hear really," he shot back, his manner turning laconic and taking McQuaid by surprise. It seemed he minded a great deal. Almost as fast, however, his mood shifted back and he broke into a sheepish grin. McQuaid's expression reflected his concern he had overstepped, but Laddie clapped him on the back. "Don't give it a care mate. I just don't think about that time much anymore and you caught me a bit off guard." He stood up and looked out the windows facing the harbor, hands shoved deep in his pockets, contemplating what seemed to be a tenebrous doorway to the past. He began speaking without turning around. His eyes were fixed on the dying sun.

"I wasn't supposed to be in Hong Kong when the Jappers sailed into Victoria Harbor." His voice was low and far from the present. "In less than a week, I was supposed to be headed north, to Hanzhou, the largest city in the Zhejiang Province, just west of Shanghai. If you remember, the Jappers captured Shanghai near the end of '37. What a bloody affair that was. They massacred over three hundred thousand people, rapin' and pillagin' their way through that city. I was to be inserted ahead of their western campaign, allowin' them to roll over me, so to speak. I would have remained in deep cover, hidin' out with the local underground, to report on troop and supply movements to British command from behind their lines."

McQuaid could tell Dunross was in the full throes of it now. He began to pace, waving his arms, his eyes glowing in the deepening gloom, more in conversation with himself. It was fascinating and chilling to watch at the same time. McQuaid had fought from the air and it was rare when he could make out individual combatants struggling on the ground. Laddie had fought a much more personal war, at street level and behind enemy lines.

"They bombed Kai Tak, right after their attack on Pearl, killin' a number of my mates and destroyin' most, if not all of the military aircraft there. They followed up shortly with over twenty thousand Imperial Japanese soldiers descendin' on the colony, initially from the mainland and then up from the sea to the south. Major General Christopher Maltby, was the British garrison commander for the New Territories and Hong Kong Island. He was a tough old cock if there ever was one. Maltby had been a commander of the Jhelum Brigade forces in India, along the North-West Frontier. He was furious at the British blue-blood politicians when Sir Mark Young, the Governor of Hong Kong, told him they wouldn't be sendin' reinforcements; like the bastards promised us. They abandoned us, to fend for ourselves against the Jappers." He stopped and glared at McQuaid, crossing him arms across his chest. "It seems the British Chiefs of Staff never intended to defend the colony. They considered Hong Kong 'an undesirable military commitment', or so we were later informed." Not bothering to hide his disgust, he resumed his pacing.

"The Brits just deserted us – ten thousand men and god knows how many civilians, to the mercy of the Jappers. And as we well know, they rarely showed much mercy to prisoners. I went deep underground here, workin' with several

Chinese resistance groups, but hidin' in plain sight you might say." McQuaid was curious about that.

"How did you hope to stay under cover in China? You're, what – a little over six feet tall?" Dunross chuckled at this.

"What? You don't think I blend in so well? You're quite perceptive, Mister McQuaid. I don't look much like a Japper, or a Chiney. But there are ways to deceive the senses mate. I'll prove it to you sometime when we have more time for tomfoolery." Dunross had pulled an ornate, Calabash pipe off the end table near the window, loaded it from a ceramic jar standing nearby and struck a match to light it; puffing away until the bowl glowed bright red.

"I'm sure you managed somehow. I was just curious. Go on with your story Laddie." Dunross nodded and continued, his face transforming back to a grim mask of reflection, puffing on his pipe and filling the room with the sweet aroma of an exotic blend of tobacco.

"Well as you can imagine, the bomb attack on Kai Tak caused quite a panic in the colonies. People flooded the streets in Kowloon, nearest the airfield. They were fallin' all over each other, tryin' to escape. But they had nowhere to go. There was a huge pall of thick black smoke over the harbor from destroyed planes and flames leapin' up fifty feet in the air from burnin' fuel tanks. Maltby had a plan to retreat from the colonies, across to Hong Kong Island, if the Jappers should attack and cross over the Gin Drinkers Line." McQuaid raised his hand to stop Laddie's monologue.

"I've heard that term before, but what is it?"

"That was slang for a line Maltby drew on the map, ten miles above the British colonies on the mainland. He figured if the Jappers crossed that line, they'd have to evacuate." McQuaid nodded.

"Right, British gin drinkers. I get it."

"Anyway, there are a lot of stories I could tell, but basically it was one giant cock-up. The Jappers overwhelmed the British and Chinese forces and we were forced to surrender the colonies in just under eighteen days. Almost five thousand Commonwealth troops were killed and nearly seven thousand taken prisoner." He stopped pacing and looked out the window again, watching the last glowing ember of the sun wink out and disappear below the dark ledge of the horizon. As the room descended into murk, McQuaid heard him mutter, almost to himself. "Then the real battle began."

Dunross finally turned on the lights in the room and walked over to pour himself another whiskey. He offered one to McQuaid, but he declined. The big man continued relating the sordid days of occupation under the cruel hand of the Japanese, puffing on his pipe and conjuring up old ghosts from the past. Laddie's training with the Coast Watchers had been essential to him staying alive during those next few years, living a nomadic existence, often holed up in the basement of a bombed out building, or under a soggy pier for nights on end. Nevertheless, he helped keep money, food and arms, supplied by the older merchant cartels, flowing to the underground resistance.

"The Japanese hunted the resistance fighters down like dogs, executin' anyone they discovered on the spot; leavin' their bodies to lie in the street, to serve as a warnin' to others. Meanwhile, the war in the islands of the Pacific ground on. Food and potable water became scarcer, as the Japper's supply lines dried up. People turned feral, fightin' over tins of rations and drinkin' water. A lot of casualties fell victim to other citizens of Hong Kong, especially those raised in formerly privileged households. They were ill equipped and too ignorant street-wise, to fend for themselves. The ranks of the rebel fighters swelled, despite the dangers, when the supply lines of the resistance movement were expanded to include provisions for anyone the Jappers decided to punish and had left to starve."

"I thought the Japanese tried to protect the local businesses and keep the economy running, so they wouldn't have to deal with angry mobs of starving Chinese," McQuaid wondered.

"Oh they tried, for sure. Some of the local merchants were even crazy enough to think they might be able to cheat the system and profit from the dwindlin' supplies. Under the Britsh, they would have been fined, or jailed. But when the Jappers found 'em out, they just hauled them out in the street and lopped their heads off. Between the resistance, nippin' at their heels and the Jappers bleedin' the local economy, to make up their war losses elsewhere, it wasn't too long before anarchy finally broke out and the violence escalated. Only the strong and those under military protection survived." McQuaid could only imagine.

"One night, I heard screamin' in an alleyway, near North Point, off Tin Chong Street. It seems a couple Nippers had a young Chiney girl cornered and were takin' their usual liberties. Normally, I would have just scuttled by, quiet like; stayin' out of sight. I couldn't get tangled up being a vigilante. There were way too many bigger and I'm ashamed to say it, more important battles to fight. I couldn't risk bein' discovered. Too much depended on me. But this young girl happened to see me and caught my eye, pleadin' for her life. I couldn't just leave her there in good conscience. There were two Jappers on her. One holdin' her down, the other watchin', laughin' and cheerin' his buddy on. I caught that one from behind and snapped his scrawny little neck, before he even knew I was there. I yanked the second one off the girl and cut his throat before he had time to sound the alarm. He sprayed blood all over me and the girl, before I could toss him aside. He was still lookin' up at us, eyes wide, pleadin with us, tryin' to hold his hands against his throat, to slow the blood. This girl, she couldn't have been more than fourteen, squatted down next to him, spit in his face and pulled his hand away, watchin', as the life slowly drained out of him. She'd already become a killer at fourteen. It sickened me to see a young girl, still a child, becomin' so cold and heartless. But she'd already been robbed of her childhood. From that day forward, she'd never be that innocent young girl again."

Dunross paused here and pulled a chair over across from McQuaid, slid an ashtray on the table over and tapped some of his dead pipe ash into it. He pulled out a matchstick to relight the remains, while he stared into the ashtray, without noticing the flame creeping up toward his fingers on the still lit match. After a moment's silence, he recognized the danger and shook it out. Then he started up again.

"It was around this time that old witch you refer to as Madam Chin, reopened a number of brothels around the island and on the mainland waterfront over near Kowloon. She catered to the eccentric tastes of Japper officers. There were plenty of young girls, like the one from the alley, who needed work and ended up sellin' their bodies for her. She didn't call herself Madam Chin back then. From what I heard, she didn't want to call attention to herself. In return for drugs and sex she provided the Jappers, they cut her in on the better rations and protected her from gangs of belligerent soldiers roamin' the streets, takin' out their anger on local woman and old men;

anything, or anyone they could vent their growin' frustrations upon. The resistance was after her too – for aidin' the enemy. They almost got their hands around her scrawny throat a couple times. But somebody would slip her the word somehow and she always escaped." Dunross slugged down the last of his whiskey and clunked the glass down on the table. He cast a stern look over at McQuaid.

"This little girl of yours, how old did you say she was?" Leaning over to the ashtray again, he tapped out the remaining dottle from his pipe.

"Nine." Dunross gave him a slow understanding nod in return, staring into his face, but McQuaid could tell he was seeing through him; somewhere else in time. Returning to the present again, he stood up to walk into the kitchen and wash his face in the sink. Coming back into the sitting room, he toweled himself dry, while he regarded McQuaid with quiet resolve.

"C'mon mate." he said, his voice changed. "Let's get back to work." A half hour later they loaded McQuaid's duffel bag in the car, loaded with two Owen sub-machine guns, a couple silenced Browning 9mm Inglis automatics and McQuaid's grenades. It was almost nine o'clock by the time they eased into an alley across from Pier 18, a half block from the warehouse on Hoi Wan Road. Dunross had parked the car so they could see the front of the building and the docks at the far end, where the Lin Yao was still tied up. Her decks were ablaze with strings of lights festooned along the deck rails. Strands of brassy, big band music echoed around the wharf. They were both slumped down in the front seat of the car, in the shadows alongside another building at the pier. McQuaid checked his watch. They had about an hour to kill.

There were a number of cars parked near the back of the warehouse on Hoi Wan Road, across from where they were sitting. As they watched, they could see men dressed in evening attire getting out of the cars and strolling over to board the riverboat. There were festive colored, Chinese paper lanterns lining the gangway and white coated waiters greeting the men and handing them drinks as they came aboard. Dunross had a pair of binoculars out and was watching the groups of men heading onto the Lin Yao, trying to make out their faces. The time crawled by, while they continued to wait.

Suddenly, headlights appeared behind them and an elegant black sedan cruised by on the street to the left of them.

Someone in the back seat was lighting a cigar, illuminating his face and those of the men seated around him. Dunross ducked his head down.

"Bloody hell," he hissed, as the car continued past them, turning into the parking area behind the warehouse across the street, the tires crunching on the gravel.

"What?" McQuaid asked, alarmed they may have been spotted. Dunross pulled a small notebook out of his pocket and jotted down a few lines. He made a sour face at McQuaid and explained.

"Three of those men in that car were cabinet members on the governor's staff. From what I spotted with the binocs, more than a few mucky-mucks will be on board the Lin Yao t'night. Must be somethin' mighty special goin' on." He stuffed the notebook back in his pocket. "All's the better for us mate. With that crowd, they're sure to roll out the red carpet for 'em. I don't expect too many will be left hangin' around the warehouse." Sure enough, the row of windows near the roof line of the warehouse showed only dim lights within now. McQuaid was relieved to see the open space in back, where the cars had been parked, was pitch dark. It would be easier to slip around to the rear door without being observed. Luck was with them tonight. He was growing more anxious to get inside and find Kiko.

A shrill whistle from the Lin Yao made him jump. Smoke was pouring out of her twin stacks and they could see several of her crew casting off lines. They pulled back the gangway and the paddlewheel began to churn the water at the stern. Slowly, she pulled away from the dock, her lights reflecting off the water and they could hear the steady chugging sound of her engines. Dunross slapped the dashboard with his hand.

"Time to get a move on mate." He reached over the seat and dragged McQuaid's duffel bag into the front. Handing him an Owen gun, a silenced pistol and the grenades, he pulled out an Owen and pistol for himself as well. Laddie shoved some spare ammo magazines in his pocket and gave McQuaid the rest. "Ready?" McQuaid racked the Owen, making sure the first round chambered, likewise with the Inglis automatic and gave him the high-sign back.

"Ready." He started to get out of the car, but felt a hand on his shoulder. He stopped and looked back at the other man.

"Remember McQuaid, get in, grab the girl and get back out here as quick as you can. I'll cover you and have the car waitin'. If you're not back in ten minutes, I'll assume the worst and come for you. Got it?"

"Got it." McQuaid slipped the strap for the Owen gun around his neck, stuffed the pistol and grenades in his jacket pockets and made his way out into the night. Laddie got out the other side and disappeared into the shadows, where he could key an eye on the front and both sides of the warehouse.

McQuaid crossed the street, holding the sub-machine gun just inside the opening of his jacket. His manner was casual and inconspicuous – just a man out on an evening stroll. It was dark, but a nearby street light provided enough light for anyone to observe him if they were looking. Alone on the street, he made his way into the deep shadows at the back of the building without being challenged. He pulled a small flashlight from his pocket, covering the lens so just a small amount of light shown on the back door.

Trying the knob, he confirmed it was held by a restraining bar from the inside. Next, he pulled out the long, slim strip of metal Dunross had given him and inserted it through the doorjamb; nearest the knob. Careful to remain as quiet as he could, he probed up and down until he felt resistance and gently worked the tool upward, pulling the door toward him; to take pressure off the bar. At first it didn't move, but pulling the door back and forth a little, while continuing to push up with the metal strip, produced the desired effect – the bar moved. Working with a steady hand, he continued pushing upward with the bar until he felt the door give way. He was in.

Pulling out the metal strip, he slid it under his belt and being as gentle as he could, he pushed the door inward. He was relieved to see the room beyond was dark. There was no light behind him either, so he should be able to slip in unseen. Closing the door behind him, he squatted down, remaining motionless, while his eyes adjusted to the dark. After a few seconds, he began to make out shapes in the room. The lighted windows they had observed outside must have been from a room above him. There were no windows showing here and the only light was coming in under a doorsill, at the far end of the room to the left.

He had been careful, waiting in the car, to keep from looking at any street lamps around the docks so his eyes were able to adjust to the very low light in the room without much time lost. Dim forms materialized around him. He discovered he was crouched in a narrow open space, between rows of small mattresses on either side of him. Across the room there was another row and parallel to the one where he had squatted down. There appeared to be sleeping forms lying on the mattresses. He counted twenty-five. That was the right number, according to Dunross. Each girl they brought in must have her own mattress. The only question was, which one belonged to Kiko?

Keeping low, he crept closer to the mattress on the immediate right and peeked at the girl lying there. She wasn't covered with anything and wore a simple cotton smock. Making sure not to shine his light in her face, he used the indirect illumination to see her face. It wasn't Kiko. He was relieved the girl was a sound sleeper. With slow, careful steps, he made his way down the row to the right, but didn't recognize any of the girls.

Working his way around the back of the room, he crossed to the row on the other side. The first mattress he came to was empty. That was odd. He stopped and looked around to see if any others were missing. There was a dark shape of a person lying on each of the other mats. This was the only one without a sleeping form on it. Only one girl was missing? Maybe she was using the bathroom. Then he saw the lavatory buckets next to each mattress. So that couldn't be it. It worried him to know someone was missing and might be returned to the room at any moment, exposing his presence. He needed to work fast.

Moving along to the next mattress, he could see this was also not Kiko. As he was creeping along to the next mat, he heard a metal clinking noise. The girls were all wearing manacles and the girl on the mat to his right, had just sat up. He froze, hoping she wouldn't notice him in the dark. She was crawling toward him, drawing nearer to where he was crouched.

"Missar McQuaid?" she whispered, just inches from his ear. A chill went up his spine. He didn't move. "Missar McQuaid, I am friend of Kiko," she whispered again, putting her hand on his arm. He spun around to look at her.

"Yes, I'm McQuaid," he whispered back. "Where is Kiko?" She scooted closer to talk with him, causing her manacles to make clinking noises again.

"Dey take her. She no here."

"What?" he could barely contain himself. "Where did they take her?" he asked.

"I not know where she is, Missar McQuaid. Kiko tell me you come. She tell me wait fo' you." McQuaid was puzzled. How did she know he was coming? He had no time to wonder about this however.

"Is she here in this building?" He imagined having to search the whole warehouse, room by room. It would be time consuming, so he'd need to get back to Laddie and report this change in events before he came looking for him. The girl whispered to him again.

"I not know where dey take her. Fat man come, tell her he take her to Lin Yao. I not know dis' Lin Yao person." McQuaid's blood ran cold. They took her onboard the Lin Yao? He turned to go back the way he'd come, but the girl grabbed him by the arm.

"No! You take me with. Kiko tell me, you take me with." She was frantic, whispering louder now. One of the girls on the mat next to her stirred and mumbled something. McQuaid stopped, considering this new twist. He needed to get out of there without her sounding the alarm. Maybe he should take her with him. It would keep her quiet and she might be able to give them more information on how to get Kiko back. He turned back to her.

"Alright, but you have to be very quiet." He could see her shake her head up and down.

"I be quiet. Take me with!" She looked to be smaller than Kiko and he could see both her hands and feet were shackled with the metal cuffs. He made a decision, reached out to her and pulled her onto his back. She clutched at him, throwing her arms around his neck, her manacled hands at this throat now. He stood up, holding her against his back and moved to the door, taking careful steps and making as little sound as possible. Once they were outside, he turned and used the metal strip to hold the locking bar up, until he pulled the door closed and could drop it back into place. The girl was holding onto his neck, her thin body warm on his back. *Now what*, he thought to himself. Somehow, he needed to get aboard the Lin Yao tonight.

Dunross moved out of the shadows, when he saw him coming across the street toward him, with the young girl on his back.

"Good work mate! Put her in the car and let's hightail it out of here." He opened the back door and McQuaid dropped the girl back onto the seat. Laddie looked down at her, held his finger to his lips and winked before closing the car door. "Welcome home Kiko," he whispered, then turned around and slapped McQuaid on the back. "See? This is the sign of good plannin', Yank. Mission accomplished on time and budget, with no casualties!" He was grinning back at McQuaid. Then he noticed he wasn't saying anything, just scowling back at him. "What? Too easy for you?"

"It's not her," he said simply. Dunross stared at him.

"What?"

"That's not Kiko." It was Laddie's turn to scowl back him.

"Then what the bloody hell did you bring her for?" he asked. McQuaid glanced in the window at her before answering.

"She was waiting for me to come; says she's Kiko's friend. I was afraid she'd raise hell if I didn't bring her along and I couldn't afford to wake up the rest of the girls. Besides, she told me where to find Kiko." He glanced out at the harbor, seeing the lights of the Lin Yao passing by the shoreline now, a few hundred yards out. Dunross grabbed him by the shoulder.

"Well let's get crackin'! We haven't got all night you know." McQuaid was still watching the Lin Yao, thinking about how best to get onboard unseen. He motioned with his chin, past Dunross, toward the harbor.

"She's out there," he said; still deep in thought about how to solve this newest problem. Dunross looked at him a moment longer, trying to decipher what in the world he was getting at; then turned to follow his gaze. It only took him an instant figure it out. He looked back to stare at him, mouth open in dismay.

"She's aboard the Lin Yao?" he asked, incredulous. McQuaid just nodded, keeping his eyes fixed on the river boat.

"Afraid so." At last he looked back at Dunross. "We need a boat."

"Well no shit we need a boat!" Laddie rubbed his hand across his face in frustration. Then looked down toward the wharf. "Well lad, it's never dull with you, I'll give you that." He grinned back at McQuaid. "C'mon mate, let's go get us a boat then." He slapped him on the shoulder, ran around to the other side of the car and jumped in. McQuaid got in on the left and slid in next to him. Laddie turned to look at the girl in the back seat. "Hello lassie, welcome to the circus!" She just stared at him with her mouth open. Then he turned back around, started the car and spun it around on the road, pointing them toward the other side of wharf. Meanwhile, McQuaid started quizzing the young girl for details about hers and Kiko's experiences with Madam Chin.

"What's your name?" he asked.

"I am Lilibeth. I am from Palawan Island. You know Palawan?" McQuaid nodded his head.

"Of course. I've flown in there many times. Did the pirates, or the old woman who runs that place hurt you or Kiko?"

"No hurt me. No hurt Kiko. Dey hurt udder girls. Dey berry bad persons. I not like dem, Missar McQuaid. I feel happy you help me." She smiled back at him, but her eyes welled up and tears rolled down her cheeks. She tried wiping them away with her hands, careful not to scratch her face on the metal cuffs. McQuaid looked over at Dunross.

"Any way we can get those bracelets off her Laddie?" Dunross just reached over and pulled open the glove box.

"In there. Look for the leather case with lock-picks in it." He was swinging the car back and forth, navigating the narrow streets, down along the harbor front. McQuaid found the case and pulled out a pick that looked about the right size. He motioned for Lilibeth to put her hands over the seat, so he could reach the locks on her manacles. Fortunately, the locks were very simple and he had her out of the metal restraints in under a minute. She leaned back and raised her feet up, so he could reach those as well. Soon, she was free and hanging over the front seat, a huge smile on her face. McQuaid continued with more questions.

"How is Kiko doing Lilibeth? Has she been eating?" Lilibeth frowned back at him.

"Dey feed us. Kiko no eat. But she eat today. She tell me you come. Kiko want be strong. She say she need kill bad men. She want make dem let all girls go." She was frowning at McQuaid now. Laddie glanced over and made eye contact with McQuaid, raising an eyebrow in sudden concern.

"What do you mean she wants to kill the bad men?" The girl responded with a hunted expression.

"She berry scary Missar McQuaid. Dis old woman try scare all girls. Kiko no scared. She look in face of old woman and bad man from ship, with berry scary face. Man tell Kiko, he come kill you. Kiko say to me, she kill him and old woman," she said and shuddered. McQuaid wondered if she was referring to one of the pirates who smuggled the girls in from the ship, or someone from the Lin Yao. Kiko was strong willed, but he hoped she wouldn't do something stupid before he could reach her. Dunross had been listening and asked a question.

"How do you know she's on the Lin Yao?" Lilibeth looked over at him, brushing her dark curls out of her face before she spoke.

"Fat little man come in night. He take Kiko. He say she need go to Lin Yao. Say, old woman want her go to Lin Yao fo' big party. I not know Lin Yao. Fat man berry bad man. He laugh at Kiko. Say he take her to Lin Yao. Say she no come back." Both Dunross and McQuaid became alarmed at this last bit of news. McQuaid corrected her.

"Lin Yao is a boat, not a person, Lilibeth. Are you saying this man was taking her onboard the Lin Yao tonight?" Lilibeth reacted as if she'd been slapped. Her hands flew to face, her eyes wide through her fingers.

"Boat berry bad. Dis' bad place fo' girls. Udder girls say old woman make girls go on boat. I not know boat is Lin Yao. Kiko say old woman want girls fo' fat old men. Say she know old men only want young girls. Dey give money to old woman fo' young girls." She was crying now. "Missar McQuaid, you need find Kiko. She no afraid of old fat men. She say she kill men fo' udder girls. Say she no let men take more girls." She had grabbed McQuaid by the arm and was shaking him, imploring him to find her, before it was too late. McQuaid was inclined to agree with her. They needed to hurry.

It was an easy task for Dunross to find a small motorboat and load them all aboard. There was no need for a key. The boat he selected had the portable gas tank removed for the outboard motor, but he found another one on a different boat, where they had removed the motor and left the gas tank. He hooked it up and pulled the starting lanyard until the engine caught. Soon, they were heading out into the harbor, toward the unmistakable Lin Yao, alight from stem to stern and music blaring, now a short distance in front of them.

Dunross was sitting close to McQuaid, speaking into his ear to be heard above the engine noise and wind.

"I'll pull up next to the stern, as close to the paddle wheel as I can get you. They won't be lookin' that way. You should be able to climb up and over the rear guard rail. Keep your coat buttoned and they won't see your weapons. Most of the men onboard are Brits. Your English will get you by the Chinese and you should be able to blend in. Once you find her, signal me. I'll be ready and we'll have your back out here mate."

He glanced over at Lilibeth, who was sitting at the bow of the small boat, clutching the the gunwales to steady herself and leaning into the wind. She was staring at the paddle wheeler with worry written across her face.

"I sure hope she's right about Kiko being aboard. Remember, try to get her away with as little ruckus as possible. We don't want to create a scene. There are a lot of important men aboard, who wouldn't take to bein' identified with the sort of entertainment provided on the Lin Yao." He gripped McQuaid by the arm before continuing. "Don't let your emotions run away with you McQuaid. Get Kiko out and we'll deal with this vermin later. They have armed guards aboard too. You start shootin' up the place and you may not be able to get away without a lot of bullets flyin' from all directions. Am I makin' sense?" McQuaid looked back at him with a quick nod of reassurance.

"Don't worry Laddie. I'll take it slow and easy. Right now, my only concern is getting Kiko out of there safely, with as little commotion as possible." Dunross grinned and patted him on the shoulder.

"That's the ticket mate – quiet as a mouse! The less of a row, the sooner we'll all be back singin' over pints in the pub."

Chapter Twenty-Four
The Lin Yao, Aberdeen Harbor, Hong Kong Island, China

Dunross steered their boat into the wake of the Lin Yao, into the blind spot at the stern. Within a minute or two, the bow of the motorboat was bouncing up and down in the wake, just to the right of the massive paddle wheel, churning the water along next to them. McQuaid moved Lilibeth over to her extreme right, to help counter balance the hull, when he stepped up to grab a hand rail on the river boat and swung a foot up to hook a leg over the gunwale. Then he eased his head up, just enough to scout out the deck, before swinging his other leg up and over. There was no one around the stern near the noisy paddle wheel. He dropped down onto the deck and then flattened himself against the rear cabin wall. Moving back and forth to the left and right, he surveyed the long expanse of the narrow deck on either side, making sure he hadn't been observed. Satisfied, he moved around to one of the salon windows and peeked in.

"Damn it!" he hissed, under his breath. The room inside was the stern lounge, with a well-attended bar at one end and a number of small, white linen draped cocktail tables, with attractive women sitting around them. The worst part was, it was also full of older men standing around the tables, ogling the women, with drinks and cigars; all in tuxedos. Even the wait staff was dressed in stylish dinner attire. There was no way he could slip in there, unnoticed, in what he was wearing. He ducked back from the window, thinking about what to do next. He could see Dunross and Lilibeth out in the motorboat, bobbing up and down on the waves, cruising along fifty or so yards out. Dunross would have his binoculars trained on him, wondering what the hell he was doing just sitting there.

His thoughts were interrupted by the sound of a door opening around the corner to his right. Ducking back around the corner of the cabin, he looked back to see who it was. A Chinese man was stepping up to the railing to light a cigarette. He looked to be a foot shorter than McQuaid and stockier. It looked like he was one of the wait staff, wearing a white dinner jacket, black bow tie and black slacks. While he was watching, the man turned to his right and began to stroll toward the stern, coming right at him. McQuaid ducked back and was just about to slide around to the other side, when he realized this was the break he was looking for.

He pulled the silenced Inglis out of his waistband and waited. When the man appeared around the corner, he hit him in the solar plexus with the butt end of the pistol. The man doubled over, the wind gushing out of him. McQuaid followed the initial attack, by bringing the hard edge of his right hand down hard, just below the base of the man's skull. He went down neatly; face first, without another sound.

McQuaid stripped him to his shorts and exchanged clothing with him. It took him a little longer to manage the bow tie, but before long he was, to all outward appearances, just another waiter. The trousers were about an inch too short and the jacket was a little tight in the shoulders, but at least he could button it, since the man had been a good deal more round than McQuaid.

He decided he wouldn't be able to hide the Owen gun under the jacket, so he threw it overboard and stuck the Ingless in the black cummerbund, along with two extra magazines and buttoned his coat over it. He had three grenades, so he tossed one overboard with the Owen and stuffed one in each of his jacket pockets. They bulged a bit, but he didn't think anyone would notice them, unless they were looking right at them. The crowd in the lounge was probably busy enough, no one would give him as much as a second glance; he was just another waiter and not worthy of particular notice. That suited him just fine.

The man at his feet began groaning and rolled around, coming to. McQuaid gathered up his clothing and threw it over the railing into the harbor. He squatted down next to the man and lifted him up by his neck. The man looked at him, his eyes rolling back in his head again. McQuaid gave him a sharp smack, with open palm, across his cheek. The eyes came back into focus and got a lot bigger when he saw the fierce face of the big Marine glaring at him, only inches from his nose.

McQuaid tightened his hand around his throat, until the eyes began to bulge, then put his index finger to his lips, showing him he meant him to stay quiet – or else. The man nodded his head, staring back at him now. McQuaid smiled, keeping his hand around his neck and stood up, bringing the man to his feet with him. Then he reached around with his other hand, grabbed the man by the seat of his shorts, lifting him off his feet and in one swooping motion, pitched him over the railing into the harbor. Then he straightened his clothing and walked around to the door of the lounge and entered the smoky room with a confident stride. He grabbed a drink tray he saw sitting on a stand to his right and nodded to the nearest man, smiling.

"Another drink sir?" The man barely looked at him.

"Absolutely, old boy. Make it a double gin and tonic." The man dropped a ten pound Hong Kong note on his tray and continued talking to his female companion; a stunning, young Chinese woman, in a black gown with an enticing, deep plunging neckline. She was much more interesting to look at, than an oversized waiter, in ill-fitting clothes. He continued on his way through the inner lounge door, holding his tray high over his head, threading a route between all the guests. The din of band music was loud, coming from somewhere farther forward and a cacophony of voices and laughter enveloped him while he moved deeper into the main floor.

There were two decks above him, topped by the pilot house at the very top between the smoke stacks. He knew nothing private was likely to go on at this level, so he was looking around and spotted a lush carpeted, ascending staircase, beneath a huge, crystal chandelier. Making his way towards the staircase, he was intercepted several times by a number of, already wobbly, men and a slurring, matron looking, gray haired woman, who insisted he drop everything and replenish their drinks. He remained patient as he took down their orders, then continued working his way toward the staircase. Joining a group heading upstairs, he smiled and nodded to everyone he passed coming down.

The second deck was more of a mezzanine, surrounding and overhanging the main deck, with a picket-railed passageway along either side; leading both astern and forward. There were a number of cabin doors off the passageways and he was uncertain in which direction he should head first. He spotted another waiter coming up the steps and matched his stride to get close enough to speak with him.

"Excuse me. I was told to come up and take drink orders for a private group somewhere up here, but I'm embarrassed to admit I wasn't sure where to find them." The man was in a hurry, but gave him a tolerant smile in return, trying to appear as not to notice him.

"You're obviously new here. Which group are you referring to?" He was Chinese, but spoke impeccable King's English. The man refused to break stride and McQuaid had to avoid several collisions in the crowded passageway, in order to keep up with him.

"I'm not sure which group, but I believe Madam Chin is with them and a few of the governor's staff." The man slowed, looking a little confused, then he seemed to hit on who he was trying to find.

"Ah, I think you might be looking for the Quemberly party – next floor up to the right." He leaned a little closer, speaking out of the side of his mouth. "A word to the wise, we don't use their real names here. And never refer to the Madam that way, péng yǒu – if you want to keep your job. She prefers Madam Ching Shih."

The man was shaking his head and tsking him, as if admonishing a child. He turned to look sideways at McQuaid, to ensure his instruction was well taken. Apparently the man had not looked at him up to this point and he did a slight double-take, when he noticed he wasn't Chinese and was at least a foot and a half taller, with steel gray eyes and a sun bleached crew-cut. McQuaid returned a rakish smile at him and with a conspiratorial wink, he turned to make his way back in the opposite direction; now at a brisk clip. He thought he had seen another staircase, across from the one he'd ascended, coming up from the main deck. The helpful waiter had stopped in his tracks and was watching him disappear into the stream of party-goers, jostling him on their way by.

McQuaid was almost to the smaller staircase leading to the next deck up. It was much narrower and he noticed two bulky looking, bullet headed men standing on either side of the banisters. He slowed his pace and looked around for an alternate route. It seemed however, that was the only entry to the third floor deck. As he was contemplating his options, an over gassed, portly man in a rumpled tuxedo, with bow tie askew, ran into him. His drink splashed down the front of his shirt and he turned on McQuaid; his face beet red.

"Bloody hell! Watch where you're bloody going you ignorant Chinky bastard!" The man had been busy looking down and wiping at, what looked like a dark whiskey, running down the front of his white shirt. When he realized he wasn't hearing a profuse apology back, he raised his bloodshot eyes to look at the insolent offender. He was about to level another "just deserved" barrage of profanity at him, when he realized he was looking eye-level at McQuaid's bow tie. His fleshy red lips fluttered in confusion, while he continued cranking his gaze upward to meet a pair of now stormy looking, flint gray eyes glaring down at him. McQuaid had been taken aback at first, but was in no mood to be slobbered on by a pompous drunk, who seemed quite comfortable lashing out at the smaller Chinese wait staff.

The man was just looking up at him, slack-jawed now, the puffy lips sagging open, trying to get his feeble brain around the anomaly standing before him. McQuaid smiled down at him, taking his now empty glass from his hand.

"I beg your pardon sir. Why don't you allow me to buy you another drink on the house, Mister...?" He raised his eyebrows, keeping his generous smile intact.

"Brumley – Walter Brumley." The man began dabbing at his shirt front again.

"Of course, Mr. Brumley, why don't you let me bring you upstairs to the executive suite for another drink – on me this time, instead of you?" McQuaid laughed at his own joke, putting his arm around the man's shoulder and steering him toward the third floor staircase. Brumley seemed congenial now and stumbled along beside him. He looked up at McQuaid and grinned, his blubbery lips wrapped around crooked, nicotine stained teeth.

"You're kind of large for a Chinky, aren't you, old boy?" McQuaid clapped him on the back and laughed, overloud, drawing nearer the two bullet-heads at the stairs, who were locked onto them now, like a pair of domed turrets.

"You're quite the comedian Mr. Brumley. Of course I'm larger than the rest of the Chinese waiters. I'm the headwaiter and management needs me to keep watch over all those skinny little bastards, so they don't steal all the liquor and fine cigars. By the way, can I get you a nice cigar to go with that complimentary drink this evening?" He nodded to the bullet heads, who were eyeing them with mild suspicion, as he reached the first step. Leaning closer to the one on the right, he whispered, "This one got away from the Quemberly party and Madam Ching Shih asked me to round him back up before he creates a scene." He winked at the man, who glanced at Brumley, noting indeed he was a mess, with his drink down the front of his shirt. He nodded to his fellow bullet head and they stood aside to let McQuaid guide the stumbling man upstairs.

While helping Blumley navigate the steps, he glanced back to check the room behind him and noticed a taller Chinese man, wearing a senior waiter's black tuxedo, eyeing them, with a slight frown on his face. McQuaid just nodded to him, smiling and gestured with his head to the besotted guest he was assisting up the stairs. The man seemed to hesitate, but then started moving toward them. His eyes were following them up, as he moved past one of the two guards, ignoring the man's show of waving him through. McQuaid helped Brumley up to the landing and looked around, hoping to find someplace to duck into. Sure enough, there was a restroom door, marked "Gentlemen" off to the right.

"Why don't we stop off in the men's room, so you can freshen up a bit sir? Maybe we can get some of that whiskey off your shirt before it stains."

"That sounds like a fine plan my dear fellow," Bromley slurred back, his eyes at half-mast. "Although I must say, old boy, ne'er a drop of whiskey ever touches my lips – I'm a strict scotch man. How about you?" McQuaid was busy moving him toward the lavatory and whipped open the door, just as the waiter topped the stairs behind them. The restroom was large enough for two urinals and a stall, with the door standing ajar. There was also a low bench adjacent the entry door and he plopped Brumley down on it, leaning his head into the corner to prop him up.

"Just sit right there and rest for a spell sir, while I use the loo. I won't be long and then I'll get that drink for you." Brumley seemed content for the moment, leaning back and closing his eyes. McQuaid stepped over to the sink and began rinsing his hands, watching the door behind him in the mirror. It didn't take long. The door swung open and the Chinese waiter walked in, eyes catching McQuaid's in the mirror. The man stepped inside, just enough to allow the door to shut behind him, but a good six feet away, out of reach from McQuaid leaning over the sink.

"Who are you sir? I didn't see you at the waiter's meeting earlier." Before he could answer, Brumley ripped off with a stupendous belch, that reverberated off the walls of the small room and the man glared at him with contempt. "Who is this man you've brought up here? This is a private floor and not accessible by all our guests." He was looking at McQuaid again now and frowning. McQuaid remained unperturbed while he dried his hands on a small linen towel and regarded him from the mirror. Offering him a patient smile, he explained in a tone that sounded official, yet deferred to the man's rank on the wait staff.

"That," he pointed at the drunk, "is one of the governor's special guests and you aren't supposed to know about me. Or didn't you hear?" The man's confidence waivered, but he remained suspicious.

"What didn't I hear?"

"The Governor's office wanted to make sure they had a few of their own men around tonight, just in case." The man's confusion turned to concern at this last and his eyes widened in alarm.

"Why, what is happening tonight?"

"The Governor received word there may be a Chinese agent onboard somewhere, trying to get some of the government officials drunk and reveal secrets about a new British weapon they're bringing to Hong Kong to protect against future attacks on the colonies." He brought his finger to his lips. "Very hush, hush." The man was staring at him now.

"What is this? Are you a British agent?" he asked, still skeptical, but beginning to be more curious. "You don't sound British."

"Well of course I don't sound British! If I did, you'd know I was a British agent wouldn't you?" McQuaid tossed the towel aside and turned to face him with a look of disdain. The man was growing flustered. McQuaid pressed on. "Look, I don't have time to stand around here with you all night. I need to get this man back to the room with the rest of the officials in the Governor's party." He stopped abruptly and shook his head. "Dammit, I wasn't supposed to tell anyone that. I meant the Quemberly party." The man stared back at him, his eyes very wide now.

"Those men are with the Governor?" he asked. McQuaid stepped closer to him, holding his finger against his lips again.

"Keep your voice down!" He looked over at Brumley, as if to check to see if he was listening. Satisfied he was passed out at this point, he flashed a stern look back at the waiter. "What is your name sir?"

"My name is Chou Lin Wong. Why do you ask?" The man was on the defensive now; right where he wanted him. McQuaid stepped even closer.

"Can you keep a secret Mister Wong?" The man nodded. McQuaid pointed over at Brumley.

"That man is a very important member of the British Consulate here in Hong Kong. He's here under an assumed name tonight. I was supposed to be keeping an eye on him, but he somehow got himself completely shit-faced and now I have to sneak him back into the suite with the rest of the 'Quemberly' party," he gave the man an exaggerated wink, "before anyone notices he's been running around making a fool of himself. I need your help, Mr. Wong. Is there a back door, or some other way I can sneak him back in without being seen?" Wong brightened up at once.

"Yes! They are in suite 302 and they also reserved the suites on either side." He glanced at his watch. "They were just served dinner a half hour ago. You could take the man into suite 300 and lay him on the bed." He gave McQuaid a broad smile, happy he could help with some official sounding British subterfuge. McQuaid bestowed him with a benevolent smile in return, happy to know where he could find Madam Chin, but almost as relieved he would not have to injure, or kill this man to keep from being discovered aboard.

"Thank you Mister Wong. You've been a great help to her Majesty's secret service here tonight. I will be sure to mention this to the Governor when I see him next." The man beamed back at him. "Could you do me one last favor Mister Wong?"

"Of course, sir."

"You seem to be resourceful and someone I can trust with this. Could you please go down to the main deck and watch for a man named Moriarity – James Moriarity? That's an assumed name by the way. I can't tell you his real name, but he will also be in disguise. Look for a man, a little shorter than me, with bright blue eyes and dark hair. But he really has red hair under that wig. Don't let him catch you looking at him too closely though, or he'll know you're spying on him." The man looked willing, but completely confused.

"How will I know it's him if he's wearing a disguise?" he asked, starting to look nervous again.

"He'll also be wearing round, steel rimmed glasses. He's thin, has a beard and probably looks like a college professor. Look closely for signs around his beard and eyebrows, to see if he's dyed his red hair brown." Wong seemed to find this reassuring. "If you see him, come right back up to find me in suite 302. I'll be there waiting." He put his hand on the man's shoulder and looked him in the eyes. "Will you do this for me Mister Wong?"

"Yes, yes of course...Mister...?" He waited.

"Call me Mister McQuaid. If I don't answer the door, they'll know who I am." Wong nodded again and smiled back at him.

"Don't worry Mister McQuaid." He glanced back at Brumley, snoring away in the corner now. "I'll keep our secret and find this Mister...James Moriarity!" McQuaid reached over and shook his hand to seal their contract.

"Off you go then, Mister Wong and don't forget to keep me posted." The man was on a mission now and strode out of the men's lavatory door with purpose. McQuaid stood there a moment longer, then looked over at Brumley, slumped against the wall snoring. "Well, I'll have to get you that drink a little later it seems," he said more to himself. By this time it, was obvious Brumley was in no shape to hear anything. He walked out and started down the hall, looking for suite 302.

It wasn't hard to find. The third floor was laid out like a hotel and had only penthouse-like suites off the main corridor. The odd and even numbered rooms alternated, so rooms 300 and 301, were across the hall from each other. He found the door numbered 302 near the far end and put his ear against it. There was the unmistakable sound of silver clinking on china and he could hear occasional laughing, along with both women and men's voices in conversation.

He moved down another door to suite 300. He could still hear the noises from the other suite, but more subdued now. Otherwise it seemed things were quiet on the other side of the door. He reached down and tried the handle, but it was locked. Pulling out the thin strip of metal he'd used on the warehouse door, he inserted it through the doorjamb and pushed it against the resistance of the latch, securing the door inside the strike plate. It took only seconds and the door gave way.

With a quick look around, to make sure he was still unobserved, he pushed the door inward, slow and as quiet as possible, one hand on the knob and the other on the handle of the Inglis 9mm in his cummerbund. He winced as the door squeaked. Opening the door enough to slip in, he found himself in a dim room, with a small sitting area in front of him, an open door to the left and another door to the right with light shining into the room from the threshold. *That had to be the adjoining door to suite 302.* The room was good sized and he figured the door on the left led to a bedroom.

Moving over to stand against the wall near the door frame, he looked around the corner into an even darker room beyond. Someone was lying on the bed, but he couldn't make them out in the dim light. Keeping the Inglis handy, he tiptoed into the room and squatted down next to the bed; waiting for his eyes to adjust to the light. After a few seconds, he could begin to make out the form and face of the person.

It was a young Chinese girl; probably in her later teens – definitely not Kiko. He realized he'd been holding his breath and let it out through pursed lips. He walked over and closed the bedroom door with a soft click, then walked back to the girl's side. Trying to be as gentle as possible, he shook her by the shoulder. After several attempts without effect, he turned on the lamp near the bed and felt her pulse. She was alive. Lifting one of her eyelids, he noticed her pupils were dilated, but still showed weak response to the light. McQuaid shook his head; disgusted. The girl had been drugged.

He sat down on the bed next to her and slapped her with his open palm. Her eyes fluttered open, but she just stared at the ceiling, without moving. Moving her head over toward him, she continued staring back at him in a daze. So this is what these guys were into. McQuaid could feel the burn moving up from his gut. Looking around the boat, he had noticed a few Chinese civilians in formal wear, who weren't waiters, but most of the guests aboard the Lin Yao were English. It disgusted him to think of how these girls were being abused by supposed gentry of a civilized society.

There was no one else in room 300. Maybe Kiko wasn't with the Quemberly party after all. What the hell was he supposed to do now?

He didn't have to wait long to find out. There was the sound of a door opening in the other room. McQuaid took two quick strides to the wall behind the bedroom door, the gun metal of the 9mm flat against his cheek. The doorknob turned and the door opened, shielding him from the man who entered the room and walked over to the bed. He wasn't Chinese, so probably one of the local British. He looked like he was in his fifties, thin and balding, with gray hair. The man was standing next to the bed now, holding a drink in one hand, the other in the pocket of his tuxedo trousers. Setting his drink down on the table, he sat next to the girl on the bed, laying his hand on her bare thigh. She was wearing a thin, short silk skirt and the man was there to sample the wares. He slid his hand up her thigh under the skirt, making his way north, when the cold muzzle of McQuaid's Inglis pressed against his head, just above his right ear.

"Don't move a muscle, or I'll will blow your head off with this." he said, his voice soft, but grave with portended violence. The man froze. "Just sit there, don't turn around and let's have a little chat, shall we?" The man didn't move, or speak. "Nod your head if you understand what I told you!" The man gave a quick nod in return. "Good. Now take your hand off the little girl's thigh and put it in your lap, with your other hand, so I can see them." McQuaid pushed the muzzle of the pistol against his head, to remind him to be careful. The man placed his hands in his lap and kept his head turned away. "Now, tell me who is in the other room." The man cleared his throat and McQuaid pushed the gun harder against his head. "Keep your voice low." He kicked the bedroom door closed with his foot, as the man began to speak in a low voice.

"Do you know who I am?" he asked, his voice a deep baritone, with a heavy English accent. The man didn't seem to be pulling rank; he just wanted to know if McQuaid already knew his identity.

"My hunch is you're one of the Governor's party." The man gave a slight jerk and McQuaid had to "remind him" again with the Inglis.

"Sorry," he muttered. "You just surprised me for a moment. No one is supposed to know we're here."

"Who is 'we'?" McQuaid asked.

"Kimberly, Bartlett, Norbert, some Chinese official; I'm not sure of his name. It might have been Peng."

"Who are you?"

"My name is Cowlsby," he said. "We're just here to have a little fun. That's all." His voice was taking on an annoying twinge of indignation. McQuaid didn't recognize his name, but then he wouldn't know any of them. It was good info to pocket for later though.

"Who else is in there with you?" The man harrumphed before speaking again.

"A few female guests. You know; some of the local color provided by the Madam."

"Madam Chin?" The man nodded.

"Is she in there too?" The man moved his head side to side.

"She was, but she left a few minutes ago. Listen here, if it's about money, I can pay you." McQuaid frowned.

"I don't want money. Where did she go?" The man hesitated. "I asked you where she went!" he growled.

"She went to the other suite," he said, hedging on any further details. McQuaid remembered the waiter had told him they had reserved three suites, he was in 300 and the party was in 302. He lashed out with his gun, cracking the man across the side of the head. He fell sideways, stunned, but still conscious. McQuaid grabbed him by the collar and yanked him upright again, twisting his collar around his neck and giving him a rough shake before putting the gun muzzle back to his temple.

"Let me clear something up with you, Cowlsby. I don't have a lot of time to play 'guess my game'. Don't try to stall for time and spoon feed me what you think I need to know. Start telling me what the hell you gentlemen are doing on the Lin Yao exactly, why Madam Chin is involved and where she went. I won't ask you again," he finished, with an unmistakable ominous tone to his voice. He noticed with some satisfaction, he had put a large bluish welt on the side of the man's head.

"Okay, just bloody relax. You don't need to crack me. I'll tell you what you want to know." He took a deep breath and let out a sigh. "We were invited aboard tonight, along with everyone else on the main and second decks, for a big party. It's all very posh and on the up-and-up. Some of the men even brought their wives. But a select group of us received special invitations up here, to the penthouse deck, for an exclusive private party..." He hesitated, but felt the gun push against his head in warning and continued. "...to have sex with young girls. We were told some of them are virgins; so that means she gets to charge us an even more outrageous sum of money. This one here," he motioned with his head to the young girl on the bed, "is more my type." He sighed again. "But a couple of these blokes like them much younger than her."

"Children you mean?"

Cowlsby nodded. "Not really my taste, mind you."

326

"I thought you had girls in there already."

"They aren't the virgins. These two are. Well, I mean this one and the one Madam Chin went over to fetch."

"From room 301?"

"That's right." The man continued to blather on about how he was too much of a gentleman to take advantage of virgins, especially if they were drugged, like the girl on the bed. He'd just been "curious". McQuaid had stopped listening. So, there was another girl, laid out like this one, in the other room across the hall. That might be where they were keeping Kiko. He was relieved to find out they hadn't had time to begin their more depraved activities yet. There was the sound of the door opening to the adjoining room again.

"Cowlsby, what the bloody hell is taking you so long in the loo?" McQuaid needed to act quickly. He swung his gun arm back and smacked Cowlsby hard, at the base of his skull. He caught him as he slumped forward and dragged him off the bed and around to the other side, laying him out on the floor and shoving him under the bed on the far side. Then he flattened himself against the wall again, just as the door to the bedroom opened. A dark haired, younger man eased in and walked over to the bed to admire the girl. McQuaid clunked him on the noggin too and stashed him alongside his friend – two down and god only knew how many to go. He was about ready to sneak out the door and over to suite 301, when he heard loud voices and laughter from the adjoining suite. The voices were muffled by the door, but he heard a man's voice rise above the rest.

"Oh my, isn't she a darling little thing?" McQuaid walked over and knelt down to peek through the keyhole into the room beyond. There were three men, so Cowlsby had lied, or someone new had joined them. There were also some scantily clad young women, all of them standing facing away from him, looking at someone who had come through the main door of the suite. He couldn't quite make out who it was, but he heard a woman's voice speaking now.

"I brought her special for anyone who would like to join me in the suite across the hall. Or, you could stay here and these ladies will be happy to entertain you. There is another special girl in the next room, which allows for privacy. That girl is also untouched, like this one, but not as young." A babble of voices started up all at once. McQuaid couldn't make out what they were saying, but it seemed they were crowding around whoever this woman had brought in with her. He was straining to see, but couldn't quite get the right angle through the keyhole. Suite 302 was a long and narrow room layout, the same as the Suite 300, but reversed, with the bedroom on the opposite side. It might be Kiko, but he needed to bide his time. There were too many people in the room and only a perilous route of escape, down the stairs past the guards and two decks crowded with guests and wait staff. If only he could tell for sure she was in there.

Across the room to his left, he had noticed some drapes, maybe over windows along that wall. He hurried over and drew back the curtains. Sure enough, there was a double set of windows and the end ones were hinged, to push outward for fresh air. He unlatched the one on the right, swung it open as far as it would go and looked out.

The harbor breeze felt soothing on his face. The water about thirty feet below, rushed by, as the paddle wheeler was making five to six knots, cruising around the bay. He looked out across the water and thanked his good luck he was on the starboard side of the boat. Somewhere out there, he hoped close, Dunross was waiting for a signal. It was now or never. The longer he stayed on board, the worse his odds got for remaining undiscovered. He took out his flashlight and flicked it on and off out the window three times and waited. Nothing. He did it again and almost at once, he saw a return signal of three flashes back. Good, now it was time to get this show on the road.

Fortunately, there was a small ledge underneath the windows, so he climbed out and with great care, worked his way around to the left, easing his face around to look in the windows of the adjoining cabin. The curtains had been left open, so guests could see the harbor lights beyond. He could see the well-dressed men and young women in clinging, sequined gowns, crowding around someone, holding the hand of an older woman, dressed in a red silk evening gown. Her black hair was piled on top of her head, held with tall, Japanese looking coiffure combs. There still wasn't a clear view of who she was holding onto, but it appeared the person was small enough to be reaching up to hold the woman's hand. The windows to the room were open, so McQuaid could hear the voices much better now.

The women were making cooing sounds, like they were admiring a small dog, or maybe a child. The men's faces reflected varying emotions; none of them particularly decorous. In fact, a couple seemed to be taking unusual interest in the young girl being offered. He gritted his teeth, disgusted at them ogling a child as a sex object. There was a loud knock at the door and the older woman turned toward it. As she did, a couple of the women encircling the little girl moved to the side. At long last, he could see who the woman was holding onto. His heart skipped beat or two. It was Kiko!

They had dressed her in an elegant shift of shimmering green and yellow silk. Her short, bobbed hair had been brushed back and tied with a green satin ribbon and she had little black sandals on her feet. McQuaid looked hard at her expression. Her eyes, the most animated feature of her face, were dull and lackluster. His lips pulled back from his teeth in a snarl. Those bastards had drugged her and were planning to offer her to the highest bidder in this sickening group of men, old enough to be her father and in one case, even her grandfather. That had to be Madam Chin. She had called out to the person at the door and he heard a man's familiar voice reply.

"I am looking for Mister McQuaid. I have a message for him." He could just see the side of Madam Chin's face and even from over twenty feet away, he could see the color drain from her cheeks. She pulled Kiko around behind her and answered the man in the hallway.

"What do you want with Mister McQuaid?" she asked in a shrill voice. The atmosphere in the room had become deathly quiet and electrified, as everyone noticed the alarming change in the older woman. They were all facing the door, away from the windows, leaving him the chance he'd been hoping for. Moving cat-like, he slipped in through the open window and dropped to the floor. He pulled the Inglis from his cummerbund and started working his way closer to Kiko. She appeared out of it and wasn't watching him, even though she was closest to him and the only one in the group facing the windows.

"Mister McQuaid told me to come and find him when I was finished looking for the man downstairs."

"What man did he tell you to look for?" Madam Chin asked him, her voice like ice. Everyone was engrossed with curiosity, but a few of the men mumbled back and forth now, asking if anyone knew who this McQuaid fellow was. As he was stepping closer, he was trying to keep an eye on everyone, but watching Kiko for any sign she might have noticed him. As he watched, she looked up and seemed to realize he was there. A light began to glimmer in her dark eyes. She was struggling to come to her senses. Her mouth started working up and down, trying to form a word. The word began to work its way out. He could hear a low soft sound of two syllables being repeated, over and over.

"He told me to find a man who looks like a professor, named Moriarity – James Moriarity." Madam Chin didn't appear to recognize the name one way or the other, but the men around her began to chuckle. She spun around to one of them and queried him, her eyes flashing daggers.

"How do you know this man?" she asked, her tone belligerent; no longer concerned with being the gracious host. McQuaid froze, hoping she wouldn't spot him until he got close enough to get a hold on Kiko. He knew if he could reach her, no matter what followed, they would never get her back from him while he was still alive. Madam Chin didn't seem to notice him, but was fixated instead on the man to her left. The man was grinning back at her, amused at her ignorance.

"Well, I've never heard of this McQuaid fellow, but every school boy knows Moriarity!" Madam Chin was in no mood for guessing games.

"Who is this Moriarity?" she hissed at him, on the verge of flying into a rage. The man was taken aback, the smile frozen on his face. He stammered, but was able to answer her.

"Professor James Moriarity is the arch villain in all the Sherlock Holmes novels. Holmes was a famous English detective, who could solve any crime, but he could never seem to catch his nemesis, Moriarity. Every British school boy knows the stories. I'd say this fellow McQuaid, whoever he is, might be pulling the man's leg out there." Madam Chin continued to stare at him and then turned back to the door.

"You said Mister McQuaid told you to meet him here?" It sounded like more of a statement she hoped was false.

"Yes! I am certain he told me I would find him here," he replied. McQuaid was trying to work his way closer, but was fascinated by the metamorphosis coming over Kiko. She was staring at him, her eyes struggling to focus, her mouth continuing to work up and down and the word she was so desperate to vocalize, came out at last, just before he got within reach of her. He put his finger to his lips, trying to shush her. But it was too late.

"Gunna," came out low at first, then a little louder, "Gunna," and then, she blurted it out with enough volume, the rest of the room noticed and turned to look down at her, "Gunna!" She began stretching her free hand toward him. He leaped forward, covering the last few feet and grabbed her hand. The older woman hadn't turned around yet. She was screaming at the man on the other side of the door.

"Call the guards immediately, you idiot!" she shrieked at the top of her lungs, along with a few Chinese expletives, then switching back to English, "Hurry, or I'll have you keelhauled under this boat and stretched out to rot in the sun at daybreak!" Everyone but her had turned and was watching McQuaid by this point. But he had Kiko by the hand now and there was no force on Earth that would pry her loose from him.

With one quick motion, he snatched her other hand out of the clutches of Madam Chin, who whipped around, to see what had happened. Her eyes narrowed to evil slits, as she spotted the big Marine, dragging Kiko around behind him. Then she noticed the muzzle of the pistol, moving closer to a spot between her arched eyebrows, as McQuaid stepped toward her, almost placing the barrel of the silencer against her forehead. Had he been in a better mood, he might have thought her funny, watching her eyes growing wide and crossing, as they fixated on the muzzle, now a mere inch or two from the bridge of her nose.

Everyone else in the room had turned to statues. But then, one of the women began to emit the beginnings of a scream. McQuaid's eyes flicked her way, the dark storm reflected in them and the set of his jaw, suggesting he could kill her without a second thought. Her mouth clamped shut and his eyes, growing even more dark and foreboding, snapped back onto those of Madam Chin, who was staring back at him, her initial shock being replaced with an expression like a cobra; vile and deadly. No one in the room could determine which of them appeared more malevolent, or determined to meet out death to the other one.

"I ought to shoot you in your despicable face, you horror of an excuse for a woman. Just give me the slightest sniff of a reason and I promise you, I will turn your head into a bloody pulp, along with everyone else in this room!" he said, his voice low and hard.

There was a near imperceptible change in her eyes, but he could tell she had decided not to do anything rash. Moving Kiko back to his side, with his arm secure around her, he began backing up, their eyes still deadlocked. Then he noticed a slight movement to his left. The distinguished looking Chinese man's right hand was making a slow, casual move toward the inside of his tuxedo jacket. Without taking his eyes off the old woman, he swung the pistol toward the man and lined it up with his crotch.

"Mr. Peng I presume?" The hand at the man's waist froze. "If you move your hand toward your weapon again, I will shoot your balls clean off. At this distance, it would be hard for me to miss." He flicked his eyes to the man just long enough to see him staring down at the muzzle of the Inglis and slowly moving his hand out and away from inside his jacket. "Please use your left hand, just the finger tips and carefully remove your weapon. Take it out and toss it over here to me." The man hesitated for a heartbeat. The Inglis made a popping noise. A small hole appeared, as if by magic, in the man's left trouser leg inseam, a bare inch below his fly. One of the girls standing next to him jumped, making a high squeaking noise, as the bullet smacked into the wall just behind her.

"Alright!" he gasped. "Don't shoot me." Slow and with exaggerated care, he pulled his jacket open with his left hand, revealing a pistol butt sticking out of a belt holster. He pulled it from the holster, using his thumb and forefinger and tossed it over toward McQuaid. It landed with a heavy clunk on the thick carpet at his feet. Using his foot, McQuaid slid it behind him toward the windows, all the while keeping his eyes and gun fixed back on Madam Chin. He could feel Kiko squirming at his left hip and pulled her even tighter against him, while continuing to back a few more feet away from the group. Then he addressed the room.

"Everyone step toward me and then lie face down on the floor, with your heads facing this way. They all moved as one, to comply. No one doubted he would shoot the first one who tried to make any move but the right one. "Not you Madam. You remain standing – right where you are." She stopped, looking back at him, confused and apprehensive; wondering why he was singling her out from the others. The rest of her guests did as they were told, flattening out on the carpet around her. "Now, walk toward me – slowly." She just stood there, looking back at him, fear beginning to show in her eyes. "Madam, if you don't do exactly what I'm telling you, the next sound you hear, will be a bullet ripping through your skull." She began to move forward. McQuaid reached down and scooped up Li Peng's gun. It was an American made .32 caliber Colt automatic. He noted it was a typical Chinese army officer's gun. Sticking it in his cummerbund, he continued backing toward the windows.

Kiko, still fairly woozy, knew Gunner had a good grip on her and trusted he would take care of her, no matter what. But he had been holding her against his hip and was pressing the side of her face painfully against a hard lump in his jacket pocket. She reached her hand in to try and move it away and got her fingers around one of the grenades. When she pulled it out to look at it, even in her dazed state, she realized what it was. Gunner had warned her away from them several times in the past, when she had come across his box of grenades stowed away in the Goose. He also showed her how the ring on the side of the handle was attached to a safety pin, to protect the firing mechanism. Many times he had warned her she should never handle them. Once, he demonstrated what would happen if she disobeyed him.

They went out to large field outside of town and he had her stand behind him as he pulled the ring on one and threw it way out in the field behind some big rocks. She heard him counting and when he got to five, there was a very loud blast and big cloud of smoke flew out from behind the rocks. The explosion scared her, but then they walked around behind the rocks and he showed her how the explosion had created a shallow crater in the ground and jagged shrapnel from the grenade had gouged out chunks of rock, on the side facing the blast. Gunner explained it was very dangerous and could kill anyone near the explosion.

She had seen Japanese soldiers throw grenades into huts in their village, with families tied up inside so they couldn't get away. Later, she had seen them burying the torn and bloodied bodies of the dead. She remembered how she had hoped she might find a grenade and throw it back at the Japanese soldiers.

Holding the heavy metal grenade in her little fist now, it looked like a miniature, dark green pineapple. Had her mind been clearer, she would have been afraid to touch it. Instead, she was fascinated by it, noticing the ring on the pin was still intact. Gunner had told her it was safe to hold it, so long as the pin wasn't pulled out. She looked up at Gunner, to tell him about the grenade, but he was looking at the people across the room, with a mad face. She looked over at the people now too and saw Madam Chin standing there, glaring back at her.

It seemed to Kiko, like she was seeing her through a gray fog. Bad memories of her worked their way through the cloud in her mind. Gunner was talking to her like he was very angry with her. Kiko remembered how mad she had been at her too, though it seemed like it was so long ago and far away. She was very tired. She hoped Gunner would stop and let her sleep soon. But she needed to remember to tell him about the grenade – better just to hold onto it for now.

Then she heard a loud bang and felt Gunner jerk backwards. People were screaming and she saw a large scary man, with a bald head, bursting through the door, firing a gun that made such a loud booming noise, it shocked her to her core.

The bullet head brothers must have sneaked up to the door outside. McQuaid hadn't heard them coming until the door splintered inward with a loud bang and one of them charged through the shattered remains, with a big gun in his hand. The women lying on the floor began screaming and Madam Chin turned around, ducking, throwing her hands to her ears. McQuaid saw the man a split second before he spotted him and maybe because Madam Chin was standing right in front of him, he hesitated for a heartbeat or two. McQuaid squeezed off three shots in quick succession, careful to space them just enough to bring the gun barrel back down to realign his aim, after the recoil of each shot.

The first round hit the man in the middle of the chest, driving him backward and spoiling his aim. He still got off two shots from his large bore automatic. His gun boomed and the shock wave was felt by everyone in the room. His first round whizzed by McQuaid's right ear, the big .45 caliber round cutting a palpable, supersonic swath through the air, exploding the plate glass window behind him. McQuaid's second shot caught the man in the throat, tearing right through tissue and bone. The spent round lodged in the wall, past the head of bullet head number two, who had been coming through the door right behind him, spattering blood, bone chips and tissue in his face.

Bullet head number one's second shot went wild, smacking into the ceiling above the people cringing on the floor, knocking out a large hunk of plaster, which rained down around them, causing renewed shrieking from the women. McQuaid's third round hit the man square in the forehead, making a loud cracking sound, as it tore through the bone of his skull. He fell backward into the bloodied man behind him, like a falling tree, pinning him against the wall of the passageway.

Kiko was fully alert now, watching in horror at the pandemonium in the room and shocked by the guns firing in the confines of the small space. One thought seared her brain like no other – Gunner was in trouble – the bald men were trying to hurt him. She had to do something to protect him. She looked down at the grenade in her hand, put her finger through the ring and pulled the pin. The handle flew straight out in front of her, cartwheeling end over end and she heard a popping noise, followed by a sizzling sound like meat cooking over a fire. Kiko stared at the grenade, knowing she needed to throw it away, like Gunner had shown her. Raising her arm, she flung it as hard as she could at the men in the doorway, put her hands over her ears and clenched her eyes shut.

McQuaid was just about to fire at bullet head number two, who was struggling to get out from under the body of the bleeding man lying on top of him, when the arming handle of the grenade flew through the air in front of him. At first he wasn't sure what he'd seen, then he felt Kiko wrest herself away from his grip and before he could grab her back, watched as she threw a grenade toward the front of the room. McQuaid watched in horror as it tumbled through the air toward the open door, bounced off the floor just inside the threshold, then off the chest of bullet head number one and rebounded back into the room.

Everyone in the room had their eyes locked on the grenade now, as it rolled over and stopped at the feet of Madam Chin, who gawked at it, unsure of what it was she was looking at. McQuaid's mind snapped back into gear. He spun around, grabbed Kiko around the waist and ran the two remaining steps to the window and jumped out, head first, just as the room exploded in a roar behind him. He could feel the fireball searing his back, as they sailed through the air toward the water below.

He tried to get himself and Kiko turned around in time, so they would hit the water feet first. But it was difficult to judge his angle in the dark. They landed on their backs instead, with Kiko just ahead of him and after falling near thirty feet, he hit hard, the wind gushing out of him. Trying not to black out, he struggled to the surface.

He'd lost his grip on Kiko when they hit and couldn't find her when he broke the surface. The Lin Yao wasn't going very fast and was still sliding past him, illuminating the surface of the water around him. Debris from the explosion was still splashing down around them on all sides, but there was no sign of Kiko. He took a couple of quick breaths and dove underwater to see if he could spot her.

She was down a few feet to his right, arms outstretched, sinking into darkness of the depths below. Kicking hard, he dove down after her and grabbed her under the arms. Looking into her face, he could see her eyes were open and looking at him, semi-conscious, with the wind knocked out of her as well. Dragging her toward the surface, he saw her smile at him and mouth his name, then she closed her eyes and sagged down against him.

Dunross had seen them ejected out of the upper deck windows, along with a hail of flaming pieces from one of the top deck rooms on the riverboat. He feared they had caught the full force of the blast and expected he might have to pick them up in pieces. Looking around where he had seen them hit the water, he could find no trace of them. Circling the boat around, he began a desperate search, while the area was still being lit by the passing windows of the riverboat. After a few moments, the Lin Yao had gone by and the harbor surface turned pitch black again. He killed the motor and was just stripping off his shirt to dive in, when Lilibeth pointed to their right.

"Look! Over there!" Snapping his head around, he spied a head in the water, then a second one. He restarted the motor and spun the boat around to pull alongside of them. McQuaid handed up Kiko's limp body first, then grabbed Laddie's outstretched hand and pulled himself in as well. Dunross was already working on Kiko, by the time he was able to sit upright in the boat. He had wrapped his arms around her chest from behind and jerked his arms tight against her diaphragm, forcing her to spew water out of her mouth. Then he flipped her onto her back and blew air back into her lungs, mouth-to-mouth.

After only a few breaths, her eyes flew open and she started retching, coughing out the remaining water and gasping. Lilibeth was holding her hand, crying. Kiko came to and sat up, still hacking and coughing. Lilibeth threw her arms around her and they both began sobbing at the same time. Dunross looked over at McQuaid, great relief reflected in his face. The water had been cold, so between the shock and the night breeze on the water, both he and Kiko were already shivering.

"Best get you two into some dry clothes right quick," he said, as he cranked the outboard motor to the side and aimed for shore. McQuaid grabbed him by the shoulder and squeezed.

"Thanks Laddie," he said. His eyes said it all. Dunross looked back at him and grinned, his teeth white in the reflected moonlight, beneath the dark handlebar mustache. Behind them, the Lin Yao's top deck, aft of the pilot house, was engulfed in flames. She was blowing her whistle and turning toward shore. On the far side of the wharf, they could hear sirens and saw red lights of police and fire trucks heading toward the docks. A couple police boats were en route, across the harbor at top speed, sirens whooping, their spotlights sweeping back and forth across the sides of the Lin Yao, bathing her in circles of brilliant white light. They could see a couple lifeboats being lowered over the side and the dark silhouettes of passengers, running out on to her decks, ship's crew blowing whistles and shepherding people toward the open decks at the bow and stern. Dunross and McQuaid watched the unfolding panic on the harbor with impassive eyes. In a few minutes, they would be back at the dock and without further delay, on the winding peak road again, leaving the mayhem on the harbor behind them.

"Well you certainly know how to keep things lively; I'll give you that, McQuaid," the Aussie hollered back over the sound of the motor. "And I was wonderin' mate, did you somehow miss my full meanin' about not raisin' a row back there? I thought you'd blown the whole bloody top off the Lin Yao, you crazy Yank!" McQuaid had stopped listening and was looking forward, watching Lilibeth, her arms around Kiko, using her body heat to try and keep her friend warm. They looked like a couple happy and innocent young school girls. Kiko must have sensed he was watching her and returned his gaze. Then she smiled the most beautiful, radiant smile he had ever seen. He reached over and rumpled the wet mop of her hair.

"It's good to see you again, little pigeon " She just nodded, her teeth chattering, as Lilibeth squeezed her and lay the side of her face against the top of her head. McQuaid couldn't stop grinning all the way back to the dock. It felt great to be alive.

They stopped at Dunross' flat only long enough to towel off and change into dry clothes. McQuaid had little trouble fitting into some of the man's spare jeans and a shirt, but they had to roll up the pant legs and shirt sleeves on the clothing he donated for Kiko. She looked like a midget scarecrow before being stuffed with straw. Dunross slapped together some pork meat sandwiches on thick peasant bread, along with a couple bottles of lemon flavored soda pop, to take with them in the car. Kiko and Lilibeth munched away and slurped down the sodas on the ride back to Kai Tak. Both he and Dunross decided they shouldn't waste any time getting him to his plane and winging back toward the Philippines.

The whole southern shore around Aberdeen was awake and on full alert now. After the explosion on the Lin Yao, the entire harbor was lit up and they had emptied all the police and fire houses in the area. Dunross announced that he couldn't imagine the extent of the repercussions, once they determined the casualty count aboard the riverboat; in particular the third floor suite, where it was probable McQuaid had damn near wiped out the Governor's personal staff. McQuaid was concerned about the potential fallout for Laddie, but he reassured him, there would be no overt public inquiry into any of his staff being injured, or killed aboard the floating brothel. It was however, his sincere hope, they had seen the last of one, Madam Chin.

McQuaid had the girls strapped into the plane for the flight back and was standing on the tarmac saying goodbye to Dunross. Only a few words needed to be exchanged. McQuaid had given Laddie the Chinese intelligence officer's pistol for his collection. Somehow he was able to hold onto in the explosion and subsequent high dive into the harbor. He knew it was only a token gift and apologized for having to throw his Owen Gun away. Dunross understood and told him he knew it couldn't be helped and waved the American off when he offered to pay for it.

"It was a small price to pay mate. I'm just happy we got the little girl back and now a bonus child to boot – in case you were lookin' for a spare." McQuaid laughed. "And now that I know you're the man to build a party around, I'm offerin' you a standin' invite to come back anytime you feel the urge. Give us some time to repair the island before you return for a rematch though. Oh, and make sure you tell Jake Wilmouth, when you see him next, he owes me more than a few pints at the pub now. And mention he should bring a few of those extra Sheila's he claims he has followin' him around." McQuaid assured him he would pass along the request. He would miss Laddie and told him he'd look him up next time he was in Hong Kong.

"Just make sure you give us fair warnin' before you do McQuaid," he replied. As he taxied the Goose out onto the runway, he waved out the pilot's window at him, standing there where he first saw him, next to his Tilly, in the long coat and Fedora. Dunross waved back, then climbed in his truck and sped off toward the gate. McQuaid got takeoff clearance and a few minutes later, they were winging their way over Victoria Harbor, climbing into the starlit night, a fat crescent moon just peeking up over the edge of the dark sea horizon.

Kiko came forward and climbed into the co-pilot's seat, with her new friend Lilibeth on her lap. They were both looking out at the night sky, the ruddy glow of the instrument lights against their faces, watching the moon rise; chattering back and forth in their native language. Kiko was being the willing guide for her friend, who had never flown in an airplane before. The Goose seemed content as well, her engines throbbing in synchronized harmony. Her controls felt firm under his hands and moving in gentle rhythm to the cool night air currents, flowing over her wings. He grabbed a fresh cigar out of his flight coverall and clamped it between his teeth. It would be a long flight back, but he welcomed the solitude high above the dark sea below them.

After an hour or so, both the girls had fallen asleep, their arms tangled up with each other and their heads resting against the padded armrest on the co-pilot's seat. McQuaid had decided to make straight for Clark, assuming he would need to pick Mattie up for the quick hop back to Lubang. By two in the morning he was within range and called Clark tower for his approach. There was always someone on duty, even if the rest of the field was sleeping. He requested landing approval and was quickly cleared in. As he was beginning to reduce airspeed for his descent, the tower called him back.

"McQuaid Air Cargo, Clark tower, over." He picked up the mike and acknowledged. "Mister McQuaid, we have a message here for you, from a Major Jake Wilmouth. Are you ready to copy?"

"Roger, Clark tower, ready to copy." He had pulled out his notepad by force of habit and had his pencil poised to take down the message.

"Roger McQuaid Air Cargo, message follows. Major Wilmouth says you are to proceed direct to Lubang airfield and I quote here: 'The bird is back in her nest'. I was told you would understand, over."

"Indeed I do, Clark tower. Thanks. Belay that landing request, I'll be diverting direct to Lubang field." He was grinning to himself. Jake had flown Mattie home.

"Roger McQuaid Air Cargo, understand you are canceling your request to land and diverting to Lubang Island. Good night and have a safe flight. Clark tower, out."

"Roger Clark tower and thanks. Good night to you sir." McQuaid shoved the throttles forward and banked to the southwest. As soon as he established the correct course heading, he dialed in the radio frequency at the cargo office.

"McQuaid to Baacay, do you read?" He let up on the mike button and listened. There was no response, so he tried again and still there was no response. Baacay was probably sound asleep; even though he had told him he would wait for his call. He decided to try the General Store, short wave radio frequency, but got no response back from there either. If Mattie was there, she may have turned off the radio set for the night. Within a half hour, he could see the Lubang lighthouse beacon and right after, the lights on the airfield tower. It was unfortunate that the tower was never manned and the runway lights weren't lit. Even with the moonlight, he couldn't see any details of the field around the tower. This was a problem.

With his auxiliary tank installed, he still had fuel left, but he didn't want to chance a landing, even if he decided to land the Goose on her floats in the water, if he couldn't see anything. Descending to a little over a thousand feet, he decided he would buzz the airfield and see if he could wake up Baacay. He crossed the field at almost full power, roaring right over the air cargo hangar, which had a radio antenna with a light on top, marking its location. The noise from the twin Pratt & Whitneys would be near deafening at low level, for anyone on the ground. Pulling up and banking around, he glanced back at the airfield and started a circling pattern. Sure enough, in less than a minute or so, the runway lights flicked on. In another five minutes, he was wheels and flaps down, drifting in over the runway threshold, flaring to let the airspeed bleed off, until the Goose settled onto the pavement.

He had wakened Kiko and Lilibeth and sent them back to belt in and when he turned onto the taxiway he could hear them talking back and forth in excited voices. As he taxied toward the hangar, he saw Baacay in the beam of the landing lights, waving him over to one of the tie-downs. The cargo hatch was opened, while he was still switching things off in the cockpit. A peal of happy shrieking went up in back and McQuaid wasn't sure if it was Baacay, or Kiko, who was shriller. Making his way back, he jumped out onto the tarmac to see Baacay and Kiko, holding onto each other and dancing around. Lilibeth was standing to one side watching them. McQuaid came up behind her and slipped his arm around her shoulders. She looked up at him and even in the dim, predawn light; he could see she was happy. She put her arm around his waist and he pulled her tight against him. He wasn't sure what they were going to do with her, but for now, she was part of their family, until otherwise decided. Baacay pulled back from Kiko long enough to look at McQuaid, his eyes teary, not sad, but grateful.

"Ho Gunna'. So happy to see you too!" McQuaid extended his hand and Baacay began shaking it with unabashed enthusiasm. They walked over to the hangar together and McQuaid was pleased to see he had somehow found time to start a fresh pot of coffee. He was tired and could use a good cup of Joe. He filled one of the big white mugs and downed a few sips before Baacay came over to talk with him again.

"Sorry if I scared you earlier, flying over so low. I tried calling you on the radio, but you were probably asleep." He slugged some more coffee back, waiting to hear his reply.

"No sleep Gunna! I go out to pee. Run back, but you no answer radio!" He was serious now and seemed nonplussed McQuaid might think he'd been shirking. But he just chuckled back.

"I tried calling the radio at the store right after I called you. I guess when you were trying to reach me back, I wasn't on your frequency anymore. Sorry about that." Baacay gave him a toothy grin in return.

"You talk to Mattie at store?" he asked, his expression suggesting he hoped they had. McQuaid shook his head.

"No, she must have the radio off. Were you able to get the store repaired for her in time?" Baacay broke into an even bigger grin.

"Yah, Gunna. I fix stor' good. All pretty fo' Mattie!" McQuaid was impressed. He'd only been away a full day.

"Did you have enough money to cover everything?" Baacay's face fell and McQuaid was concerned he had hurt his feelings.

"No cost, Gunna. I fix stor' good." He waggled his hands back and forth. "No cost fo' you, no cost fo' Mattie." He dug into his shorts pocket and pulled out the same wad of bills he'd been handed him before his flight to Hong Kong. McQuaid was puzzled.

"What about materials, paint and food merchandise to restock the shelves?" Baacay waved his hand back at him.

"Rajan bring. You no pay. Rajan say, you boss. You no need pay." McQuaid pushed his ball cap back on his head and looked down at Baacay in disbelief.

"Who paid for materials and repairs then?" Baacay squinted back at him with a smug look now. He pointed in the direction of the town.

"Lubang people come, help fix stor'. Nguyen help fix too. He bring udder police men. All help fix stor' fo' Mattie." McQuaid just shook his head. Baacay looked very pleased with himself. He clapped him on the shoulder and smiled down at him, touched by the open generosity of people in the town. Baacay was still trying to hand him back his money. With some reluctance, he took the bills and shoved them in his pocket.

"Nguyen helped too, huh?" he asked, still incredulous, trying to imagine Nguyen and his deputies wielding hammers and paint brushes. Baacay was nodding, and then glanced over at Kiko and her friend, sitting around the chairs in the cargo office, whispering back and forth to each other, their heads held close together.

"Who dis' girl, Gunna?" McQuaid looked past him over at Lilibeth. He pulled Baacay outside with him so they could talk in private.

"They had Kiko locked up with a bunch of other girls. I guess these two got to be friends and she didn't want to leave her behind." Baacay looked back toward the door.

"Dis island girl?" McQuaid scratched the stubble on in cheek in absent minded reflection and looking back toward the office now as well.

"Yeah. She told me she was from Taytay, on Palawan Island. She probably has family there. How do you suppose she ended up being taken by the pirates?" Baacay just shrugged. "Do you think it's possible her family sold her to them?" Baacay looked up at him with narrowed eyes; but remained silent. McQuaid pulled his ball cap down, almost covering his eyes, nodding his head in answer to his own question. "I think I'll take a little trip over there after things settle down here a little. Would you mind going with me? I could use someone to interpret, in case the villagers don't speak English." Or, he thought to himself, they don't want to. Baacay's mouth turned up in a lopsided grin of appreciation.

"I come with Gunna." Then he looked back toward the office again. "Mebbe now dis' girl have no family. Dey sell girl, take money fom pirates." He looked back at McQuaid, deep lines of consternation creasing his forehead. "Why dey do dis', Gunna?" he asked, his dark eyes wide and incredulous. McQuaid just shook his head.

"I really have no answer for you Baacay. But, I do plan on asking them exactly that." He turned back toward the door. "C'mon. Let's get over to the store and see Mattie. I don't think she'll mind how early it is, do you?" Baacay beamed back at him. No answer was expected. When they walked back in, Kiko jumped up to make an announcement.

"Gunna, dis' my new sister!" she said, pulling Lilibeth to her feet to stand alongside of her. Lilibeth seemed really happy about the idea and then blushed when she saw McQuaid looking back at the two of them, like he wasn't sure how to respond. He walked over to squat down in front of the two of them. Taking his ball cap off, he placed it on Kiko's head and yanked it down over her eyes until she giggled.

"I cannot see Gunna," she laughed, pulling it back off and putting it on Lilibeth's head instead. She pointed at her friend and laughed. McQuaid couldn't help but laugh along with her. Lilibeth looked back at him, her dark brown eyes innocent and fragile from under the bill of the cap. *This was not going to go easy*, he thought. He had seldom seen Kiko so happy and after her ordeal in Hong Kong, he couldn't imagine how he could take this moment away from her. He rubbed his hand over his face, realizing he needed Mattie now, more than ever before.

"C'mon you two. I think we need to go over and wake up Mattie to tell her the news." Kiko jumped up and down, clapping her hands.

"Yeaaah! C'mon Lilibeth. We go see Mattie now!" She grabbed her hand and started yanking her toward the door. McQuaid looked over at Baacay, who just shook his head in sympathy.

"Dis' big problem, Gunna." he said low and under his breath, so the girls wouldn't hear. McQuaid nodded back.

"Well, one thing's sure. We're not going to try to figure this all out on our own. This is definitely one reason God made women." Baacay seemed to understand his meaning, but a frown lingered. He followed McQuaid out to the company jeep, climbing into the jump-seat in back with Lilibeth. Kiko took her usual place in front with McQuaid. It was almost three-thirty in the morning before they pulled up in front of the General Store. The headlights shined on the screen door, which had been replaced, along with the front windows. Everything looked like it had gotten a fresh coat of paint.

McQuaid turned off the engine and was just heading up the steps with his entourage in tow, when Mattie flew through the screen door and leaped into his arms. Her head was sleep tousled and she was wearing an old faded, knee-length nightgown. She had always been self-conscious about her appearance, so he was certain he would hear about not giving her ample warning later. But to McQuaid, she was the best sight he'd seen in a long time.

Her legs were locked tight around his waist and she had a death grip around his neck at the moment. He could feel her face against his, then her lips, then her face again. Just holding her against him now, made all the problems of the recent past and those he knew would face them in the future, evaporate like smoke in the morning breeze.

Kiko ran up and began tugging on her bare legs, calling her name and at last getting her attention. She pulled her face away to look at him, her eyes wet, but she was smiling and kissed him on the lips, watching his eyes looking back at her. Then she disengaged herself and knelt down to gather up the impatient Kiko into her arms. Now she was laughing and crying at the same time, dragging Kiko off her feet and rocking her back and forth, swinging her little legs side to side like a rag doll.

"God you feel good to me little girl!" she breathed in her ear. "I knew Richard would bring you back, no matter what he had to do." Kiko was holding on for dear life and McQuaid could see her eyes were bulging from the pressure of Mattie's arms squeezing her. But Kiko was laughing and he could see the only imminent danger was Mattie might lose her balance and they might tumble down the steps in a heap together.

McQuaid noticed Lilibeth out of the corner of his eye, standing to the side, his ball cap still pulled down low over her face. She was watching Mattie and Kiko together, her expression a touching mix of happy and sad. He could tell she was glad to see her friend was loved, but he wondered if she was torn between joy and pangs of grief. Standing apart from all these people in joyous reunion, he could imagine the thoughts going through her mind.

Kiko began squirming after a few moments, but Mattie was relentless, kissing her all over her cheeks and forehead. Resigned at last, she allowed her to escape her clutches and noticed Lilibeth standing there for the first time. She recognized McQuaid's ball cap on her head and looked over to him for an explanation. Before he could say anything however, Kiko pulled her friend up the steps and introduced her.

"Dis Lilibeth, my new sister!" McQuaid was impressed with Mattie's poker-face.

"Well I am very pleased to meet you Lilibeth," she said, beaming down at her and holding out her hand. Lilibeth shook it with great formality and smiled back at Mattie with an adoring expression that seemed to touch her heart. Catching sight of Baacay, he noticed he also appeared smitten with this little girl. McQuaid was struck by how easy she had made it all seem thus far. He hoped he was watching the beginning of the best to follow, not the last best moments of the days to come.

Mattie invited everyone inside the store, holding hands with the girls and only letting go long enough to turn on the lights and overhead fans. McQuaid was glad to see everything looked normal and a little brighter, which he attributed to the smell of fresh paint. Kiko had started to get tense. But seeing there was no evidence in the room, or on the floor, of the earlier attack on Mattie, she seemed to relax. Mattie grabbed a towel off the bar and began mopping the table tops in the room.

"How about I make us all some breakfast? Anybody hungry?" Happy cries of "Yes!" resounded from all sides.

"Can I have Coca?" Kiko asked. Mattie responded with a patient smile, foregoing the expected "Before breakfast?" question McQuaid expected was on her mind and simply pointed to the long steel ice chest near the door. Baacay was laughing. It was evident Kiko was using Mattie's relief over having her home again, to push her limits.

"You know where they are. Maybe your 'sister' would like one too?" Kiko nodded and grabbed Lilibeth's hand to drag her over next to her, so they could paw through the sodas together. Mattie was shooting him a look now and she motioned with her head for him to follow her into the small kitchen area in the back room. They ducked under the bar and through the door leading to the kitchen.

Mattie closed the door with a soft click behind them and grabbed McQuaid by the front of his shirt; pulling him hard against her. She kissed him, long and insistent, holding the full length of her body against him. He pressed her against the wall and kissed her back, moving his hands to her hips and pulling her even harder against his loins.

"I missed you too," he breathed, his voice husky in her ear. Her hands were holding the back of his neck, pulling his lips even tighter against her own. They could hear laughing starting up in the next room and Mattie drew back, her eyes looking deep into his. She smiled up at him, content and then a hint of fear crossed her face.

"You scared me Richard." He responded in reproach.

"What? You didn't think I'd make it back?" She lowered her eyes, hiding her thoughts. But then she looked back up at him, her eyes still brimming with worry.

"I never doubted you'd come back to me, I just..." Her words trailed off as she placed her hands flat against his chest, chagrinned at having to admit such weakness. McQuaid took her hands in his and kissed her on the forehead.

"I hate worrying you, but there are plenty more dangers ahead and we can't allow our fears to hold us back." She nodded her head and kissed him back on the lips, then with a gentle shove, pushed him away from her.

"Come and talk to me while I make breakfast." She moved off into the kitchen, pulling an apron off a hook on the wall and tying it around her. She smirked at him. "You haven't mentioned how impressed you were with my sleep attire. I guess I'll have to find something a little more exciting to wear, if you're going to be hanging around my bedroom." She looked back at him, offering her vulnerable side. He was leaning against the door frame – appraising her and debating his response.

"It's kind of ugly alright, but not with you in it. Right now, you could be wearing an old saddle blanket and I wouldn't be able to keep my hands off you!" She blushed and shot him a skeptical look.

"Yeah, that's your story now. I know your type, Marine. Tell them anything to get 'em back in the sack." He looked hurt.

"You confuse me with my evil brother, Jake," he parried. She laughed and moved over to the icebox to pull out some eggs and a side of bacon.

"He was wonderful to me Richard. I felt like he was watching over me like my big brother." She dropped the items on the counter and turned back to face him, wiping her hands on her apron. "I told him I needed to get back here to the store, but he wanted me to stay at Clark for another day. Finally he agreed to let me go, only if I had Major Dennehy check me out one more time and give me the official blessing. Honestly, I think he was more worried about me than anyone. There's a heart of gold inside that cowboy chest." McQuaid just nodded. She hesitated and then changed subjects. "You'll tell me all about your trip to Hong Kong eventually, right?"

"Right."

"Okay, so in the meantime, what's the short version on Kiko's new sister?" She reached over and grabbed a pan off the wall and handed to him. "Slap some of that bacon in here and put it on the stove, while you talk. I'm all ears." McQuaid took the pan and walked over to place it on one of the gas burners, lighting it with a kitchen match.

"Lilibeth is from a village on Palawan Island, south of here." He pulled a hunk of bacon out of the package and used one of her large knives to cut it into slices, while he continued. "They were holding her, along with twenty-four other girls from around the islands, including Kiko." Mattie was cracking eggs in a bowl, but turned around to question him on this.

"Don't you think that's sort of bold of these pirates? That's a lot of girls to steal from the local villages. How do they get away with that?" McQuaid had turned up the gas jet on the pan and was looking down at it, his eyes lost in thought while he was waiting for it to heat up. Mattie pointed out a bread keeper on the opposite counter. "Since you're so good with that knife, try your luck on slicing up some of that bread over there." He still didn't respond and she shot him a quick look. "You don't mind helping me out in here do you? I mean I know it's not exactly 'man's work' and I probably should have asked first." McQuaid just waved his hand at her.

"That's not it. I'm glad I can help." He grabbed for the bread and started hacking off some of it for toast. "I guess I'm not really sure about this yet, but I think some of these villagers have been selling young girls to the pirates." Mattie spun around in surprise.

"What?" She looked horrified.

"Like I said, I'm not convinced that's the case yet, but I have heard some stories like that from Chief Mahutra too."

"How could a mother sell her daughters to these animals, knowing what they do with them?" The eggs were all but forgotten.

"It's common practice still in the interior of China. Lijuan told me as much, but I had heard things like that before. I just didn't know it might be going on in the Philippines." Mattie's face was drawn, her eyes becoming fearful again.

"Richard? Did anything happen to Kiko?" She needed to know, but he could tell she was afraid to find out. McQuaid had stopped slicing the bread and was leaning his back against the counter, caught up in the memory of recent events.

"No. I got there in time." He paused. "Do you really want to do this now?" he asked. She shook her head fiercely back and forth.

"No, not yet. I'm not ready to hear all the details right now." He understood her reluctance.

"It was ugly for her Mattie, but she's home safe now. Let's just take a breath and enjoy having her back for a spell, okay?" Mattie stood blanched and frozen, looking back at him, while she mulled that over. Then she jabbed the fork she'd been using toward the closed door to the bar. Her eyes were tormented.

"You think Lilibeth's parent's sold her?" McQuaid cocked his head to the side, considering how little he did know.

"Maybe. But I intend to fly over to her village on Palawan and find out for sure." Mattie's jaw was set, with her mouth a twisted line of despair. He could tell her mind was working through the implications and he was curious about what she might want to do about it, if he discovered Lilibeth really was an outcast. She turned around and began beating the eggs in the bowl with furious strokes, not quite ready to reveal her thoughts. McQuaid waited. After she had finished with the eggs, she turned back to look at him, an odd and worried look on her face now.

"How do you feel about adopting this child with me, if you find out her parents sold her into prostitution?" McQuaid offered a knowing smile back and walked over to look into her eyes, reaching out to hold her hands in his. She looked back at him, uncertain and nervous. "I know we're just getting started Richard and I..." He put his finger against her lips.

"That little girl out there is not only very brave, but she helped me find Kiko, when I thought I'd lost her. Lilibeth and Kiko became fast friends; in the worst of conditions. I think she deserves a better family." His eyes gauged her expression, appreciating her even more. "And I'm glad you feel the same way about it." She reached up and put her arms around him, laying her head on his shoulder.

"I love you Richard. You are a kind and decent man. I couldn't hope for anyone better." He just kissed the top of her head, his gaze lost in contemplation of the changes that lay ahead of them.

Breakfast was slow in coming and everyone crowded around the tables in the bar, when Mattie and McQuaid brought out the heaping bowl of scrambled eggs and another large plate piled high with toast and bacon. They all attacked the food with gusto. Mattie was watching Kiko helping Lilibeth load her plate, smiling at her when Lilibeth began eating and her eyes wide, leaving little doubt she found the food tasted wonderful. Baacay wasted no time either and within a fraction of the time it took to prepare, only a few crumbs of breakfast remained on the bare plates in front of them.

Mattie instructed the girls to clear the plates and meet her back in the kitchen for KP duty. Meanwhile, McQuaid walked out through the screen door onto the front veranda and flopped down in the chairs with Baacay. He'd brought out a big mug of coffee and a bottle of brandy from behind the bar.

350

Pouring a liberal dose into his mug, he stretched out his legs in front of him and sipped the black, fortified brew for a few minutes, enjoying the quiet of the early morning. Pink clouds were already forming along the eastern sky and wildlife was stirring in the palm trees around the jungle thicket, across the street from them. Baacay seemed content to just sit there with him. McQuaid glanced over at him.

"There's going to be trouble here again before long Baacay," he offered. Baacay nodded his head. McQuaid took another sip of his coffee, feeling the brandy working its way into his bones. "The pirates will be back and probably soon." Baacay looked over at him with alarm.

"Dey no come back fo' Kiko!" McQuaid just shook his head.

"I doubt it. But they will be coming back for me." He watched his reaction and felt compassion for the man. This was his fight, not Baacay's. He would need to work with Jake and Mahutra to draw them out in the open, where they could deal with them in the only way those people would understand; and before they could ever get anywhere near Mattie and Kiko again. If this was going to be a war, he needed to be ready and to better his odds, while keeping the people closest to him safe; well behind the front lines. He looked back at the eastern sky, growing lighter by the minute and watched the palms swaying, as the morning sea breeze hissed through their fronds.

It was so beautiful and peaceful here. Mornings and early evenings were his favorite times. The heat of the day would be upon them soon enough, but for now, it was still cool and pleasant. In the store behind them, he hear the muted sounds of laughter in the kitchen. Mattie was having the girls wash dishes and clean up from making breakfast. They were gentle beings and shouldn't have to worry about the evil, following him back from China, to this small, tranquil island paradise.

Baacay remained quiet, knowing McQuaid's moods well, after working with him over the last couple years. It was one of the many things McQuaid appreciated about these island people. They seemed to have an instinct about the rhythms of life Westerner's rarely took the time to ponder and so were seldom able to enjoy. McQuaid nodded his head to himself. Life was funny like that. Chief Mahutra had advised him to follow his heart, not his feet. He smiled, reflecting on that decision he had made, which seemed so long ago now.

Chapter Twenty-Six
Lubang Village General Store, Lubang Island, the Philippines

It was late afternoon when he heard Nguyen's jeep pull up out front. McQuaid wasn't sure yet how he wanted to deal with the police chief, now that he had Kiko back. He knew the man had betrayed him and had damn near gotten Mattie killed; not to mention enabled the pirates to steal Kiko away in the first place. There was a side of him that still wanted to just shoot him. But he also suspected Nguyen really hadn't known the full potential for consequences his alliance with the pirates might unleash. He hadn't shared any of this with Mattie, though he knew he would need to at some point.

Mattie was busy talking on the radio to Mindoro Island. They still had to get that medical delivery off to them and the other half of their bill paid for the shipment. She had also been making a list of other sundry goods they still needed from Manila to get the store restocked. A constant stream of customers from around the village had already been through earlier in the morning, depleting much of their inventory. Business tended to go in ebbs and flows, but with the store shut down for a few days, local families needed to catch up on their supplies. Things had been very busy as soon as she had opened. Now, at last, they had some time to regroup on the cargo business side. Naturally, that would be the time Nguyen decided to show up. Mattie was still working the radio, so McQuaid met him when he walked through the screen door. It seemed by his expression the police chief hadn't expected to see McQuaid back yet. A parade of mixed emotions crossed his face before he removed the stub of his cigarette hanging from his lips.

"Ho, Gunna! You back soon." He flipped the butt out the door and flashed a gold toothed grin at him, pushing his Aussie hat back on his head with the stiffened tips of his fingers. McQuaid nodded back to him without returning his greeting. The police chief waved at Mattie behind the bar, but they had already caught up on things while doing repairs on the store together. So she just nodded back. But Nguyen seemed distracted already, looking around the room for something, or someone.

Then he spotted Kiko, standing on a stool putting small glass jars on one of the back store shelves. Nguyen's face lit up and he grinned so wide, McQuaid thought he might split open the corners of his mouth. His excitement and relief at seeing her back appeared genuine. He brushed by McQuaid and strode over to her.

"Ho Kiko. So good to see you!" he said, slapping her on the back. She turned around and smiled back at him, happy to see him too, but she also seemed unnerved at his unusual exuberance. She pointed to Lilibeth, who was squatting down handing jars up to her from out of a box on the floor.

"Dis my sister, Lilibeth," she said, quick to distract his attention from herself. Nguyen looked down at the girl somewhat confused, but he recovered enough to offer his hand to her in greeting.

"Ho, Lilibeth," he offered, glancing back at McQuaid for some clue to this new mystery. McQuaid motioned him toward the veranda and walked out to wait for him. When Nguyen joined him, he was at once put on the defensive, seeing McQuaid standing there facing him with arms crossed and frowning when he walked through the door. Nguyen looked nervous, but smiled back.

"Good to see you get Kiko back, Gunna." He paused, waiting for a reply and receiving none, he continued. "You go to Hong Kong, find Kiko, heh?' McQuaid nodded, still staring at him. Nguyen's expression turned belligerent. Putting his hands on his hips, he started in on a tirade. "Why you look mad Gunna? You be happy you get Kiko back. Dez pirates berry bad. I not help pirates hurt Mattie, take Kiko!" He pointed his finger in McQuaid's face, his voice growing louder. "Dis yor' problem Gunna. I not make problem for you. You make big problem for me." McQuaid balled his fists and was about ready to wade into Nguyen, when the screen door banged open and Mattie marched out and wedged herself between the two angry men.

"I knew you two were going to get into each other's face today!" She glared back and forth at the two of them. "Do you really need to do this? Kiko and Lilibeth don't need to see two grown men, who should know better, getting into a brawl with each other on top of all they've been through." They both knew she was right. But neither of them was quite ready to stand down yet either. "Alright. If that's the way it's going to be, let me set a few things straight with you two first. Then, if you still want to beat each other's brains out, you have my blessing. Just take it down the street – no knives, or guns – just a good clean head bashing is all I ask." She turned to McQuaid, glaring up at him. "Okay, first of all, Nguyen had no way of knowing the pirates would come and take Kiko away, much less shoot me. They were supposed to be coming for Lijuan!" McQuaid looked down at her, appearing confused. "That's right, he told me he tipped off the pirates you would be out of town and they could come and steal Lijuan back while you were away." McQuaid looked over at Nguyen, arching a skeptical eyebrow at him.

"Is that right, Captain?" Nguyen dropped his arms and turned away, looking down the street, then folded his arms across his chest before looking back to McQuaid.

"Dez pirates tell me dey take Lijuan. You make big problem Gunna." He pushed his face toward McQuaid, starting to yell. "I try fix problem!" Mattie put her hand on his chest and shoved him backwards, then pointed her finger in his face.

"Shut up while you're ahead, Captain! Richard wouldn't have had any reason to start shooting up pirates, if you hadn't been taking payoffs from them in the first place!" McQuaid gawked at her in surprise.

"You knew about this?" She glared back at him, her hands on her hips now too.

"What do you take me for? Of course I knew he was getting paid off! I've been on this island a lot longer than you have Richard. Everybody around here, BUT you, seems to know he's been on the take for years. In fact, just about every Philippine official around these islands takes bribe money. He'd practically be a local saint if he hadn't been." Nguyen continued to look uncomfortable and was about to offer a word or two in his defense, when Mattie turned and gave him a withering look. Nguyen's pressed his mouth into a thin line, but remained quiet. Mattie swung back around on McQuaid. "And you, even though you know I adore you, are also not the easiest man to work around sometimes. When you first came to town to start your cargo business, I tried to explain how things worked in the islands around here. Everyone isn't always noble, or acts like a Marine Corps officer. Culturally, the islands are very different than what you're used to. But people here mostly get along. You bulldozed your way into Lubang, like a typical Yank and the first time Nguyen put his hand out for a little palm-grease, you acted like he was some kind of traitor to the flag. And you two have been at each other's throats ever since!" She took a quick breath and started in again. "Nguyen may be a pain in the ass a good deal of the time," she looked back over her shoulder at him, "and I'm sorry Captain, but you are a royal pain sometimes." She faced around to continue addressing McQuaid. "But he would never intentionally cause me, or Kiko any harm. The pirate situation has been a problem for us all. We need to work together now, more than ever, or they will surely divide us and cause more bloodshed in the future. I'd personally like to avoid that again – if you don't mind. But we won't, if we're all fighting among ourselves."

Finally she stopped and just glared back and forth at the two of them. Then she turned on her heel and flounced back into the store, banging the screen door behind her. Nguyen flinched at the sound. Then he and McQuaid stood looking at each other in uncomfortable silence for a few moments longer. McQuaid cocked his head toward the store and rubbed the back of his hand across his lips.

"Captain, I don't know about you, but I'm a little dry after all that ass-chewing. How about I buy us a couple beers?" Nguyen looked back at him, his face poker straight.

"Beer sound good now Gunna. Happy to hear you buy. Mebbe I buy next beer, okay?" McQuaid slapped him on the back.

"Deal." They trooped back into the store together, passing Kiko skipping out the front door with Lilibeth. She was told she could show Lilibeth around the town when they finished their work. They offered happy waves to the men on their way past. McQuaid headed over to the ice chest where he pulled out two beers, snapping off the tops and handed one to Nguyen in mock ceremony. Mattie was back on the radio, but noticed them wandering over to the ice chest together and stifled a smile. She turned away so they wouldn't get any ideas about being back in her good graces just yet. McQuaid was just taking a second pull off his beer, when he remembered something he'd been meaning to ask the police chief.

"Hey Captain, I haven't seen any of Chief Mahutra's men around since I got back. I thought they were supposed to stick around and help keep an eye out for pirates returning to town." Nguyen waved a hand back at him, swallowing his beer before he replied.

"My men look for pirates now. I tell dez men for Mahutra – 'go home'. Pirates no come back now. Dey take

Kiko, shoot Mattie, you gone to Luzon. Pirates no need come back. Mebbe, dey come back for Lijuan. I give dem Lijuan – no problem! No need men from Mahutra." Nguyen nodded to him smiling and took another drink from his beer, satisfied he had everything under control now. McQuaid was just staring at him; wondering: *could he be that stupid?* His one deputy, Cho, was near useless and he couldn't even remember when he'd last seen his other deputy. On the other hand, he had no idea what had gone on in Hong Kong and McQuaid hadn't let anyone know about the pirate leader telling Kiko he was coming back to kill him. Nguyen was going on about having to take Lijuan to Manila anyway, so she wouldn't even be in town much longer – "problem solved".

McQuaid wasn't listening anymore. He was thinking back to the earlier conversation he and Jake had had with Nguyen. The police chief seemed to be plenty worried about the pirates then; even asking Jake for assurances he would get help from the military if he needed it. Now he didn't seem to be worried in the least. Something didn't feel right. Baacay had brought in some cold cuts and was arranging them on the ice under the glass counters at the other side of the room. He looked like he was just finishing up, so McQuaid motioned him over.

"Baacay, can you run over to the airfield and bring back that duffel bag I took with me to Clark?" Baacay nodded and headed out. He heard him start up the company jeep and tear off toward the airfield. It wouldn't take him long to get there and back – he hoped. Nguyen reached in for two more beers, popped the tops, keeping one for himself and handed the other one to McQuaid. Mattie ducked under the bar and headed over to join them.

"I spoke to the hospital on Mindoro and they told me to get the medical supplies over there by tomorrow and they'd be happy with that," she said looking cheerful once again. She reached in and grabbed a beer to join the two men. "Whew, that's a relief. I thought they were going to be more upset about it taking us so long to deliver their shipment." She looked over at McQuaid and winked. "She says she'll have the cash to pay the balance of our bill on delivery. That should help pay a few bills around here, huh?" Nguyen popped the cap on her beer for her and she toasted the two of them. "Glad to see you boys are getting along a little better," she said, before taking a longer swig from her bottle. Noticing McQuaid had grown quiet, she looked at him sideways. "You are getting along better, right?"

Suddenly, they heard a loud scream, just outside the door. Mattie dropped her bottle and it broke, splattering the floor with beer and shards of glass. The screen door opened and Nguyen's deputy, Cho, stumbled in looking confused. Mattie's hand flew to her mouth, as he turned toward them and they could see a bright red stain soaking the front of his white uniform shirt, still spurting blood from a jagged wound in his chest. He just looked at them with his mouth hanging open, like he wanted to say something. Then his eyes turned glassy and his legs buckled, pitching him face forward onto the plank wood floor. McQuaid noticed his gun holster was empty and felt a sliver of ice up his spine.

"Oh my God Richard, he's been stabbed!" Mattie started towards him, but McQuaid reached out and grabbed her by the arm before she could get past him. There was a dark figure standing outside the screen door now, looking in. Mattie recognized him and let out a scream. McQuaid pulled her behind him and started backing toward the bar, away from the door. The man's features were dark and he looked Chinese. He wore his hair in a long, braided pigtail at his back.

Then he pulled open the screen door and walked in, shoving a short, thin sword back into the scabbard on his belt. In his other hand, he was holding a large caliber pistol, pointed at Mattie. He was staring at her, the black oriental eyes bugging out in surprise, as if he was seeing a ghost. Outside in the street behind him, stood two other rough, swarthy looking men, each holding a rifle and gripping Lilibeth and Kiko by their necks. The man inside took another small step toward Mattie, still staring at her. Nguyen was making a move toward his revolver, but the man noticed and swung his pistol toward him.

Things were beginning to slow down for McQuaid. It seemed like the man's gun arm took forever to line up with Nguyen's chest. Meanwhile, his warrior mind was moving faster, using every split second to try and figure a way out of their predicament; but his options were few and all of them appeared futile at the moment. He heard the man hiss something at Nguyen in Tagalog. He used the word "unggoy" and waved his gun back and forth in a warning at him, then swung it back toward McQuaid. Rajan had bought Kiko a stuffed monkey in Manila and he called it an unggoy. The words this man spoke to Nguyen were clear and he understood what he had said to him.

This was the pirate who had shot and stabbed Mattie; the one Kiko had told him about. He was the pirate leader, Jiang, who had been ordered by Madam Chin to kill him. The man had just warned Nguyen against pulling out his gun; saying: "Your job is done little monkey." Still moving in slow motion, he turned to see Nguyen's reaction and saw a deep scowl cross his face. But, he moved his hand away from the big revolver he kept holstered low on his leg, like a gunslinger.

McQuaid's mind was still working away, even faster now, musing to himself about Nguyen. He always loved American Westerns and probably imagined himself as some sort of dangerous gunfighter. What a joke he was. The pirate was looking back at McQuaid now, his pistol back to line up on his chest. McQuaid moved to his right and stiff-armed Mattie, shoving her hard. She was off balance and tumbled, splaying her hands out in an effort to break her fall and screamed again.

"Richard, noooo!" The words came out so slowly, he thought she was just being dramatic. It was all too crazy, like a bad dream he needed to wake up from. The man in front of him was a Chinese pirate, about to gun him down, an American ex-fighter pilot, in an old ramshackle saloon in the Philippines, with a British saloon girl, screaming for him to stop and a Vietnamese Sheriff, who thought he was a cowboy, but who had just been told he was a monkey. It was all too weird. The pirate turned to watch Mattie falling to the right, taking his eyes off him and Nguyen for a second.

McQuaid dropped into a crouch, coiling the muscles in his legs, hoping he could spring over Cho lying on the floor at his feet and somehow tackle this pirate before he shot him. If only Jake was here to see this amazing move. He was watching the pirate's eyes swiveling back toward him as he launched himself into mid-air. He just needed to cover the three feet between them. Dim hope flickered somewhere in the far recesses of his mind. Maybe he could make it in time. But the gun had centered on him again and he saw the man's eyes squinting as his finger tightened on the trigger. In that moment, McQuaid knew he wasn't going to make it after all.

Somehow, in the midst of all of it, out of his peripheral vision to the left, he spotted Nguyen's gun hand moving as a blur. Almost faster than the eye could follow, even in slow motion, Nguyen slapped the big pistol out of his holster and fanned the hammer back, firing three times so fast, McQuaid was still just halfway to the man in front of him. He was getting closer, his outstretched hands almost touching him, when he saw three red holes appear in his chest, just below the collarbone and as McQuaid continued to fly toward him, he began staggering backward; almost as fast.

The man's gun boomed, as he squeezed the trigger in reflex to being shot. The ceiling fan overhead, took two rounds, right through the motor casing and sparks showered down in front of McQuaid's eyes, blinding him for a second. The pirate continued to stagger backward, staring down at the holes in his chest.

Then McQuaid heard the unmistakable, sharp clattering sound of his Thompson firing and the two men holding Lilibeth and Kiko were knocked flat on their faces. The pirate in front of him, turned and stumbled back through the screen door, gun arm hanging limp at his side, just as McQuaid hit the floor where he had been standing. Time returned to normal, as he jumped up and tried to get through the screen door after the wounded man, who had made it out to the top step of the veranda, the door banging shut behind him. He could see him standing there through the screen, at the top of the steps looking down at his men sprawled out in the street. And then, the end of the blade of his sword seemed to magically poke through his shirt, out of his back and he dropped to his knees. McQuaid whipped the screen door open in time to get a clear view over the top of his head.

Kiko was standing on the step below and in front of him, both arms extended, holding the sword she had just stabbed him with, buried to the haft in his chest. She was staring into his eyes, watching him kneeling in front of her now. Then she stepped to the side, as he fell forward and tumbled face first down the steps.

Lilibeth started screaming, but Kiko just stared down at the man, her face devoid of expression, watching his mouth working open and closed in the dirt, like a gasping fish out of water. His blood puddled out in the gravel from under his body, soaking into the thirsty sand. She raised her eyes to see McQuaid standing there watching her.

He heard the screen door open behind him again and felt Mattie move up next to him and then Nguyen appeared on his left. They were all staring down at the dying pirate at

Kiko's feet and the men who had been holding the two girls, laid out on either side of him. Movement out in the street caught his attention and he was amazed to see Jake walking toward them, grim faced, gripping a still smoking Thompson submachine gun. Baacay trailed behind him, holding the rifle from the cargo office. His face was hard and still red with rage. The smell of gun smoke hung heavy in the air between them. Jake looked up at McQuaid, a bitter grin starting to work its way around the murderous glare he'd been wearing.

"If I didn't know better, I'd swear this was the O-K Corral," he drawled; walking over to check on the man at Kiko's feet. It looked like he had stopped breathing. "This the pirate leader they sent over to finish you off?" McQuaid nodded. Mattie ran down the steps now and gathered up the still quaking Lilibeth and Kiko, who couldn't seem to tear her eyes away from the man she had stabbed. Mattie was on her knees now, her arms encircling the girls, holding both of them tight against her. Jake handed the Thompson over to Baacay. "Good thing I decided to hightail it over here. Guess I almost got here too late." McQuaid gave him a wry smile in return.

"I'd say, you're still a great wingman. You got here just in the nick of time, Snake." Jake smiled.

"Yeah, well I got here as soon as I could, after the urgent wire message I got from Laddie." McQuaid looked up at him, his brow creased with sudden interest.

"Must have been important." Jake nodded back and moved over to sit down on the top step. McQuaid sat down alongside him. They were both watching the hospital truck in the distance, barreling down the dusty street toward them. Jake rubbed his eyes with the heels of his hands and then looked over at McQuaid, his face serious again.

"Well, he warned me this Jiang character was on his way over to take you out on orders from Madam Chin. He also mentioned the attack on that boat, I guess it's called the Lin Yao, pretty much got everybody's attention, from the British Governor, all the way up to the Chinese Committee Chairman overseeing the colonies. By the way, nice work getting in and out of Hong Kong without anybody noticing there, Houdini." He smirked at McQuaid. "I thought I was supposed to be the loose cannon around here." They both paused to watch the ambulance from the hospital screech to a stop in front of them and Doc McCawley pile out with a couple of nurses and medical bags. McCawley ignored the men on the ground, leaving them for the nurses and jogged over to see how Mattie was doing. She reassured him everyone was alright, except for the men lying in the street. McCawley cast a curious look up at the two Marines sitting on the steps together.

"Glad to see you two didn't get your hair mussed. Any bullet holes anywhere you haven't noticed yet?" Both McQuaid and Jake waved him off. Nguyen was walking down the steps toward the bodies now, needing to bring some vestige of law enforcement back into the picture again. McQuaid jerked a thumb in his direction.

"You might check with Wild Bill here. He did most of the shooting." Nguyen just shook his head and waved a dismissive hand at McCawley.

"No person shoot me," he responded. "Dez men dead?" he asked. McCawley was looking them over and glanced over at one of the nurses, who had been checking them for a pulse. She returned his silent query with a rueful shake of her head. He frowned back at Nguyen, seeming to be disappointed there was no real medical attention needed by anyone.

"They all appear to be dead alright." He looked down at the pirate leader lying on his face, with the bloody sword tip still protruding from his back. "This one looks like he was quite thoroughly killed. That sword is a nice finishing touch. Whose handiwork do we have to thank for that?" No one volunteered anything as he looked from one to the other of them, his usual doctor frown becoming even more pronounced. "What? No one wants to own up to that one?"

"Me," a small voice piped up from behind him and he turned around to see who had spoken. Mattie had been holding on to Kiko, but she pulled away from her and stepped forward now, still looking down at the dead pirate leader. "Was me," she said again, her voice flat and emotionless. Everyone stopped moving and looked at her. She lifted her eyes to those of Doc McCawley, watching him staring back at her, his mouth open in surprise. Then her eyes welled up and her face crumbled. Mattie pulled her face back to her breast and held her there, as she began to convulse with deep, uncontrolled sobs. Lilibeth joined in and then Mattie began bawling as well. McQuaid stood up and walked down the steps to console them. Doc looked at Nguyen.

"Captain, there isn't much left for me to do here but load these men up and take them over to the morgue. Do you need to conduct any sort of investigation before I do that?" Nguyen looked down at the revolver, still in his hand, like he just noticed it was there. He stuck it in his holster and looked back at Doc.

"No need," he replied, his voice tight. Then he pointed back up the steps into the store. "My man Cho in there. He dead too." Then he walked down the steps and over to the police jeep still parked in front. Climbing in, he grabbed the radio mike off the hook to call his other deputy over from the office. McQuaid was pulling Mattie and the girls over to the chairs on the veranda, not wanting them to have to view Cho's bloody corpse lying on the floor just inside the screen door. Mattie was careful to keep their eyes averted, while she walked them over to the chairs and sat them down.

Doc motioned to Baacay to assist him and his nurses to load up the men from the street into the truck. McQuaid and Jake went down to help them too. It was quick but gruesome work, in particular, lifting the over-sized body of Cho up, out of his pool of blood in the store. Within a few minutes, it was all done and the hospital truck started back up the dusty street toward the hospital. Doc stayed behind, standing next to Jake and McQuaid.

"Should I be getting ready for another attack? There's a big blue trawler anchored in the harbor, you know. I believe it belongs to the one with the pigtail and sword sticking out of his back. That's the son-of-a-bitch who almost killed Mattie, right?" McQuaid frowned over at Jake.

"Maybe we should saddle up and head down there before they start wondering about all the shooting." Jake cocked his head toward the company jeep sitting on the other side of the white police jeep.

"Your other Thompson's in there, along with extra ammo and a few grenades." McQuaid nodded and started walking over, motioning for him to follow. Jake took the Thompson back from Baacay and walked over with him to talk to Nguyen. He had just finished up on the radio and looked back at them; puzzled, wondering where they were going.

"Come on, Captain. There's a pirate ship anchored in the harbor. We're going down to pay those fellows a little visit, before they decide to start shooting up the rest of the town. I reckon you'll need some help." Nguyen stared back at him, his face grim, but without protest. McQuaid moved around to the company jeep and pulled the other Thompson out of his bag, along with extra ammo magazines and a couple grenades. He also strapped on his Colt .45 automatic. McCawley was watching him from a few feet away.

"You know Richard, I'm getting really sick of these bloody bastards. They just march into to town anytime they feel like it, shooting and stabbing people around here I care about. It really pissed me off when they tried to kill Mattie." McQuaid could see him wrestling with his emotions. "I guess what I'm trying to say is, if you need any more help, I can do more than just stitch 'em up." His face was hard now, more like a warrior than a healer. McQuaid returned an empathetic nod; understanding what he was feeling. He reached back into his duffel bag and pulled out his other .45 automatic and tossed it over to him. McCawley caught it deftly in his right hand.

"You remember how to use one of those, Doc?" McCawley worked the slide back and forth, his eye squinting, as he watched to make sure a round chambered. Then he dropped the magazine out into his other hand to make sure it was full, jammed it back in and snapped off the safety with this thumb. He peered back at McQuaid with a determined look on his face. McQuaid just nodded.

Nguyen racked the shotgun he had just gotten out of the police jeep, replaced the spent shells in his revolver from the loops in his belt and pushed his holstered sidearm lower down his leg. He put on his sunglasses and pulled his Aussie hat down lower over his eyes. Looking back at McQuaid, he just nodded to let him know he was ready. McQuaid had retrieved his ball cap and pulled the bill low over his face. Yanking a fresh cigar out of his pocket, he clamped it between his teeth and gazed down the road toward the harbor ahead.

"Alright then. Let's go boys." Nguyen fell in step beside them as the four men strolled down the dusty main street together, in a line abreast, looking for all the world like a modern rendition of the Earp brothers, a version of Doc Holiday and...well, Nguyen seemed the odd man out, but now that McQuaid knew he was a true gunslinger, he was glad to have him along. Jake spoke to McQuaid quietly out of the side of his mouth.

"You know Madam Chin lived through that explosion." McQuaid kept his eyes pointed straight ahead and just continued walking. "She didn't much care for you blowing the shit out of her expensive party boat either." McQuaid's eyes narrowed and his mouth tightened. "I figure this is all just getting started Gunner." McQuaid kept walking.

"Yep, 'fraid so, Snake." The glare of the dying light was at their backs. Holding their rifles high, they topped the hill on the road down to the harbor; marching shoulder to shoulder; relentless, dark and ominous silhouettes against the blinding rays, under a Pacific sun.

About the Author

The author of **Under a Pacific Sun**, DC Musgrove, writes novels in a number of genres, including: *historical fiction, aviation, sci-fi and science*. He is an active blogger and posts to Facebook and Twitter.

American born, Musgrove lived and attended school in Europe as a teen, is a USAF veteran and former flight crew in an air rescue squadron. He's a private pilot, business owner and lives with his wife in Southern California.

You can find DC Musgrove on Facebook and the author's page at: www.*StarWand Publishing*.

www.ingramcontent.com/pod-product-compliance
Lightning Source LLC
Chambersburg PA
CBHW060157260626
47160CB00001B/308